To Bill,

Thanks for supporting me! I hope you enjoy the fantasy, anyway.

James Joseph

SHADOW OF THE SERPENT

A Coyote Moon Story

James Joseph

Audenreed Press
1997

ISBN: 1-879418-80-0

Printed in the United States of America

Audenreed Press
PO Box 1305 #103
Brunswick, ME 04011
207-833-5016

For my wife, Catherine,
whose unique experiences
on the road of life
have added so much
to the dimension of this story.

Acknowledgments

Thanks to the many people whose insight, wisdom, inspiration, sincere help and technical assistance, past & present, made this book possible: Julie Zimmerman, Irene Howe, Maine Writers & Publishers Alliance, C.A. Schmutz, Tom Brown, Roland Legare, Tom Raven Ford, Maura Mulcahy Seymour, Janot Mendler, Steve Chappell, Jonathon Stevens, Nancy Hancock Hayward, Laurie LaMountain, Thomas H. Marks, Dr. K and Squeaky Patterson.

Contents

Introduction

Long, long ago, before recorded history, even before the written word, people from every race and heritage maintained oral traditions that were handed down from one generation to the next. The North American continent once thrived with more than 500 different nations: some were permanent, some were nomadic, some were migratory. Though there was minor friction between many of them, rarely did they engage in massive invasions or genocide. For the most part, they learned from each other, shared and traded.

The original natives of this continent relied on their ancient lore when they were first inundated with foreign immigrants. Some can still recite the old stories even now, despite centuries of inhumane treatment and countless attempts to eradicate those who clung to their traditional ways. They were forced to integrate into more "civilized" views, often ridiculed and condemned as ignorant pagans. Intoxicated with proclamations of "manifest destiny" and "survival of the fittest", their foreign guests turned on them, plundering their lands, resources, farms and wealth, and forcing them into agreements that were invariably overturned.

To the south of this continent, large-scale civilizations already existed, with writing systems, intricate technologies and considerable wealth. Yet, unlike Europe and Asia, where civilization spread into even the remotest of regions, it could barely get a toe-hold on this continent. North America is one of the most fertile lands on the face of the earth, the climate is pleasant and natural resources are abundant. It just doesn't make sense that civilization wouldn't have taken root here even long before Europeans arrived. It prompts us to ask, why, if civilization is so desirable, was it always resisted rather than embraced? Why, after conquering millions in the ancient cities of Mexico and Central America, did the Spanish run into a stumbling block with the sparse populations of what is now known as the desert southwest? Why, after 300 years of constant battles and skirmishes, did they have little more control over these people than when they first arrived? Why, with its millions of citizens, its extraordinarily superior technology, its insurmountable wealth and its inexorable greed, did the US finally have to turn these indigenous nations against each other in order to defeat them? Did they resist for logical reasons? Spiritual? Just plain stubbornness?

Perhaps they understood that the gifts civilization had to offer were little more than illusion. The stories they had heard since birth conflicted with the ideals of civilized peoples. The treasures offered by these strange people would soon become necessities, and they would become trapped in a perverse social system that increasingly isolated them from nature. They would become dependent on the fruits of society, and in turn, a weaker, more isolated species of the natural world. Though civilizations generated formidable power, in the long term, individuals would be catastrophically weakened when nature reclaimed what had been taken from her.

The ancient lore of these nations was told around the fires of many wigwams, teepees, wickiups, longhouses and kivas. The meanings to these stories were generally lost to the uninformed. Different colors, animals and entities were often symbols of human behavior. Countless gods were merely facets of the true Creator. The tales were so metaphorical, that outsiders would need to learn dozens of cross-references to comprehend even the simplest of stories. They spoke of origins and history, of tradition and spirituality, of wisdom and morals, of humor and catastrophe, but they were created to entertain as well.

Shadow of the Serpent: A Coyote Moon Story is written with the same intent–mostly to entertain, but also to bring some of the underlying meanings of Native American spirituality and philosophy into a more universal light–something to amuse and something to ponder when we find ourselves isolated during our own "coyote moons".

CHAPTER 1

The damp and humid air lured even the sun to rest lazily on dawn's horizon as the night rain hung in misty vapors, steamed up from the warm, moist earth. Sequannah perched in the crook of a gnarled oak, half daydreaming and half following the routines of his father. Petawahin finished packing the food and weapons and hid their camp sign. He caught the boy's attention, then grunted his intention to leave. Two small sparrows appeared in the branches close to the boy's face, chirped alarmedly at him, then flew in tight circles just above his head. Sequannah scanned fruitlessly for the nest they would defend, then swung down beside his father.

"What does my young scout find this morning?" mused the seasoned warrior.

"Only a couple of sparrows," Sequannah answered meekly.

"Did you notice the sun move higher in the sky than we wished it to be when we leave?" Petawahin chided. Sequannah stared blankly towards the musty, wet buffalo robe at his feet.

"Know what others can see as well as yourself. Many will depend on you for their survival," Petawahin warned. "Carry the food and those buffalo robes today. You need to make yourself stronger."

"I will grow strong carrying meat back to the clan," Sequannah said confidently. Petawahin glanced sternly at him. Their hunting plans did not include large game on this trip, and arrogance was not tolerated until after a successful hunt. Sequannah's expression showed a sudden realization of his lack of humility, but his father became distracted.

Petawahin held a hand over his mouth to signify silence. He leaned an ear to the west. Sequannah noticed a faint buzzing, then silence. Petawahin appeared uneasy with the sound of cicadas at dawn. The air would become that of a sweat lodge.

"You will have to be stronger than me," Petawahin warned. "There are more Paccu tracks around here every year. During the coyote moon, there were more new stories about the Snake people than old ones. From what the other clans say, they have come back, and the words that have filled our lodges in the coyote moon...words older than the grandfathers' grandfathers, are true."

"Do you think the Paccus will be friendly?" Sequannah

worried. "Or are they with the Snake people?" During the winter gathering, many horrifying stories had been circulating through the southern villages. The Snake people were not new. The old legends were laced with tales of a vicious people and their strange snakes. But they were thought to have disappeared long ago. And many thought they were just stories, created to pass the time in the dead of winter, when the people huddled in wickiups, and coyotes cried their hunger to the moon.

"We will not know that until they know we are here, that we claim this to be ours when we come here each summer...and this they shall know soon," Petawahin stated. "This we must show them, but first we must find out what kind of people they are before we decide how to show them."

"How do you know the Paccus do not already know we are here?" Sequannah asked.

"If you hid your tracks well, you would not have to ask. But I hid them for you. It is late for worry now. No one has seen any of their tracks around the camp, only out here beyond the lake. They do not hide their moccasin sign, so they must not know we are here," said Petawahin. "We'll scout the small ponds and see if we can find some geese to hunt."

Sequannah and Petawahin moved cautiously ahead, well beyond the lake where the band had been staying for nearly a moon. Although the Minnecou had only frequented this area for a few summers, they considered it their territory to use as they pleased. Contact with other tribes this far north was rare for the Minnecou, and establishing territory was accomplished simply by returning each year. Further south, most of the lands had been established for countless generations, and the only way of acquiring more territory would be through invitation or by routing a tribe out of its own domain. The Minnecou, though, had always preferred to summer well north and into the vast unclaimed areas of the plains, tundra, and up to the foothills of the Dark Mountains. Like the many other Minnecou clans, they lived by the trails and roamed the vast prairies to the north and west. During the winter months, they would return from their journeys and have great reunions with those clans called relative to the Minnecou who lived in the permanent villages in the south.

Most of these had been established farming communities for generations that provided fruits and vegetables to sustain the entire

Minnecou tribe throughout the winter. In return, clans like the one Sequannah and Petawahin belonged to would bring in supplies of pemmican from bison, antelope, and elk; furs and hides for tanning and trading, flint and anything else of value they could manage to bring back with them. Petawahin was teaching Sequannah how to hunt geese so they would have meat to smoke and cache for the clan's journey back from their northernmost hunting areas.

As they approached the first in a series of small ponds, Petawahin motioned for Sequannah to stay low. Geese take flight if they sense any immediate danger, and like any other animal, they are much more difficult to hunt if they see you first.

"It is best to crawl," whispered Petawahin. "Until we reach those rushes, we will be in full view."

Sequannah crouched down low and carried his decoy carefully so that it slipped silently through the unyielding brush. He enjoyed hunting with his father more than anything else, but spent many more of his days fishing with his grandfather. He liked the fishing and Kwoita's stories, but fishing required no long journeys or tracking or sleeping outside of the lodge. Petawahin spent more time scouting and on the trail than in the Minnecou camps, and the times when he was with the clan, Sequannah most often lingered around the council lodge waiting for him to finish his long meetings with the chief and the Washan. But Petawahin knew the animals, their secrets, and the skills needed to find their trails and ambush them. Although his father had gained most of his knowledge from other elders in the band, Sequannah was certain it was all of his own design.

The two hunters crawled silently, yet skillfully through the rushes. They waited patiently for gentle breezes. The rustling wind obscured the movement of reeds and the crunching of dead leaves and straw. During the still moments, they planned their silent maneuvers.

Midway through the bulrushes, they reached a marshy area and kneaded their way through the warm, soft muck. Still, their pace quickened as it was much less noisy than stepping on dry leaves. Close to the open water, they submerged in the warm pools of the marsh and placed the decoys over their heads. They were made in the old way: from gourds that had been dried in the sun, then cut, shaped, and sewn together in the common shape of waterfowl. Their tawny color seemed to contrast sharply with the colors of real birds. Instead, they aroused the curiosity of ducks and geese that would swim close by to get a look at the new creatures.

Two slots located above the water line allowed the hunters to breathe and find their way around. They carried their spears submerged for when the geese would not swim close enough. But most often, when their quarry was lured in, the hunters would reach out and grab the duck or goose's feet, yanking it underwater quickly so that there would be no time for the bird to honk out a warning. They would then throttle the bird and tie the legs to their breechclouts with rawhide.

The two hunters moved slowly, grabbing onto strands of weeds to pull themselves through the mire until they reached the open water. Here, they scanned the area to see if they could find the geese once again. Sequannah spotted them off to the right in a small cove. About thirty birds floated aimlessly around, occasionally diving or honking.

Petawahin signaled to move in closer. They tread on their knees through the muck and wilted rushes lying on the pond bottom until only a patch of water lilies stood between them and the geese. Petawahin grabbed Sequannah's arm and whispered to him, "Face to the left of the geese and keep them out of your view. I will circle slowly around you and draw their attention to us."

Petawahin moved cautiously around his son, always facing him and glancing through the slots at a small group of curious ganders slowly approaching the edge of the lily pads. Petawahin kept circling as one of the boldest ganders advanced close to the two hunters. Suddenly the gander swerved and all of the geese swam rapidly away. Even the ones in the cove began to paddle down the shoreline. Petawahin sensed something was wrong and whispered to Sequannah, "Quick, move back into the rushes."

The two hunters maneuvered themselves into the tangled weeds, removed their decoys, and waited. They heard the sound of voices and then laughter. Moments later, a man and woman came into view.

The surface of the pond was thick with the green seed of pickerel weed, yet the young couple quickly tossed off their deer hide clothing and dove into the open area of water. The surface was warm, but beneath this deceiving layer the temperature rapidly chilled. They knew just where to find the spring that fed this small pond. The ascension from the icy depths back towards the warm layers near the surface provided just the relief they sought on hot summer days. The two young Paccus reappeared and posed like frogs surveying the surrounding flora for dangers, but they did this more as a game than because they sensed they were in any real danger.

After a short time of stifled laughter and affectionate splashing, they waded back out onto the grassy banks that made up the western shore of the pond and lay down on their clothing. Here they became involved in a more serious romantic encounter.

On the other side of the pond, Sequannah tried desperately to get a better view, but the breezes kept blowing the rushes back and forth in front of him. He heard a muffled snort behind him and turned to see Petawahin with both hands over his mouth, trembling with laughter. Sequannah's ears burned red as he realized that his father had been watching his desperation. Then a refrain of unusually loud grunting and moaning reverberated from the far side of the pond. Petawahin and Sequannah looked at each other and both Minnecous had to dunk their heads underwater to keep their laughter from being heard. The raucous grunting slowly climbed a torturous peak, then they fell apart from each other in a tumble of exhausted sighs. A movement in the bushes some distance behind them caught Sequannah's attention. An angry boar grizzly raised up on his hind legs, towering over the surrounding brush and sniffing in every direction.

"Run! Grizzly! Run!" Sequannah screamed.

Petawahin missed Sequannah's breechclout in a futile attempt to keep the boy down. The seasoned warrior followed the boy into the water, his jaw clenched in anger at Sequannah's foolishness. He clutched his spear with one hand and slashed away at the reeds with his chert knife. The young Paccu on the other side of the pond sent the woman scrambling through the bushes while he stood defiantly with his spear against what he perceived to be two enemies on the attack. Rushing suddenly into the water at the two Minnecou, he charged no more than a few paces when he realized they were not attacking, but trying to warn him. The Paccu turned slightly and glimpsed the oncoming blur just in time to dive quickly under the water before the grizzly reached the pond's edge. He swam until he could hold his breath no longer and burst up within a couple of lengths of the Minnecou clansmen.

The summer-fattened bear advanced rapidly through the churned water towards the three warriors. Petawahin signaled to split up, and the Paccu struggled in the opposite direction of the two Minnecou. The grizzly chose to follow the Paccu. Immediately, Petawahin turned and took pursuit on the grizzly. The water felt thick as he ran hip-deep trying desperately to catch up with the bear. Once within striking distance, he lunged with his spear at the grizzly's ribs, praying to hit a vital organ. The bear howled ferociously and turned on his unseen assailant. At that moment Sequannah forced all of his strength into his spear-throwing arm, and caught the silver-haired beast in the throat. The Paccu turned back, poking at the grizzly's face with his spear to keep him at a distance.

Though the heavy bear began to founder in the muddy water, he was still extremely dangerous. Soaking wet, hair bristled fury on his neck and down along his spine. He lashed out repeatedly at the Paccu warrior, narrowly missing with his deadly swipes. Petawahin attacked the bear from behind once again, this time with his knife. He latched onto the bear's neck, his arm locked under the snout, and repeatedly stabbed into the chest and throat. Sequannah yanked out his spear and maneuvered for another thrust. The enraged grizzly shook Petawahin off, raking deadly claws over his back, and in the same motion, lunged at Petawahin, and bit into the soft flesh of his side.

Sequannah and the Paccu warrior immediately attacked the raging bear, Sequannah stabbing violently with the spear he had retrieved, and the Paccu jabbing at any part of the bear within reach. The grizzly became confused and let go of Petawahin. Bleeding and dazed by the onslaught, water-laced lungs stifled his screams as the beast finally let him surface. Sequannah hooked his father's arm and dragged him towards the water's edge. The Paccu backed away in the same direction. The bear snarled ferociously, a bloody froth ringing his mouth, but he was exhausted and severely injured.

The Paccu helped Sequannah drag his father up the bank on the west side of the pond, while the grizzly howled, grunted and twisted in the water, slowly advancing towards the level shoreline to the left of them. Petawahin, still pale from the shock of close combat with a grizzly, sputtered, choked and forced his speech at Sequannah and the Paccu.

"Keep him in the water; throw spears, stones or anything you can find. He'll be much quicker on land if he's not injured enough, and there's a lot of meat to be lost for the fighting we've done."

Sequannah grabbed a tuft of grass and handed it to his

father to press onto his bleeding wound. He then scrambled frantically, searching for stones and anything else that could be used as a weapon. He tried to make the Paccu understand, but the bear was getting too close to the shoreline. Sequannah strained with the heaviest rock he could lift and heaved it at the bear, missing him by a full length. The bear diverted some, but paddled furiously to get out of the water where he could easily outrun a human.

The Paccu warrior picked up a couple of jagged, fist-sized rocks and hurled them with deadly accuracy, hitting the bear directly in the eye with one. The stunned beast foundered and slipped under the surface of the water, only to reappear a short distance away, even closer to the shore. Petawahin stepped in between them, heaving a huge boulder onto the base of the grizzly's skull, and the bear slipped underwater for a second time. Air bubbles burst through the churned surface.

The three of them waited intently for the raging grizzly to reappear, but its lungs had filled with water and the carcass had sunk to the murky bottom. Petawahin tore off a piece of his breechclout and tied it over the grass he had pressed onto the wound at his side. Sequannah was relieved to see that his father was not mortally wounded.

"Sequannah," Petawahin admitted proudly, "You were as brave as a true warrior. As much if not more than the Paccu. The People shall know of this when we return. Everyone will be proud to have you in their camp for your first deeds as a warrior, though they may be upset that your actions have caused the Paccus to be aware of us."

"I did not know what I was doing," Sequannah said modestly. "I saw the bear and warned the Paccus, and when the bear came after us, I just tried to keep him from killing us. I only did what you told me to do."

"Or so you thought I told you," countered Petawahin. "I did not want you to go after the bear again after we had split up with the Paccu, but I am thankful that you did because you saved my life. I am proud of a son who is brave enough to stand against an angry grizzly in order to save another's life. Facing a grizzly is the same as standing up to an enemy warrior, and you will be honored and respected as such from this day forth."

The young Paccu warrior was poking around with his spear in the mud-churned water when he called out to the two Minnecou, announcing that he had found the sunken carcass. Although neither Petawahin nor Sequannah understood his language, they both waded into the water to help retrieve the beast. The huge grizzly was moved with relative ease through the water, but had to be rolled once they got it close to shore.

The three warriors butchered the carcass into quarters, blood streaming down their arms. Then Sequannah scraped the excess meat off the hide while Petawahin went to retrieve their sleeping bundles, and the young Paccu made two small travois for hauling the heavy slabs of meat. As they set the meat on the travois, the Paccu motioned for them to put one quarter on one of the travois and the remaining three on the other. Then he picked up the travois with the lightest load, put the yoke around his shoulders, and began to drag it off towards the west.

Petawahin motioned for him to stop. He was pleased at the amount of meat the Paccu was willing to give to them, but there was too much to carry back to the Minnecou encampment.

"We have a long way to go," said Petawahin. "We cannot carry all this meat that far. It will go bad."

The Paccu didn't understand. Petawahin and Sequannah rolled one of the quarters off their travois and put it on the Paccu's. He looked disappointed, but tugged against the yoke, and grunted and strained his way up the grassy bank, out onto the scrub. Petawahin couldn't tell if the Paccu's disappointment was because he truly felt that the Minnecou deserved a larger share, or if he just didn't want to carry such a large load himself.

Petawahin tried the yoke over his neck and shoulders, and began to pull the heavy load. "The Paccus do know how to make a good travois," he admitted to Sequannah. But his injuries could not withstand the constant jarring and chafing, and he was forced to take turns with Sequannah. Sequannah wasn't much help either; he could only drag the travois at a very slow pace for short distances. After that, he was totally exhausted, having dragged three times his weight over a coarse, bush-laden terrain. They hadn't gone very far when Petawahin decided it would be better to carry the meat suspended from two stout poles than to drag the heavy load over the bumpy ground, jarring his raw and aching side the whole time.

"Sequannah," Petawahin said, nearly out of breath, "Grab your spear from the travois and guard the meat. Stay hidden in the bushes. Keep the buzzards and coyotes away from the meat. But if the Paccus should try to follow or a pack of wolves should appear, I'll be down in the valley next to the stream where those trees are in the distance. Move quickly and find me, but signal so I will know that it is you. I'm going to get a couple of strong poles from those trees. These are too heavy for carrying," he said, pointing at the travois.

Sequannah picked up his spear and bow and blended into the brush.

"And remember to think first before you act," Petawahin added. "We could both be dead right now if our Creator didn't see fit to help us. Your actions caused us to be known to the Paccus. Keep your mind on the people and your family, Sequannah. Doing a good deed for strangers does not mean that they would do the same for us...or even that they would not still see us as enemy."

Petawahin moved swiftly through the bush country, fully aware of the perilous position in which he'd left his son. The earth became gravely, though the brush remained thick. Thoughts of being known to the Paccus distracted him, and the trying terrain demanded all of his attention.

Petawahin crossed a stretch of horsetails before reaching the stream. He remembered chewing on the young shoots as a child. He thought to himself how tough and tasteless they are at this time of the year. Moments later, the stream sparkled before him. A catbird whined from among the reeds; red-winged blackbirds trilled like burning logs, screaming in the flames. The morning sun slowly climbed the sky.

Petawahin shimmied a slender alder until his weight caused the tree to bow. He rode the sapling to the ground and forced down on it, causing it to snap just above the base. By walking the end around in circles, he twisted the tree off its unyielding trunk. He repeated his efforts and doubled back towards Sequannah with two lightweight but durable carrying poles.

* * *

Sequannah sat sweltering in the hot summer sun. Crouched in a swath of sweetgrass, he was completely surrounded in an impenetrable barrier of brush and thicket. His bow at the ready and his spear at his side, he slowly maneuvered himself to a standing position so

17

that he could barely see over the tops of the surrounding brush. As he surveyed the area for danger and felt increasingly secure, he began to relax.

He absorbed the blend of grasses and brush, and the enchanting specters of cedar and juniper that stood sentinel over the graceful knolls, then thickened into forest in the lower reaches of the vales. The pinkish hue of clover tinted the grassy meadows in the distance. Sequannah heard a hawk screaming somewhere in the clouds, and craned his neck to scan the hazy white skies in search of the winged hunter. He focused near a sun-brightened cloud and gazed at the slowly soaring bird for quite some time before he noticed another hawk circling to the east of the first, and still another further away. A sudden feeling of irritation or fear crept into him as he watched the distant birds; he couldn't tell which. A slight humming off to his right distracted him as it became increasingly louder and seemed to be moving in his direction. The humming gradually turned into the distinct sound of voices, steadily approaching.

Sequannah tensed and slowly crouched, cringing as each branch clung to him, then sprang back with a stifled swish. As the voices became clearer, he thought he heard a few words of Minnecou. Then he recognized the voices of Mahkawan and Tamahna, the two Wolf warriors. He heard them talking about the Paccus. Suddenly, a crash in the thickets behind him—Sequannah froze. But no further sounds came from that direction. He heard the voices of the two Minnecou gradually fade away, but he dared not move; something began to rustle in the brush far in back of him. Although he didn't see the two Minnecou, he sensed the location of their trail. But he didn't know whether he should run to them for protection and to warn them, or if he should just stay where he was and avoid being detected by whatever was in the brush behind him.

The Paccu warriors could be trailing them on a parallel course, trying to ambush or follow them to the Minnecou encampment. Sequannah crept through the tall grass and thickets, painfully aware that any movement of the dense brush could result in an attack against him or the Wolf brothers. His knees knotted in the sharp pain of jagged stones pressing into his skin, but he knew he had to keep moving and catch up with the Wolf brothers. He discovered what appeared to be a freshly traveled path and followed in pursuit of the two Minnecou. Their trail led east for a short distance, then arced to the left. He crouched down lower as he realized he was steadily circling back towards his initial starting point. Soon, he detected the faint scent of the grizzly's carcass. He snaked his way through the brambles and thickets, moving elbow over elbow to get even closer. Broken twigs and ruffled grass told him that the two Minnecou had to have come this way. Peering through the bushes, he caught a glimpse of the bloody carcass. A fierce looking warrior with mud caked on his face squatted next to the meat, peering in his direction. Sequannah lowered his head slowly to avoid being detected.

He waited for quite some time before daring to lift his head again, only to find that the warrior had disappeared. He had heard nothing and knew his enemy was close by. The strange looking warrior must have seen him. He set tense and motionless as a hare.

Something crawled unto his foot. Sequannah dared not move–he knew he was being watched. The insect crawled up his leg and down to his foot again, then stopped. A steady piercing pricked into the soft part of his sole. The pressure increased until he realized that no insect could possess that kind of strength. He leapt forward and glanced back before breaking into a full sprint. Then he saw his father lying down with a stiff piece of straw hanging out of his mouth. Here lay the perpetrator of this cruel prank, smiling mischievously at his cunning.

"This is no time for tricks. There was a strange warrior near our meat," whispered Sequannah. "Tamahna and Mahkawan are not far away if we need help," he assessed the situation.

"We'd better go after the warrior," Petawahin became serious. "If we go after the Wolf brothers, he'll surely escape and probably steal our meat.

Petawahin grabbed his sapling pole and elbowed his way towards the fly-ridden carcass. Sequannah followed closely behind, keeping an eye out for what his father might miss. They crawled up to within a few lengths of the carcass but remained hidden in the dense underbrush. After a short time, Sequannah crawled up alongside his father.

"Do you think he's still around?" Sequannah whispered.

"Umm," answered the boy's father, "Still here."

"I don't see or hear anything," Sequannah countered after a long silence. "How do you know he's still here?"

"Would you recognize him if you saw him?" Petawahin

asked.

Sequannah shivered at the thought that this man could be within their midst, and yet he still didn't have a clue as to where he was. "I think so," murmured Sequannah.

"Then why did you follow him all the way over here on your elbows just to look at a dead bear?" mused Petawahin, suddenly bursting into laughter.

"Why did you do that?" asked Sequannah, angry, yet in awe of his father's skills.

"To demonstrate what is possible for you to do with a little practice. A young warrior knows little, and it was easy for me to guess what you would do," Petawahin grinned. "Should we go find Mahkawan and Tamahna to help with the load?" Petawahin joked.

Sequannah, suddenly realizing that his father had imitated the Wolf brothers, looked up and grinned, shaking his head in disbelief.

"But what made the big noise behind me when you were imitating the Wolf brothers?"

"Sequannah," Petawahin questioned, "How many carrying poles do I have with me?"

"One," answered the boy.

"And how many did I say I was getting?" Petawahin continued.

"Two?" Sequannah asked, though he knew he was correct.

Petawahin fell into a fit of laughter once again, so proud was he of outwitting his son in this manner. He knew Sequannah would learn these tricks simply because the boy was now aware that they were possible and very effective.

Petawahin removed the strip of hide from his side and replaced the tuft of grass with a mat of coarse and stringy willow bark to ease the pain and stanch the wound. Luckily, the grizzly didn't have enough time to tear the flesh away before Sequannah and the Paccu had attacked and confused him again. Petawahin had Sequannah rub some of the moist stringy bark into the deep scrapes across his back. Only one of the scrapes was serious, but the others were just as painful with his sweat soaking into them. He now regretted not swimming in the stream to cleanse them.

Petawahin found some tough vines to lash the meat to the

two poles. Sequannah tied them together in a manner that would not allow them to separate by more than the width of his shoulders. Many of the hunters would return to the camp with their loads tied in this manner so they could allow their arms to remain free.

"I see others tie their poles like this," Sequannah announced proudly.

"How many had grizzly meat tied to theirs?" his father smiled.

Petawahin stood up and signaled to move. Sequannah picked up his spear and his father placed the heavy load on the boy's bony shoulders. Sequannah dropped the spear and grasped the two poles as his shoulders began to droop.

"It's not easy killing a bear, is it Sequannah? Their ways are simpler. They just eat what they want and bury the rest for later. But we don't eat that much, so we have to take it with us, just like the ants do, to feed everyone or the meat will be wasted." Petawahin picked up the back end of the load and pressed on in a different direction then they had been traveling. "Big ants," he laughed.

"We'll change direction so no one can follow. You can't hide your trail using that thing," Petawahin said contemptuously.

Although the load wasn't very heavy for Petawahin, the boy appeared uncomfortably awkward with it. Sequannah's shoulders were numb and his arms throbbed from holding them up to keep a grip. Finally, he let go and was astonished to find that the load was no longer such a burden once his arms were rested. His shoulders no longer shrank from the pain.

They carried the meat down to the stream where his father had gotten the poles, and cast off their heavy load. Petawahin jumped into the icy water, finally relieving his stinging back. He washed off the traces of mud still clinging to the long black hair pushed back behind his ears, and floated on his back in the cool brook. Sequannah hadn't even noticed that his father's hair was unbraided. Petawahin always wore his hair in two braids when he was on the trail; he only let his hair down within the encampment. Sequannah dropped into a pool, drifting with the slow current, and Petawahin thought to himself that the boy was probably in as much pain as he was, carrying such a heavy load on his small bony shoulders. Petawahin had calluses there from years of hunting.

Sequannah basked in the emerald reflections shimmering

over the pool. Water shield hovered on the surface of the lazy current and arrowhead dotted the edges of the bank with pointed leaves and pure white flowers. The bank was covered with ferns, some still unfurling from their fetal beginnings. And, though further away, the boy could smell the pungent, wild amaranth as it misted its aroma through the sparkling pool. As he drifted downstream with the current, he spotted some small reddish-purple juneberries, but none had ripened to a bright blue quite yet; there was little sunlight penetrating the thick canopy overhead.

Petawahin watched the young warrior from a pool upstream and let him rest a while longer. These types of experiences would give the boy something to work for and defend, rather than to let the boy think he should toil and battle just for the sake of honor.

Later, Petawahin was still reluctant to push the boy back on the trail, but there was no time to waste. Sequannah, though, felt prepared to face the prospect of hauling the meat until long after sunset. When Petawahin placed the poles back on his shoulders, however, he was disappointed to find that the pain was just as bad as it was the first time, but he knew that eventually his body would adjust.

* * *

Petawahin was truly proud of his son. After they had put the first half of the journey behind them, he marveled at Sequannah and the children of the clan. What would seem nearly impossible for them to accomplish, they would undertake without so much as a whimper. If only he could get them to treat the minor irritations in life with the same attitude. But, then they would be better than the adults.

"Will we make it back to the camp today?" Sequannah asked weakly.

"I'm amazed we made it this far so soon," Petawahin said proudly. "But we are still only half way back and there is not much daylight left. If you can still go on, it will be that much less we will have to travel tomorrow, but it may be better to rest now."

"I want to go on," said Sequannah. "We can bring this meat when everyone is dancing around the fire and they will make a celebration for us right then."

Many hunters would go on so that they could walk in on the twilight songs and dances and bring honor to the clan. They would gladly suffer overwhelming difficulties in order to walk into such a reception. Petawahin had done this many times himself and could not bring himself to deny the same satisfaction to his son. They grunted and sweated and stumbled their way through the dense brush and forest, Sequannah forging ahead with amazing determination and Petawahin keenly alert to the dangers on the trail.

As the sun drew closer to the western horizon, though, Sequannah began to stumble more frequently. He tried desperately to move ahead, but his body was stooped and he was losing his footing; his strength was giving out. Every rise seemed to steal his breath and sap more of his strength. He thought that maybe with a little rest, he would recover his strength and be able to finally make it back into camp that night.

"Father," Sequannah sighed exhaustedly, "I have to stop for a little while to catch my breath. Then I think I can go the rest of the way."

"You had to stop a long time ago. You will be lucky if you ever catch your breath again," Petawahin said with a hint of admiration. "It is your choice. Whatever you choose to put yourself through, I will follow."

Sequannah felt proud to think that his father had to work to keep up with him, though he wasn't sure that this was actually true. He removed the heavy load from his shoulders and lay down in a soft bed of sweetgrass.

Petawahin went to relieve himself and slowly took in his surroundings. The sun was down but the sky still cast enough light for travel. Mosquitoes hummed around them as crickets chirped gleefully through the thick, matted grass. Petawahin checked his wound and saw that he was still bleeding on his side. Each tooth mark left a dark purple hole of clotted blood, and the skin was beginning to discolor like a bruise. But the itching and burning he felt was only from his sweat. It was not infected yet. The long scrapes on his back had scabbed over.

He went to rouse Sequannah so they could still make headway in the warm and purplish twilight. When he got to the boy, he found him flat on his back, snoring loudly. He woke the boy and reminded to sleep on his stomach to avoid snoring while they were out on the trail. Then he lay down himself. His thoughts drifted to visions of the young warrior stumbling and struggling with the heavy load of meat. Slowly he turned over onto his stomach and fell into a deep sleep to the mournful song of a whippoorwill in the distant brush.

Petawahin awoke early the next morning. A faint light illuminated the eastern skies where the sun would eventually rise. Finches and meadowlarks announced the impending dawn, while small rodents rustled through the dry leaves near the grizzly's butchered carcass. He looked over to Sequannah and saw that the boy was still asleep, then went in search of water. This was the time of year when drinking water became scarce. Stagnant backwaters often tainted many of the streams. Petawahin found a ravine with a small spring-fed brook bubbling its way over a bed of sand and pebbles. He stooped to drink at one of the bubbling springs and spotted a spearhead in the soft sandy bottom. The blade was as long as his hand. Never had anyone crafted such a work of art from the clan, and the shiny black stock used to create it was rare in this part of the land. There were clever notches for fastening to the shaft of a long spear, but there was no shaft to be found. A short distance upstream, he spotted what appeared to be stumps protruding through the eroding sandbank. On closer examination, these stumps appeared to have been made of a soft, chalk-like substance rather than wood, though the color was more gray than white. Petawahin couldn't recall any wood that had this texture, although he had frequently seen the grayish color on driftwood. He wrapped the artifact in leaves and twined the bundle with long strands of bur-reed. Dropping the bundle into his moccasin legging, he headed back to the boy so they could finish their trek early in the day.

Petawahin noticed that the boy's shoulders had become raw from the chafing of the carrying poles, and it was obvious that the youngster was totally exhausted. He shook the boy into wakefulness, but even that took some doing as Sequannah would strain to keep his eyes open, but then drift back into unconsciousness.

The lake near the encampment would be visible over the next rise and Petawahin began to walk in that direction. As the water came into view, he could make out the tiny forms in and around the shore on the opposite side of the lake. A trace of smoke sifted through the bluish-green spruce. These spruce seemed to be peculiar to this lake only; probably one time passengers, drifting from distant and foreign lands, then finally deposited with the melt off in this glacial moraine. On the north side of the lake, dark, smoothed bedrock protruded through the earthy surrounding. Through the thin mist, he could make out where the glacially carved hillock suddenly dropped off as a jagged cliff, effectively containing the entire north shore of the lake. The east and west sides of the lake were woodland and meadows, thick with grass and brush, while the southern end was strewn with boulders of every type and description; leftovers in the same glacial moraine that had created the deep, spring fed lake.

Petawahin approached the encampment by the southern end of the lake, where an easily maneuverable, though cleverly concealed path, served as a means of escape and a way to disperse unwitting enemy shadows. Once off the barely discernible path, wanderers exposed themselves to tricky crags and boulders, interspersed with swampy, wetland areas and quicksand. A screen of blueberry, laurel, and mulberry bushes, and thickets made it impossible to see far enough ahead to plan a course through the marshy area as it wound its way south through a long and shallow valley. The Minnecou had found their way across through trial and error, and recognizing the value of this area as a natural defense, never let the path get run down to the point where it would be visible.

As Petawahin labored his way through the arduous pathway, he came across a well placed log that would cleverly divert those approaching into an uninviting mire. Mokotak must have seen him approaching and placed it there as a precaution. Mokotak was most often alone and appeared that way even in the midst of a crowd. His loyalty, however, was nearly obsessive as he guarded the encampment constantly, diverting approaching strangers and attacking with the fervor of an enraged grizzly, if necessary. He watched over everyone and kept himself aware of every possible danger lurking near the people.

Mokotak came from a family that lived in one of the permanent villages to the south. His father was of the clan, but after he died, his mother stayed in the village. Since he was a young boy, Mokotak always begged to return to the clan, and when he was old enough, his mother allowed chief Ketanka to adopt him back into the westernmost clan of the nomadic Minnecou.

When he wasn't watching over the encampment, he spent most of his time hunting and fishing, almost always alone. He usually conveyed few words in his brief messages and rarely took part in any of the games or festivities involving the clan. Some of the children would be afraid of him because of his constant scowl, but as they grew older, they learned to accept and respect the formidable warrior.

Petawahin was always leery of approaching this particular encampment from this direction, knowing that Mokotak was lurking somewhere off the path, waiting to hack up any enemy that had found their way through his diversions. Mokotak might not recognize him in time during one of his lightning-like attacks. As he approached a huge boulder, he sensed that Mokotak was crouched in waiting behind it.

"Mokotak," Petawahin called softly. "Are you here, Mokotak?"

Mokotak stepped out from behind the boulder with the huge hatchet he usually carried hanging limply from the fist of his large, meaty arm. A scowl of disappointment hung over his sharply featured face. He looked up at Petawahin with one of his rare smiles and motioned for him to pass. Petawahin walked towards the menacing and sometimes mischievous warrior, tripped over a vine that had been hidden in the leaves, and fell face down in a pool of mud. Petawahin looked up and noticed that his head would have been right in line with the edge of the boulder and ready for a pummeling from this massive warrior.

He expected to find Mokotak smiling or maybe even hear him laugh, but he was just standing there with that same look of disappointment on his face. Petawahin got up to his feet, embarrassed for having been tricked, and found no solace in the fact that Mokotak remained solemn. He felt a deep anger rising up within him and was about to explode at Mokotak, when the silent warrior smiled broadly and handed him a bunch of leaves to wipe the mud off his face.

"Mokotak," Petawahin said, "Sequannah and I and a young Paccu warrior killed a grizzly yesterday. I carried our half of the meat with Sequannah until we reached that far ridge last night," he said, pointing to the west. "This morning, Sequannah would not move, and his eyes would not stay open. His shoulders are almost bleeding. He won't be able to carry that load with me again today. Help me carry the meat back and maybe Sequannah will be able to walk. I came by this way so that no one would see me, and Sequannah could still surprise the clan."

Mokotak understood and followed Petawahin over the next ridge and through a series of vales to where Petawahin had left

Sequannah. Mokotak could smell the carcass as they approached their destination. Petawahin spotted Sequannah peering at them through the brush. "At least the boy's awake if not alert," Petawahin thought to himself.

Flies had discovered the carcass again and buzzed over the butchered meat. Sequannah tried to fan them away as the two men approached.

"Mokotak will carry," Petawahin spoke without looking at the boy.

Sequannah was relieved, but as he walked into the camp, the people would not realize all the work he had done. They moved infinitely quicker with Mokotak on the other end of the load, following the southern route as always when returning from a hunt or journey. From any other direction, the approach to the clan would be visible for too great a distance. Not only would this allow enemies to locate their camp, but it would take the element of surprise away from successful hunters.

When they came to a small clearing, just out of view of the camp, Mokotak stopped and maneuvered the heavy load unto Sequannah's shoulders, then disappeared ahead of them, strolling casually among the clan.

Though wavering under the strain of the heavy load, Sequannah was determined to walk straight and tall. The trembling in his knees and his unsteady gait, though, increased his self-consciousness. But, he was resolved to appear as a strong young warrior as he shouldered the meat to the main firepit.

Shamira stared in wonder as her little brother strutted through the camp. For the first time, she noticed that his skinny legs had begun to take on muscle. People gathered from every direction as the two solemn hunters strode through the pathways with their enviable haul. Two, or maybe three times a year, a hunting party returned with bear meat, but very rarely would it turn out to be grizzly. To see such a young warrior return with a heavy load of grizzly meat was unimaginable.

Sequannah tried his best to remain humble, but this was not what was expected of him. Usually, it was the one who boasted of his exploits who received the most respect, as long as it wasn't done too often. He heard announcements of their arrival echoing throughout the camp. "Petawahin! Petawahin!"

Petawahin smiled proudly at Sequannah, shifting recognition to his son. But most of the clan was inclined to believe that their success was due to the older warrior; Sequannah couldn't possibly have taken the grizzly on alone. The youngsters in the crowd gathered around in awe of Sequannah. One or two winters ago, he was just another playmate, but now he was a warrior.

Women gathered wood for the huge firepit that was integral to the spirit of the tribe. Although the central firepit was generally reserved for twilight gatherings, there was no dissension about starting the festivities at midday—there was a new warrior to be honored, and grizzly meat was rare in a band of this size.

Mahkawan and Tamahna erected a spit for the choice pieces of meat and a larger spit for the remainder of the two quarters. The Wolf brothers always amused the clan with their antics, directing them towards the children and bringing smiles to the faces of the adults as well.

"Do you think we still have enough room to fit Quetatsu on the spit?" Mahkawan teased. "With a few berries and hazelnuts, I think we could get him to taste almost as good as the bear meat."

Quetatsu, however, returned the taunts of the men. At four winters, he already knew what was expected of him, or rather, he knew what the Minnecou would enjoy.

"You couldn't catch me," he taunted.

The Wolf brothers kept building the spits, pretending that the child hadn't even spoken. Quetatsu repeated his taunt, moving steadily closer, smiling and laughing.

"You couldn't catch me!" he repeated.

Suddenly, Tamahna jumped up and dashed at the youngster. Quetatsu turned and ran on his short skinny legs. He ran around and around the firepit while the whole clan cheered at the spectacle. Tamahna pretended that he was running as fast as he could, and that he was almost out of breath. He stumbled and appeared near to collapse.

Quetatsu raced in front of the warrior, laughing and teasing. Tamahna appeared as though he couldn't go another step and fumbled his way around the circle. He fell to the ground, pretending to catch his breath. Shamira encouraged Quetatsu.

"He's not playing. He can't run anymore. You tired him out, Quetatsu."

The youngster loomed closer and closer with his taunts. He tapped Tamahna on the shoulder twice and quickly darted away. But on the third try, Tamahna reached out and grabbed the boy by the ankle. He hoisted him up over his shoulder and sauntered towards the spit, the toddler screaming and laughing simultaneously as he dangled upside down in Tamahna's powerful grip.

"Sharpen the end of that spit, Mahkawan. We've got some more fresh meat here," Tamahna goaded the child.

"I'm not afraid," laughed Quetatsu.

"Light the fire, Mahkawan," Tamahna demanded.

The boy jeered and laughed at the Wolf brothers in such a flaunting manner, they grinned and put him down. Everyone laughed as the two Wolf brothers were left smiling sheepishly in defeat. Petawahin was amused that the child had enough trust in the Wolf brothers to realize that no matter what they did, they would never hurt him. But, had this been perpetrated by someone like Mokotak, he wasn't so sure the outcome would have been the same.

Chief Ketanka strolled in with his heavy body and deliberate step. A strong man, though not as quick as he had been in his youth, he could run as fast as anyone for short distances, but he couldn't endure the long run. His experience, however, more than compensated for his lack of endurance; he wasted no energy and his every move was effective.

While he appeared to be intolerant, he was actually a patient and pensive leader. He was devoted to the traditions of the tribe. His deeply rooted belief in the ancestral and traditional lore handed down through the generations, bonded each one to an unshakable faith in the whole.

Chief Ketanka was considered among the wisest of chiefs and was often sought out for council or support. His decisions were usually final because he was extremely persuasive and seemed to be divinely guided in his instinctive wisdom. And though there was a natural fear of him, his presence also lent great comfort to the people. He loomed in front of Sequannah.

"I see you and your father give us cause for great celebration today," the chief croaked in his deep voice.

Ketanka placed a pudgy paw on Sequannah's shoulder, feeling for muscle and noting the boy's raw skin. He looked at the surrounding faces with an admirable smile, then directed his honor to

Sequannah. Sequannah never felt so proud and never before realized how much the chief meant to him. Ketanka held an arm out to Petawahin, and the two men slowly walked away from the crowd in quiet discussion, as they usually did when Petawahin would return.

CHAPTER 2

From outside the council lodge, a stream of smoke drifted listlessly through the venting atop the largest of structures within the encampment. Throughout the day's games, feasting, and celebration, there had been much talk and quiet concern about the two hunters' encounter with the Paccus.

Petawahin and Sequannah were to give a complete account of the incident regarding the Paccus. Sequannah was apprehensive at the prospect of speaking on the same terms as the seasoned warriors of the tribe. Changes in his life were rapid and he sensed they would run much deeper than he could fathom. He wanted to be outside playing with the other children, protected from the trials and uncertainty that haunt the fledgling warrior, but at the same time, he wanted to be a man and part of the strategy involved in running the encampment.

Ketanka settled on a pile of mats directly across from the lodge's only entrance. This was considered to be a place of honor, and the closer one sat to this place, the more authority they held over the particular meeting. The point was brought across more effectively during the winter months, though, when visitors would lift the flap to enter and allow the cold breath of winter to follow. Mokotak, however, held little regard for place setting and would sit wherever he chose. Sometimes, he would sit in the most important position to humor the council; his expression pompously somber as Ketanka bellowed his displeasure, then laughed along with the rest of the council. Other times, he would sit outside of the lodge, just to keep everyone aware of his quiet mischief and lack of enthusiasm for authority.

This night, however, Mokotak took the position to the left of the chief while Sequannah and Petawahin sat immediately to the right. The arrangement seemed agreeable to the rest of the council, and Ketanka removed the long-stemmed pipe from its tripod, lighting the contents of the sacred soapstone bowl. Though most of its length was of cherry wood with a long draw hole burnt through it ages ago, the bowl itself seemed to be of even greater antiquity. A strange creature with long upturned tusks, large flopping ears, and a nose like an arm seemed a divine creation to those who partook of its use. It is said that this pipe was a gift to one of the old Minnecou chiefs from those people who dwell in the cities of stone far to the south. Even these people had never seen such a creature, but traditional lore had it that the pipe originated from far to the north and east of them and that these creatures still remained there at the time the city dwellers had given the pipe to the old chief. It was said that when the last of these creatures was gone, the Creator's children would change.

As Ketanka presented his offering to the Creator, the spirits entrusted to the four sacred directions, and the mother of earthly continuity, the other members offered their own contemplation. A man with no contemplation was thought to have nothing but mere existence within the universe. Each man in turn smoked the sacred pipe and passed it on. As the pipe was passed to Sequannah, several of the others watched in anticipation. When he did not cough, he was looked upon with questioning eyes. The chief began the ceremony again and passed the pipe around once more until every face betrayed nothing but trust. Ketanka would not allow even the slightest imperfection into the sacred ceremony. After the pipe had made its second round and Ketanka was satisfied that the proper influence prevailed over the council, he began with his deep, croaking intonations.

"Everyone seems content with their bellies full of grizzly meat. It is a fine gift from one of our best hunters and a new young warrior who will now sit with our council. I see that you both endured much suffering in order to bring this great gift to your people. I'm sure that the band will be satisfied for many days with the fruit of your great generosity. Many seem to be ill at ease, though, that the Paccus will probably know there is a Minnecou encampment close by to them...that they may send scouts to find out more about us. As I understand what occurred between Petawahin, Sequannah, and the Paccus, there was no cause for anger or disagreement. You left each other in peace. However, it would be wise for us to send out scouts and find their village as soon as possible. Then we will have knowledge of them at the same time that they may discover our own encampment. If Petawahin could give us an account of the incident, we may use this to discover their camp and know a little more about them."

Petawahin told of how they had been hunting for geese with decoys when they became aware of something approaching and then found a place to hide in the rushes. There was much laughter as Petawahin imitated the grunting and moaning of the two Paccus.

"I saw the grizzly stand up looking for the human scent that was irritating him, but before I could stop him, Sequannah jumped up and ran out to warn the Paccus. I ran after Sequannah, but the two Paccus thought we were attacking them. The warrior sent his woman off towards the direction of the summer wind and bravely stood alone against us. But, when we pointed out the bear behind him, he jumped into the water in time to avoid being mauled. The bear was in a rage and would not stop at the water line, but came in after us. We split up and the bear went after the Paccu. I came up behind the bear and thrust my spear into his side, but he did not die. When he turned on me, Sequannah threw his spear and hit the bear in the throat. The foolish Paccu started poking the bear with his spear. The bear was confused, but he went after the Paccu. I attacked the bear from behind again and cut his throat with my knife, but it was too short to kill him. He threw me off and began to claw and bite at me."

"The Paccu and Sequannah both attacked him again and he let me go. The bear was hurt, but he was still dangerous. We got out of the water. Sequannah and the Paccu tried to keep the bear from getting out of the water. The Paccu picked up two stones and hit the bear with them; one of them hit the bear in the eye, the other was very close. The bear sank, and I thought it was dead because it took a long time to come up again. But when he did come up, I threw a heavy rock on his head, and his spirit flew away," Petawahin made a flapping gesture with his hands. "We cut the bear into quarters, while the Paccu made two travois. He dragged his off to the west and we came around the pond to the east."

"Their camp must be a good distance from that pond," Ketanka determined. "Otherwise the girl would have been able to get help for the Paccu warrior. But also, they may have been right behind you all the way back here."

"We threw the travois away and used carrying poles instead so that we would leave no trail," Petawahin explained, "...but I'm not sure that the Paccu could afford to do the same; he was alone and his load was too heavy to carry."

The chief nodded approval, "So he may have left a trail if we are quick enough to follow."

Ketanka looked to the Washan, the clan's seer and healer. The Washan was always asked what unseen difficulties might lie in the path of the clan. His intuition was accurate much more often than not, and his insight and observations compensated wherever his instinct was lacking. Many refused to gamble with him. Sometimes his insights were genuinely prophetic, though these could be counted on one hand over the years he has been Washan.

"How long before rain?" croaked the heavy chief.

"Maybe thunder and rain tomorrow night, maybe not," replied the seer. "The Paccus throw rocks for weapons?" the Washan asked. "From what Petawahin tells us, they are very accurate."

"They could be dangerous warriors," the chief thought aloud. "But they do not cover their trail sign, and they do not seem to be aware of who may be around them, which could make life very dangerous for them," Ketanka encouraged his warriors.

"Sequannah seemed more reliable a warrior than the Paccu," Petawahin added. "The Paccu was brave, but foolish as well. But he was also very young. Maybe two, three winters older than Sequannah."

"Many young warriors start out brave but foolish," Ketanka bellowed as he turned to Sequannah. "You have obviously showed your potential as a warrior," Ketanka praised him. "And we trust that eventually you will learn to make wise decisions quickly, as well, when it should become necessary. Think of the people first, then of your own survival, and the survival of strangers last. While it is possible that we may make good and lasting friendships in the future because of your actions, they also may not be the type of people we would want to call friend. What was your opinion of the Paccus you had met?"

"They did not seem to be bad people," Sequannah announced, honored to have his opinion requested at his first council meeting. "The woman was very pretty, but she ran as soon as she saw us coming at them. The warrior was very brave. He was going to fight both of us before the bear came. He also held the bear off with his spear and the bear was never quick enough to hurt him. When we split up the meat, he was going to give us most of it and he gave us the hide.

He also built a travois for us to carry the meat. He did not seem to be an enemy."

"Petawahin," Ketanka requested. "What did you think of the Paccus."

"I cannot tell by what little I could understand of them. The brave was foolish, like many young braves are. If he had any sense he would have run off with his woman. He was brave, as Sequannah has said, and this speaks for his people. However, his reason for giving us the meat may have been so that we would let him live. And he may have built the travois so that it would be easier to follow us back to our camp. He wanted to give us three quarters of the meat, but I insisted that he take half. This would make it harder for him to discard his travois, and we could not bring that much meat back here without it all going bad. Also, with Sequannah's help, we could discard the travois and carry the meat back in a manner which would still allow us to conceal our tracks. But, from what I have seen, it still remains a question as to whether the Paccus are to be trusted or not."

"Trust does not begin with one act alone," said Ketanka. "Trust will only come after we have known and dealt with them over a period of time. Suspicion may make this period of time much longer, but the consequences could be grave if we were to consider them honorable before we truly know them. I know, Petawahin, that you have just returned from a long hunt, and that you have been wounded as well, but I must ask you to go back as soon as possible and see if you can find the Paccu's trail and their village. Take Quitkwa with you. The Wolf brothers will stay in the camp to protect the clan. Sequannah will watch from the top of the cliffs. Mokotak will guard the trail to the south of the lake. That will be the Paccus' most likely route if they can follow any of the trail sign you may have left behind. Washan, stay in the camp so you can warn us if you sense any unforeseen danger. No one else will go anywhere west of the encampment, including the lake. The women and children will have to go to the east to gather berries and whatever else they have to do to prepare us to leave before midday tomorrow. Quebathe and Shatomi will keep watch over them wherever they go."

Petawahin reached into his moccasin and revealed the long black obsidian blade he had discovered in the spring. All eyes were fixed on the object as Petawahin displayed its unique craftsmanship.

"Is that a Paccu blade?" Ketanka inquired.

"The Paccu we saw had a smaller gray stone on the end of his spear," Petawahin replied. "But some of their better warriors may have black ones like these. I found this a short distance from here, near the spring-fed brook over the first ridge west of here. It is larger than any blade I have seen. It's a spearhead...maybe for large buffalo or grizzly."

Petawahin passed the artifact around and each one who received it found different qualities in the unique blade. Tamahna held the projectile up to the fire as he felt the sharp edges, and noticed that he could see through this stone where it became thin. As he held it closer to his eye, he saw the fire blazing through the center of the strange stone.

"The stone looks black, but it is clear," declared Tamahna.

Ketanka looked through the object and felt its weight and sleekness. "We must find some of this stone," Ketanka demanded. "It is a powerful stone, and if others have it, then we will need the same if we are to survive."

Ketanka handed the stone back to Petawahin and told him it would be best if he could leave with Quitkwa tonight. "It would be best if we all left now," Ketanka bellowed. "I will relieve you from time to time so that each of you will have time to rest."

The men filed out of the council lodge, though the sun had not yet set. Each went to his respective hut to prepare for the night ahead. All of the dome shaped huts were fashioned from bent spruce or pine boughs covered with grass and bark to insure that the wickiups remained dry. Each had a firepit in the center and animal skins on top guided by long poles to act as smoke flaps. The entrances faced toward the east so that the sun would be their first sight in the morning and to ward off the prevalent westerly winds with the thickly thatched backsides of the wickiups.

Petawahin and Sequannah went to the hut they now shared. Sequannah had been living in Petawahin's hut for only the past two moons. He had grown to the age where it was no longer practicable for him to stay with his sister and grandmother, but still, he spent most nights alone in the hut. Petawahin was usually either hunting or scouting ahead for the clan. He had been living alone for the past eleven years, since the death of Sequannah's mother. She had died of the coughing sickness. One moon to the next saw her change from a sniffle to ashen-faced wheezing. Petawahin was shocked and grief-stricken. For years, he wouldn't stay in the camp but for brief periods. During this time, his mother and father looked after Shamira and Sequannah while he went out on his long, solitary wanderings. He nearly always came back with meat, and once in a while he would bring back things that had been left behind by other tribes. Often he marveled that these things could have been lost anywhere from moments to generations ago and sometimes there were no clues to tell him the difference. On his lonely treks he often discovered beautiful places that he would describe to the clan. Many times, the whole clan would pack up and move at his word. The camp they were situated at now was one of Petawahin's discoveries from nearly five years earlier, and the Minnecou had returned there every summer since. Nine or ten days walk from here was another one of Petawahin's discoveries, now their northernmost outpost before they returned southward to the winter villages. Once every moon or half moon, they would pack up and move everything they needed that would not be readily available at the next encampment. Each year, they traveled from the small farming villages where snow never falls, all the way to the foothills of the Dark Mountains and back again by the following winter. They moved frequently so that the game and wild fruits, nuts and tubers remained plentiful. Petawahin had a great influence on their travel patterns and was often scouting for new sites while he hunted. But his desire to constantly seek out newer and more exotic retreats for the people not only separated him from his family, but left the clan increasingly isolated from the other Minnecou bands.

Sequannah barely remembered his mother; she was gone before he saw his third winter. Shamira, however, had the similarly sad, though wizened expression of her father. Four years older than Sequannah, she remembered the secure and intimate family that once shared the same cook fire.

Now, at eighteen, she was relatively old to be unmarried and without children. But during the past few years, they had been ranging further west and contact with the other Minnecou clans had been cut off during most of the year. Many thought that she looked more beautiful than her mother, Mesarah, and felt that it was shameful for her father to allow her to live on in loneliness. She, herself, felt that Petawahin was using his influence with the band to keep her isolated. All of her life, she didn't want to marry into one of the families in the Minnecou villages to the south because she knew she would never be happy. Even though the villagers were called relative to the wandering clans, their ways were vastly different. They contemplated the spirits over their corn and tobacco fields. They spent their lives working in the dirt and repairing their enormous lodges. All of the ceremonies that took place on the trail were unknown to most of the villagers. But now, as she got older, a certain fear began to creep into her lonely life. Her wandering lifestyle was turning to isolation, and the stable, stationary ways of the south became increasingly appealing. Living with the clan was different for Sequannah; as a warrior, he would have more freedom to roam between the different clans and other tribes. But she had to stay mostly within their temporary encampments tending to the needs of the band. Petawahin, himself, sensed that she was becoming restless, and knew that if he didn't put her in contact with the right type of men–the kind he would find suitable as potential husbands for her–he would live to regret it. But, this year's travels were nearly set to wind down with their return south, and still he hadn't managed to merge with one of the other clans and break the bonds of her isolation. Perhaps the other clans had ranged much further east to avoid the Snake people. It had been said that the big river swarmed with these strange people. Perhaps the other clans could no longer cross so easily.

Petawahin found it difficult to believe that the grotesque people from the ancient legends could suddenly return. The stories had been passed along for so many generations that most people no longer believed in them. They seemed to be just another episode out of the many stories that had always been handed from the grandmothers and grandfathers down to the children. Although they were said to be sacred and true, Petawahin had always thought them to be just stories for entertainment or to teach valuable lessons to the young in a way that would be easy for them to remember.

* * *

Sequannah sat in front of the hearth in his father's hut, tying his leggings and gathering food and weapons for the long night ahead. He took a pinch of his father's smoking mixture along with a small pipe he had fashioned out of a ball of clay and an old discarded pipe stem. He never knew what was in the mixture, but it was often different.

Sometimes it would make him dizzy and nauseous, while at other times, he would feel pleasingly soothed.

There were usually many good sources of smoking herbs in the vicinity of Petawahin's discoveries; this was considered an added pleasure by many of the adults in the clan. While the Washan leaned toward the more narcotic herbs, most seemed to enjoy the milder mixtures.

Petawahin was also preparing. He took his best bow and a quiver of arrows, a chert knife and his spear, some meat and berries, and a sac of water. He would leave the black spearhead with his father, Kwoita, to fasten onto a meticulously crafted shaft, balanced for hunting.

"You would have been going with me if it wasn't for your behavior with the Paccus," Petawahin wanted Sequannah to know why Quitkwa had been chosen instead.

"I know," said Sequannah. "That's why I didn't complain when I was told to keep watch by the cliffs."

"If you had spoken one word of complaint, you would have found yourself regretting. Your ears would still hear cricket sound now. It is good that you know. You will learn to control yourself and gain the respect that you and the rest of us both need from each other. Keep your eyes open out there. I should be back sometime tomorrow. Take care of the family when you have the chance."

Petawahin left the young man alone and walked on to his father's hut. Kwoita sat solemnly smoking his pipe, but a smile appeared as his son walked through the familiar old elk-hide flap. This same flap had always protected Kwoita's huts. Petawahin's mother had died several years earlier, and so the old man lived in the way of his son. Sequannah and Shamira's maternal grandmother set up camp with Ketanka's roving Minnecou when she heard of her death so the children could remain among their friends and relatives and still have a proper upbringing. Kwoita and Petawahin both brought meat to Meequaw's hut often because there was no formal provider. Meequaw was in much the same position with the Titank Minnecou before she came here. Her husband was killed long ago in one of the large stone cities far to the south of the Minnecou wintering areas. She was told that the earth trembled and he was covered with stones. When he never returned, she knew him to be dead.

While living with the Titank Minnecou, she also had no

provider, so she would take care of orphaned or lonely young children, and the camp would provide for her in return. She left the Titank Minnecou in favor of caring for her own blood relatives. Bitter old women were often left to fend for themselves when they had no formal provider. Meequaw, though, would never be subjected to this type of rejection, because she was revered by every known clan of the Minnecou tribe, and her pleasant manner was always welcome. Petawahin had hoped that Kwoita and Meequaw would have married, but instead, their relationship never grew beyond their constant playful teasing and humorous insults.

Kwoita spent quite a bit of his time teaching Sequannah how to fish, but he was mostly reciting the old legends and relating the wisdom of the ancient ones to him. With Kwoita being the oldest of all the northernmost Minnecou, Petawahin felt proud to have some of the forgotten stories and traditions being handed down to his son. He handed the long, black projectile to his father.

"Make me a shaft to use with this as a spear," Petawahin requested. "I'm leaving tonight with Quitkwa to find the Paccu village, and rather than make one for myself, I would prefer that your wisdom be entrusted with making the shaft for such a powerful blade."

Kwoita's smile widened at his son's praise. He turned the blade over and over, measuring every angle and admiring the uniqueness of the spearhead.

"This was made for animals much larger than any I've seen, but not larger than those I've heard of. Long ago, when I was a boy, we used to go to the ocean at the mouth of the great muddy river. Some people from the stone cities far to the south stayed at our beach for a time. They came in a very large dugout canoe. One of them spoke of huge fish in the sea, some of them much longer than the canoe they came in, and there were fourteen people in that canoe with food and many trading goods."

"He told of huge animals that lived in caves in a big land far to the south and east of the beach where they stayed. And he also told of people who lived far to the north and east of the great muddy river who had spoken of huge animals with long noses and big ears. When he saw the council pipe, he said that these must be the same animals. Maybe one of these animals is what this blade was used for," Kwoita mused, though he didn't know whether to believe if they actually existed or not.

"It is well balanced and will be good for buffalo," Petawahin stated. "I wish I could stay longer, but I'm on my way to meet Quitkwa and then we will set out in search of the Paccu camp."

"And Sequannah?" Kwoita questioned.

"He'll be staying here, keeping watch from the cliffs," said Petawahin.

"I'm glad he was accepted," mused Kwoita. "I wouldn't want to look after a long-faced young warrior."

"I'll be back by tomorrow," Petawahin cut his father short. And with that, he quickly walked to the hut where he found Quitkwa waiting and they commenced their westward journey, picking their way through the swampy trail at the southern end of the lake.

* * *

Sequannah sat alone in his lodge. He pulled a burning twig from the fire and held it to the long stemmed pipe he'd filled with Petawahin's smoking mixture. This kind looked different than any he'd smoked before. His lungs felt cool as he drew the smoke in deeper. He held the smoke in his lungs for a short time; a smile of confidence and contentment radiated from the young warrior's face as he slowly leaned unto his backrest. As he exhaled, he felt the coolness spread to his throat and lungs. But as he drew in his next breath, he felt a sudden twitch in his chest and began to cough. With his next breath, he began to choke and cough uncontrollably. Tears flowed down his cheeks as he dumped the contents of the bowl into the fire. He reached for the sac of water and guzzled its entire contents. His mouth began to burn and he spit out the remainder as he recognized the hot peppery flavor that had been laced into the drink. Even more tears began to stream down his face and he was nearly blinded as he felt his face flush, red and burning.

He took out the small pouch he had used to hide the mixture he had stolen from Petawahin and dumped its contents under a stone by the side of the fire. This was his punishment for stealing his father's mixture. He was still coughing when he heard a scratching on the flap of the wickiup. Lifting the flap and peering out into the twilight, Sequannah found Sabatt standing meekly outside of the lodge. He had a small bow draped on his shoulder and a bundle under his arm.

"I'll go with you tonight," Sabatt posed, almost in question.

"Ketanka told you to come with me?" Sequannah questioned the twelve-year-old.

"No."

"Your father says you can go?"

"No."

"Why don't you ask them?" Sequannah asked.

"They will say no."

"Then how can I help you?" Sequannah asked in sympathy.

"You are warrior now," Sabatt shifted on his feet, "And you are in the council. I could ask you."

"No," Sequannah said softly. "Ketanka has already decided how things will be done and everyone agreed. We can't change anything now without another council meeting. Some of the warriors have already left." Sequannah paused for a moment until he saw the disappointment in Sabatt's face. "Why aren't you with your brothers? I'll bet they're having fun."

"I cannot become a warrior by having fun," Sabatt said stubbornly. "They are still children. That's still good for them."

Sequannah thought for a moment. "I need a warrior to do something for me, and I don't think there will be need of a council meeting to decide anything about it," he announced.

"I'm here!" Sabatt volunteered.

"It's getting dark now and I need someone who's not afraid to be out in the night," Sequannah warned.

"I'm not afraid anytime," Sabatt smirked.

"I need someone to go all the way to the edge of the camp and watch for me while I climb the cliffs. I may not be able to see the enemies in the darkness if they should try to follow me," Sequannah whispered.

"I'll do it," Sabatt said bravely.

"Good," Sequannah breathed a sigh of relief. "If you see anyone out there, go and tell Ketanka right away. Don't stop for anything. My life could be in danger and so could yours."

"I can do it. Nothing will stop me."

"As soon as I get to the top of the cliffs, though, you'll have to go back to your lodge," Sequannah told the boy. "We'll both be in trouble if someone has to call for you. Remember, this was not mentioned in the council meeting. It's just something that smart warriors do."

"Okay!" Sabatt said with a big grin on his face.

"Do you have arrows for that bow?" Sequannah questioned. Sabatt displayed the quiver on his back.

"Got a knife?"

Sabatt shook his head.

"Go home and get your knife and meet me at the fire pit," Sequannah demanded.

"Okay," Sabatt smiled and ran off to the other side of the encampment.

Sequannah took his pouch and pipe and hid them under his buffalo robe. Moments later, he pulled them back out and placed them on top of his bed.

CHAPTER 3

Sequannah gathered the remainder of his gear, exited through the hide flap of his father's hut, and walked out into the smoky encampment. Many of the clan still strolled about, wearing scant garments of deer hide and ornamental bracelets and necklaces of bones, teeth and shells of various animals. Most seemed to be nearly naked, though, to accommodate themselves in the late summer heat. Their jewelry appeared to be the larger portion of their dress. Hollow sounds of twilight and the resonance of even the slightest murmurs reminded Sequannah that autumn was almost upon them. Soon they would be wearing heavy buffalo and deer hide clothing to keep from freezing to death as they made their way southward. He hoped they would turn back earlier this year.

Some of the women stood next to the dying embers of the fire as the men headed out to their destinations. Sequannah caught a glimpse of Shamira carrying a bundle of dead branches to rekindle the dwindling fire, and noticed the distracted and lonely air surrounding her. He knew she needed the company of one of the other clans and hoped that they would move near one of their camps after they had found out about the Paccus. He also wanted the young boys and friends he had made in the various clans to see that he was now a warrior.

Sabatt ran up to Sequannah as sparks crackled from the

tinder Shamira had placed on the hot embers. He had his knife in his hand, showing Sequannah that he was now prepared for anything. Sequannah grunted and turned his head in the direction they would go, using his chin to point. The two young men strode off to the west in the diminishing light. Tiny sparks of light flashed in the tall grasses.

"You want to catch some fireflies on the way?" Sabatt questioned in his child voice.

"No talking."

* * *

As he turned towards the bluffs on the northern edge of the lake, Sequannah noticed the more sharply defined formations in the sunset clouds, an indication of cooler weather to come; the winding down of summer. The night would bring on a chill and he wondered if he had dressed warmly enough. As he reached the top of the first hillock of the ancient basalt ridge, the exertion deluded him into thinking he had overdressed. But he knew that later, as he lay motionless in watch over the tiny village, he would become much colder and wouldn't have the luxury of moving about to warm up.

The top of the ridge was nearly flat and strewn about with heavy, round boulders. To the north and west lay a vast plateau of tundra, speckled with shallow, stagnant ponds rimmed in cattail and bulrush. To the east and southwest, a hilly terrain formed a barrier to the plateau. Directly south and straight down, lay the lake which the band used as its principle water supply as well as a source of fish and freshwater mollusks. The black cliffs formed a rough arc on the northern perimeter of the lake with plummets greater than ten times the height of a man. The lake, itself, appeared to be nearly bottomless on the north side, and became increasingly shallow throughout its elongated shape southward to where a marshy area ended abruptly in a jumbled collection of huge boulders at the edge of a dense conifer forest.

Sequannah settled in between two large boulders at one of the highest points of the ridge. From this vantage point, he could see nearly a half morning's walk in every direction, with the exception of the heavily forested section to the south and the hilly areas to the southwest. As the last rays of sunlight strayed along the broad landscape, Sequannah observed the tiny figures of Petawahin and Quitkwa treading their way over the series of hills and dales far to the southwest. A few deer were venturing out onto the plateau to the north-east. Sandpipers, wood ducks, and night herons had already settled into their nests in the deadwood stand on the southern end of the lake. The water was smoother than new ice as it mirrored the brilliant colors of sunset, and though Sequannah knew the clan was nestled close by to the east, neither smoke, nor sight, nor sound gave testimony to this. Sequannah began to feel that he truly was alone.

As the hours passed, the stars filled the sky with an exceptional brilliance. This was the night of the new moon. At first, Sequannah had taken his duty lightly–the Paccus would not be as quick as the Minnecou to act. But as the night wore on, he grew apprehensive. Wouldn't they take advantage of the cloak of a new moon? Even in the open, they would be difficult to discern; Sequannah could barely see the lake beneath him in the impenetrable darkness. The occasional lapping against the base of the cliffs provided the only sense of the water below. Earlier, he had heard the baying of wolves far off to the west. He heard trampling and the rattle of antlers to the north. Every so often, a nearby rustling would nearly stop his heart. But, as the hours passed, a fear crept over him that none of these noises were real; that everything was contrived either to distract or test him. He feared that the Paccus were out there and maybe within arm's reach of him; that they'd known he was there right from the beginning. He thought to himself that maybe they'd always known that the Minnecou were here. They may already have discovered that the clan returned here every summer. They would probably have even guessed that there was a lookout here on this ridge. They would try to kill him silently and then ambush the rest of the clan.

Sequannah shivered when a cool breeze began to blow. As the constellations climbed the sky, the night grew colder and the breezes became more frequent. Sequannah remembered the goose hunting technique and watched intently as each puff of wind rustled the grasses and brush. And as each died down, he listened for the inadvertent snaps and rustlings. The cold gnawed at him as he determined to remain completely motionless. He thought to himself that if he was being watched, the Paccus would probably dismiss the thought that anyone could still be here after this length of time; he had not moved for more than half the night. Drowsiness was not even a factor. Sequannah felt that he could remain awake through the whole of the next day as well as the night. His exhaustion of the previous day had evaporated into a memory. But any thoughts that were distractful to his task were immediately pushed aside, and he would watch while the wind blew and listen for those who stepped out of rhythm when it stopped.

Sequannah was relieved to see Ketanka finally approaching the cliffs; not so much because he needed a rest, but because this oriented him as to what he could actually see in the dark. Being able to see Ketanka from the considerable distance to the foot of the ridge reassured Sequannah. That Ketanka made no attempt to conceal his movements seemed to dissuade the notion that any Paccus were lurking about. The night had settled into a stifled drowsiness, as mists floated aimlessly off of the warm surface of the lake and out over the surrounding meadows.

Ketanka interrupted this tranquillity with his heavy step and heaving breath as he reached the top of the ridge. He walked slowly along the crest of the black cliff, scanning from side to side, trying to locate Sequannah and stopping occasionally to peer between clumps of boulders. Sequannah remained still, partly because he was amused that the chief had not known exactly where he was, and because he wanted to find out just how well he was hidden. Ketanka meandered his way among the glacial rubble until he came to rest on a huge boulder within whispering distance of the young warrior.

"No sign of anyone?" mumbled the heavy chief.

"Nothing," Sequannah answered, surprised to find that the chief had known where he was. "I had not hidden well enough," Sequannah admitted. "How far away could you see me?" he wondered.

"I could see you all the way from the edge of the woods by the side of the lake," the chief whispered as if he would embarrass Sequannah in front of the whole tribe.

"How could you see me here, crouched between these boulders in the dark?" Sequannah questioned, trying to defend himself through the implication that the chief had supernatural powers.

"That was easy," the chief whispered with his gravely overtones. "I watched you come here before the sun went down. I was hoping to find you in another place; that's why I was looking around for you. What you should have done was to find a good place to watch from, and then when you have observed for a while and found nothing out of the ordinary, you should have crept over to another place that would be better or almost as good to watch from, in case someone had seen you. You must always be aware of what others can see. But at least you are awake. It shows that you have a good and healthy fear, and that you care about the protection of the clan."

Sequannah looked up with a solemn face. "I have no fear of the Paccus. I am a warrior now and will have no fear."

"Fear is what makes the best warriors," Ketanka stated. "Your fear can keep you awake. It can keep you alert and free from other distractions. Fear is what makes you plan your next move. If you have no fear, then you will make no plans. And if you make no plans, then you will not be a good warrior. Fear teaches the best way to survive, if you know how to use it and not let it use you by allowing yourself to panic...or imagine things that are not there. It is a voice that tells you when you are not prepared. Listen to it...You did well. Tamahna is at the bottom of the cliff," he gestured to the west end of the ridge. "If you had been acting foolishly, he would have been up here. Go back to the camp and get some sleep and be back here shortly after midday."

Only Venus was visible in the brightening eastern sky as Sequannah wound his way down the ridge, thinking over the chief's remarks. "If the chief expected me to move to different places, then why didn't he tell me?" Sequannah thought to himself. It seemed as though he couldn't do anything right and that the other warriors were probably going to spend their time ridiculing him, too. But, in actuality, this was Ketanka's crude, but effective way to teach and keep things interesting for the teacher as well. He had learned long ago that there's almost no better incentive than a person's pride to help them learn quicker. The trick is not to crush that pride, but to irritate it in a manner that causes people to question themselves. Then they will either reinforce or change their particular view to a better position.

As Sequannah strode into the encampment, he was surprised to find the clan awake and moving about. Everything seemed normal with the exception that there were no cooking fires. From his perch atop the cliffs, it seemed as though the whole clan had abandoned the area. Not a sound or hint of people could be detected, though everyone was preparing to move. As to whether they would move north to the next and outmost hunting area, or begin the long journey back to the south, seemed to hinge on the return of Petawahin and Quitkwa. Sequannah picked out a small piece of bear meat from the stew that was kept warm by the hot stones of the firepit in front of Meequaw's half dissembled lodge. Everything would be carried on their backs, with the exception of the heavy pine and spruce boughs which would be scattered or burned in the central firepit, whichever was most practical. Sequannah decided to take his rest, as the camp was nearly packed and ready to travel.

The women and children were just beginning to head out in small staggered groups to a wetland area east of them where many ripe berries could be harvested and cached for the trip back. Shatomi and Quebathe went with the first group and the stragglers quickly readied themselves in order to have time to catch up. Sequannah leaned against the outside of Petawahin's lodge as the last of the women and children drifted out of hearing range. He lapsed into the memories of the mist shrouded lake.

As the sun rose higher and the deer flies became more active, Sequannah became immersed in irritating and disturbing dreams. He could see a long edge of brush with many enemy warriors, barely discernible, peering through the branches at him. Each, in turn, would lunge out at him, then scramble back into the dense bramble. As he hit one of them particularly hard, his face began to sting and he awoke abruptly, only to find he had squashed a deerfly that had been biting him as he slept. As he looked around, after what seemed to be a momentary dream, he realized that most of the women and children were back now, quietly packing the berries they had picked. They had probably stirred up the deer flies that were now pecking away at him.

The conversations among the women were noticeably stifled as they tried to keep the camp noise to a minimum. Meequaw dished out a large portion of bear stew and berries to Shamira for her brother. As she handed the wooden bowl to him, she whispered, "I hope we move south. We have not seen anyone from the other clans all summer." Sequannah began to eat without answering. Shamira's eyes showed her irritation. "We will never see them if we head north. Do you think something is wrong? We have always run across at least one of the other bands."

"Maybe they all went further east this year," was all Sequannah had to offer. This underlying uneasiness had been with the tribe for some time now, though this was the first time anyone had spoken to Sequannah of it. He guessed that they actually would move south now, no matter how long the weather stayed good. In the past, whenever the clan began to feel uncomfortable, they always headed south. Sequannah savored every last bit of the grizzly stew and as he got up to return the bowl to Meequaw, he noticed the Washan walking into the encampment. He spoke in whispers to several women and when he caught sight of Sequannah, he gradually edged his way over to Meequaw's lodge where he could see that the young warrior was headed. As Sequannah thanked Meequaw for the stew, the Washan hooked onto his arm.

"Go down to the spruce trees by the lake and meet Ketanka. Three Paccus approach from the west and he wants you to meet him there."

Sequannah grabbed his spear and bow and raced silently towards the lake while the Washan stayed on, talking quietly with Meequaw. Sequannah noticed that Mokotak was now within sight of the band and that Quebathe and Shatomi had moved closer to the women and children. Apparently, the Washan had already spoken to them.

Sequannah skirted the open field that would normally have been the shortest route to Ketanka's position. He kept low and well hidden, and when he reached Ketanka, he could see the three Paccus climbing to the top of the black ridge. Ketanka turned to Sequannah, acknowledged his presence, and immediately focused back on the Paccus to observe their movement. From their position, they were a fair distance from the Paccus. Even so, Ketanka restrained his coarse voice.

"Be prepared to move quickly. Mahkawan is in the same boulders up there that you were in last night. Tamahna is still at the bottom of the cliffs." Sequannah looked up to the point where he was hidden last night and realized that the Paccus would probably work their way up the cliffs very close to that cluster of boulders, if that was not their destination to begin with. His heart raced to think that he could have been in the same situation that Mahkawan was in now, had the Paccus come earlier. He tensed as they climbed closer and closer to Mahkawan. When they were nearly upon him, they stopped and surveyed the area, talking and laughing as though they felt confidently alone. They shed their clothing and two of them dove into the lake from their lofty perch. The Minnecous looked on in amazement at the daring of the Paccus. The two divers surfaced, laughing at the Paccu remaining on the cliff. They taunted him in the Paccu tongue and tried to goad him into diving off the cliff, but he apparently had an insurmountable fear of diving from that height. As the Paccu warrior stood fully absorbed in the task before him, Mahkawan took advantage of the distraction and crept up to within arm's length, giving the coward a shove he would never forget. The Paccu fell end over end until he hit the surface of the water with a loud slapping sound. Even Ketanka cringed at the smack the surprised Paccu had just received. The chief shook his head and broke into a grin as Mahkawan stood at the top of the cliff, laughing and holding up the Paccu warriors' clothing for all to view.

"Let's go!" Ketanka told Sequannah, and they walked out along the eastern shore of the lake to effectively cut off that escape route. Mahkawan scrambled down to the base of the cliff with his spear and bow, effectively cutting off that direction, because now the Paccus had no weapons. Tamahna walked down to the western shore of the lake with his own array of weapons to cut off the final escape route; the southern end of the lake was distant and the Minnecou could walk there faster than the Paccus could swim. Tamahna and Mahkawan howled fierce war cries and threatened menacingly with their spears and bows from their separate positions. The only permissible route out of the water was in line with chief Ketanka and Sequannah. Ketanka stood somberly, holding his ground on the eastern shore of the lake while waiting for the Paccus to wade submissively out of the water, his arms folded across his chest to demonstrate his authority. Mokotak, Quebathe, and Shatomi joined Ketanka and Sequannah on the eastern edge of the lake, making this the most impossible route of escape. The Paccus, however, understood that this would be the only permissible route to undertake, knowing that the Minnecou could get to any point on the lake faster than they could swim. The whole clan suddenly appeared on the shore as the Paccus waded naked through the last few steps of knee deep water to the sandy beach. They held their heads high and appeared undaunted, despite their subdued position.

The women and children giggled and the men of the clan wore smiles of superiority, but the chief remained solemn and stared the Paccus down as though they were a pack of sheepish dogs. When the last of them relented, Ketanka croaked out the words to fill their stomachs.

"Start the fires," he bellowed. "These Paccus will be our guests until Petawahin and Quitkwa return."

Mahkawan tossed their clothes to them, but walked off to the council lodge with their weapons. Not one of them had the black spearhead, now sought by the Minnecou. The Washan was inside the council lodge when Mahkawan entered. He examined the weapons with a keen interest: two chert knives, modestly crafted; a very blunt tomahawk, obviously meant for crushing rather than chopping; and three spears, all made exactly the same except for some identification markings. The spears were not crude, but still lacked in refinement.

"I think they are a simple people," the Washan spoke softly. "Their weapons are simple. Their manner is not aggressive. They are isolated up here. Nothing I have seen or heard of them would cause me to think of them as a people with bad intentions. If they were, they would probably have stolen something or ambushed one of us by now. But, I am sure there will be much to learn from them later, especially about this area. I think they live here all the time. They didn't try to get accustomed to the cold water before they jumped off the cliffs."

Mahkawan was inclined to agree with the Washan's assessment. "They seemed surprised when I did not give them back their weapons. Most would wonder why we did not kill them."

Ketanka stepped into the council lodge and dropped down into the seat reserved for the chief. He, too, looked at the Paccu weapons but cast them aside like a pile of children's toys. He smiled a sigh of relief that seemed to suggest they had all been worried over nothing, yet it never hurts to be cautious when dealing with the unknown. He felt confident that Petawahin and Quitkwa would return soon without the Paccus ever detecting their presence; three of them had just nearly walked into the Minnecou encampment without even realizing it.

"After everyone is fed and comfortable, we will meet back here and try to talk with the Paccus," the chief spoke. "Washan, maybe you will be able to act as interpreter. You know more words than anyone else. We will keep the Paccus here until we are sure that Petawahin and Quitkwa are safe, but we will treat them as guests.

* * *

Melonak began the preparations with Meequaw and Shahte. They made stews with grizzly meat, wild onions, garlic, and yam-like tubers that grow off the roots of certain vines. Shamira took

Keshtahr and Petana to gather firewood for the feast. Sabatt and Kalashte went down to the lake to see if they could catch a few fish for the feast. Tamahna and Shatomi tried to communicate with the Paccus through sign language, though with very limited success. The Paccus took a greater interest in the two boys bow-hunting for fish. Soon, they were all fishing for the feast; the Paccus were allowed to use the bow one at a time. They apparently had never fished in this manner before because they were astonished to see even young Kalashte latch onto a large walleye. One of the Paccus caught a small trout under his foot as he chased it into the shallows, amusing everyone with his antics.

Kwoita made his way around the encampment, his long and thin gray braids hung loosely from his cocked head as he danced and chanted in his reverie with the Creator. Old men and Washans needed no excuse to dance, only the inclination. Shamira threw the first kindling into the firepit, and the old grandfather walked over to give thanks and respect to the Earth Mother, the heavenly father in the sky, and to the four directions, so the fire would keep the feast sacred. He moved on to tease Meequaw and to check on the progress of the preparations. He always snooped around the women and he always teased Meequaw, but this time, he was gradually working his way over to the lake to get a good look at the Paccus. He wasn't sure if he'd ever seen one before. As he walked towards the lake, he could pick out the Paccus quite easily, even from a distance. They were of a slightly lighter skin tone and a more slender build. They come from the mountains, he thought to himself. Their hair, too, was lighter. They must stay here in the north throughout the year, he mused, because their hair didn't have that hint of a bluish sheen common to southern dwellers and migratory tribes.

As he reached the shoreline, he saw that they were having quite a time for themselves in the water, unafraid of strangers and apparently unaware that they were being held as hostages of sorts. One of the Paccus looked up at him and nodded in respect. Kwoita nodded back and gave him the welcome sign customary to some of the mountain people he'd known long ago. The young Paccu looked astonished, and returned the same gesture. The Paccu went over to his two companions and spoke to them, pointing at Kwoita, but the old grandfather was walking away towards the black cliffs on the north shore of the lake.

He picked his way along the rugged terrain, slowly enough so that his breathing remained comfortable. The black, rain-smoothed basalt threw off an intense heat during the height of the day, and Kwoita's sweat began to run. Sometimes these rocks could be an old man's greatest comfort. On a cool summer night, their retained warmth would bring his sore old joints and bones to ecstasy, but during the day, they were absolutely torrid and of no comfort to anyone. As he reached the uppermost levels of the ridge, he spotted Sequannah eyeing his approach.

Sequannah scanned for any other Paccus that may have ventured into the area. He felt confident there were none. Even if there were, he would be little more than a messenger at this point, as the Paccus seemed to be fairly comfortable in the Minnecou encampment. He studied the slow and feeble ways of his grandfather's last few steps to the top of the ridge, but only as a source of curiosity; he didn't see himself as eventually being at the same stage. Kwoita appeared to be nearly helpless on the trail, but Sequannah didn't know if this was true or even if Kwoita himself had thought about it. Kwoita seemed to be living just to make sure that the tribe continued to live on in the old ways and did not forget their ancestors. The old man stopped a few paces from Sequannah and looked around, taking in the view of the area from this height for the first time. He looked down the face of the cliff to the surface of the lake below. He was stalling to catch his breath.

"The Paccus are a mountain people," he finally spoke. "When I was a young man, about your age, we traveled west for a time while we followed a huge herd of buffalo. When we reached the end of the plains, we came to a land where there were many tall mountains and clear rivers. We had killed so many buffalo that it became impossible for us to carry all of the meat back with us, and it was at a time when we should have been heading back to the south. I was just a young boy then, and there was a big council meeting where everyone argued. Some wanted to move back to the south because the days were getting colder and they were afraid we were going to get stuck there for the winter. Others said that we could only go if we left some of the meat to rot there, and the Creator would punish them for their wastefulness. Everyone was more in fear of the Creator than they were of spending the winter there, so we ended up staying and eating as much meat as we could, and making pemmican until we could carry it all back with us. But we were only there for a few days when the wind blew cold out of the north and the sky became gray and smooth. We piled many pine and spruce boughs on our wickiups because we knew that a big storm was coming and we could all feel that it would not be rain. The first snow came lightly and then gradually the flakes became smaller, but many more of them. It was not a hard snow like a blizzard but a steady, regular snow. After a day of this we thought it would be over when we woke up the next morning and then we would head back south. There was only a little snow...maybe just above our ankles. But the next morning came and it was still snowing. Not any harder, but not any less. Some said we should leave because there was not enough snow to stop us and it would end soon anyway. But the wiser ones said that it was always foolish to leave before you know which way the weather is changing and so we waited another day. But when the next day came, it was still the same, only the snow was up to our knees instead of our ankles. That storm did not end until five days later and by that time, the snow was almost up to our shoulders. And even after it did stop, two days later another storm blew in and it snowed for three more days. It was a good thing we stayed where we were because if we had left all that meat behind, we would still have been stranded, but with not enough food for the winter. Two moons later, when the ground was frozen hard and the trees popped in the night from the cold, our warriors grew fearful that we would run out of food before the spring greens had a chance to grow. They decided that maybe the buffalo herd we had chased all summer was stranded nearby some-where and that it would be worth going out to have a look. It was then that we came across a tribe of mountain people. They lived at the bottom of the mountains in the winter and roamed the plains in the summer and fall. Both of our peoples began to see more and more of each other, and when the spring finally came, we made one big camp together.

But, just like these Paccus, they always liked to dive from high places. That summer, all of us boys learned to dive, some of us from pretty high up. We really enjoyed that. We learned some of their speech and they learned some of ours, but mostly we talked with our hands. Our hand talk was also different, but it was still much better than trying to speak because many things were still the same in hand signs, but nothing was the same when we spoke. The Paccus recog-nized the mountain peoples' sign for welcome and so I know that they are related to them. They also are thinner than most people, but have bigger legs. I noticed this when I met the mountain people many years ago. When you see two or three of them, you don't notice this, but when you see many of them dancing together, you will always remember their big legs."

"When we left the mountain people at the end of that summer, we almost did not make it back to the south again because it began to snow on some days, so we never went that far west again. And now they are here. They must have traveled far this year," the old man mused.

"Grandfather," Sequannah said dejectedly, "Why do I have to stand guard here when it is plain to see that we are not the enemies of the Paccu? If any other Paccus come, they will see their own among us and see that we have not harmed them."

"It is always good to have someone watching," warned Kwoita, "Because we do not know what has happened with your father and Quitkwa. Suppose they found them, and Petawahin and Quitkwa killed one of them to get away? Then, they may chase them or try to follow them here. What will these three Paccus tell their people if they see that we have no one as scout here? Someone must always be watching." Kwoita stared into the distance, his eyes squinted as he tried to recall his thoughts before Sequannah distracted him.

"But also, I remember that when we were living with the mountain people, they had a very powerful Washan who they said could make the ground shake by talking to the spirits. He did not do it while we were there, but we did see him make the sky talk and that was enough to make our own Washan believe. When we were leaving, he told us that once we were both the same people...that we lived the same life. He said that a different people would someday come here and steal our spirits, and we would live only for them and their ways. He also said that we must always remember each other as lost brothers and sisters, because we could only survive together."

"Grandfather," Sequannah asked, "you have traveled for many years and have seen many different peoples. How will you know which one the mountain people speak of? Have you not told me that different tribes are as different as the different clans within each tribe?"

"Yes, and that is true," Kwoita assured him. "Some clans would be more suited to other tribes and some tribes would be more suited to other nations, but all of these different peoples and different ways add to the knowledge and survival of the people. We could go on for many winters living the way we do. But one year could come along where we would not be able to survive that one time, and by knowing different ways, at least we will have a chance to survive. There are people who live in one place all of the time because they have so many things that they need to survive, they could never carry them all. There are people far to the south who live in stone lodges and walk on stone paths. They pray to the Creator in structures as big as mountains, made of stone from the ledges and wood from the trees. These people work always on the fields that surround their villages of stone. They take the seeds of certain plants and sew them in the ground, and then they work all year bringing water there and making sure that no other plants grow there by constantly pulling them out. They take fish from the rivers and lakes, and instead of eating them all, they throw many of them into the soil with the seeds. They also throw animal dung in there to make the plants grow better."

"I don't think I would like to go there, Grandfather, I think I would be sick if I ate their food."

"They do not eat the dung and the rotten fish," Kwoita laughed, "The plants eat them."

"I'm not sure," Sequannah went on. "I don't think it would be good to eat something that eats dung and rotten fish. If I found berries or roots that had rotten fish and dung on them while I was out on the trail, I would not eat them."

"Well, I will tell you the truth," Kwoita went on. "You have already eaten of this food. The Minnecou in the villages to the south do the same thing, but we are already on the trail by that time. And the food is very good to taste. They have many kinds of pumpkins instead of just one kind like our village relatives have. They have things called squash, beans, and many hands of different kinds of peppers. They have melons which are very sweet. They have many trees with sweet fruit on them. But, the best thing is their corn. It is better than the corn our Minnecou relatives in the southern villages can grow. They grow many different types of corn and they make all kinds of food with it. They make breads and cakes, they make stews, and they eat it boiled like we do. I've even seen them dry it so that it is as hard as wood, then they would cook it in animal fat and the small kernels would burst into bigger food, like little clouds. Their Washans would make this at their festivals and everyone would be happy."

"They kept goats and some other animals they called llamas

to use for food and to make clothing with the hair of these beasts. They make containers and vessels for cooking and eating out of clay. They have many beautiful things in their stone camps. They carve many things out of stone and wood, and they decorated many things with a yellow metal that they said was sacred. Anything made of this metal belonged to the gods and the Washans. But all of these things are very heavy. It would take all of our clan a full year to move just one of their lodges from here to the next ridge, and they have many more things to move besides that. Even if they could move all of their things, they would never be able to move the fields where they grow their food. So, they must stay there all the time. They almost never go on the trail except to trade; sometimes for the things they need, but mostly for the things that they want. I lived there for a time, but the food did not make me feel strong and I grew stiff and sore from working in the fields and helping to drag the stones to build their lodges. I knew that I would feel good once I was back on the trail with the clan again and eating fresh meat, and so I left."

"Did you ever go back to the stone village, grandfather?" Sequannah asked.

"No, I never did," Kwoita said in a reverie. "After being there for so long, I missed the woods, the mountains, the plains, and the wild animals. I did not like staying in one place for so long. At first it seemed like a very amazing place to be, but I felt as though I didn't know anything. I was like a child and the people there taught me and took care of me as long as I worked with them. But, if I did not want to work, they would not feed me or even talk to me. They used to call me wild. I didn't know what they meant by this. Then one day, one of them who was my friend pointed out a wolf at the edge of a field. The wolf's ears lay flat and the grin on his face was gone. He knew he was in a place where he did not belong. My friend told me that I was like the wolf. He pointed to some dogs, playing in the village, and said that his people were like the dogs. I knew that he was right. Soon, everything began to look the same all the time. It all became too familiar, and I no longer wanted to work all the time or learn their ways. I remembered the trails I used to walk on when I was a child and I yearned to go there. So I left and I went back far to the north, to the woods where I roamed as a boy in the winters; the same woods we return to every winter now. The clan had already gone north long before I got there, so I spent a few days living alone in the woods near the Minnecou village of the Sachu clan. I was very happy to be with them because they are relatives and we had much to talk about. But, soon I grew tired of still being in the same place all the time and I could not wait for my own clan to return. The next year, when I was traveling with this clan, I knew that this was the best way for me to live, and I never went back to the stone village. When you grow older, you, too, will remember the times you are living right now and they will become sacred to you."

"Grandfather, I would like to stay on the trail like you, but I would also like to see the stone villages and the marvels of the people there. There are powerful Washans there and I have heard they have big sacred places where the gods come to them. I would also like to see how the Paccus live and where they travel to. They do not seem like bad people and they live almost like us. When I was smaller, I was afraid of these things, but I'm not anymore."

"You have passed the fear of your childhood because you are no longer helpless. You know what is going on and you can take care of others, as well as yourself. But, remember that once you become older, these fears will return, even though at that point you will know what is going on, because you will once again become helpless. You will realize that you are becoming a burden and you will not know from day to day when people will weary of carrying you any further. Fear will come more readily, too, because you will realize the consequences of exposing yourself to danger by remembering what happened to all the others who are now gone."

"The fear I had before and the fear I have in front of me will soon be overcome," Sequannah declared. "I will fear no more when I become older because the Creator will provide no power to those who have not learned to stay brave. I will die like a warrior and not live in fear, no matter how old I get."

"That is the true spirit of a warrior, my grandson, may you live out your life as a reminder to all. But, may you also learn which fears to avoid and which to listen to."

Kwoita still remained standing in the same spot as when he first came to the top of the ridge. He removed the old blanket he usually had draped over him and placed it before him. He stepped onto it, clad only in his breechclout, and chanted his song of praise to the Creator. On the last word, he did not hesitate, but dove headlong into the deep blue surface, a perilous distance from the top of the cliffs.

Sequannah ran to the edge in a panic. I have shamed my only grandfather into killing himself, he thought. There was no excuse for his insensitivity.

But the old man surfaced with a broad smile on his face, though he was sputtering with water he had taken in.

"Did you think I would die?" he laughed. "I like to remember my childhood." He rolled onto his back and paddled himself back to the beach.

CHAPTER 4

Petawahin and Quitkwa moved swiftly through the first part of their journey, unconcerned with inadvertent noises or trail sign they might leave. They ran at a steady pace until they came to within a small valley's width of the clear stream where Petawahin had made the carrying poles. Here, they moved stealthily and kept under cover; they were in Paccu territory. The two scouts crept slowly towards the small pond where the grizzly had been slaughtered. They stopped occasionally to listen in silence and to smell for campfire odor on the gentle current drifting in from the south. But, they found no sign of the Paccus until they reached the pond. They approached from the north under cover of the southerly wind flow.

When they reached where Petawahin had last seen the Paccu, they found the ground still darkened with blood, though scavengers had consumed the entrails. Large black flies feasted on the blood that had accumulated in globs and then dried flat against the dead leaves strewn about the water's edge. The travois marks were plainly visible, and the two Minnecou left immediately to follow the Paccu's well marked path.

They moved cautiously as they trailed the furrows westward. The humid air became stifling; not even the slightest of breezes stirred. A forbidding silence pervaded the area as they entered a shallow, darkening valley, where the last rays of sunlight lingered on the wide floor. Only the occasional whine from a lone catbird interrupted the steady rhythm of cricket song. They crept ahead, keeping the travois marks in view, but remaining under dense cover. Several crows cawed and squawked just ahead of them. Further along, a drone of buzzing flies obscured the ceaseless cricket song. Petawahin signaled to stop. The grizzly carcass lay ahead; he could just barely smell it. But the Paccu may have deliberately left a visible trail in order to ambush any following Minnecou.

They waited silently for several tense moments, but heard nothing. The twilight was fading rapidly and there had been almost no visible movement anywhere. In the stillness, a thickening haze began to ooze over the valley floor. Darkness came quickly and fireflies danced brightly in the steamy, moonless night. Mosquitoes tormented as a horde of other insects had taken to crawling over them. A chilling howl shattered the stifled night air. The Minnecou eyes flashed towards the crest of a gentle slope that served as the western ridge of the barely discernible valley. Several sharp barks emanated from somewhere beyond. Soon a pack of wolves loped hungrily towards the carcass; the yelping had not been Paccu imitations. Petawahin could hear the snarling, barking and ripping of the nearly two-day-old flesh. They gorged themselves for most of the night, mostly in silence, with occasional outbreaks of snarling and ferocious admonishments. Near dawn, the wolf pack abruptly left to return to their dens and pups. Petawahin and Quitkwa lingered to make sure there were no remaining animals, and to determine if anyone else could be waiting in the darkness. Petawahin felt assured they were alone. He walked over to where the wolves had gorged themselves on the grizzly's corpse, and tried to determine how much of it the Paccu had left. Quitkwa, following behind, searched for stray grizzly bones, and anything the Paccu may have left behind. The wolves had eaten everything down to the bones, which now lay scattered over a broad area. Quitkwa managed to find the dismantled travois in the midst of the scant remains. But from the few bones they had found, it was impossible to determine if the Paccu had left the entire load, or carried one of the quarters on his shoulders. Nothing could be done in darkness, though, so they crept back to their first location, where they would sleep until sunrise.

Neither had spoken since they first entered the shallow valley, but each understood the necessary course of action. They lay on the bare ground, fearful of making noise gathering grass to make a bed. But there was no need for such precautions. There was no one in the valley, nor had there been since the single Paccu had last passed through. But the Paccu had had the same sensations many times as he passed through these small arroyos, because they were ideal for ambushes. He dragged the grizzly meat to the closest one, in the hopes that anyone following would soon become anxious and perhaps turn back, or at least lose much valuable time.

Quitkwa and Petawahin slept lightly, but sufficiently, until a changing wind blew in from the west. The listless haze of the drifting, southern current, dissolved in an intensifying breeze from the west. There was no accompanying rain and the haze settled as dew on the surrounding flora; the grass and leaves crisped. The two scouts soon found themselves in a chill, and were thankful when the first hint of light began to soften the morning stars. They would be able to move, and warm themselves.

Petawahin was confident there was no one else in the area, but there was no way to be certain, so dense was the underbrush. He crept to various positions, watching and waiting, before he dared to stand. Then he sent Quitkwa to find the Paccu's trail, while he searched for clues to determine the Paccu's course of action. Quitkwa made increasingly wider circles in an effort to locate the Paccu's fading prints. On the third trip around, he found the hint of a moccasin in the dirt and traced a straight path back to Petawahin.

"The Paccu's trail goes west from here," Quitkwa said. "Should we follow now or find food first?"

"You did not bring pemmican with you?" Petawahin asked in astonishment.

"Yes, but it is all gone now," Quitkwa replied. "Do you have any more food?" he asked sheepishly.

"Yes, I have plenty," Petawahin stated. "For me."

"I'm hungry, Petawahin," Quitkwa begged.

"There are some fine grizzly bones over there for those who plan their moves like dogs," Petawahin admonished.

Quitkwa knew that no matter how much Petawahin seemed possible to dissuade, he was not. He picked up a large bone and tried to break it by jumping on it, but was unsuccessful. He then tried to snap it by using leverage between two hickory trees. Again, he was not successful.

Petawahin grabbed the bone from him and rapped it hard several times on a rock, then he peeled back the splinters to reveal the marrow. Quitkwa stood at his side, waiting patiently. Petawahin wrapped the splintered bone in rawhide, then stuffed it into the side of his breechclout. Quitkwa's jaw tightened as he realized that he wasn't going to eat unless he broke his own. He grabbed another large bone and started rapping it against a rock, but was getting nowhere. He banged a little harder and managed only to break off the end. Petawahin grabbed the bone from him and rapped it against the rock in just the right manner to cause it to splinter. Then, he wrapped this along with the other bone and stuffed them back into his breechclout. Quitkwa's face tensed visibly in frustration, and Petawahin handed the bones to him laughing.

"If you were my son, you would not have gotten them," Petawahin said after handing him the bones. "I would have let his hunger teach." Quitkwa was thankful for that. He lifted the splintered bone to his mouth, only to have Petawahin stop him before he could even get a taste.

"That is bear meat!" Petawahin stated.

"I know!" Quitkwa became upset.

"You will be sick if you eat bear meat—we will be making no fires today."

They stopped at a few blueberry bushes to sustain themselves. Petawahin's pemmican was all they had left, and there was no telling when they would have time to hunt down suitable prey.

Petawahin discerned that the Paccu had indeed carried one of the quarters away with him, making it even easier to track him because now his moccasin tracks would be deeper, he would disturb more brush, and he would have to rest more frequently. His trail led immediately out of the valley towards the northwest. Once atop the ridge, they could see for a considerable distance over a flat, bushy terrain. Directly north of them was a herd of elk, feeding on the thinning summer grasses. Petawahin could see the racks moving back and forth amongst the shoulder high growth. West of them stood a grove of pine and spruce, an immense island of boreal forest, unscathed by the glacial passing thousands of years earlier. A dense column of smoke drifted upwards from behind a ridge amongst the conifers.

"They are a foolish people to make such smoke for everyone to see," Petawahin muttered to Quitkwa, "but it could be difficult to cross the bush country to get there. They could watch from the edge of the forest or from the tall brush."

They waited for a short while, but the area seemed deserted. They crouched down low and nearly crawled as they made their way towards the distant conifers. The dense brush became more of a challenge with each passing step. Thorns and brambles appeared before them, growing in long strips, too lengthy to evade. Then, they began to flush grouse and quail, signaling their every move. Three times, they crossed well-traveled paths where it was impossible to see in either direction, unless they stood directly in the middle of the trail, in plain view. The footpaths, however, were abandoned. When they were nearly across the thick meadow, Petawahin could smell the smoke emanating from the pine forest; an acrid odor assaulted his senses.

Quitkwa's face grimaced. "What are they burning in there?" he asked in disgust.

"Smells like hair or feathers, or maybe hides," Petawahin suggested. "Let's keep moving. We'll find out where they are and whatever else we can, so we can head back soon."

As they crept through the shoulder-high brush, a heavy herbal fragrance permeated their senses, and though the air had dried out dramatically, the dense cover of flowers, brush and herbs seemed to emit a strong humidity of its own, hampering the very breath of the two Minnecou scouts. When they reached the first conifers, they could see easily into the forest. The trees had grown tall, and there was only scant vegetation from the ground to at least twice the height of a man. A crowd of jays screamed incessantly as the two scouts tried to maneuver quietly into the forest, making it nearly impossible to detect any noises that the Paccus might make.

As they slipped under the cool canopy, they were attacked by swarms of voracious gnats and mosquitoes, causing them to move too quickly in such a dangerous area. The terrain had changed abruptly from a flat tableland meadow, to a series of ridges that increased in size as they headed in a westerly direction. Each of these ridges was separated by marshes that unleashed onslaughts of mosquitoes, gnats and deer flies that would follow for as long as necessary to snatch a bite of flesh, or a drop of blood.

"I wish your father could be with us now," Petawahin whispered sarcastically.

"Ketanka does not enjoy this type of feast," Quitkwa laughed. "He likes to be the one who is eating."

They climbed over several ridges and forded the streams between, trying to avoid the swampy areas. Still, they had seen no one. The next ridge was much higher than the others, and smoke billowed out over the crest while the acrid odor sharpened. Wailing and shouting pealed through the din of an incessant slashing sound; the smell of blood and sweat mingled with the acrid smoke. At top of the final ridge, they found themselves near the edge of a sprawling encampment that reached down to the bottom of the next valley, to a large and swiftly moving river. The Paccu lodges were of animal hide and most had been set ablaze. Many butchered bodies lay scattered between the burning teepees. In the distance, a line of Paccus was being forcibly marched along the bank of the river. The village, itself, was deserted and pillaged.

They ran quickly down the hill and hid where they could get a better view of the victors hauling off their captives. The invading warriors were the most vile looking that either of them would ever have imagined. Their hair was caked in mud and their bodies were painted in sharp, jagged lines of yellow and black. The eerie grimaces in their brightly colored faces made the stomach wilt. They carried large clubs and spears, bows and arrows, knives, and some had long snakes in their hands that had been dried and tanned with the heads intact. They whipped their captives with these, and the fangs that had been filed down to half their original size, scraped into the Paccus' flesh.

Petawahin was not sure if these were men or demons. He had never seen or heard of war paint before. Every tribe had always looked different, but he had never known men as evil as these. He could see that the Paccu village was much larger than that of a Minnecou clan. Even the surviving captives would outnumber his own encampment by more than three to one. They now marched slowly in the distance, wailing in rebellion, fear and sorrow as they were pushed or tugged by those they had been shackled to with thick, grass-braided ropes. The two Minnecou warriors looked on in horror as the invaders drove their traumatized victims southward along the riverbank.

The gruesomely painted warriors were in complete control. Each knew his function and carried it out in its proper time, much like the clan would do on a buffalo hunt. They moved almost subconsciously, as if they had performed these same tasks hundreds of times. In the midst of the murderous swarm stood their sadistic and cruel looking leader, whose face was the only one left unpainted. While the others' bodies were emblazoned with jagged marks of yellow and black, this warrior had one stripe beginning at the back of his neck and running down between his shoulder blades in a black and yellow checkered pattern. In one hand, he held a long wooden staff with the triangular head of a viper carved into its handle. The other arm was covered with ringlets of carefully arranged hawks' feathers that fluttered in the wake of his movements. He walked slowly down the length of the procession as his principal warriors buzzed around him, awaiting his orders. Four effeminate looking attendants followed behind at a respectful distance, ready to fulfill his slightest whims, while trying to stay out of the way of his war chiefs.

Quiktkoata hadn't even looked over his latest acquisition of captives, but arrogantly retained the faint trace of a satisfied smile as he surveyed the scattering of butchered bodies, and the fanatical devotion of his hideous warriors as they raced around, desperately trying to please him. When the last of the captives had been dragged out of sight of the Paccu village, Quiktkoata's four attendants came quickly with the litter they would use to carry their oppressive chief. Petawahin seethed as the litter conveyed the arrogant leader out of view.

"Go back to the Paccu village and see if anyone survived," he ordered Quitkwa. "I will follow them till sundown and then I will meet you back here." His face clearly enraged, Petawahin glared sternly at Quitkwa as he spoke. Quitkwa nodded in compliance, relieved to have someone of authority in the aftermath of this sadistic massacre.

As Quitkwa made his way back up the slope, he found an arm that had been hacked off of a rebellious captive. He cautiously edged into the stench of the burning village and was surrounded by human corpses, butchered bloody and strewn haphazardly. He saw dead women left in prone positions, who had been raped, and then stabbed in the back repeatedly until the life force had been shocked out of them. But most of the Paccus had been shot through with arrows. Some had as many as eight arrows in them. None were alive. Anyone who lay even unconscious had been bludgeoned.

Quitkwa began to feel nauseous and nearly vomited as he strayed through the village. He did not want to wait here until dark for Petawahin to return, but he wasn't anxious to follow along with him either. As he looked around, he couldn't help but take in more of the gruesome details. Eyes had been plucked out and thrown onto the bodies. Some had been decapitated. Many dead dogs lay at the feet of the Paccus. This was indeed a traveling band, though much different than the Minnecou.

Intermingled were the dead corpses of the gruesomely painted warriors, none of which had been butchered. Along with these, Quitkwa found the remains of a surprising amount of snakes; all of which had been decapitated. The old legends of the Snake people whirled in his head. He bent down and touched the paint on one of the invaders' bodies and found that it came off rather easily, revealing these demons as ordinary men, painted with gruesome designs. But the overwhelming carnage forced him to look at other things to cushion the shock of the disaster surrounding him. He began instead to take an interest in their lodges, clothing and surroundings. The fires from the teepees had diminished to ashes and the smoke had cleared.

He had thought that most of the encampment was on the slope of a hill, but now realized that the largest part lay on a level area, and only the teepees at the fringe were on an incline. This was an encampment as large as the whole Minnecou encampment was in the winter, when all of the clans gathered in the south, near the salty water. He wondered if this was just such a gathering or if it was only a single clan like his father's. They had chosen a peaceful setting. He could hear the river rushing over a small set of falls below. Crows squawked from across the river; small birds chirped gleefully after the din of the battle as if nothing had changed at all. The sun shined down in rays through the clouds, as small patches of sunlight drifted eastward over the valley floor. He could picture the campfires cooking, with women preparing and stirring, while babies crawled about on the grass and children played by the river.

Now, he saw these same children trampled and their mothers butchered or tied up and marched away for some unknown, but surely unjustifiable reason. Some of the campfires were still burning and he noticed the smell of cooked meat intermingled with the wafting stench of the disembowelment of a whole tribe. He found some large pots made of clay, broken among the embers, their contents spilled upon the earth. One still remained standing and intact in the hot coals of a large cooking fire. It was a very deep, round pot with intricate designs sculpted into the sides of it, apparently through the use of a stiff piece of grass or some other small tool. It tapered to a point on the bottom so that it could be pressed into the embers, and yet still allow the pot to remain upright. Inside, wild leeks, watercress, and seeds from shepherds purse slowly flavored a stew of chunked grizzly meat. The Paccu warrior they were following had made it back with food to strengthen his relatives, but had witnessed their destruction instead.

Quitkwa's eyes teared as thoughts of his own family surfaced, and he empathized with the Paccus. His own clan had feasted in the same manner just the day before, and he thought, now, how strange it was that at that time the Minnecou were worried about the Paccus.

The sound of distant voices alerted him and he scrambled to the nearest bushes. He squatted; his bow notched and aimed. The horrid scene became meaningless. Previous feelings of sympathy and disgust vanished. He heard laughter and yelling, but they remained a respectable distance from him. Crawling down the hill to get a better look, he thought he heard children's voices. He was nearly at the river's edge when he finally caught sight of them. He couldn't tell how many there were because some were in the water, splashing and constantly moving towards the riverbank closest to him where they were out of sight. But, there were two young women standing on the bank, one of them holding an infant, while four or five children splashed in the water. They were Paccus, wearing the same type of clothing he had seen on the slaughtered bodies. They must have come down the path atop the riverbank, but from the north, the opposite direction from which the Snake warriors had just marched their captives.

As he tried to get a better view of the group, a sharp cry of warning came from his right and the two women scrambled into the bushes. The children swam under the overhang of the undercut riverbank and hid between the gnarls and roots of the huge trees that would one day be flotsam in the river. Quitkwa instinctively turned to the right just in time to witness the release of the arrow that simultaneously tore into his shoulder. There was just a pinch of skin surrounding the outside of the arrow, but Quitkwa pulled it through rather than rip the flesh. Before the boy could release another, Quitkwa had scrambled through the brush and pressed his chert knife to the boy's throat. The boy was no more than twelve and he alternately opened and then shut his eyes tight as he expected his untimely finish.

At seventeen winters, Quitkwa proved to be too much of a challenge, although, had the boy been slightly more accurate, or Quitkwa less fortunate, one of them may now lie dead or crippled. Quitkwa removed the knife from the boy's throat, and dragged him by the arm to where he'd last seen the rest of their party. He looked up and down the riverbank, but they were gone. Slipping down the bank and into the water, he dragged the boy with him. From here, he spotted them upstream from where they had originally entered the river, huddled under the roots of a large cottonwood where the current had undercut a particularly deep recess. He waded upstream in the waste deep water, still dragging the boy behind, but taking care not to look in the direction where the small party hid. They might think that he hadn't spotted them after all. When it was too late for them to escape, he turned directly towards them and let the boy go. The boy let out a loud scream, expecting the Paccu village to come to his rescue, and praying the Minnecou warrior would take flight as well. But the Minnecou stood his ground, his expression somewhat sorrowful; he didn't seem at all unnerved at the prospect of a whole Paccu war party at his throat. Surely, the boy thought, he must know that he is within hailing distance of the village.

Quitkwa had no idea of how to tell them that their families had been overrun. A line of blood traced the length of his arm as he motioned with his hands to tell them of the disaster in the village. The only thing they understood was the greeting in Minnecou sign language, and that was only because a little old woman, who apparently had been in swimming with children out of Quitkwa's view, understood this handsign. But this was getting nowhere as they remained huddled behind the thick entanglement of roots. Finally, he handed the bow and arrows back to the boy and motioned for them to follow. He knew of no other way to prepare them for the catastrophe but to coldly lead them onto the bloody scene. They climbed up the bank and Quitkwa followed them with the boy behind him, an arrow at the ready, but not yet notched to the bowstring. Quitkwa pointed towards the Paccu camp.

As they walked the narrow path, the children remained quiet, their shoulders slightly hunched as if they expected a blow to the neck at any moment. The old woman, however, spoke to them in a calming manner. She turned back and smiled at Quitkwa, while the children laughed nervously at something she uttered in Paccu. She sensed that he didn't really intend to harm them and that perhaps he was a friend to someone back at the village.

They ascended the gentle slope towards the village, to a point where the smell of burnt hides became noticeable. Quitkwa ran ahead and stopped the small party. They glanced at each other, sensing that something was very wrong, not knowing whether they wanted to continue or not. The village was eerily silent. Something terrible had happened. Quitkwa grabbed the young boy's arm, for he appeared to be the most capable to handle the grisly scene, and led him towards the camp. The others began to follow and Quitkwa yelled once again for them to stop. But the old woman shouted back in a mixture of Paccu and Minnecou admonishments, and they continued to follow him into the camp.

The old woman moved ahead of Quitkwa and the boy, right into the midst of the horrible stench of butchered and burnt bodies. Her expression was blank; the children screamed and wailed. Two little girls tried to run away, but Quitkwa caught them and convinced them to stay outside of the encampment, but still within view. The two older girls hugged each other, crying and wailing loudly; the young infant held between them looked around in uncomprehending bewilderment. The young boy stood, tears streaming down his face, but not a sound uttered from his open mouth. Quitkwa looked to the old woman to see what she would have him do. He felt that if she was strong enough to walk in amongst her own dead, she could bring some order and sensibility back to their small party. But when she turned around, her face was ashen, and she swayed and then fell to the earth.

Quitkwa yelled to the young boy for help, but he stood open-mouthed until Quitkwa went over and shook him. He couldn't even imagine his own reaction had this been his encampment, but he hoped that he would have the strength to continue on with what had to be done. They found some blankets woven from goat's hair and placed the old woman on them. The two young women at the edge of the village were given charge of the infant and two other small children, while Quitkwa sent the boy to the river to fetch water.

When the boy returned with the water sac, Quitkwa dumped the entire contents on the old woman, hoping that her heart had not given out and that she would regain consciousness. She snapped upright, screaming at him; he knew she would be alright. She crawled off of the blankets to vomit, then lay down again, chanting and wailing. When she finally regained her composure, she beckoned the two older girls to come to her, and explained to them how they must prepare the bodies for their journey into the next world.

The two young women laid out many pine boughs and then began to strip and wash the bodies, placing each on its own pile of boughs. The old woman had the boy pounding stakes through the bodies of the Snake warriors so that they would have to remain in their rotting carcasses and not be allowed into the next world while still being staked to the earth. Later, they would be buried where they lay so that no person or animal would drag them away from their stakes and allow them to continue on into eternity.

Quitkwa could see that there would not be near enough pine boughs to place all of the bodies on, so he got all the children involved, not only to help with the work, but also because he seemed to be the only one left to watch them. He left the oldest of the children to supervise the others while he helped the boy pound stakes through the remainder of the Snake warriors, and carry the Paccu bodies over to the two young women. The old woman went through the charred teepees in search of red ocher in order to dress the bodies properly.

Quitkwa wandered back to where the pot of grizzly stew remained embedded in the warm coals. The stew had cooled to the point where he could reach his hand into the warm broth and extract a tender cut of rich, slowly simmered meat. As he savored his first mouthful, he noticed that the children had left their work and run down the hill towards the river. He stood erect to see where they were going. Another party of Paccus was approaching the burned out village.

* * *

Petawahin walked southward along the riverbank, following the strange warriors and their captives. There was no doubt in his mind but that these were the vicious Snake people who had destroyed the Paccu encampment. The stories that had once seemed absurd, now appeared to have some foundation. He climbed the slope to the top of the ridge, where he would not be easily detected, and able to see on both sides of him. He had his bow at the ready in the event that he was spotted first. He knew they couldn't have gone very far in the short time he had watched Quitkwa, and that they would be traveling slowly anyway. He took his time walking the ridge line, being careful not to make any inadvertent noises or to walk blindly through possible ambushes. As he paralleled the trail of the Snake people, he thought they'd be in view as he came around each bend. But they weren't visible until he'd traveled around many hillsides. The captives were driven at a frantic pace, considering how they were nearly hobbled. They were sweating into their scrapes and bruises, but too out of breath to wail at the same time. The Snake warriors jogged alongside, whipping and clubbing, as the Paccus jerked and dragged each other along through the tangle of rope that kept them lashed together.

Petawahin began to trot along the top of the ridge to keep pace with them, but was extremely wary of the painted scouts. Their tactics were very effective and well thought out. By moving swiftly, not only did they get a good start, but anyone following would be easier to spot as they raced through the many open areas. He took to stopping and observing, and then sprinting from one position to the next. Overtaking the procession, he sought to reach their turning point before they arrived, hoping that they would not move south along the entire length of the river.

Petawahin moved downstream, quite a distance ahead of them. There were no scouts other than those staying right along the riverbank. Two lead scouts steadily retraced the attack route, not venturing far enough off the trail to run into Petawahin. He paralleled them until they stopped to wait for the procession. Then he moved ahead until he reached a small ravine heading eastward. Here, he found where the trail led away from the river. But, if they headed back to the east from this point, and if his own people had decided to move south, there was a good chance that the Minnecou could meet up with the Snake people or cross paths ahead of them. The Snake warriors couldn't wage another battle with so many captives to guard, but there would be reason for them to return if they found Minnecou in the area as well as Paccus.

He studied the hundreds of footprints and noticed that there was a lump in the arch of each print. This distinction would always tell him when they were around and where they had been. He moved further up the ravine, as he was a considerable distance ahead of the war party, and found holes dug into a sandy area, filled with paint mixtures. Apparently, they had mixed colored powders with water right in the ground, and then painted themselves or each other to give them the most horrible and frightening appearances. There was a wallow of thick and fine grained mud from which they had caked their hair. He found several knives of a reddish-green metal, apparently dropped and thought to be lost in the mud. A spear had a similar copper point. Both were thick, but not very sharp. A sudden movement distracted him.

A long, black snake wound along the length of a gray-weathered, fallen tree. It lifted its head. Petawahin, not looking directly at the strange serpent, became aware that it was following his every move. He'd never known of a snake that would follow a man's movements unless it was close enough to be in immediate danger. Petawahin remained aloof and pretended to be studying a trail of footprints that led to within a few steps of the large snake on the log. He picked up a stout stick and turned on the snake with stunning speed, but it took flight along the length of the log the moment Petawahin had even touched the stick. His first swipe missed the serpent by a full length and it slithered rapidly away in a baffling swirl. The next swing caught the very middle of the snake's body. It turned, and in a screaming hiss seemed to curse every shred of Petawahin's existence. The serpent bolted once again and Petawahin noticed the long stripe that began between its nostrils and ran down the length of its back. He immediately recognized the yellow and black checkered pattern that filled out the width of the brilliant stripe, but he couldn't remember where he'd seen it. He took another swing, trying to smash its vile looking head, but the serpent stopped short and began to slither away into an unseen hole. Petawahin was stunned as he watched this most unusual snake vanishing lengthwise into the air. In a desperate effort, he dove and caught the end of the snake's tail. There was a little resistance, then the piece broke off in his hand. He grabbed again and tried to pull the serpent out of the dimension into which it was making its escape, but there was no way to pull it back. With all of his strength, he couldn't budge the snake back out, but if he let up for an instant, the snake would wrangle in a little further, and Petawahin was left with that much less to hold onto. He held on as tight as he could with one hand and reached for his chert knife. He hacked away until he had cut off almost the entire back half of the snake. A chilling shriek rang in his ears and the wriggling piece of snake fell through his fingers as dust, vaporizing into a thin, foul-smelling smoke before reaching the ground.

Petawahin had heard of such things happening before, but he'd never believed they were actually true. As he thought about this, he realized that he was actually standing some distance away from where he had just had the experience with the serpent. He swore to himself that what had just happened was real, yet not even his own footprints came close enough for him to reach the snake, even with the stick he had used to club it. He then realized that the experience had occurred in his mind, but not in the physical reality of his world. He dismissed it as a strange dream.

In the distance, the yells and taunts of the painted ones grew louder as they drove the captives toward him. As the procession approached, Petawahin heard the low moaning and wailing of the Paccus' suffering, and hid in the nearby brush. The procession suddenly halted. There was some confusion among the Snake warriors; messengers were running back and forth along the trail. A rumble of thunder echoed in the distance, but there were no clouds in the sky.

At the head of the procession twenty Paccus were tied together, with eight painted warriors driving them along. But most of the Snake warriors suddenly ran back along the procession to protect the rear, leaving only two, their bows at the ready and aimed directly into the group of hobbled and unarmed Paccus, to guard over the lead group in the string of captives.

Petawahin waited till the other Snake warriors were out of earshot and pulled back with all of his strength, piercing the back of the nearest painted warrior at a point where he determined his heart would be. He immediately loosened two more arrows into the throat and eye of the furthest Snake warrior. Neither let out a loud cry, for they had been fatally stricken.

Petawahin moved quickly and slashed the heavy braids that enchained the suffering Paccus. Those who were freed took the copper knives from the dead guards and cut their friends and relatives loose. They seized the weapons from the dead Snake warriors and Petawahin led them swiftly back along the hidden side of the ridge line, towards their ravaged encampment.

*　*　*

Petawahin and the freed Paccus moved quickly into the Paccu village, and after locating Quitkwa, determined that they must leave immediately in the event that the Snake warriors had followed their trail. Twilight was upon them and the glow of sunset was fading. Petawahin pulled Quitkwa aside.

"We must get back to our own, now," Petawahin demanded. "The snake people may be heading directly towards them. There are not enough Minnecou in our clan to fight them off, especially without warning and without us. The Paccus must either follow or go their own way, but the Snake warriors will surely come back here, even if they didn't find our trail. If they catch up with us, they will not be taking captives. If the Paccus want to follow us back to the clan, it would be best for all of us, because with them and the clan together, the Snake warriors would be foolish to attack. We may be able to free more of the captives later."

Quitkwa went to gather his weapons, then ran back to Petawahin. They headed out towards the east, back through the conifer forest. The Paccus, at a loss of what to do or where to go, left everything and followed the two Minnecou with what few weapons they could find. Two of the Paccus remained behind and gathered food and more weapons.

Petawahin led the way through the small forest and quickly crossed the flat and open meadowland; those who could not keep up would be left behind to fend for themselves, because Petawahin would allow no time to be wasted in getting his warning to the clan. When they reached the eastern side of the meadow, they scrambled down the embankment; even the children kept pace–their survival depended upon it. They followed the long, shallow ravine back to the pond where two days earlier Petawahin and Sequannah had come to the aid of the Paccus for the first time.

Here, there were two Paccu warriors awaiting them with a cache of food and more weapons. The young Paccu with whom Petawahin had battled the grizzly had been among the group of freed Paccu captives, and after following for a short distance, had ascertained Petawahin's intentions. Knowing a shorter route, he arrived ahead of Petawahin with the other Paccu and brought the cache to a place of dire need, risking only his and another Paccu's lives. Petawahin placed a hand on the young man's shoulder, acknowledging him as a warrior with strategy. The Paccu still had no idea of what he was saying, but nodded in appreciation of Petawahin's compliment. Each took what they needed and raced eastward.

CHAPTER 5

Shortly before dawn, Mokotak raced through the Minnecou encampment, arousing the sleeping clan–a group of Paccus was about to descend upon them. Ketanka had everyone gather their weapons and lay low in the underbrush. They watched in readiness as a band of Paccus headed towards the cliffs from the far side of the lake. The Minnecou could have fled, but with a large group stumbling through the darkness, they couldn't possibly have covered their trail, and would have been more vulnerable on the run.

The Paccus appeared ragged and weary as they slowly ascended the steep trail to the top of the black cliffs. Two of them scrambled quickly over the heights and ran directly into the camp, shouting in Minnecou. Ketanka was surprised to discover that Petawahin had led the Paccus right to them. The Minnecou came out of the underbrush, while the Paccus stumbled into the camp behind Quitkwa and Petawahin.

"These Paccus are with me," Petawahin shouted. "They have seen battle with many evil warriors. These enemies are very dangerous and kill anyone they do not hold as captives. They may be the Snake people we have heard talk of through the winters, but now they are coming here. I brought these Paccus so we will be able to fight them if they come this way."

"We will not wait for them to find us," Ketanka bellowed. "We will send out a large scouting party and find them now. Any of the Paccus who want to go are welcome, but from what I can see, most would do better to rest. There is no time for a council meeting. Every able warrior gather your weapons and return here immediately while I talk with Petawahin and Quitkwa."

The old woman whom Quitkwa had encountered with the children began to shout to all of the Paccus. The Minnecou were amazed to see her shouting at the Paccu warriors, but when she walked over to Kwoita, the old grandfather, and seemed to recognize him as she spoke softly in Minnecou, they realized that she was merely translating. Quitkwa was amazed to hear her fluent, yet strangely accented Minnecou, but realized that he had never even tried to speak with her.

As the battle-ready warriors headed back to the center of the encampment, Ketanka drew a long line, starting in the west, and curving to the other side of an arc facing the southeast. As each warrior came into line, he was paired off with another warrior to make ten equally strong teams of Paccus and Minnecou. Ketanka stood at the focal point and all teams faced outward from him.

"All pairs will go forth in the direction they are facing," he bellowed out. "Move quickly to the top of the next ridge. But from that point on, be cautious, and keep guard against any movement of strangely painted Snake people. Keep in view of the team on either side of you, so you can signal to them when you find the enemy. Retreat to a safe place if you find them, letting everyone in view know what is going on. Avoid fighting unless it is necessary, but find out how many there are, what they are doing, and where they are going. Then send messengers back to let us know. Soon, the light of dawn will begin to brighten the eastern sky. When the sunrise color fades away, return here, whether they are found or not. There will be no fires, so if you smell smoke, it will not be ours. Go quickly and return in the bright daylight."

All of the warriors ran swiftly in their appointed directions. Those heading west or southwest gathered in a small war party on the single trail through the swampy interlude at the southern end of the lake. Tamahna and Mahkawan each paired off with young Paccu warriors. The young warrior who had killed the grizzly with Petawahin and Sequannah, was now keeping pace with Mokotak, and the more he saw of this massive warrior, the less sure he became of whom he was actually more afraid. He felt more secure with their combined strength, but he also sensed that this warrior would attack the whole of the painted warriors without fear or even thought of his own life. The young Paccu was not quite prepared for this type of sacrifice yet, but to live and be known as a coward would be equally punishing.

Sequannah was paired with what seemed to be one of the most capable of the Paccu refugees. He announced his name as Woltah, doing a brief and graceful dance with his spear. Sequannah merely stated his name and signed a greeting to the muscular, though pompous warrior. He wondered if all of the Paccus would announce themselves in this manner, but the three who had come to them the day before had not done this. By all appearances Woltah seemed clever, tricky, strong and enduring. But, Sequannah had already heard much of what had happened at the Paccu village. If he was truly a great warrior, Sequannah thought to himself, wouldn't he have been counted among the dead instead of the captive. Sequannah and Woltah moved directly south, with Mokotak and Karnack on their left. Quebathe and one of the three Paccus who were taken in with the Minnecou the previous day, stalked to their right.

Each team was comprised of one Paccu and one Minnecou and two of the teams were made up of just Minnecou so that at least everyone who was Minnecou would be able to understand the handsign of their parallel teams. Many of the Paccus were too exhausted to scout out the Snake people, and remained in the Minnecou camp. Petawahin and Quitkwa were also forced to remain behind. Though they protested, Ketanka reminded them of the possibility that the painted ones could also come from some unexpected direction. This, however, was not quite enough to stifle their complaints. Kwoita and the Washan were allowed to prowl around behind the scouting party; two of the most feeble and defenseless warriors imaginable. While it was risky, Ketanka felt that their combined wisdom and experience would be indispensable to the ten teams in front of them.

As the silvery beginnings of dawn spread flames of red, orange and purple across the sky, two of the teams dangerously out-paced the rest of the scouting party. Though they could see each other, the warriors behind became indistinct and too distant for handsign. Mokotak and Woltah respectively were at the head of each, sprinting in a south-southeasterly direction, as if they knew exactly where the Snake warriors were. There was no sign of smoke in the air, however, and no movement anywhere.

Kwoita and the Washan, quite a distance behind the line, noticed the gap and pressed ahead to try and fill it. They thought that perhaps it would be better to have an advance party, but if either end of the line was to be first in encountering the hostile enemy, it could lead to disaster, especially on the western end. Ketanka should have foreseen this and placed the most experienced team there. Everyone would be in jeopardy if the line were to cross ahead of the Snake warriors instead of behind them.

Just as Kwoita and the Washan caught up with the rest of the line, the Washan experienced an overwhelming sense of evil and disaster lurking ahead, and signaled in both directions for all teams to halt. Mokotak, Karnack, Woltah and Sequannah were now completely out of view and therefore out of touch.

The Washan remained motionless, scanning for a visible sign to confirm his instincts. The others stood in patient curiosity, wondering what it was that should hold them up. Some distance ahead of them, Kwoita noticed a large black shadow maneuvering its way along a path that would lead directly between the two advance groups and the initial line of scouts. He pointed this out to the Washan because he couldn't see clearly enough to determine exactly what it was. The Washan signaled the others to remain still while he went ahead to investigate. The further he proceeded, the more fluid the shadowy mass appeared. The other teams noticed the object of the Washan's foreboding as well. The Washan froze as he finally crept close enough to see that the slowly moving shadow was actually a mass of wriggling serpents. All were heading in the same direction, some of them twice as long as a man. Very rarely had he seen snakes even close to this length, but never moving in numbers. The Washan remained motionless; snakes cannot see that which does not move, nor perceive what they cannot smell. They were swirling along at a quicker pace than the Washan had originally thought, and in greater numbers. Three large huts lashed together would take up less space than this nearly solid tangle of thick, black snakes.

The leading edge of the mass stopped suddenly, and the trailing serpents slithered right over them. Out of the wriggling confusion, several large snakes wound their way off in a southeasterly direction along the freshly traveled path of Woltah and Sequannah. Several also headed in the direction of Kwoita and the Washan, along the same path that Sequannah and Woltah had come from. The slithering mass then continued on, leaving three small vipers to mark the trail. The dark, creeping shadow had not gotten far when it stopped cold, as if it had run into the base of a cliff–they had scented the trail of Mokotak and Karnack. Once again, several large snakes broke off from the boiling throng and wound their way down both directions of the trail.

Kwoita looked up to see the Washan trembling in fear: his face in a sweat, his color pallid. Kwoita knew they were in more danger than he himself could perceive, because he knew the Washan to be fearless. Most Washans could shed their emotion in order to allow their instincts to remain unencumbered. Kwoita became alarmed as the snakes approached the fear-stricken Washan.

"Washan! Do we kill them?" he whispered loudly.

There was no reply. The Washan didn't even turn back. There was an odor of moist clay in the air as the serpents crept to within striking distance of the Washan. Kwoita picked up a heavy piece of wood to swing at them–he might not be quick or accurate enough to kill them with his spear. The serpents immediately perceived his movement and diverted from the Washan in a straight line to Kwoita. Kwoita was shocked into a frozen paralysis as he merely glimpsed the hypnotic stare in their golden orbs. It was too late to realize that what had tried to overcome the Washan, now had complete control over him.

The Washan's spell broken, he grabbed his spear to help the aged grandfather in his helpless state. The serpents were totally absorbed with Kwoita. The Washan thrust his spear into the base of one of the wide triangular heads, then pulled back quickly, ready to bolt. The viper turned halfway, but immediately recoiled to its fix on Kwoita. The Washan warily stepped up to the serpents once again and speared the same viper, severing its head. He ran several paces in anticipation of their immediate diversion to him, but they never moved. They appeared to be as entranced as their victim. Four serpents were beheaded before Kwoita's trance was broken and he was able to help kill the remaining two. The Washan poked under leaves and into the underbrush to insure that they had disposed of them all.

The warriors on either side of them closed in to investigate. As the first team from the east crossed the trail used by Mokotak and Karnack, they glimpsed another contingent of serpents, and they too became entranced. The Washan moved only when he saw the team freeze and he could get a fix on their traumatized gaze. Again from the rear, he beheaded every snake, apparently unperceived. All of the warriors had gathered within a few short moments.

"These snakes are not normal snakes, they are with the painted ones. Do not look directly at them or you will not be able to move," the Washan stated. "If you have seen the snakes that crossed in front of us, then you know that this is unusual and that for them to send out groups that follow the scent of a trail is unnatural, especially where humans are concerned. There are snakes left to mark the trails, and others that went off in both directions of each path. They are still following Mokotak and Sequannah, and we must get to them quickly, but first we must kill these snakes that sit in the trail."

Two clusters of vipers were coiled on the path, awaiting the advance of the Snake people. The Washan and the others spied from a distance, deciding who would distract the snakes so they could creep up from behind. Those who had already fallen under the serpentine spell adamantly refused to volunteer, and the others became leery themselves. Two Paccus stepped forward aggressively, though their nervousness was apparent. They signed their intentions and the Washan immediately sent them off in a wide circle to come up behind the snakes. Once they fell under the spell, the snakes would already be facing away from the attacking warriors.

The two Paccus paralleled the trail for a short distance, then doubled back to where the vipers remained coiled. Sensing movement, the snakes reeled to face the two Paccus and, like the others, the Paccus immediately fell under the mysterious influence of the serpents' power. As the Washan and the others stood upright and took their first few steps, the Paccu who was with Quebathe called out a short and stifled halt. Behind them, two gruesomely painted warriors poked around the underbrush, then climbed a small hill to get a better view of the surrounding area; they were scouts in advance of the main party.

One of the Snake warriors spotted the two Paccus, spellbound in the snakes' trail. Both warriors whooped ecstatically as they raced towards the two victims transfixed to the evil stare. Quebathe and the Paccu crept swiftly through the underbrush and tripped the scouts up with their spears, impaling them where they fell. The Washan and the others killed the vipers that marked the trails, freeing the two Paccus from sacrifice. But there was no time to follow Sequannah or Mokotak; the clamor of the advancing Snake warriors' procession could already be heard. They fled north over the nearest ridge, closer to the Minnecou encampment, carrying the two bodies with them. The Washan gathered the dead snakes and threw them well away from the trail, while taking the time to place a few of the severed snake heads in the satchel hanging from his breechclout.

The Paccu and Minnecou warriors hid and waited for some time at the considerably distant ridge before the main party of Snake warriors finally came into view. Many now felt that they could have saved the two advance parties had they tried, but there was no way of knowing just how far ahead they had strayed. Their fates appeared to be grim; they would be overtaken by an ambush from the rear. Even if they looked back frequently, they would not be on guard for an enemy slithering at ankle height. The Paccus watched with disgust, fear and anger as their relatives trudged along in the distance like so many fish on a string. The Snake warriors strutted along, unleashing their sadistic impulses with sickly laughter or even casual indifference. Several captives were dragged along individually with knives to their throats, apparently to deter any other Paccus from trying to escape. Each group consisted of twenty to thirty Paccus and six to ten of the painted warriors prodding them along with spears and the whips made from snake skins. Two bands of a dozen Snake warriors each constantly patrolled the flanks of the procession, scrutinizing the prisoners and their forested surroundings.

In the middle of the procession, a cruel looking chieftain posed arrogantly on his litter, a thatched canopy shielding him from the elements. By the size and effectiveness of the umbrage, the scowl on his face was plainly of cold contempt for his underlings and not the beginnings of a squint. He didn't appear to be looking at anyone in particular, but rather over everyone. It was evident that he was in complete control and that those who fell under his icy gaze would not expect to be lavished with praise. So effective was his demeanor, that none of his warriors would risk looking directly at him. Yet, the instant he raised his hand, the whole procession came to à halt. Four warriors raced from each direction.

The procession hushed as everyone awaited his commands. The Minnecou scouting party heard a vague mumbling from the distant litter. Soon, Snake warriors began beating about in the bushes with their spears, while a group of six painted warriors sprinted ahead in search of the two advance scouts. Two attendants helped their chief down from his litter. A large black crest on his head fanned from front to back. Starting at the base of his skull and running down the length of his back, was a long stripe in a yellow and black checkered pattern. He shoved the two attendants away as they propped him up, but fell immediately to the ground from whence he began to swing at them with his staff for not catching him. It appeared that his legs were paralyzed and he was in a rage. They picked him back up and propped him against a tree which he held onto with both hands as he turned himself slowly about to survey the area. It seemed strange to the Minnecou that the Snake warriors would obey and fear one in such a disabled condition.

Still, almost no sound came from the procession, except for the low grumbling directed unrestrainedly towards the two attendants. They hurried to carry out his every command, running to prepare everything quickly and in a meticulous manner. The two of them once again escorted him to the litter and when one of them tripped over a stone, even though the leader had not fallen again himself, he batted the fallen attendant unconscious with his staff. One of his chief warriors kicked the slumped body into the underbrush.

Many of the warriors began to return to the procession with the limp carcasses of dead snakes in their hands, most with severed heads. As each warrior brought in a dead snake, he was placed in a formation consisting of two lines on either side of the procession. Four of the six warriors who had gone ahead, came back with the news that there was no sign of the two advance scouts. The chieftain cursed and screamed, waving his staff in the air. Dark clouds began to appear on the horizon as rolls of thunder boomed in the distance. The Snake warriors hadn't found a trace of their enemies, other than dead snakes. The cruel one looked down to the ground and noticed the faintest trace of a moccasin print headed towards the southeast. He immediately dispatched six warriors in that direction. He then shouted out to the two lines holding the dead serpents, and they began to beat and whip viciously at the captive Paccus with the snake corpses. The chief of the Snake warriors bellowed out at one of his warriors for severely injuring one of his Paccu slaves and had him whipped as well.

The Minnecou had to hold several of their Paccu allies at bay; there was no way to even conceive of getting to the captives without being captured themselves, though the Paccus couldn't bear to watch their relatives being whipped. The cruel chief of the Snake people hoped to flush the escaped Paccus out with this vicious display, but with the Minnecou holding them in check, he resorted to yelling out taunts and laughing haughtily as his soldiers tortured their captives. But there were just too many Snake warriors, capable and well-armed. Any attempt at rescuing more Paccu captives was certain to end in disaster. The vicious chief of the painted ones sneered as he scanned the wooded ridges for signs of movement. He rested back upon his litter, convinced that the escaped Paccus were some distance away, but within view of their suffering relatives. He reveled in their fear of him and his fierce warriors. From over the ridge behind the procession, another band of Snake warriors suddenly appeared. The Washan was relieved that he and the other Minnecou had been able to quietly subdue their Paccu allies, but dismayed that all these warriors were patrolling in back of the procession. They may discover the two teams that had strayed.

Shortly after these warriors had appeared, six warriors dragged Woltah and Sequannah out of the brush and up to the Snake chief's litter. Woltah's legs were tied together with his hands lashed behind him. One warrior held onto a crop of Sequannah's hair, pushing him along in front of him. His feet barely touched the ground. Only his hands were tied.

The Washan sent everyone back to the Minnecou encampment to defend it in the event it was discovered. Only he and the Wolf brothers would trail the Snake warriors. He felt it necessary to go himself in order to find out what other powers they possessed. The Paccus began to follow along, but the Wolf brothers and Quebathe threatened with their spears; they didn't want the Minnecou camp to be threatened because of foolish maneuvers from the Paccus. Tired and weary as most of the Paccus were, there was little they could do to resist.

Quebathe and Shatomi led them back through the swampy trail at the southern end of the lake. Their trail sign was meticulously concealed once they entered the swamp, and diversions were set up everywhere to send followers into the bogs, sinkholes and pockets of quicksand. The quicksand was of a loose consistency, where a body would sink immediately up to the chest, but became more viscous after this point. The feet of the victim would then become helplessly mired, with the head almost completely submerged. When they stood on their toes to reach for the next breath of air, they sank further into the deep pockets, drowning within moments of slipping into the mire. The Minnecou showed the Paccus how to set up diversions and false trails that would lead their enemies into clusters of such mires.

Quebathe smelled fire and noticed that the others were also becoming aware of the odor of burning leaves, sifting into the swampy area. He and Shatomi led them quickly towards the Minnecou encampment and as they ascended the last few steps out of the low-lying, alluvial swamp, billowing pillars of smoke became visible towards the southeast.

CHAPTER 6

Petawahin wakened abruptly. The scent of burning forest meandered into his dream, and he jerked upright in alarm. He crawled to the entrance of his small wickiup and lifted the old flap; his eyes stung as he perceived columns of smoke rising in the distance. Down near the lake, Ketanka's roaring hurled the returning scouts into motion. He couldn't see Sequannah, nor Mokotak and the Wolf Brothers. The group seemed to be quite thinned; especially of Minnecou warriors. Petawahin shook off his stupor and raced to intercept them.

"Where is Sequannah?" he asked. "Where is Sequannah? The Wolf Brothers? Mokotak? Washan?"

"Your son and one of the Paccus were captured by the Snake people," Ketanka explained solemnly as he placed a hand on Petawahin's shoulder. "The others are trailing them."

"You knew he was too young," Petawahin said gruffly as he pushed the chief's hand away. "A boy becomes a warrior for one day and you send him out against a war party of Snake warriors? There are too many of them for the Wolf Brothers, Mokotak or even all of us and all of the Paccus to fight and still have some of us to walk away. Tamahna, Mahkawan, Mokotak; they are not his father, they will come back to tell us of how hopeless it is to try and free him. I will find a way to get him back even if I have to die. I have lived a good length of life. Sequannah just begins to walk like a man and you send him out on his final trail."

"Every able warrior was needed, including Sequannah, to find out where the Snake people were," Ketanka defended himself. "If our warriors were detected, they must know that we have many. If they see a scouting party of this size, then maybe they would think again about facing a war party. Sequannah was sent out because we needed Minnecou warriors on every team. Everyone must be prepared to sacrifice in order to protect the whole. And you are needed much more with the people than out on the trail, unable to protect the clan."

"You are taking the clan away from danger," Petawahin countered the chief. "My son stands within it. Who needs my help more? Is not a man's blood his first loyalty?"

Ketanka's expression softened. "Even as chief, I would not try to prevent you from trying to save your own son. If you go, you may save him, but realize that you may have no one to return to if we also are attacked. We are only a small clan."

Ketanka read Petawahin's eyes, then spoke in resignation. "We will go north to the lakes where the geese feed as they head south for the winter, until we can safely return to gather with the other clans. We will go as far as the foothills of the Dark Mountains. I know that you will not stay with us until you find Sequannah, so I ask you to send back the Wolf brothers. No one has seen Mokotak, but if you should find him, send him back also and take only the Washan with you. Find their village, learn as much as you can about them, and remember that the lives of the clan may depend on your information. You could place the clan in danger trying to rescue Sequannah. Remember also that you have a daughter and father among your relatives here. The Snake people would fare well if they could cause you to lose focus on your people through Sequannah. Don't forget us," the chief warned him. "We can only wait for a short time and then we must head south."

A short distance away, Petawahin saw Shamira and Meequaw standing by their pile of possessions, ready to flee. One of the young Paccu warriors offered to ease some of the beautiful young girl's burden, while in the background, another Paccu looked on with envy. Petawahin turned to Ketanka, who was also watching.

"Take care of my family while I'm gone," Petawahin asked of the chief. "And keep those Paccu coyotes out of her range," he grumbled with obvious disdain. "Make sure those two go along with every scouting and hunting party that goes out. And if you have to make a war party, tell them how brave they are and put them in the front."

"I thought you wanted to see her married," Ketanka almost laughed. Petawahin scowled at the chief and looked again at the two young Paccus with disgust.

"I want my daughter to marry a warrior who can protect and provide for her, not just look at her with the eyes of a pup. Kwoita sees with my eyes also," he spoke sharply.

"Kwoita sees with his own eyes," the old man returned, "and Shamira will see with her own eyes, just as her mother and grandmother saw with theirs. The more you try to fight their vision, the less they will see of yours; just as right now you struggle to see less of mine. Find Sequannah and be patient. If you can free twenty Paccus, I'm sure you can find a way to free Sequannah. Beware of the snakes and do not look them in the eyes. They are allies of the Snake warriors and scout their trails for them."

Petawahin looked at the chief questioningly. "What is he saying? Does he mean real snakes or good scouts?" The chief shrugged.

Shatomi and Quebathe, though, nodded in testimony to Kwoita's statements.

"Thousands of snakes move in front of the painted ones. They are the eyes for the Snake people and capture those in their path," Quebathe testified in his soft voice. "If you look at them, their eyes are magic, and you cannot move. It didn't happen to me, but the others looked sickly and sweat filled their faces. If the snakes are holding someone, they do not see anything else, so even a child could kill them easily. But it would be dangerous to try and follow the Snake people alone."

"I will be with the Washan," Petawahin said confidently. He squinted at the southern horizon. "How did the fire start?"

The warriors shrugged, looking around anxiously. They preferred to leave immediately rather than end up one step ahead of the flames all day. Just in the short time they took to exchange information, the separate columns of smoke had joined together into an unbroken wall of fire. The women gathered everything together; all of their belongings had been readied since before dawn. Many were already on the trail towards the northernmost camp at the foothills of the Dark Mountains. Petawahin glanced in their direction as the first people moved northward and saw Shamira shading her eyes as she looked over the group of warriors in search of Sequannah. Meequaw tugged at her arm, pointing towards the fire, but Shamira began walking towards the men.

Petawahin went to intercept her. She stopped and stared at the ground when she saw him; he had come alone.

"Where's Sequannah?" her barely audible voice faltered. "Is he alright?"

"I don't know," Petawahin looked away. "He was captured by the Snake people along with the Paccu they call Woltah." Shamira shrugged, not knowing who he was, then shifted her gaze back to the ground.

"Are the others going to get him back?" she insisted. "You freed those Paccus, why aren't they getting Sequannah back for us."

"They are useless. They would only get captured again. It is best to have more warriors to protect the clan anyway...Mokotak may be captured too. Nobody knows where he and the other Paccu are either. I'll find Sequannah with the help of the Washan."

"And what if you are captured too?" she pleaded. "I will

have no family."

"Kwoita...and Meequaw," Petawahin said meekly.

"Kwoita! How many winters did we count as his last? He is the oldest grandfather in all the clans. How will he provide for us while I wait for a husband? How will he make me feel like I am part of a family when he could go on to the next life before the next sunset or sunrise?" she cried. "I want to go with you, he is my only brother and I would rather die or be captured with you and Sequannah than to be left here alone."

"You are a shadow in the woods...and good with your weapons. But there are too many questions about these people to separate you from the protection of the clan. If they captured you, that would be one more hostage they could use against us," Petawahin argued, trying not to add to her fears of his own fate.

"I will fight to the death and take many with me rather than let them capture me," she cried.

"That does not comfort my worries," he answered. "Do not cry over Sequannah and I. We will be back, both of us alive. I would never leave you at a time like this unless there was no choice. Go with Meequaw and stay with her until I get back. The air will change with the fall weather, soon, and even these painted ones will have to move south or suffer through a freezing winter. I don't know how the Paccus and the Minnecou will get along, but if it is not good, go and live with Ketanka and his family. I will send a message with the Wolf brothers to tell you what is going on, but after that, you can only wait for our return," Petawahin said, clasping her hands.

He turned and left before she could reply. But she knew she would have been a danger and a burden had she gone along. She watched him disappear into his hut to gather food and weapons. Fumbling through her bundles, she found a small pouch that she quickly filled with berries. She pulled out a parfleche filled with dried venison, then ran down to give them to her father. Petawahin was already outside of the wickiup, trying to learn the best way to find the Washan from Quebathe when she ran up and handed him the food. He nodded, met her eyes briefly, then shooed her back to the clan. One small glance would tell her more than he could say in a morning and more than he would ever demonstrate in front of others. She watched as he tore the flap off his hut and tossed it to Kwoita, putting a hand on his shoulder. She couldn't hear the words he spoke; his lips were still moving as he bolted towards the flames. When she could no longer make him out through the smoke, she turned slowly and heavily away, though she should already have been fleeing with the clan. Fires like these often fan a scorching rush of roaring wind ahead of the flames, sometimes igniting the air itself.

She trudged to her pile of bundles, turning several times to catch another glimpse of Petawahin as each puff of wind cleared out a swath of smoke. But he was beyond her view, stealthily avoiding the watchful eyes of Snake warriors. Kwoita waited with his own belongings as well as some of Shamira's over his back. Only the returning Paccu and Minnecou warriors trailed behind them as he hurried her along to catch up with the rest of the clan.

"So I hear I may die any day now," Kwoita took her off guard.

"I did not mean it that way. I meant that you have lived a long time and your time to go is closer than most. If my father and brother do not return, then what would you do if Ketanka wanted me for his wife, or if one of the Paccus tried to take me? Even if you could stop them, they might only have to wait a short while for you to go, because you are the oldest of all the clans' people." She paused for a moment. "Does my father always tell you everything I say?"

"Not knowing everything, I cannot say for certain," he smiled, "but I'm sure he tells me everything as long as it does not interfere with my view of him as a perfect human being."

"Would you like to hear some secrets about him?" she smiled.

"I knew him as a child, Shamira," he laughed. "People change much less than they think," he laughed again. "Let's hurry, my eyes are stinging and this old body cannot do much in all this smoke."

Shamira had a hard time keeping up with the old warrior. "Don't kill yourself trying to show me how strong you are. I know that you are not going to die today."

"Your have become a disrespectful young woman," he sneered. "I travel slow so you won't have to walk alone, and you try to slow me down even more so you can enjoy your laziness."

Shamira looked away, rolling her eyes. A noticeable wheeze became distinct as he huffed and puffed.

"I am not lazy," she said stubbornly. "I'm just not strong enough to keep up with you."

"Now you are telling the kind of lies your grandfather likes to hear," he said laughing, still straining to breathe. "Do not worry. If I live through the trials I put myself through, I always become stronger."

"Grandfather, why do you always tell me not to worry and then give me a reason to worry more. My father must have learned this from you."

"Well we are still here aren't we, and I am the oldest grandfather in all of the northern clans, so why worry if something works?"

"Because the one time it doesn't work will be the last time you try anything," she retorted.

"I realize that eventually there will be a last time. That's why I choose smaller trials to put myself through," he confided. "I know that as I get older, there is less I am capable of doing. If I forget, I am usually reminded very quickly."

As they caught up with Meequaw, she joined in with the last bit of conversation she overheard. "Yes, and we are growing weary of having to remind you. Don't let him convince you that everything he does is good for him, Shamira. Sometimes he thinks he is his son, and then other times I swear he thinks he is his grandson," she said shaking her head, though smiling.

"You are not so young yourself," Kwoita pointed out. "How many teeth do you have left."

"A mouthful of teeth does not make it any wiser to dive off a cliff or go out scouting after enemy warriors who could catch you without ever having to run."

"To sit back constantly saying I'm too old to do anything would really make me pleasing to have around. If I am to worry myself into not doing what I can, then of what use am I to anyone? I would be like a child, but a child will eventually grow into something useful. I would grow into another bundle to drag along the trail."

"Grandfather, why didn't the Paccus help my father? Why are the Wolf brothers coming back here? My father cannot fight all those Snake people with just the Washan," she said angrily. "Why are all those Paccus back here where it is safe when it is mostly their people that the Snake people have captured?"

"Petawahin is not going to fight them, he's just going to try and get Sequannah back when he has an opportunity," Kwoita explained. "The Paccus might have tried to fight them which may have resulted in all of us being killed. We didn't know their plans, so we forced them all to come back."

"But at least if Mokotak or the Wolf brothers went along, my father would have a chance if he had to fight them."

"Mokotak went too far ahead, too. We don't know what happened to him because we had to leave to get back here. With all of the Paccus here, too, we need the Wolf brothers and every Minnecou warrior to make sure that the Paccus do not try to run our clan. Many of them are injured and exhausted right now, but what will happen when they are better? I felt the same as you, but when I thought about it, the Washan chose the best thing for the people."

"When will we find out what is going on?" Meequaw asked impatiently. "We all must know what is going on in order to protect ourselves."

"Do you think that we should all stop now and hold a council?" Kwoita asked sarcastically. "Or do you think it might be better to wait until we are in a safe place."

"I think it would be best if we all had one big council, women included, when we make our camp for the night. I hear so many stories. I would like to know what is true and what is not," Meequaw demanded.

The three of them stopped their conversation when they heard Ketanka bellowing out far in back of them. They turned to see the chief throwing his arms up and roaring at the Paccus, showing them how to cover their trail. He left Quebathe and Shatomi to teach them more and to cover up any inadvertent clues the band may have left behind. Ketanka stormed off, heading towards the front of the line, in an unshakable display of authority.

"Here comes Ketanka now," Kwoita said innocently. "Now you can tell him about the council meeting tonight."

"Old moose turd!" Meequaw snapped. "He's just showing the Paccus that he is the chief of this band. And I *will* talk to him about the council meeting."

Kwoita nudged Shamira, "Let's watch her chin quiver as her words stay tied to her tongue." Shamira seemed to relax a little and smiled as the two hecklers fell back to their old antics. No matter what the situation, these two would eventually find a weak spot to needle each other. Ketanka lumbered up in back of them, shaking his head as he make contact with Kwoita.

"Kwoita, go back there with Quebathe and Shatomi and show those Paccus how to cover the trail. They're supposed to be hiding the clan's trail and they're leaving it even more visible with their own clumsy shuffling."

Ketanka grabbed Kwoita's bundles and walked along with Meequaw and Shamira. "Let's catch up with the others. The faster we move, the faster they'll move in back of us. If we move quickly, we can make it to the Dark Mountains in two days. I don't know how far the Snake people are camped from here, but another three days hike will make it that much more difficult for them. We have nearly a full day ahead of us and I intend for us to move swiftly till nightfall and try to reach where we usually camp on our second night."

"We have had no council meetings or talks about what is going on since we first heard of these Snake people," Shamira cut in ahead of Meequaw. "My father is out after Sequannah now and no one knows the fate of our best warriors. All we know are stories about snakes, and no one seems to really know what is going on. Could we have council meeting where everyone can hear what is said? Our lives are at stake, too, and we all need to know."

"Yes, let's hear the stories from all the men," Meequaw joined in. "Everything we hear cannot be true."

"Perhaps not," Ketanka croaked. "But I would like to have distance between us and the Snake people until we can find out more about them and know exactly where they are at all times. I don't know if it would be a good idea to hold a council meeting about the Snake people right away. I think it would be best to wait until either the Wolf brothers or Mokotak returns and we have more information about what these Snake warriors are doing. For now, I think it would be best to show the Paccus how to travel swiftly. I will talk to the old woman and maybe she can explain to them. We will invite her to any council meetings and she can tell the rest of them what is going on because they won't understand anyway. If they want to stay with us, they can follow and do as we do; if not, they can return to where they came from."

"Do you think we should try to teach them our words and maybe learn some of theirs?" Shamira asked. "We may need to stay together if these Snake people decide to follow us, and it would be best if we understood each other."

"It may be necessary for all of us to stay together," Ketanka sighed. As they approached the main party, three Paccu women and two young boys were just ahead of them and Ketanka quickened his pace to overtake them. "Here is a good place for you to start," Ketanka smiled, as he handed Kwoita's bundles to the empty-handed Paccus.

Ketanka walked quickly towards the front of the procession, leaving Meequaw and Shamira with the Paccus. Shamira pointed to herself repeating her name and pointed at Meequaw telling them her name. The two young boys jumped up and down telling Shamira their names, but the three women appeared to be shy and hesitant. One of them looked almost indignant at having to carry one of the bundles Ketanka had given them.

"We saved them from the Snake people who were whipping and beating them, and because we ask them to carry a few small things, they act as if we are making them our slaves," Meequaw mumbled disgustedly. The three of them perceived Meequaw's tone, dropped the bundles, and walked away. "I wonder if they acted this way with the Snake people," Meequaw muttered. "Now I know why they were being whipped."

"Help me pick up these bundles," Shamira asked. "Maybe if we show them that we wish to be their friends, they will become good allies with the Minnecou."

"They are just a lazy and ungrateful group," Meequaw said matter-of-factly. "They only have respect for those who would take their lives from them, or beat them senseless for the slightest mistake."

"But they would always hold hate in their hearts," Shamira said. "And was it not you who told me that no matter how small or weak a person, their hate can have a bad effect on everyone."

"Your mother and grandfather always used my words against me, too. I guess it's only fitting that you would grow up to do the same. You may be right, child. I'll try to see with my heart instead of my eyes, but you talk to them; I don't think they would appreciate my words now."

Meequaw and Shamira caught up with them once again, even with all the bundles they carried. Shamira, walking alongside, held out a sac of water and sounded out the Minnecou word for it. They seemed unimpressed, but one of them did take it when Shamira gestured for them to drink. When she went to hand it back, Shamira gestured for the others to drink. After they drank, they spoke to each other and then took some of the bundles from Shamira and Meequaw. They smiled at Shamira as they relieved her of some of her load, but scowled at Meequaw as each of them plucked one of the smallest items off of her heavy load. Meequaw, however, still managed to maintain a weak and forced smile as she voiced her appreciation to the impudent guests. The small group of Paccus then quickly hurried off and maintained a deliberate distance from Shamira and Meequaw until they caught up with another group of Paccus. These were the injured Paccu warriors who had not gone out with the scouting party at dawn, but were forced to remain behind in the Minnecou encampment to rest and treat their wounds.

The band moved at a rapid pace until after the sun had reached its highest point before they finally stopped. During their brief rest, Shamira and Meequaw noticed the three Paccu women and the two young boys sitting off to one side, talking. They went over to join them. Shamira sat down and smiled, but they just glanced at her and stopped talking. A tense silence kept up for several moments as Meequaw and Shamira sat beside them, neither one knowing how to break it without any understandable form of communication. The Paccu warriors, obviously not in much pain from their minor injuries, laughed and talked and seemed to be bragging to each other as they frequently glanced over at the two Minnecou women. The Paccu women knew and the Minnecou women sensed that they were talking about Shamira.

But she wouldn't allow their laughter and leering to make her uncomfortable in the midst of her own clan. When Shatomi, Quebathe, and Kwoita came up with the other Paccus from the rear, however, she felt much more at ease. A tall, pleasant looking Paccu warrior walking alongside Shatomi, came up to the injured Paccus and spoke briefly with them. One of them spoke out in Paccu and the whole group of them laughed and stared at Shamira alternately. The tall Paccu muttered something that obviously irritated the outspoken Paccu and the whole group jeered at the one who had been speaking of Shamira.

Shamira saw Kwoita walk up last in line, covering the group's trail sign as he went along. In the distance behind him, she could see two figures running up. She ran to Kwoita, pointing behind him at the two approaching warriors, but before she could reach him, she recognized the Wolf brothers. Her uneasy feelings faded as Mahkawan and Tamahna strode into the group. The laughter and boisterous conversation diminished to a few weak smiles and idle conversation in the presence of the powerful Wolf brothers.

The only one who appeared even capable of challenging one of the Wolf brothers was the tall one named Ceptke. But his manner was friendly. He walked off towards the front of the procession with a gesture of greeting and a subtle smile as he passed Shamira and the Wolf brothers. Tamahna was pleased that at least a few capable and level-headed warriors were among the Paccus, but he also noticed the smile Shamira had returned to the tall warrior. Her immediate attention to the Wolf brothers quickly dispelled Tamahna's notions. Meequaw joined them and helped Shamira prepare something for Mahkawan and Tamahna to eat as they finally returned to the clan. Their families were among the very first to leave and were traveling at the lead.

"Were you told about the snakes?" Mahkawan asked the two women.

"Yes, we heard many stories about snakes," Shamira replied. "But no people can tell snakes where to go or what to do. Someone must have stepped on their nest."

"Well, it didn't appear that way," Mahkawan said. "The Washan said he thinks they are Snake people magic. Many clans train wolf and coyote pups for pets and protection, maybe they do the same with snakes. But, I don't see how anyone can make a snake listen to him..."

He thought for a moment. "I think it is magic. We stayed behind with the Washan to watch their painted warriors and find out where they were going. The Washan sent everyone else back. After they left, the ugly looking one that they carried around started to scream at us into the woods, but he could not find us. He tapped his snake stick against a tree. Soon after that, the snakes came back over the ridge and began to move toward us. The Washan told us to light fires in a long line to stop the snakes from finding us...or heading towards the clan. Then we moved further south, in a different direction than they would look for us. We hid behind another ridge, and the Snake people left in a hurry. The fire spread quickly and we heard the hissing of many snakes as they burned in the flames. That is when Petawahin came down from the ridge behind us. He told the Washan that we were to get back to the clan, while only he and the Washan would follow the Snake people. He said to tell you that he was only going to get Sequannah and that he would come back to meet the clan before the leaves change. He said to tell you that they will watch always from a distance until they have a chance to get at Sequannah when no one was looking, or until they find their village. "

"We waited around there for a while after your father and the Washan left, but all the snakes were burned in the fire and the Snake people were gone. The fire got very big and we had to get out of there quickly. The rest of the morning we spent following behind the clan, but there were no Snake warriors and the trail was well hidden. In a couple of days, no one will be able to find our trail. Petawahin said he and the Washan will go to the Dark Mountains when they return, and if we are not there, they will go to the south where the clans gather for the winter."

"Were there many Snake warriors in their war party?" Shamira asked.

"With us and all of the Paccus we have here, they still have ten warriors for every person in this band, including women and children. We could not attack them without every one of the other Minnecou clans to help us. There will be much to talk about this winter," Tamahna admitted.

"What did they do to Sequannah?" Shamira asked. "He has only just become a warrior."

"They tied him and dragged him by the hair, but they didn't whip him. They beat the other Paccu that was with him, though, and then they tied him to the rest of the Paccus. Then they beat another group of Paccus that they had lined up. I'm not sure if they noticed that Sequannah was any different than the Paccus," Tamahna said.

"We have to do something to them," Meequaw demanded. "They will torture us like the Paccus. They will get worse unless we find a way to teach them to stay away from the Minnecou."

"They were fools to anger Ketanka. If he doesn't find a weakness, he will make one. We killed two of their scouts, but they never found them because they had to run from the fire," Mahkawan stated. "Petawahin freed twenty of the Paccus and killed two more of their warriors. And we made them run from the fire, but I am not sure if they know that we are Minnecou. If they do know, perhaps they will prefer to fight Paccus than Minnecou from now on."

Meequaw gave them pemmican that she had made by mixing ground up dried venison with the berries they had picked the previous day. Shamira repacked the large packets of food into her bundles and handed the two men the sac of water. She then poured some of the water into a smaller sac and put in a mixture of sassafras roots, raspberry leaves, and ground rose hips. By next morning, the tea would be ready to drink—it would give the people strength on the trail. The tea could have been made much quicker if it were possible to make a fire, but the Minnecou have always been adaptable to living on the move. Most Minnecou clans spent forty to fifty days traveling during the course of a year and had discovered many ways to make the frequent trips more comfortable. They knew where they were going and which materials would be on hand. Whatever would be available at the next encampment would be that much less they would have to carry.

The Minnecou had many sacred places to return to each year, and couldn't understand how their relatives from the south and some whole tribes could live in the same place all the time. But those people who lived in year round villages acquired many more possessions and couldn't understand how the migratory peoples roamed around in what seemed to be a constant state of poverty. Tribes like the Minnecou, however, felt stronger eating the wild foods and grew restless if they remained in the same place for any great span.

The Paccus were different. They spent their winters in one area and their summers in another. Staying with the Minnecou, however, could prove to be quite trying. With the Snake people around, though, the Paccus had no choice unless they were to move west of their hunting areas, exposing themselves to other hostile tribes.

"We are only going to be at the Dark Mountains for a short time," Mahkawan said. "Tamahna and I talked on the way here. We thought we could make one big lodge for both of our families. If you and Shamira would like to stay with us, you are both welcome. Wanashta and Tumaris are probably far ahead. When we start moving again, you two could catch up with them and tell them that we are traveling behind the band. It would be good for them to know that we are safe. Maybe you could all talk together and decide what kind of a lodge we should build."

Shamira's eyes lit up as Mahkawan spoke. Meequaw looked to Shamira to see if she would be interested in the new arrangement, but she didn't have to ask. She was glad to see Shamira smiling and eager, instead of distracted and quiet as she had been most of the morning. Normally, she would have had the Paccus talking and laughing by this time, and she would have learned a good deal of their language. But there was too much confusion and uncertainty.

As the Wolf brothers crammed handfuls of pemmican into their mouths, Shamira reached into one of her bundles and pulled out a small packet of hazelnuts. Their eyebrows rose.

The Paccus were rationing the food that Karnack and another young Paccu had brought to where the grizzly had been killed, but now, with not even one day's passing, their food was nearly gone. The Minnecou were not over laden with food provisions themselves, but they did have enough to get to the Dark Mountains. Trying to feed the Paccus, however, could leave the Minnecou hungry as well. Looking to the head of the line, Tamahna saw that they were on the move again. He slung his bow over his shoulder.

"They are starting to move again," he said, addressing everyone in the rear of the procession. "Let's keep up with them and stay closer together. Be careful where you step. Don't break any branches or leave anything behind." The Wolf brothers helped Shamira and Meequaw repack their bundles and placed them in a manner where they would be much easier to carry.

"See if you two can move a little easier now and catch up with Tumaris and Wanashta," Mahkawan said. "They may need help with the children and you could let them know that we are here. Maybe we will camp with them tonight, I'm not sure, but we will be there to eat. You had better move quickly or you may not catch them until we stop."

After they had gone a short distance, Shamira looked back and saw the Wolf brothers checking the area where the Paccus had sat, fluffing up the grasses with dead branches. Looking towards the front, they could see Ketanka walking back, stopping to talk several times as he went along. He could move easily back and forth along the procession as well as most of the warriors because they were carrying very little besides their weapons. The women, however, were heavily burdened, and the children were given as much as they could carry and still keep pace with the rest of the band. The only warriors that were carrying heavy articles were the injured Paccus who were strong enough. The Paccu women were nearly empty-handed; there were only scant food provisions and most of their possessions were left in the ashes of their former village.

"We're not going fast enough for you two?" Ketanka questioned as he intercepted them.

"We're trying to catch up with Wanashta and Tumaris to tell them that the Wolf brothers are here."

"Tamahna and Mahkawan are back?" his low voice rose. "Good! Then Petawahin found the Washan. Did Mokotak return, too?"

"No," said Meequaw. "Maybe Petawahin and the Washan will find him, but the Wolf brothers came back alone."

"Did you teach anything or learn anything from the Paccus?" Ketanka questioned Shamira.

"They are not friendly. They kept a distance between us all morning," Shamira said in frustration.

"The old Paccu woman is up in the front with the families you seek. They are trading stories with the Paccus while the old woman translates. You would be better off with them." Ketanka grabbed a few things from each of the women.

"Come!" he croaked, "I'll help you catch up with them."

Ketanka took up a frantic pace towards the front of the procession and the two women glanced at each other, though neither would say that they would rather have carried everything at their own pace than to get rid of a few items and put themselves through an exhausting trial. It was especially true at this point because they were on one of the steepest inclines between the lake and the Dark Mountains. As the smiling chief's vigorous step brought them to within shouting distance of the Wolf brothers' families, he still remained unaware of the angry and impatient eyes trained on his rotund form as the two women strained to keep up.

"Why does he choose us to prove that he can still move with all that weight?" Meequaw muttered.

"I know he is the chief, and we are supposed to show respect," Shamira whispered. "But I hope all of this sudden movement doesn't stir up his gases."

Meequaw started to giggle and Shamira soon lost her composure. Every time they laid eyes on the chief, they both started to laugh. Ketanka pretended not to hear, but after a few moments of this, he turned abruptly and handed the two women the rest of their bundles.

"You should be able to catch them now," he said. "I have to get back to Tamahna and Mahkawan."

"Thank you, Ketanka," they both said smiling. "We would

never have gotten here this quickly without you," Meequaw said, still smiling. The chief walked off with an uneasy feeling, but shrugged it off before he had gone a dozen paces.

Though the clan was discomfited with the presence of Paccus and the threat of the Snake people, they remained self-assured; everything seemed be going accordingly. They had planned to head north on this very day, even before the demise of the Paccus. The Paccus had no choice in the plan, except to follow if they chose, or return to their ransacked village. Fleeing with the Minnecou gave them a chance to compose themselves and remain in the relative safety of numbers; the Minnecou, no matter how arrogant or intimidating, could be trusted. Even so, the Paccus grew more uneasy with each step as they widened the gap between themselves and their captive relatives, ranging ever further into unfamiliar Minnecou outlands. They were familiar with the area near the lake, but they had no idea where the Minnecou were leading them now.

Shamira and Meequaw caught up with the Wolf brothers' families, but at a much slower pace than they had endured with Ketanka. Mahkawan's three sons ran to greet them, each with a large spear in his hand.

"We protect you!" they exclaimed. "We protect everyone with our families," they said, as they proudly displayed the warrior's spears that their mothers allowed them to carry as they traveled. They were obviously too big for them to handle, but Tumaris and Wanashta knew this would help to allay their fears; an underlying tension hummed along the entire procession. The spears instilled a feeling of confidence in the youngsters that they would need if they were going to be effective as warriors in the future.

Along with the Wolf clans were four more Paccu women, including the older woman and her complement of children. Two old Paccu grandfathers also kept pace in this section of the procession, while the young Paccu boy who had let an arrow fly at Quitkwa walked along in back of them, his bow in his left hand and an arrow in his right. Even as a youngster, he was obviously lethal with a weapon. He was one or two years older than the eldest of Mahkawan's sons, but at that age, he may just as well have been a decade older, so great was the difference between them. His solemn stare and manly disposition stood in sharp contrast to the playful and clumsy pack of wolf pups. Shamira and Meequaw caught up with the head of the procession while

Mahkawan's three sons fell into a solemn march behind the group, wielding their spears in imitation of the young Paccu boy with his bow. Wanashta carried Washeena in her arms and Shamira immediately offered to take her. Wanashta smiled in appreciation as she handed over the sleeping child, but she still appeared burdened.

"Tamahna and Mahkawan are with us now, they're following in back of the band," Shamira told her.

Wanashta's expression changed immediately as she called to Tumaris. "Our husbands are behind us!" Tumaris smiled and seemed to step more quickly in her relief.

"Now they will be coming to scout ahead of the band!" Tumaris exclaimed.

"They said they wouldn't be back until nightfall because they would be staying behind the band instead," Shamira stated. "Ketanka kept Kwoita back there, too, to make sure that our trail was well covered. I hope they bring Kwoita here with them tonight. Mahkawan said that they would at least be here to eat if not sleep. There was no way of knowing until they had spoken with Ketanka."

"Shatomi and Quitkwa are scouting ahead now," Melonak cut in. "They are just as capable as the Wolf brothers when it comes to scouting," she defended the present arrangement. But even as she spoke, Quitkwa appeared in the distance, his second run back for food. Shatomi would let him go back with the band just to be rid of the complaints and the constant grumbling of his stomach. If Petawahin were there, he would probably have sent him to scout for meat for the band. But Shatomi let the chief's son do as he pleased, as long as he didn't steer them into danger.

*   *   *

Shatomi observed the Paccu scouts for some time and discovered that they used the same sign language for hunting and scouting as the Minnecou. In their silent world of stealth and observation, they could just as well have been Minnecou as they flashed the same signs for berries, even to the degree of which type. The same signs for deer and antelope herds, and fox and bear tracks caused Shatomi to feel as if he were scouting with some distant clan of the Minnecou. At first, only one Paccu scout by the name of Boaka was with Shatomi and Quitkwa. He was a wiry old scout close to fifty winters, adept on the trail, bearing no hint of slowing with age. A dark green paste camouflaged parts of his face and body, making him nearly impossible to perceive in the brush. The other Paccu was equally adept and surprisingly silent as he maneuvered his large frame through the maze of thicket and timber, keeping low as they crossed through the many heaths and meadows.

Ceptke was sent to scout ahead as an emissary between the scouting party and the Paccus traveling within the procession to allay their anxiety about entering into an unknown territory, and further separation from their suffering relatives. The Paccus were wary of straying so far from the captives that rescue would become impossible. The old woman had spoken to Ketanka of the Paccus concerns and they agreed that Ceptke would be best suited to smooth over any difficulties that might arise. Ketanka realized that as soon as the wounded Paccus were fit, they would send a war party out to rescue their captive relatives. While this may jeopardize Petawahin and the Washan's designs to rescue Sequannah, to prevent them from going could put the whole clan in danger, and prove to be impossible anyway.

Wanachan also expressed their concerns that if Petawahin and the Washan were killed or captured, then they may lose all hope of ever finding their relatives again. Ketanka himself knew that if Petawahin and the Washan couldn't rescue Sequannah before the Snake people reached their village, there may be no way for them to get him out of there. Even the Minnecou villages were heavily guarded, though they were generally peaceful clans. These war-like people probably had very elaborate defenses for their own village. They were making many enemies.

Ketanka, however, was relieved that a warrior like Ceptke had been among the rescued party of Paccus. Most of the others seemed resentful. Ceptke's calm manner would seem to be the only influence to prevent the Paccu warriors from taking any rash action. Ceptke realized the risks of separating themselves further from their suffering relatives, but he also knew that they could all be killed or trapped in the ropes of the Snake people if they did not use their small numbers wisely. Cooperation with the Minnecou was essential for the time being, and probably from this day forth, but he couldn't allow the Minnecou to dominate him or the Paccu council. Tonight, he would hold a council with all of the Paccu warriors, and together they would determine the best course of action.

* * *

Quitkwa strutted back to the front of the procession with an empty food pouch held open in a gesture for Melonak to prepare more food for him and the other scouts. His demanding manner didn't strike his mother in a very pleasing way.

"Can't you find anything to eat out there on your own?" she snapped. "I haven't seen Shatomi or the Paccus come running back here for food yet."

"We are scouts," he boasted. "We don't have time to hunt and protect the whole tribe at the same time. When we go out on a hunting party, I will make sure that every empty food pouch you own will be full," he smiled.

Melonak reached into her bundles once again with a smile. Even if his voracious appetite could be irritating at times, at seventeen winters, he was a very capable hunter, and more than once had he filled every packet and pouch she owned with fresh meat. Everyone in the tribe, however, was anxious for him to grow into a more normal appetite, as his constant hunger seemed to distract him from every chore other than seeking out more food.

Quitkwa noticed irritable expressions on the faces of Tumaris and Wanashta as Meequaw told them of the Wolf brothers invitation to her and Shamira. Shamira rocked Washeena as she walked, oblivious to the uneasy feelings that Meequaw sensed from the Wolf brothers' wives. Quitkwa, however, knew that they wouldn't put up with their husbands' attentions to Shamira. His heart quickened as he calculated that she would eventually end up in Ketanka's lodge with his family. Quitkwa had dreamt that Shamira would someday see him as an important warrior; he was the chief's son, and some day she would hold the same desire for him as he held for her.

"All of the scouts are thankful for the food you send them," Quitkwa thanked his mother with an air of importance. "Perhaps we will bring back much more than we have asked for. We are far ahead now and we will hunt while we wait for everyone to catch up," he said, trying to impress Shamira and everyone else who could hear. He disappeared more quickly than anyone had ever seen him move before, and although Meequaw was aware of his motives, she was still quite impressed with his agility and speed.

* * *

The Wolf brothers returned early at the end of the day's march. The band had stopped for but a few moments, when they strode up to see their families for the first time since they had returned. The three young warriors of Mahkawan's charged, howling as they threatened with their spears. The Wolf brothers retreated into the brush, pretending they hadn't recognized the children and that they appeared to be fearsome warriors.

"Surely, two strong warriors like you would not run from children," Shamira teased as they hid in the underbrush. "Come out and help us set up camp for the night, I'll make sure they don't hurt you."

"Is that you Shamira? Are you sure they're just children? They look too dangerous to be children."

"They are very strong boys, but I don't think they would hurt their own father," Shamira chided. "Are you two going to stay with us tonight and protect us. With five warriors, we will feel safer after all that has happened."

A short distance away, Tumaris and Wanashta watched their husbands approach as they prepared the food and raised a temporary shelter for their families.

"She acts as if both of them were her husbands," Tumaris whispered contemptuously. "All of the men are always gawking at her. If she's going to be tempting our husbands, we'll have to be very careful. I don't even know if she's aware of what she does, but I've never seen her shy away when the men make eyes at her."

"She does not fool me," Wanashta stated. "She knows what she's doing. She is a grown woman now; she's no longer Petawahin's little girl and all women know what they are doing when it comes to tempting men, no matter how innocent they pretend to be."

"Well, we will have to get rid of her. Make her feel unwelcome here," Tumaris said.

"As soon as Meequaw told me that Mahkawan and Tamahna invited them, I knew there would be trouble. I could see them talking nicely to the grandmother while all the time trying to get Shamira into their own lodge so they could stare at her when no one is watching."

"Maybe Petawahin asked them to look after her," Tumaris attempted to be positive.

"Those two would be the last he would trust to look after Shamira!" Wanashta's whisper sharpened. A look of satisfaction drifted into her expression. "I've seen a tall and handsome Paccu that could lure her off the Wolf brothers' trail. You and I will not have to be at all unpleasant with her and when we talk to our husbands, we can find a way to make her appear distasteful to them as well."

Tumaris smiled, "I've seen him looking at her."

CHAPTER 7

Sequannah grew apprehensive of Woltah's frantic pace. The determined Paccu raced against Mokotak and Karnack in an effort to dominate the scouting party. Behind him, Sequannah could barely perceive the other pairs, advancing at a slower and more cautious rate. To his left, he occasionally caught a glimpse of Mokotak's team as they strove to keep up or move slightly ahead of Woltah. The two seasoned warriors were competing vigorously, and though he preferred that Mokotak prevail, they were moving too quickly; the Snake people's scouts would see them first, and they were too far ahead to expect any help from the other teams. Several times he thought they'd slow down so they would at least be in visual contact with the other teams, but Woltah would lead them through thickets and over ridges where there was no possibility of communication. Even Mokotak was becoming increasingly remote in the event they should run into trouble.

As they whisked through the forest, Woltah's frenzied chase showed no sign of slowing. Sequannah glanced frequently behind and to his left in the hope of catching sight of at least someone from the advancing line of scouts. But even warriors coming up in back of him could be enemies. The chief had told them to stay in view of each other in case they were spotted by the Snake people first. He couldn't understand why Mokotak was also leading his team at such a dangerous pace; even as an inexperienced warrior, he could see the obvious danger that could result from straying too far from the original plan. But Mokotak would never let this pompous warrior called Woltah even imagine that he could outmaneuver a Minnecou.

Sequannah deliberately slowed his pace as he scanned for the other teams, but soon he had even lost sight of Woltah. He looked to the ground; Woltah's moccasin prints glared as they wound through the dense underbrush. He was relieved that he would at least be able to find the foolish Paccu, but anyone else could also follow their highly visible trail and he had no way of knowing just how far this extended in back of him. He quietly snapped off a handful of green branches, a good distance from their trail, then returned to blend the clumsy footprints into the loose gravel. He had learned from his father how important it was to conceal the trail so that one could spend more time looking ahead instead of worrying about who may be following.

He concealed the Paccu's tracks, effecting a long break in the trail. Then he dropped suddenly to the ground; he heard rustling nearby. He could see for quite a distance because the brush was clumped together and not of sufficient height to where it would spread and form an impenetrable blind. He was relieved to catch a glimpse of the Paccu's high-legged moccasins. Woltah had turned back to find him. A scraping noise to his rear, however, caused the flesh to crawl on the back of his neck, and he turned slowly, peering under the canopy of dense brush. He thought he had seen movement a short distance away, but there was no place for anything as large as a human to hide. He felt relieved, but as he turned back to look for Woltah's approach, several loud scraping noises erupted from behind a bush clump nearly touching his feet.

Standing half-erect, he spread the brush to get a look at what type of creature would choose to make so much noise within obvious range of human scent. Six hissing snake heads sprung to his face; his heart exploded in his chest. He was frozen in place by the sudden terror, but as his instinct took hold and reacted to jump back, he couldn't move. The serpents' eyes were of a golden glow and he found that he could not divert from them. The same initial shock that had paralyzed him for an instant when he first saw the snakes, as when he had ever been startled by the sudden hiss of a serpent, would not let go; his heart beat wildly and out of control. The six snake heads wavered from side to side in unison, just beyond his nose. He could feel their darting tongues flicking against his lips, but he could not move. Their cold, elliptical pupils were an eternity of darkness surrounded by a lure of glowing gold that somehow resembled the warmth of the sun, though not so bright and more likening to a cold light.

A feeling of vertigo and severe dizziness gripped him as the swaying heads merged into one massive and ferocious looking serpent. Only its riveting eyes were more horrifying than its screaming hiss. He felt his whole life-force being drawn helplessly into the cold and eternal darkness of the serpent's deep, black pupils and every part of his instinct warned of death. His struggle to fight from falling into the darkness left him frozen in fear; the world around him became hazy and indistinct. Every muscle in his body burned in rigidity and a numbness crept over him till he could no longer feel his arms and legs. His blurred vision slowly sharpened into a swirling pattern of checkered diamonds and he could no longer make out the serpent's features as they blended into the background of its surroundings. He felt imprisoned in a long and rigid tube.

His hearing splintered as every sound became indistinguishable in a constant volley of never-ending echoes. Coldness crept through his body and he sensed that only warm sunlight would dissipate the drowsiness that had stolen his strength. He struggled to feel his arms, but they seemed only a memory. He searched for what seemed to be an eternity for some usable function of his former self and came across a strange phenomenon when he stuck out his tongue. An explosion of senses in the form of heat, smell, taste and touch filled his being with a familiar, yet very different perception of the world around him. With his strange and stunted vision, he could make out the swaying serpent in front of him, but his tongue seemed to tell him the exact locations of the serpent's movements; the exact texture of everything in every direction; the exact degree of warmth or coolness. He could smell all of the different grasses, bushes, trees, insects. He could even smell the different components of the earth beneath him, all simultaneously and all completely distinguishable. He could taste his surroundings and could even taste the hissing of the serpent in front of him, but he could move nothing but the direction of his tongue.

He found himself darting his tongue in and out with increasing frequency as each separate flick gave him fresh knowledge, and the world around him became unique in every direction. He felt the ground begin to rumble; a herd of huge and foul smelling creatures approached his direction. An instinctive and primordial fear gripped him as he sensed the violent motion in front of him, but the checkered patterns blended into a normal vision and he could feel a warmth beginning to surge through his body and his rediscovered limbs. A violent jerk and severe pain shocked him back to reality as his feet kicked about in the air. He was surrounded by six of the ugliest and most gruesome looking warriors he had ever imagined and one of them had him hoisted by the hair. On the ground he saw a heap of thick black snakes, headless and squirming.

The warriors whooped with glee as they discovered yet another victim only a short distance away. Five of the Snake warriors headed off towards the south as the warrior gripping Sequannah's hair turned him away from the scene and forced his knee into the boy's back, causing him to arch with the taut pull on his long black hair. Sequannah heard the sounds of slapping and kicking and the crying out in pain as the Snake warriors dragged and beat a wide-eyed Woltah through the thickets and brambles of the bushy terrain. Every small tree was a delight to the warriors as they tested its hardness with Woltah's head. In the short distance between Sequannah and Woltah, the painted warriors had found time to beat the Paccu from screaming agony to a faint moaning and breathless murmuring for mercy. One of the warriors pulled out his snake whip to stifle the Paccu gibberish, but was stopped by the others with warnings about Quiktkoata's own hunger for revenge. They threw Woltah to the ground and bound him by the hands and feet. The warrior holding Sequannah turned him around and jerked him by the hair, face first to the ground, pinning him there while one of the other Snake warriors tied his hands in back of him.

The enemy warriors whisked the two captives back to the procession. Sequannah felt a trickle of blood running into his ear as the sadistic Snake warrior nearly tore the scalp from his head. He wanted to scream out, but he had seen what happened to Woltah. His rage was intense; if he was untied and armed, he would gladly have fought them all to the death. Nevertheless, he tightened his jaw and stifled even the slightest groan as they jerked him along, his feet barely touching the ground. If I am alive, he thought to himself, there is always the chance that one day I can treat them the same.

As they neared the procession, Sequannah caught sight of the elaborate litter, unable to conceive why four people would be carrying a lodge on their shoulders. Upon closer examination, he clearly perceived the dark and sadistic face of Quiktkoata glaring down at him and Woltah from beneath the canopy. There was no mercy in the eyes of this powerful sorcerer; Sequannah braced for the worst. The cold and icy feeling returned to the pit of his stomach, much the same as he felt under the serpents' spell. The party came to a halt and two of the warriors pushed the captives forward, throwing them to the ground at the foot of the litter. Sequannah looked up, and once again was confronted with Quiktkoata's icy stare; his eyes were forced back to the ground. A low muttering erupted from under the canopy, but Sequannah dared not look up. After a short pause, Quiktkoata's voice thundered down upon them, and two Snake warriors jerked both of the captives by the hair, forcing them to look up at the cruel man seated in the litter. His lips were curled in sadistic pleasure as he sneered at the two captives, contemplating the lessons he had in mind for them.

He murmured several commands, then grinned contemptuously as he awaited the outcome. Two of the Snake warriors wielded their snakeskin whips and slashed at Woltah's legs until he curled up in defense. As soon as he attempted to defend himself, another warrior would give him five or six sharp kicks to the head and shoulders until his legs became vulnerable once again. Then the two warriors would hurriedly slash away at Woltah's legs, the filed down fangs of the snakeskins leaving long and deep scrapes along the Paccu's calves and thighs. As soon as he attempted to retract them once again, another volley of sharp kicks rendered him prostrate until he no longer moved. Quiktkoata waved his hand and dismissed the three warriors after Woltah ceased to groan, providing only minimal entertainment.

His attention shifted to Sequannah. He stared the boy down as one of the Snake warriors kept his grip on the handful of hair that had forced Sequannah to witness Woltah's punishment as well as the icy glare of Quiktkoata. Every time Sequannah's eyes met directly with those of the Snake chief, the cold feeling returned to his torso and his limbs began to numb until he averted his gaze. Sequannah trembled within himself as the ruthless Quiktkoata mumbled his punishment.

But the Snake warriors did nothing to Sequannah, whipping viciously at a line of assembled Paccus, instead. Quiktkoata rumbled with vicious laughter as he threw taunts into the surrounding woodlands and sought out the movements of his enemies. Nothing moved. He seethed in frustration, then rained a torrent of frothing curses, repeatedly and deliberately rapping his staff against the litter in a steady rhythm. The mass of snakes came boiling back over the ridge from the east. Other snakes wriggled out of the undergrowth as well as from various places amongst the trees, swelling the writhing heap. Sequannah flinched and his face flushed as they suddenly burst apart and raced out in every direction, most heading in the direction of the Minnecou encampment. In the distance he witnessed an almost imperceivable movement along the ridge line. Soon, wisps of smoke began drifting through the forest. A draft from the northwest fanned the smoke into pockets of flame as Quiktkoata continued to curse and scream at his unseen enemies. The snakes were pouring themselves directly onto the rapidly spreading blaze and the Snake chief couldn't stop them. His cold and contemptuous smile changed to a raging grimace as he roared at the procession to evacuate. In the midst of his anger, he spotted Sequannah and screamed at one of his soldiers while pointing towards the boy. The Snake warriors grabbed Sequannah's arms and held them outstretched as they tied them off tightly to each pole in back of the litter. They grabbed another bunch of his hair and tied that off to the top of the canopy so that he could neither fall nor lose pace without putting all of the strain to his scalp. Sequannah was facing outward from the rear as the four attendants whisked off with their chief, forcing him to run backwards in a strain to keep up with his hair.

The captive Paccus who had been whipped were frantically lashed to the others and quickly marched out of the area. Quiktkoata's litter traveled off to the side of the procession as they went at a much quicker pace than everyone else, much to Sequannah's dismay. He stumbled frequently at first, but the effeminate attendants had little stamina and the pace soon diminished.

Quiktkoata was more absorbed in securing his forces than in deriving any sadistic pleasure from Sequannah's woes. Once out of danger, he no longer concerned himself with the slowing pace, but brooded over revenge upon the enemy he had never seen. He was well aware that he was not merely facing another clan of foolish Paccus or the woodland tribes they had been raiding to the east.

The procession was beginning to outpace the litter, yet still the painted warriors' chief brooded over this insult to his ferocious army. Sequannah was getting very sore in the calves, but he was glad that they were no longer racing from the fire. He turned around twice to see where they were headed, and the Snake chief seemed to have forgotten about him: hunched in his litter, gazing ahead. Sequannah secretly reveled in the grief his small clan had inflicted upon this massive army of fierce warriors, but he sensed that Quiktkoata would be merciless in his revenge if he learned that the Minnecou were responsible for the escaped Paccus and probably for the fire as well. Fear's biting grip sunk even deeper as he realized that eventually someone would discover that he was not a Paccu, if Quiktkoata didn't already know. There wasn't a tremendous amount of difference between the dress of the two tribes, but the moccasin prints were distinct. The darker color and the faint blue sheen to his hair also made him slightly conspicuous in this string of Paccu captives. Sequannah was certain that he would be found out; he couldn't even communicate with anyone. The Paccus could at least console each other, but Sequannah was alone, not sure if he should even trust the Paccus. He thought to himself that he was probably better off separated from them and that Quiktkoata's decision to make an example of him was actually a blessing. He feared being placed among the Paccus because he was certain that Snake warriors would torture him to death if they knew he was a Minnecou. The thought occurred to him that had he run from the grizzly instead of fighting beside his father, he would have been traveling safely with the clan now.

He turned around once again. A black curtain had been drawn around the litter, secluding Quiktkoata from any watchful eyes. Spinning back, he watched the scene in front of him unfolding in reverse as he jaunted backwards; there was no chance for escape. A sudden movement overhead caused him to stumble as he quickly ducked, nearly pulling his hair out in the process; he thought one of Quiktkoata's snakes had ambushed him from a tree. But it was a peculiar hawk, of unnatural proportions, that had swooped down close to the litter. Shortly after, another huge hawk swished by his head, its wing clipping the rope that fastened his hair to the canopy. It trailed the other hawk in a northwesterly direction. Sequannah suspected that it had come from inside the litter, but he had seen Quiktkoata before the curtain was drawn and there was nothing around him, especially not two hawks. He heard a flutter behind him, and turned in time to see a third hawk struggling its way out from in back of the curtain, only to fly off in the same direction as the other two hawks.

Immediately after the third hawk, the air became very thick

and stifled. The din of the Snake warriors' shouts and snarling took on a hollow tone. The sky grew dark to his left, strangely menacing through the trees. Swarms of mosquitoes appeared as stillness pervaded the area. Horseflies bit into Sequannah's flesh, but he could do nothing to shoo them with his arms tied tightly to the litter. A loud booming to the southeast announced the imminent storm and Sequannah welcomed it, anticipating the rain that would cool him down and rid him of these bloodthirsty insects; no matter the lightning. He would probably do better to die that way than to suffer in the sadistic hands of the Snake people.

The still and humid air caused even the most languid of the Paccus to swing out maddeningly at the swarms of horseflies and mosquitoes, their tightly bound arms meeting with resistance from the Paccus to their front and rear. Sequannah, as well as everyone else, could find no air sufficient enough to provide any cooling relief. Several Paccu captives dropped off into fainting spells and the others were forced to tow them along, further increasing their workloads and causing their bonds to become even tighter with the drag of limp bodies. Even the Snake warriors were beginning to lose stamina as their mud-caked hair and faces ran in rivulets of sweat, blurring and covering the once sharply-defined, jagged, yellow patterns. Two of the Paccus became convulsive and the painted warriors cut them loose and beat them limp, kicking them into the underbrush.

The group to which one of the convulsing Paccus was attached erupted suddenly into a frothing and red-eyed mass. The whole line swerved suddenly to their left and bowled down the painted warriors that were guarding them. Five Snake warriors went down. The Paccu captives used their knees to lash out at them; their feet and hands still tied to the captives to their front and rear. While the Snake warriors had anticipated Paccu rebellion, they had planned on individual ravings rather than a coordinated attack. Two of the painted warriors had the life snuffed out of them by the heavy Paccu knees that had crushed the air passage in their windpipes. The other three Snake warriors managed to roll away from the trampling Paccus, though badly bruised and beaten.

The two Snake warriors guarding the right side of the Paccu group ran into the midst of the mayhem, swinging their snake-skin whips and cursing the rebellious Paccus. The Paccus scrambled to their feet again and turned on the two guards, ignoring the violent whipping; they had been driven to the point where death was no longer a viable threat to them, but just as welcome as any other means of escape. The three trampled and dazed Snake warriors attempted to regroup, but suddenly went down in rapid succession as a large hatchet-wielding Minnecou raced out of the underbrush and leveled them with crushing blows to the skull. Karnack slipped through the turmoil and began hacking away at the thick ropes lashing the captives together. The freed Paccus grabbed onto the other two guards and Mokotak pummeled them. The Paccus were in a frenzy as they tore away at their shackling ropes. The other groups, witnessing the commotion, began to cheer and scream, begging the freed Paccus to untie them as well.

The procession came to a sudden halt and dozens of vicious, eerily painted Snake warriors streamed down the sides of the column towards the commotion. The freed Paccus had picked up the weapons of the dead Snake warriors and attacked the guards of the groups to their front and rear, whipping and jabbing with the Snake warriors' own copper-tipped spears. Mokotak could see that they were about to be overwhelmed and took out the first four advancing Snake warriors with his bow before slipping back into the underbrush. There was no time to help or even warn Karnack. Shortly after he'd made his escape, seventy-five Snake warriors surrounded the freed Paccus and squashed the rebellion.

But they didn't kill a single Paccu. They led them away singly and spread them out among the other groups of captives instead. They didn't beat them or treat them harshly and even led them instead of dragging them with ropes or by the hair. Quiktkoata knew they had exceeded rational limits, and that further brutality could jeopardize the entire operation, leaving them with nothing but corpses to show for their arduous journey. His object was to bring as many slaves as possible back to the city to build the empire. The procession halted as the Paccus were given rest and allowed to remain in relative peace.

* * *

Sequannah, in his restrained position, was caught up in all the screaming and cheering and the frantic bellowing of orders being shouted out all around him. A group of high-ranking warriors had quickly assembled around the litter and messengers darted back and forth into the tumultuous scene in the distance, enabling Sequannah to witness much of the rebellion. The sky remained dark and swirling to the south and the approaching storm seemed to be standing still as the Paccu rebels were led to their new groups. A young Paccu was placed in front of the group directly behind him and Sequannah found himself face to face with Karnack, the young Paccu he had encountered with Petawahin and the grizzly. Something inside him lit up as he saw the first person he recognized since being captured, but he wondered what had become of Mokotak. He hadn't even seen Woltah since he had first been tied to the litter.

Karnack signed a greeting to Sequannah as he recognized him immediately. Sequannah nodded in return but could manage nothing else in the way of communication. Sequannah was amazed the Snake people didn't even seem to notice they had a new face among their captives. But he couldn't even venture a guess as to why they didn't punish the rebel Paccus. After all the punishment they had inflicted upon the captives for seemingly trivial reasons, why all of a sudden do they allow them to get away with murder, and even allow them to rest in peace. But the Snake people had lost quite a few of their warriors and while they were in control for the moment, if the Paccus continued to rebel, the Snake warriors would eventually be worn down as well. He sensed that the Snake warriors' sudden change of heart was only a trick after reasoning what would happen once they got close enough to their village to send for help.

The humid air hadn't stirred in the slightest and the storm to their south continued to brew and swirl. It still hadn't moved any closer to them since it first blackened the southern horizon. Through the trees, the sky was an ominous blue-gray wall; occasional flashes of pink and blue lightning issued threatening echoes of crashing thunder. But the storm seemed to parallel them as they traveled to the east instead of following through with its original track. In fact, as the Paccus were engaged in their quickly subdued rebellion, the thunder was roaring and the treetops fluttered helplessly over the ridge directly to their south in the high winds. But the storm seemed to lose steam immediately after the commotion was quelled and was now swirling in place as they rested the Paccu captives. There were no birds or any other signs of wildlife about them since Sequannah had first been captured; only the irritating hum of mosquitoes and the droning buzz of horseflies interrupted the steady chorus of crickets and cicadas in the stifling late summer heat. The whisperings of the Paccus and the low grumbles of the Snake warriors were occasionally punctuated with rumblings and booms of distant thunder.

Sequannah was drifting off into a standing sleep when a painted messenger whizzed by him, a handful of bloodied sticks in his hand. He stopped at the front of the litter. Sequannah's blood curdled as Quiktkoata suddenly broke the silence with a deafening roar. He heard the sticks being snapped and tossed out of the enclosed litter on the ground to his left. He looked down at the sticks and immediately recognized Kwoita's handicraft in the blood-stained Minnecou arrows. Fear crept over him, once again, that discovery of his Minnecou ancestry was imminent, especially in such close proximity to Quiktkoata.

Several high-ranking warriors came running to the litter to offer their assistance, and Quiktkoata boomed out the orders to get the Paccus back on their feet again and get the procession moving. He ordered them to keep the Paccus healthy and the line moving, but if any more rebels should act up, to kill them immediately. Thunder from the swirling storm in the distance seemed to echo his every statement.

The sudden activity once again stirred up the mosquitoes from the underbrush and gnats were roused from their nests buried in the forest floor. A swirl of black flies formed a funnel over Sequannah's head and though they were not landing on him, they heightened the onslaught of mosquitoes and horseflies. He tried to blow them away, with little effect. But it was not until they started moving again that the gnats were finally left behind. The Snake warriors cracked their whips to get the Paccus back on their feet again, but this time, the snakes' fangs did not find their way to Paccu flesh.

Sequannah stiffened considerably during their brief rest and every backwards movement became awkward and painful, especially when they went up or down hills. He recalled carrying the grizzly meat a few days earlier and thought to himself how the Snake people considered walking backwards to be a punishment. Even with the strain on his scalp, the pain was more bearable than the carrying poles were on his shoulders when he had carried the grizzly meat of his own free will. He remembered how his father had told him that by carrying the food and hides, he would become stronger. The Snake people were trying to punish him, but in reality they were making him stronger, providing he could survive in this unusual heat.

Behind him, Karnack was more energetic than the other

Paccus and had no trouble in keeping pace with the litter. But the other captives stumbled in their efforts to keep up. They hadn't slept since they'd first been captured. With this heat, Sequannah deduced that if they didn't rest soon, there would be very few Paccus who would see this journey through to the end. The women and children were losing their footing already, and with no food or water, sickness and dehydration would set in rapidly.

Quiktkoata fully intended to feed them, but not until he was sure that they were sufficiently weakened to prevent them from becoming rebellious again. At the same time, he had to make sure that they remained strong enough to survive the entire journey or all would have been wasted; he would have lost much valuable time with few workers to add to his vast and rapidly growing stock of slaves. Quiktkoata had suffered more setbacks in this expedition than in any of the previous ones and his main objective now was to get these captives back alive. Even the Paccus could see the strain that Quiktkoata was under.

* * *

When the Paccus were first attacked, swarms of snakes invaded their village. As they attempted to beat them off, they were cut down in a hail of arrows. Immediately afterward, hundreds of heavily armed black and yellow painted warriors inundated them. Most of the Paccu arrows glanced off of the thick, hard leather of the Snake warriors' armor. It was likened to a massive swarm of huge bees. The Paccu defense was futile, and within a very short time, the cruelest looking man they had ever seen stood leering down at them, smiling in sadistic ecstasy as his underlings carved the fallen Paccu warriors and the entire village to shreds. But after the forced march began, things went awry for Quiktkoata. Early on, he had an inexplicable convulsion that caused him to lose the use of his legs. Soon after that, a large group of his new slave stock had escaped. Several of his scouts were missing and his weary army now had to deal with rebellion among the captives; apparently with outside help. Revenge against his unseen enemy was inevitable, but his anger had to be put aside if he was going to get these workers back to the empire. The land was empty with the exception of a few nomadic tribes and farming villages. After being driven from the magnificent cities in the south, Quiktkoata was determined to build the greatest empire the world had ever seen. Even the prophecies foretold of a nation of immeasurable wealth that would one day spring forth out of the vast and undeveloped continent to the north.

Quiktkoata's most pressing problem, however, was that no matter how many slaves he acquired, he could find none that were knowledgeable in the art of working stone. While he could eventually match the size and splendor of the ancient cities to the south with wooden structures and mounds of earth, everything would eventually rot and become overrun with vegetation; leaving no lasting monuments as testimony to the grandeur of his empire. He was envious of the giant stone pyramids in the city known as the "Place of the Creator" and its streets and avenues lined with dwellings and buildings of stone, but he was also aware that he would never be welcome there again; this being the third and final time he was exiled for attempting to overtake the priestly hierarchy and take possession of Teyotewakan.

Soon after he'd begun the monumental task of building his own empire, he made a discovery that gave him a certain amount of leverage with the merchants of Teyotewakan; a discovery that he determined to keep secret. While exploring the areas well to the north in search of more slaves to build his empire, a scouting party had run across a curious looking group of strange men with hairy faces and a pinkish hue to their skin. They were a ferocious lot and it took several battles for Quiktkoata and his warriors to overwhelm them, as his army was still not quite developed, but he managed to keep many of them alive.

He was fascinated with their strange village. They had erected several stone furnaces on the hills, facing into the prevailing winds. On clear days, when the wind was strong enough, they fed these furnaces with plenty of wood and large quantities of black, shiny coal. On top of each furnace was a vat of stone into which the hairy men would pile another kind of stone that left a green rust wherever it lay. The stone vat would become completely red in the intense heat, but would always hold together. Inside, however, the green stones melted into a hot and bright liquid which they would then ladle out into different molds to make copper colored objects for many uses. They would add certain other stones or sands to the molten liquid to make different strengths in the cooled objects they manufactured. Quiktkoata recognized the value in his discovery and kept the surviving hairy men as his slaves. He fed them well, gave them slaves of their own and even had slaves build more comfortable quarters for them. Many of the wooden structures in his growing empire were copies of the structures of the hairy men, though on a much larger scale. But, most of the strange men were kept in the area surrounding the furnaces. They were not even allowed to go as far as mining the copper; Quiktkoata had slaves brought in to keep the strange men occupied with their idle time and when they tired of the women and yearned to return home, he would tie one of them up in an outstretched position to four trees and leave him suspended there, just above the ground, without food or water. It did not matter who did the most complaining or the most work; one of them would be chosen at random and left there until those who had tried to escape were returned or until those who were slow in their work increased the pace. Every punishment was doled out matter-of-factly until the strange men understood that they were merely glorified slaves and not Quiktkoata's temporary guests.

With these strange and new marvels, Quiktkoata made many more inroads into the Teyotewakan markets and was once again rebuilding his influence in the huge religious community. But he no longer hungered to dominate the southern cities. He was convinced that he was to fulfill the prophecies and build the wealthiest and most powerful empire in the new world. It was foretold that the Snake would dominate the Hawk, and Quiktkoata was the most powerful of Snake Washans ever known, as well as a Washan of the hawk. Fear of him caused many to follow rather than suffer, but this same fear resulted in his many years of exile through the constant and united pressure of rivals. He determined to build his empire and as he dominated more and more territory, the southern cities would eventually fall under his domain.

Now, the overzealous Quiktkoata sat hunched over in his enclosed litter, partially paralyzed from his Snake spirit's encounter with a Minnecou warrior; the first substantial resistance to his ever-expanding empire. He was well aware that the Paccus, though capable of Minnecou strengths, were not entirely responsible for the woes that now beset him. He held them responsible for the great losses that had occurred to his ranks, even though the battle to overrun them had been brief. But the wily and unpredictable events that had upset his normally smooth slave drives were reminiscent of the same type of tactics he had encountered earlier in the summer when he overran a small band of Minnecou. He surrounded them four times before he finally prevented their tricky escapes, but in the end, he captured only a very few of them for use as slaves. Most had, at one point or another, sacrificed their own lives in order to protect the whole. Even those he had captured proved to be useless because he had to torture them to the point of being permanently maimed; still they would not carry out the work commands given to them. They would not even eat the food after being denied for days at a time. He likened them to certain wild animals that would always die in captivity, no matter what steps were taken to promote their continued good health. Whether he tortured them or left them alone, they all would eventually fade away in the same listless manner once they realized there was no hope of escape.

Quiktkoata also sensed the Minnecou shadows hovering around his procession, though he thought there were many more than the three that had actually followed. He witnessed the subtle movements out of the corners of his eyes, but he knew that to send warriors after them would prove to be futile. Every move a Minnecou makes is also a diversion. After the new slave stock has been driven into the city, ridding him of their burden, he will once again seek out his revenge against a Minnecou clan, but this time he will not attempt to take any of them alive. They are useless to his ambitions and his only interest is to rid this continent of them permanently. In the meantime, he has other means to give the Minnecou clan something to think about; his last reserve of power is already in motion. In addition to this, he left a net behind him in the form of forty painted warriors, combing the trail well in back of the procession in the hopes of picking up at least some of the Minnecou warriors who had the tenacity to harass one of his processions.

CHAPTER 8

Petawahin and the Washan watched in silence. Snake warriors lurked in the underbrush, moving only when the flames advanced too close. A few stayed out in the open, searching for signs of their unseen enemy and trying to lure the Minnecou into the midst of their concealed war party. Flames advanced in many directions instead of a steady line. Tongues of fire would quickly burn through the dried grasses surrounding an island of brush and small trees, and Quiktkoata's snakes would hurriedly take refuge in the undergrowth. Soon, they were trapped and the hissing would become frantic and vicious as the inferno advanced inward, leaving no means of escape.

The Washan smiled in ecstasy as his hastily conceived plan worked better than he could ever have imagined. He poked Petawahin on the shoulder as he pointed to yet another island of scrub erupting into a screaming hiss of flames. The fire spread in a south-easterly direction on the gentle breezes of a northwest current, but the suffocating plumes of blinding smoke began to drift into Petawahin and the Washan. The Snake warriors scrambled out of the underbrush and gathered in a quickly assembled column. They raced by the bottom of the ridge, directly beneath Petawahin and the Washan, and headed off in the direction where they estimated the fire was originally set. This gave Petawahin and the Washan an opportunity to slip through and follow Quiktkoata unhindered, but at the same time, these Snake warriors would be free to follow Ketanka and the Minnecou clan northward. They were left with no choice but to follow the war party and protect the clan as it fled northward.

They ran along the backside of the ridge in an effort to parallel them, but the further they went along, the more distant they became. When the Snake warriors were no longer in sight, Petawahin led the Washan down the ridge and headed directly to the north of where the war party seemed to be headed. He could still see the flames to his right and knew that his enemy would have to skirt these as well, so he headed northwest to give them a wide berth. When they broke through the smoke line and into the fresh air of the drifting northwest current, Petawahin cautioned the Washan to keep low and well hidden in the underbrush.

The painted warriors came stumbling out of the smoke-filled forest and scattered themselves on the ground as they gasped their first breaths of fresh air. The Washan spotted a trail across a small opening and knew this to be the trail that Quebathe and Shatomi had laid down to deliberately divert the Snake warriors from he and the Wolf brothers.

"The others made this trail for them to follow," the Washan whispered.

"We must let them see us," Petawahin returned. "But don't look at them when we cross the clearing. Let them see us walking slowly so that they will follow more cautiously and think that we are afraid of walking into an ambush from our own people."

The two of them walked across the little meadow as if they were heading out to pick blueberries, but once they fell under the cover of dense brush on the other side, they ran like antelope until Petawahin found a good place to sidetrack from the following Snake warriors. Peeking through the brush atop a small hillock, the Washan and the warrior spied the painted killers crouched down low, easing themselves along the obvious trail that led into the dense marsh at the southern end of the lake. As the last two crept by them, considerably behind the rest of the column, Petawahin sought to raise his bow and dispose of them, but the Washan halted his movement.

"Be still and don't speak or look up," he whispered.

Petawahin froze, scanning along the path where the Snake warriors had just passed. An enormous reddish-brown hawk glided silently by, following the same trail. Petawahin looked to the Washan to see if he had noticed, but the Washan's intense stare warned him to remain still. Moments later, another hawk of the same color flew in the wake of the Snake warriors. Neither bird made a sound, nor did they cause even a leaf to flutter.

"The hawks," Petawahin whispered. "Is that what you were waiting for?"

"Be still," the Washan warned him. "They are with the Snake people."

Petawahin turned his head back to the trail, and as he moved, a loud screech erupted overhead. He instinctively raised his bow and shot at the screaming hawk, but hit the branches in the tree-tops instead. A hastened second shot produced the same results and the look on the Washan's face became grave. The hawk immediately lifted out of range and circled overhead, screaming in alarm. They heard a ruckus of shrill screeching as the other two hawks returned and swooped down onto the tops of two trees just out of bow range. The three hawks glared at the Minnecou warriors, screeching their whereabouts to the Snake warriors. Petawahin grabbed the Washan by the arm and dragged him towards the swamp where he hoped to find his way to the path to the other side of the lake.

He scrambled downhill in the direction of the marshes. They couldn't see the Snake warriors, but they could hear crashing in the bushes as the painted ones took pursuit. The three hawks hovered overhead, constantly screeching as the Snake warriors followed over the difficult terrain. The two Minnecou stole quickly through the beech, birch and oak trees, and into an impossible maze of honeysuckle, blueberry bushes, and scattered clumps of cedar and juniper. When they reached the true wetland, where the water squeezed through the surface, they leapt from sod to sod to avoid falling into the thick and slippery mud.

As Petawahin led the way, he stepped onto a concealed yellow jackets' nest, and though he didn't get stung himself, he left the Washan in an angry haze of venomous bees. The Washan scrambled like a whirlwind through the grassy clumps, and though the yellow jackets no longer followed, several had clung to him and continued to pump their venom until their backsides had been torn away. The Washan dove headlong into the mud, stumbling out as he tried desperately to clear the caked mud from his eyes and then brush the stingers off of him.

Petawahin grabbed him and slung him over his shoulders as he tried to pick out a new course through the boggy terrain of the lake's outlet; the Washan had left a conspicuous trail. The Washan squirmed in Petawahin's grip as he continued to brush at the detached stingers, still pumping into his scrawny frame. Petawahin grabbed a handful of flesh and squeezed hard.

"Stop jerking," Petawahin whispered loudly. "I'm trying to get us out of here alive!"

The Washan emitted a stifled scream as he held his hand over his mouth. "Put me down," he demanded. "I can still walk." Petawahin threw the Washan down on his feet and they raced through a small patch of cattails into a dense stand of towering reeds. They crawled carefully under the tufted canopy so as not to shake the frail stalks and give away their whereabouts, but the hawks could see clearly from above and continued to circle overhead while maintaining their chorus of piercing screeches. Petawahin heard yelling in the distance and smiled at the Washan as he surmised that the Snake warriors had found their trail and stumbled into the yellow jackets' nest.

One by one, the hawks stealthily glided off in a northwesterly direction, apparently giving up on the Snake warriors ever catching up with the Minnecou in this huge stretch of marshy terrain. Immediately after the last hawk disappeared from view, a thin haze enveloped the area and the air became stifled. The mosquitoes stirred up in droves around the two Minnecou and lacy strands of spider webs became thicker and more abundant with the sudden change. They heard a distant rumble to the southeast as the sky darkened in that direction. Petawahin found a stout stick to test the ground ahead of him because he knew there was quicksand in the area. This particular marsh seemed to give certain warning signs such as the color of the water and the different types of plants surrounding the dangerous areas. Petawahin was well acquainted with these. He and the Wolf brothers had blazed the original trail through this alluvial swamp. Even if the hawks had stayed, he knew that he had led the Snake warriors into a position where he and the Washan would be well ahead of any enemies who could survive crossing through this maze of wetland flora and manage to find their way back out. It was a large flat area, but most of the plant life extended over the height of a man and at the same time was too frail to climb and establish a sense of direction. Finding a way out was largely a matter of guesswork, unless one knew which directions the various lazy currents were heading, and where they led.

The Washan found several birds' nests, but even the eggs from the second nesting were all hatched and the chicks long gone. He resorted to picking the various berries as he waited for Petawahin to slowly pick out a safe route for them. The sounds of Snake warriors crashing through the tall stalks and thick wetland flora slowly faded away, and soon the two Minnecou began to hear frantic pleas for help that abruptly ceased after a very short time. The Snake warriors had found themselves surrounded by pockets of quicksand. The Minnecou warriors smiled as each scream was suddenly stifled. They slowly picked their way through the bogs, remaining quiet and keeping movement to a minimum to prevent being seen. The Washan scooped up several large bullfrogs and batted their heads against his knotty knees to render them unconscious before stuffing them into his pouch for the two warriors to eat later.

Without any breeze to fan the unchecked forest fire, it spread much more slowly, but the hazy smoke settled in over the flat marsh and the eyes stung as Minnecou and painted warriors alike stumbled through the muddy bog. If they stood up to full height, the smoke became more intense, but if they stooped too low, they were exposed the septic odor of swamp gases they were constantly stirring up with their feet.

An arrow whirred by, several hands over the Minnecous'

heads. Moments later, another crashed into the weeds to their left. Neither Petawahin nor the Washan could see anyone from where they were, but judging by the distance that the arrows had missed them by, they ascertained that the Snake warriors knew they were falling behind and were shooting blindly in the direction from which they could hear the Minnecou. After several of their warriors had succumbed to the quicksand, many of the painted ones were afraid to move and froze in their tracks. They had made a fatal error in splitting up in the swampy area. They tried to cover more ground as there were many places in which the Minnecou could have hidden, but now, one of them had ordered them closer together. Though they were only able to follow at a much slower rate than the Minnecou were fleeing, at least they would have each other to pull themselves out of the quicksand. Once they reached drier ground, they would catch up to the insolent Minnecou warriors.

Petawahin quickened the pace and the Washan concentrated on concealing the trail behind them. Petawahin stopped short when he spied a couple of water moccasins rippling in the shallow puddles ahead. The Washan looked up to see why he was stopping and a sudden fear crept over him as he spotted the moccasins. After a few moments, several more snakes had appeared and then vanished in the weeds.

"They are not the snakes of the painted ones," the Washan whispered. "Their snakes were darker and much thicker."

"You're certain?" Petawahin questioned. "Their snakes are all the same?"

"There were different kinds," the Washan said, somewhat uneasily. "But these snakes are just swimming around one area. I think they have a nest over there because they all seem to be going back and forth to the same place."

"I pray to the Creator that you're right," Petawahin whispered. He could hear the column of Snake warriors as they crashed through the dead brush and wound their way through the thick reeds far in back of them. "Wait here," he whispered to the Washan. "I will make an easy trail for them to follow."

Petawahin backtracked to about halfway between the Washan and the Snake warriors, then shook the reeds, snapping dead branches so the Snake warriors could hear him. Moments later, a slew of arrows hailed down on him as he bolted back to the Washan, leaving deep imprints as he went along. When he reached the Washan, they carefully skirted around the moccasin nest and when they came back on the other side, to where they could see the obvious trail with the deep footprints, Petawahin and the Washan laid down another visible trail, shaking reeds and breaking more dead branches to let the Snake warriors know where they were. Another hail of arrows came raining down, but they were short of even the moccasins' nest. Petawahin once again resumed finding a safe route for them, but headed off in a slightly different direction in case the painted ones discovered the moccasin nest before they stepped in it. The Washan continued to cover their tracks, hoping that at least one of the mud-colored vipers would sink its fangs into painted flesh.

Several moments later, they heard a frantic burst of yelling. The crashing of dried reeds and dead brush erupted in hollow echoes through the still haze as the painted warriors once again dispersed in several directions. Petawahin spotted oak and birch through the maze of rushes, alder, and blueberry bushes and headed towards what he knew to be dry land. The edge of the murky swamp was bordered by a steep and slippery bank, laden with a thick, shiny, green mat of poison ivy. Petawahin ran quickly along its length, but could find no break in the poisonous barrier. Looking overhead, he noticed a long and sturdy oak branch and immediately lifted the Washan onto it. When the Washan was about halfway along its length and the branch was still bowed to within Petawahin's reach, he leapt up and grabbed onto it. The trunk of the massive oak, however, was covered with thick, brown-haired vines of the same poison ivy, and the two warriors had to climb up to a higher branch on the other side of the tree from which they would have to hang and then drop into the dead leaves of the dry forest floor. When they reached the higher branch, the Washan pointed out over the marsh with a wide grin on his face; the reeds and brush were being trampled in circles and zigzags as the Snake warriors tried desperately to find a way out of the thick entanglement.

Once they were on the ground Petawahin pointed to the northern side of the now huge forest fire. "Let's go that way and stay out of the smoke," he suggested.

"We have to find Mokotak and the young Paccu warrior and free them from the snakes or they may be burned up in the fire," the Washan reminded him. "Whatever the Snake people decide to do with Sequannah has already been done, but Mokotak and the Paccu may not have been discovered. We may still have a chance to save them if we hurry. Ketanka will need Mokotak with the clan."

"How do you know that he even fell under the spell of the snakes?" Petawahin questioned. "We may all be killed if we get trapped in the fire as well," he countered.

"It is only a short distance from here if they were stopped by the snakes, and the painted warriors behind us may not choose to follow if they see that we went directly into the fire," the Washan spoke.

Petawahin could see that the Washan was just as correct in his own view of the situation, and not wanting to appear that his son's welfare was the only matter of importance to him, he relented and went along with the Washan's plan.

They raced towards the southeast and soon they were in the midst of the still smoking and blackened earth. Their high moccasins protected them from the red cinders for the time being, but a prolonged exposure to the alkaline ashes would eventually cause the rawhide moccasins to dry out and burn. The Washan led the way he determined Mokotak most probably went, but the smoke became thicker and the red cinders threw off considerably more heat. The thick, humid air was transformed into an intense dry heat that stung as each breath was drawn into their lungs; the mosquitoes' and gnats' intensely compulsive appetites were quelled to the point where they would no longer follow their quarry, but those that had already pierced the skin of the two Minnecou, remained there and dried to hollow shells in the intense heat. They sweated profusely as they determined to cut straight through the burned out area, but they were forced to skirt to the southwest when they reached the point where flames were still flickering.

They stopped at the base of a small cliff and found the remains of several of Quiktkoata's snakes, burned to coils of hollow black shells. When they climbed to the top, they saw that they were at the perimeter of the blaze; the stone had acted as a barrier and directed the fire in a southeasterly direction. From the top of the small ridge, they could see little through the smoky haze as everything rippled in the rising waves of intense heat.

"I don't see them," Petawahin looked around anxiously. "We'd better move on or we'll never catch up with the Snake people."

The Washan scanned the area, but could find no sign of the two missing warriors. The brush had burned out to the point where there were no longer any leaves and when the smoke lifted from time to time, they could see for quite a distance. But there was no evidence of bodies left lying in the burned out ashes, and no way to determine whether Mokotak and Karnack had survived. From Petawahin's vantage, the only ways out were either to skirt around way to the south of the blaze or to go back from whence they came. To head back to the northern side of the blaze would give them more relief from the suffocating smoke, but it may also lead them back into the midst of the war party that had foolishly followed them into the marsh. By now, they could have found their way out.

"Go south of the fire," Petawahin decided. He pointed out a route for them to take and the Washan, sensing Petawahin's anxiety over his son, ran ahead of him to avoid any further delay. He stopped suddenly, however, after running only a short distance, and pointed out a Paccu moccasin print to Petawahin.

"The Paccu came this way," the Washan announced. "Mokotak would not leave any tracks behind him. Maybe they were still together."

Petawahin led at a rapid pace, pointing out the random prints of the young Paccu as he went along. The further they went, however, the closer they came to the flames. Burning embers drifted aimlessly around, falling onto the Minnecou warriors as they increased their pace to catch up with Karnack. The crackling intensified and soon, Petawahin could see that the young Paccu's tracks would lead them directly into the raging inferno.

"They must have gone through before the fire reached here," Petawahin said, hopeful that Mokotak was with the young Paccu. "We'll have to go much further to the south. It will take longer to catch up with them."

The Washan sensed that Petawahin may be hinting that they cut through the fire once again, in order to save time. He dashed off to the south before Petawahin could even think of persuading him into the thick of the blaze once again. Petawahin chased frantically after him and soon outpaced him. Perhaps, he thought, the Washan was right in going around the blaze. There was no way of telling what they may have run into and at least they were finally able to pursue Sequannah's captors without any further diversions. No sooner did this consoling thought cross his mind, when he looked back to check on the Washan, and found him running with both hands clasped to the sides of his head. A few steps further, he fell into the forest floor and lay writhing in agony as he pressed in futility against the pain in his head. The prolonged exposure to the intense heat and the vigorous activity had expanded his arteries and the bee venom was surging through them. Petawahin once again threw the Washan over his shoulders and headed off as quickly as possible in the direction of the Snake procession, searching for cool water along the way.

The smoke soon began to thin and the Washan was cooling down as well, but the need to find cool water was still apparent; the Washan was weak and nearly limp. Petawahin sensed his own need for water, as his mouth was dry as leather after running through the ash laden sauna and into the stifling humidity outside of the blaze. Nevertheless, Petawahin was not going out of his way. He had lost much valuable time already and would have to stumble onto fresh water before stopping.

In a small ditch, Petawahin noticed some skunk cabbages growing and diverted from his track to see if there was any possibility of finding water. The ground was wet. He quickly dug out a small cavity into which murky water strained itself through the surrounding mud. He soaked the Washan down and pasted more mud on him to draw out the remaining poison. Then he cooled himself off with cupped handfuls of the precious liquid that would keep him and the Washan going, even though it was not fit for drinking. The Washan finally got back on his feet, much to the relief of Petawahin, but his stunted pace soon drew Petawahin to carrying the Washan on his shoulders again. He couldn't leave the Washan behind as there was no way of knowing if the war party had indeed followed them. Though he was nearly incapacitated at this point, he may prove to be invaluable later, providing Petawahin could maneuver them to within striking distance of Quiktkoata's string of captives.

The two Minnecou warriors finally skirted the huge and ever expanding blaze and soon, the crackling and snapping of exploding embers from the intense heat faded into the background. Petawahin located a cool, quickly moving stream of clear water and stopped where they could drink and catch their breath. The Washan needed no prodding. He outpaced even Petawahin once he caught sight of the life giving artery of precious liquid. The Washan was still streaked with charcoal and mud when he stood back up and Petawahin was inclined to laugh, until he got a good look at his own reflection in the water.

The air was dead and the mosquitoes had been relentlessly hounding them since they stopped at the skunk cabbage and dug into the mud. The cool water provided their only escape from the voracious pests and every time the men stood, they found it difficult not to return to the sanctuary beneath the stream's surface.

"We should stay here for a while," Petawahin stated, knowing that the Washan would feel guilty in holding him up any longer. "But I would like to scout ahead and find out where they are so that at least we can devise a plan before nightfall."

"We still have plenty of daylight left and we have no way of knowing how far they plan to travel today," the Washan pointed out. "It's not even midday and I'm sure they're not going to make camp this close to the fire. If I remain here, you will waste time by having to return later. And we should stay together in case more snakes are around. We'll take some of this fresh water with us and find their trail. With all the captives they're dragging along and the condition they're in, I'm sure we won't have too much trouble catching up with them. We'll find them right now and find out what they've done with Sequannah so that at least you can relieve your anxiety and watch for weaknesses. After that, it will only be a matter of waiting for the right opportunity."

"What about Mokotak and Karnack?" Petawahin questioned. "They should be back with the clan."

"If we find them, we can send them back. But it would be too risky to spend our time looking for them, only to miss an opportunity to free Sequannah," the Washan concluded. Petawahin had the same sentiments, but he preferred to hear them from the Washan.

The cooling relief of the stream went a long way; the two Minnecou warriors soon located the Snake peoples' trail and paralleled it for a considerable distance before they began to feel the wearying effects of the heat again. At one point, they found a large area of flattened grass and weeds where they determined that the Snake people had stopped to rest. They kept low as they searched for clues in the area and watched for painted warriors that may have been lurking behind Quiktkoata's procession. They stumbled into a group of dead painted warriors, piled in a heap off to the side of the trampled path.

"Why do their warriors fight for them if this is the respect they earn from their people?" Petawahin questioned the Washan.

"They must be very foolish or maybe they have no respect

for their dead," the Washan said disgustedly. "Maybe they don't like themselves," he mused, turning the bodies over to find how they were killed. "They were shot through with arrows, but the arrows have been removed."

The two warriors searched the dead Snake warriors, but found no weapons or magic articles that they thought these gruesome killers would be sure to possess. The strange thing, though, was that they found no accompanying Paccu bodies. They could not fathom the notion that Quiktkoata would not take immediate and vicious revenge. They found another pile of dead Snake warriors and when the Washan turned them over, he was surprised to find out that none of these had been shot, but had been beaten and strangled to death. Three of them had large crushed areas on their skulls.

"Mokotak!" Petawahin said quietly. "Mokotak killed these warriors."

"That is why they did not kill the Paccus," the Washan deduced. "They thirst for Minnecou blood." A short distance away, the Washan found a scattering of broken and bloodied sticks. He held them up for Petawahin's inspection.

"Mokotak's arrows," Petawahin stated as the Washan nodded. "Kwoita always made those kind of arrows for Mokotak. But three of the Snake warriors were beaten and strangled. Mokotak would not waste that much time. The Paccus must have killed them unless Karnack chose to fight in this manner. If the Paccus killed their warriors, then wouldn't Quiktkoata have killed all of them out of revenge?"

"Maybe the Paccu captives are very important to Quiktkoata," the Washan guessed. "Maybe his warriors are slaves, also."

"How can you have warriors fighting for you if they would be looking to escape as well?" Petawahin questioned.

"If their families and tribes were all killed or enslaved, then they would have no one to return to even if they did escape," the Washan stated. "They would find no place to live where they would not be in danger of being attacked by the Snake people again."

Petawahin thought this over, and while it did seem possible, he couldn't conceive of anyone following a chief who didn't always do what is best for the people before considering his own desires. As far as he knew, the chief was not the one who gave the most orders and made the most demands, but the one that most of the clan thought was wisest to follow. The chief would be most fearsome to enemies, but most friendly to his own clansmen. The chief was always the one with the most to give. Ketanka's lodge would often bring in more meat than they needed and hides as well, but his power as chief came about from his willingness to share. If he kept everything to himself, he would be considered stingy and would be shamed in the eyes of the clan. Petawahin could not understand how Quiktkoata ever found anyone willing to follow him. Everyone, including his own people, would be his enemies; wouldn't they?

The area where they had rested was highly conspicuous and gave testimony to the considerable size of Quiktkoata's war party and captives. At one point, they found a place where it appeared as though Quiktkoata's servants were in the middle of preparing food for the massive procession, but dumped everything on the ground and left it there partially cooked. Something had caused them to flee, but there was no evidence of any threat to them. Certainly they weren't running from Petawahin and the Washan, nor Karnack and Mokotak.

"They must be driving the Paccus back to their village in a hurry; they are not even stopping for them to eat," Petawahin said. "Mokotak must have attacked them while the were resting. Now they may not stop until they reach their village."

"They must think we are many," the Washan said. "But they will stop. Their village must be distant, otherwise we would have seen them long before now. They must stop to at least feed their own warriors or the Paccus will not be the only ones rebelling."

The two warriors followed Quiktkoata's trail on a parallel course, keeping a careful watch for painted warriors waiting in ambush. Petawahin heard the slightest crack of a twig, and he and the Washan quietly slipped behind the cover of a small meadow of dense ferns where they laid low in the underbrush. Thirty to forty Snake warriors came whisking through the area, keeping very low and remaining nearly silent for the quick pace they were maintaining. They were fanned out in a double line, extending well to the sides of the freshly trampled trail, but not quite as far away as the two Minnecou had taken refuge. Once they had passed and Petawahin was certain they were gone, he followed them as they backtracked the highly visible trail. He and the Washan had not gotten very far when they heard the painted ones talking in their strange tongue. Petawahin signaled for the Washan to remain while he went to see what they were up to.

He maneuvered himself very close, where he could see them looking over the dead Snake warriors that he and the Washan had moved around. One of them was pointing to the broken arrows on the ground that he and the Washan had picked up and discarded haphazardly. There were many more warriors than the thirty of forty that he had originally guessed to have passed by him and the Washan. One warrior shouted out a barrage of commands and a group of about twenty-five painted warriors quickly assembled into a fanned out line and continued their stealthy combing as they went further down the trail towards the direction of the fire. Another Snake warrior was quietly giving directions to a small group of men who were preparing the dead Snake warriors for their journeys into the next world. They had deliberately left the bodies in a pile to see if anyone would disturb them.

Another painted warrior stood over a group of about forty warriors giving them orders in near whispers and pointing in sweeping circles and to vantage points as he planned to send certain ones out to ambush, and the rest to flush out the Minnecou rebels. Petawahin raced back to the Washan in complete silence.

"Follow me," he whispered frantically. "We have to get out of here quickly or they will have us surrounded in every direction. There are very many of them and if we are seen by even one, we will almost certainly be captured. We can head to the south. There are some big hills in that direction and maybe we will be able to watch them from there."

As they raced southward, they took special care not to leave any moccasin prints or make any sound. They skirted around the small rises and hills and chose instead to maneuver themselves through the dense vegetation that was characteristic of the lower lying areas at this time of the year. Rain always became scant towards the end of summer, causing most of the vegetation to brown and whither in some areas and to become considerably thinned in others; only the lower and more protected areas retained enough moisture to sustain a dense growth of flora. It was much more difficult to move without disturbing the surrounding brush, but they had to stay out of sight.

From the first ridge of considerable size, Petawahin and the Washan scanned the area in back of them, and from time to time, they caught fleeting glimpses of the Snake warriors as they fanned out southward, towards the ridge upon which they were now standing.

Other Snake warriors had been sent north of the procession's trail as well, but they were not at all visible from the two Minnecous' vantage. The Snake warriors furthest away were already beginning to turn eastward to parallel the slave drive's trail, but there was no way of telling just how far south the closest warriors intended to range before they would turn eastward as well. The two Minnecou rapidly cut across the valley south of them to the next even higher ridge. The ridge that made up the southern border of the valley was not as level as the other side, but was a series of hills, the bases of which never reached below the elevation of the valley.

Petawahin and the Washan scrambled up and down the seemingly endless series of hills as they headed in an easterly direction, and only after the sun drifted far down the western sky did they reach a crest from which they would finally catch a glimpse of the procession as the end of it rounded a bend in the valley and once again was out of sight. The Snake warriors combing the area between the two Minnecou and the trail were far behind as they moved slowly along the smaller ridge tops and through the dense flora of the valleys in a steady, silent line, hoping to catch the Minnecou warriors by surprise.

Petawahin and the Washan were more cautious as they made their way downhill and once again picked their way up the wearying ascent of the next hill from which they were certain to obtain a good view of Quiktkoata's slave procession. Silently, they crept to the edge of a steep cliff and lay low so as not to be conspicuous.

"What were they doing back there?" the Washan finally had an opportunity to question Petawahin.

"They knew we were following them because they saw that we had moved the bodies and Mokotak's broken arrows," Petawahin answered. "They sent more warriors back down the trail to see if we turned back, while other painted ones prepared the dead bodies for their journeys into the next world. But most of the warriors were sent out in our direction. I saw one of their war chiefs pointing out where they would look for us, and where they would hide in order to ambush us while the others tried to flush us out...like we would hunt deer. We have come far enough away to avoid them."

"I should have known it was a trick," the Washan whispered as they continued their nearly inaudible conversation. "No one would fight for people who would discard them like fish guts once they were no longer of any use. They're moving very slowly now," the Washan pointed to the long line in the distance. "I wonder why it took so long for us to catch up with them."

"They're looking for a place to camp for the night where they think we won't be able to get at them," Petawahin whispered with contempt. "But they will find no such place."

"If one of them sees you, you are as good as captured," the Washan warned. "And remember that I am a Washan as well as a warrior. You know that I cannot kill a man unless he first attempts to kill me."

"They saw Mokotak and he was able to get away," Petawahin said stubbornly.

"I suspect that Ketanka wanted me to go along with you so that we would find a way to get Sequannah back without bloodshed. That way, the Snake people would not find revenge so desirable. I also suspect that is why he wanted Mokotak back with him as well, but that is not the way things have turned out," the Washan admitted. "Ketanka knew that if Mokotak was here, he would kill as many of them as he could. But with a tribe as big as theirs, that would only serve to anger them."

Petawahin suddenly put his fingers to his lips for silence. Something moved below them. The Washan listened intently and soon he heard an intense scratching coming from the base of the cliff.

"Sounds like a black bear," the Washan whispered.

"As long as he stays down there we'll be safe," Petawahin whispered. "But if he decides to come up here, there's going to be a lot of noise." Petawahin began to crawl closer to the edge of the cliff and the Washan grabbed his foot.

"Where are you going?" he whispered frantically. "He might see you!"

"How can we be sure that it's only a black bear if we don't look?" Petawahin questioned. "What if it's a grizzly?"

Petawahin crawled to the very edge of the cliff and looked down its length. The Washan watched as he picked up a small rock and aimed below. The Washan moved quickly to try and stop him, but it was too late. A moment after the pebble reached its destination, the Washan heard a sharp whirring sound and caught a glimpse of an arrow as it whizzed by Petawahin's face. The arrow went straight up and came straight back down, landing between the fingers of the

Washan's left hand. The markings on one of Mokotak's arrows stood out clearly before him. He looked over at Petawahin who was doing all he could to restrain his laughter at the expression on the Washan's face.

Petawahin tossed one of his own marked arrows over the edge of the cliff, not daring to look and see where it landed. They heard the sound of muffled footsteps below them and soon after they faded away, Mokotak came strolling up from behind them.

"Follow me," Mokotak whispered. "We can see better from down there and it's harder for them to see us."

"What if someone comes up here and spots us below them like we spotted you?" Petawahin said.

"I have been following them since dawn," Mokotak answered. "They are too afraid to come this far away from the trail without a whole war party, especially after I killed a few of them. When they walk with more than two of them, they sound like buffalo trying to sneak through the dry leaves of autumn. We will be long gone before they ever get close, unless we find a good place to ambush them."

The Washan shuddered as he imagined the three of them trying to fight off thirty or forty warriors.

"We must find a way to get Sequannah back without having to kill any of them," the Washan insisted. "If we can free some of the Paccus, we will, but we'll do nothing until after we free Sequannah. Killing their warriors will give them good cause to come back after the Minnecou once they bring these captives to their village. They will hunt us down and slaughter our clan."

Mokotak looked at the Washan in astonishment. "How many painted warriors do you think the Paccus killed before they were attacked in their village? I'll tell you that it was none. If we don't kill them, then they will kill us. If they have no reason to fear us, they will run us out of this whole territory unless we want to be their slaves."

"I agree with Mokotak," Petawahin said strongly. "There is no better way to change people than to act like them. That is the only way they will understand."

"If they kill one of us for every one of their people that we kill, who is going to run out of warriors first?" the Washan asked them. "They outnumber our own clan by more than ten to one with the warriors they have here. How many more do they have left in their village?"

"We could get all of the Minnecou clans together and that would be enough to force them back to wherever they came from...or to kill them all if necessary," Petawahin said. "If we don't fight them now, then we may as well all move back to the Minnecou villages in the south and grow corn all year, because we'll never be able to come up here again. We'll never be able to enjoy the beauty of this place again. We'll just watch the plants grow in the red dirt all year and we will become great plant warriors."

Mokotak felt somewhat resentful of Petawahin's himself, had chosen the clan's way of life over the farmer's existence, where the scenery changed, and there was always something new to discover. Many of the Minnecou in the villages spent a summer or two out with a traveling clan, but if these Snake warriors were around, they may not be able to do this. There will be less things brought in from the north to trade and share with the farmers in the villages and all of the Minnecou would have to make do with much less. All of the game would be wiped out in one season and they would have to look elsewhere for food.

"We must get word to the other clans and get everyone together to fight these Snake warriors," Mokotak demanded. "We could not survive in the villages with all of the clans living there as well. There would never be enough food."

"But we have not seen even one person from any of the other clans since we left the village," the Washan stated. "Summer has nearly passed, and I don't ever remember when we didn't see anyone else. At first I thought that maybe they had gone further east than usual, but we had stuck to the same areas as last year so they should at least have known where we were. Every time we sent out hunting and scouting parties, there was no sign of the other clans. I think the reason for this lies in the valley before us. They must have attacked the other clans and killed them, or took them for slaves like they did to the Paccus. We may have no one else to help us fight them."

"The Paccus would fight with us," Mokotak said.

"The Paccus would get us all killed," Petawahin sneered.

"Karnack fought well when we tried to free a group of his people that had attacked the painted warriors," Mokotak admitted, "but he also got captured as well."

"They didn't kill him?" Petawahin questioned.

"I don't think they knew the difference between him and

the other Paccus. All of the warriors that had been guarding that group of Paccus had been killed. There was no one there to point him out. Many warriors came down towards us and I shot the first few with my bow so I could escape, but I had no time to warn Karnack or I would have taken him with me. He was quick for a young warrior."

"If we take them out on raids against the Snake people they will learn how to fight like a Minnecou. Then we could force the Snake people out of here," Petawahin said to them.

"If we want to get Sequannah back and get out of here alive, we should kill no more," the Washan said.

"Did you see the lodge that they are carrying with their chief in it?" Mokotak questioned. They both nodded. "They have Sequannah tied to the back of it. How many of their warriors do you think are going to stand back while we try to untie Sequannah over there?" Another low boom of thunder echoed throughout the valley from the dark sky to the south. "That thunderstorm has been sitting to the south all day."

"The storm cannot move if the air does not move," Petawahin stated as the men sat in the stifling heat.

"A storm does not sit that long," the Washan warned. "Many great Washans can make storms and I'm sure that this one is not natural. I think this Snake chief is a powerful Washan."

"Maybe he is Sikun," Petawahin conjectured, though he wasn't exactly sure of what a Sikun actually was. He'd only heard stories of their powers.

"Not Sikun," the Washan stated with certainty. "A Sikun would be friend to Paccu and Minnecou...and would take no slaves."

Petawahin and Mokotak looked at him questioningly, but he pointed down into the valley. "They have stopped to camp for the night."

The litter had been placed carefully on the ground, but the curtains remained drawn, and Quiktkoata did not come out from underneath the canopy. The attendants rushed about, building cooking fires and pulling out huge clay pots from a large compartment under the litter. Four men came up from the rear of the column carrying a large square box attached to poles that they placed on their shoulders in much the same manner that the litter was carried. They pulled many baskets of food from the box and dumped them in the various clay pots that servants were filling with water from a nearby stream.

The sun hovered on the horizon as the food simmered over hot fires fanned by the attendants. Many of the Paccu captives were moaning in pain, while others sat listlessly shooing mosquitoes and deerflies. Soon the smell of food drifted up the wall of the cliff and the three Minnecou suddenly realized how hungry they were. The Washan reached into his pouch and pulled out five large bullfrogs, semi-dried and somewhat misshapen, but they could not make a fire to cook them. The Washan handed one of them to Mokotak; he sniffed it and promptly threw it over the side of the cliff. "I thought you smelled strange today," he said to the Washan. Petawahin laughed quietly; the Washan dropped the other frogs over the side of the cliff as he whispered his sorrow to the Creator for having wasted what was once good meat. Petawahin pulled out a packet of dried venison and the Washan made use of the berries he had picked.

The Snake warriors were the first to eat when the simmering stews were finally ladled out of the huge clay pots. The Paccus had to huddle together when they got their share; their ropes left little room to maneuver the wooden bowls to their mouths. For the time being, the moaning had stopped and only an occasional child's crying broke the silence from the valley below. After the clay pots were emptied, the attendants once again filled them with water and heaped in many more baskets of meat and vegetables to simmer on the dying embers of the cooking fires. Next morning, they would only have to light a small fire to warm up the cooled broth.

"Wait here," the Washan said. "I have a plan if I can find what I need." The Washan wanted desperately to find a way to free Sequannah before Mokotak and Petawahin thought up some dangerous and daring maneuver to overpower the Snake warriors in the vicinity of Sequannah.

Mokotak and Petawahin waited quietly, occasionally whispering weaknesses they detected. The sun was nearly set when the Washan finally returned, displaying a large handful of red-capped mushrooms. Mokotak looked uneasily at Petawahin.

"I'm not hungry any more," he said to the Washan.

"Do you see the clay pots of food they have prepared for tomorrow?" the Washan asked. The two men nodded. "One of us must go down there and put these mushrooms into the pots and make sure they sink to the bottom so they won't be able to see them while they're eating. It's nearly dark now. Whoever is going, get as close as you can without being seen while it is still light."

"Are those poisonous?" Petawahin questioned. "How can you tell which ones are going to end up eating them?"

"It doesn't matter, these will not kill anyone. But they will make it very difficult for their warriors to fight," the Washan said.

"Umm," Petawahin nodded approvingly. "They won't be able to travel and they'll be too weak to fight if they're all sick."

"It won't make them sick either," the Washan stated.

"Then what are they supposed to do?" Mokotak asked impatiently.

"They affect everyone differently but they will find it very difficult to fight. Some will not be able to stop laughing, while others will be huddled in fear. Either way, they will not feel like fighting," the Washan stated with certainty. "Whoever decides to stay with me while the other goes down there will have the more dangerous task. Who wishes to stay?"

"What is it you plan to do?" Petawahin asked.

"If I tell you, no one will go with me, and I'm not going alone."

Both men testified to their fearlessness and Petawahin decided that he should be the one to go with the Washan since it was his son they were trying to free. The Washan looked over the Snake camp below and pointed to a large scattering of boulders just south of the cooking kettles. He tied the mushrooms together along with rings made of stone to make them sink to the bottoms of the three large cooking pots. He then found a bright, round pebble of white quartz in his pouch and handed it to Mokotak.

"After you put the mushrooms in the pots, place this stone on top of that large boulder so we'll be certain that the mushrooms are in the food. Then find a place to hide for the night because it will be very dark by then and you'll never make it back without making noise."

Mokotak took all of the mushrooms as well as his weapons and slipped silently down the side of the hill and under the cliff. The Washan watched silently as Mokotak slowly maneuvered himself into a position from which he could quickly toss the mushrooms into the clay pots at the first opportunity, and then place the white stone on top of the boulder.

The air was very still, and without the clamor of the procession, the slightest noise could bring catastrophic results. The Washan tapped Petawahin and signaled for him to follow. He led him down the backside of the hill towards the south, and soon they were out of hearing range of the Snake warriors. He stopped when he reached a small burrow in the ground and then signaled for Petawahin to lay down near the top side of the hole.

"They'll be coming out shortly," he whispered. "Throw this piece of hide over them as soon as they come out and tie them up in it right away."

Petawahin sniffed the hole and his eyes rolled back in his head.

"We can't afford any mistakes so don't miss," the Washan warned him. "I found many more holes for us to visit after this one." The Washan pulled out a pouch full of spearheads and began cutting shafts for them to which he had tied rawhide riggings. They were fitted tightly over the sharp edge of the stone so that the lines would be cut on impact.

* * *

Thunder had boomed throughout the night from some distance to the south, but still, the storm had made no advance. The sky, though hazy, still allowed the first burst of sunshine to peek over the horizon as the procession ate heartily of freshly ladled stew. Attendants had been running about long before dawn, starting the cooking fires and washing out the hundreds of wooden bowls in the stream. The air was saturated like breathing under the skins of a sweatlodge after the water had steamed up from the hissing stones. Petawahin and the Washan watched as the Snake warriors strutted about and the Paccus were marched down to the side of the stream to clean out all of the wooden bowls after they had finished eating. Apparently the Paccus were only allowed to rest before they ate. The Snake warriors were sharing long pipes filled with tobacco as they waited for the Paccus and the attendants to finish with their chores.

The Washan could see the small white stone perched conspicuously on a large boulder below, and knew that they wouldn't have to wait very long before he and Petawahin would be able to easily slip down into the valley. Though he couldn't see Mokotak, he knew he would be at their side as soon as they came to within range of the encampment. The Snake warriors seemed to be in a cheerful mood this morning and their joking became quite boisterous as they milled around the area of the encampment. The mood seemed to spread to the Paccus as they washed the wooden bowls, and they began to work slower and slower, as no one seemed to be concerned with them. The moaning had ceased and small bursts of laughter were beginning to erupt among the Paccus as well.

Quiktkoata became irritated and flung open the curtains surrounding his litter for the first time since early the previous day. A loud clap of thunder accompanied the sudden anger of Quiktkoata and the Paccus fell clinging to the earth, trembling in fear. Quiktkoata boomed out orders to the Snake warriors who came scrambling over towards the Paccus and attempted to raise them to their feet. But the Paccus were consumed in such fear that they could do nothing but tremble and cling helplessly to the ground. The Snake warriors found this to be hilarious and poked the Paccus with their spears, falling into hopeless fits of laughter at the Paccus' reactions. Quiktkoata smiled and nearly laughed himself at the Paccus' ridiculous responses, but as he boomed out his orders once again to get the Paccus on their feet, his own warriors began to laugh at him.

The Washan signaled Petawahin and they crept towards the Snake camp. Petawahin was amazed at the effectiveness of the Washan's mushrooms, but he didn't have much faith in the next part of the plan.

Mokotak watched from behind a large clump of brush as the Paccus crumbled in fear at the sight of Quiktkoata. The sudden clap of thunder had made his own heart skip, but he didn't hold onto that fear. After he witnessed the Snake warriors laughter at such a glowering figure as Quiktkoata, he knew that the Washan had given them powerful medicine. Mokotak could see the Snake warriors' eyes take on a certain glint as they fell into fits of uproarious laughter and poked at the Paccus for more reasons to laugh. A group of them would surround one Paccu and just slightly poke him. The poor Paccu would shudder and scream and nearly elapse into convulsions as the painted ones howled in laughter, then searched for another Paccu who would put on an even better show.

Suddenly, many spears descended upon the crowd. Yelling and screaming filled the Snake camp. A dozen spears had dropped into their midst, each equipped with a small black and white rodent that was instantly freed when the spear head touched the ground and severed the leather thongs holding the hides that had been wrapped around the skunks. Immediately, their tails stood erect and released powerful sprays that had been building for most of the night. Shortly afterwards, the yelling died down to a whisper and the Snake warriors and Paccus alike had scattered and lay clinging the earth. Many of the Snake warriors lay in quiet agony as they rubbed desperately to remove the stinging in their eyes while trying to keep from vomiting at the same time. A dead silence was interrupted only by Quiktkoata's booming voice and echoes of thunder as he tried repeatedly to regroup his stricken warriors. Then, from somewhere amongst the brush, a painted warrior burst out in a fit of laughter. Quiktkoata roared in his direction, but could not see him. The laughter stopped abruptly and was followed by dead silence. A few moments later, the same warrior burst out in another fit of laughter and he laughed for quite some time before another painted one joined in from some distance away. Quiktkoata tried to get off of his litter but fell to the ground with his paralyzed legs. The two warriors laughed even louder and soon all of the Snake warriors had joined in from their scattered positions amongst the underbrush.

The Washan and Petawahin took this as their cue and ran off in the direction of the litter. Petawahin saw Sequannah hanging limply from the back of the litter, a broad smirk on his face as he gazed blankly towards the ground. A sudden screeching overhead stopped all movement as three fierce looking hawks glided up to the litter. Petawahin glanced at them, then went to dash off to the litter, but the Washan grabbed his arm and pulled him to the ground. A war party of seventy Snake warriors descended upon the crowd immediately behind the hawks; they had been scouting well behind the procession and had not eaten any of the mushrooms. Hearing the commotion while at the same time catching sight of Quiktkoata's hawks, they stealthily invaded the area. The Washan led a reluctant Petawahin quickly away from the scene and when they looked back, they caught a glimpse of Mokotak pinned against a tree with several copper spear points held to his throat. He stood surrounded by half a dozen vile looking painted warriors, cursing and screaming as they kicked and spat at him.

Petawahin and the Washan were blocked off from heading back to the cliff south of the temporary camp and were forced to slip away northward. The last time Petawahin looked back, Quiktkoata was once again seated in his litter and the three hawks were fluttering intensely around him; the sneer had returned to his face. Petawahin and the Washan hid in the underbrush as the three hawks came gliding over them. Loud claps of thunder shook the ground, and the strange storm suddenly began to make its advance in the direction of the two Minnecou warriors. A violent wind picked up and the two warriors clung to the roots of trees as they awaited their fate. No rain fell and the two men witnessed three swirls of clouds heading in their direction. Each hawk flew upwards into each of the three funnels. They hovered slowly over the two Minnecou but did not touch down. Laying on their backs and looking up, Petawahin and the Washan could see deep into space through the three tunnels of swirling vortexes. Lightning flashes streaked around the inner walls of the funnels, crackling incessantly. Each whirring tornado produced an eerie hum, while slowly passing overhead in a steady course towards the northwest. "They're going in the same direction as the clan," Petawahin gasped as he looked into the grim eyes of the Washan.

CHAPTER 9

Shatomi shook his head as Quitkwa slipped silently through the brush behind him, a packet of dried venison tucked under his arm.

"You were supposed to be here with me," he said angrily. "Why do you keep running back to the clan for food when you should be gathering what you need as you go? You know that we are far ahead. Didn't you realize that we would scout for food?"

"There's no way of knowing when we would find any decent game around here. I thought it would be best if we had something in our stomachs to give us energy to hunt," Quitkwa said meekly, trying to defend his actions. "Besides, we've already found a place that the band can camp for the night."

"What if we find a better place?" Shatomi questioned. "I wouldn't have waited for you if I knew where you had gone, but I had to be sure you were safe. Now we may have missed an opportunity to find game. Three hawks came after you left, and the way they've been screeching up there, every animal in the forest probably knows where we are."

"I thought only crows and jays spooked the animals when people were near," Quitkwa said curiously.

"Hawks too, if they think you're a threat to them," Shatomi said with an air of certainty, though he had never seen this before. "I doubt if a herd of deer or antelope would be worried about a few hawks, but that ruckus could spook them or at least make them nervous."

"Those hawks will be gone shortly," Quitkwa said. "They'll find a snake or a rabbit and they'll go back to their nests."

"Let's not talk about snakes," Shatomi snapped at him. Quitkwa's eyes widened as the beginnings of a smirk appeared on his face. "If you had been with us this morning, you wouldn't be smiling about it!" Shatomi said angrily. "At least there will be four of us to hunt together," he changed the subject. "While you were gone, I kept an eye on the Paccus. They use the same hunting signals that we do."

"I'm glad that you found something useful to do without me around," Quitkwa said, the smirk returning to his face. Shatomi swept his leg under Quitkwa in an attempt to level him, but Quitkwa jumped out of the way, laughing.

"Chief's son or not, one day you will be walking in humiliation," Shatomi warned him about his constant teasing. "He who finds himself to be right in everything is the only one who does so."

Quitkwa smiled to himself as he followed Shatomi towards the two Paccu scouts. Shatomi was short and heavyset, with a face that always made Quitkwa feel like laughing. His hair was half gray and his shoulders drooped when he wasn't conscious of it. Quitkwa, noticing the sudden changes from time to time as Shatomi would throw his shoulders back, always felt that Shatomi was actually not very strong, but was constantly trying to make himself appear so. Quitkwa took to harassing him shortly after he was allowed to become a member of the council, because he appeared to be the weakest warrior other than himself. When he threw his shoulders back, however, Shatomi suddenly looked more powerful than any of the other warriors, except for Mokotak, who was as big as a moose, only more muscular. Quitkwa never became certain as to whether Shatomi was weak or strong, so he generally used his agility to stay out of range of the deceptive warrior when he felt in the mood to goad someone. Sequannah would definitely be weaker than him, but he wasn't so anxious to harass him. Win or lose, he had a strange way of always leaving the other person to look the fool. Worst of all, it was never anything that Sequannah said, but more or less the manner he had about him.

Ceptke suddenly appeared and grabbed Shatomi by the arm, placing a finger over his lips to signal silence. He then motioned with his hands to suggest the legs of a leaping animal. Shatomi gave him the hand sign for rabbits. Ceptke looked at him, somewhat surprised, and then spread his arms to suggest something larger. Shatomi gave the sign for pronghorn as he looked at him questioningly; antelope seldom ventured from the safety of the prairie where they could easily outrun predators. Ceptke looked pleased that he had guessed the animal as well as been able to communicate. Shatomi indicated that he had seen the droppings of both animals recently and pointed in the directions he thought they may have been heading. Ceptke nodded that Shatomi had been correct. Quitkwa pointed to the sky and gave the signal for hawks, but Ceptke just waved his hand as if to say: "Who didn't see them?"

Shatomi removed an arrow from the quiver that hung loosely from his hip and Quitkwa immediately mimicked his actions. The Paccus had their quivers slung over their shoulders, but either method was just as effective, depending on the way each individual had learned. However, someone would inevitably find a new reason to insist their way was best.

Through the brush, they could see the pronged horns of a large buck occasionally showing over the tops of the bushes. Other snaps and crunches in the area indicated there were several does with him as well. Boaka emitted a sharp bark from the other side of the small herd. A buck and four does bolted in the direction of the three waiting hunters. After the initial leap, one of the does caught sight of a sudden movement in front of the herd and bleated loudly while turning simultaneously to the right. The others followed in a like pattern and only one of the smaller does exposed herself to the hunters. Ceptke aimed and released with lightning speed, but was amazed to see Quitkwa's arrow stick into the broad side of the doe just as his arrow left the string. A third arrow pierced the heart of the antelope only a moment later. Shatomi's arrow, while slower in release, hit most accurately and fatally, dropping the doe as she tried to land on her feet. Ceptke signed the two Minnecou in the hunters' ancient silent language that he believed the fallen doe to be their kill. His expression gave testimony that he was surprised yet respectful to the Minnecous' hunting prowess that had left him second in speed and accuracy behind the two strange hunters. On closer inspection, he found that Quitkwa's arrow had been more accurate then his own as well, although any one of the three would have eventually caused the doe's knees to buckle after a short pursuit.

Looking down at the small antelope, they realized that while they did have meat, there wouldn't be near enough to last among the band for any length of time. Shatomi suggested that they bleed the animal and then sling it up high in a tree while they searched for more. The three hawks landed in nearby treetops, watching silently as Shatomi slit the doe's throat and the four of them drank of the otherwise wasting blood.

"These hawks will probably wait for us to finish here so they can scavenge the rest of the doe because they know it is a fresh kill. But while it hangs from the tree, they won't be able to get a good foothold and maybe they will give up after a while," Shatomi said to Quitkwa. "While they are quiet over here, I'm going to see if I can flush some rabbits. You can either come with me or try to follow the buck and the other does." Quitkwa pointed with his chin, indicating he would pursue the buck.

"I doubt that you will catch up with him now, but you can try if you want to. Just don't stay away for too long; we have to get back to the clan well before sunset to let them know what's ahead and where to set up their lodges."

Shatomi signaled his intention to go after the rabbits, and to his surprise, Boaka expressed an interest in going with him. Ceptke felt that trailing the buck would most likely prove fruitless at this point, but he acquiesced to go along with Quitkwa now that they at least had a way to communicate. Anyway, he sensed Quitkwa's lack of modesty and wanted to show him that there were many things a Paccu hunter could teach him.

Quitkwa led the way, attempting to assert his superiority on the basis of one arrow. Although this was irritating to the seasoned Paccu warrior, Ceptke knew that eventually the arrogant young Minnecou would find himself in a situation where he wouldn't be sure of himself and would either have to ask the Paccu for advice or dangerously put them at risk with his own limited knowledge.

They followed the tracks for quite a distance, where they

could see that the antelope were still running. The pronghorns had bolted for a considerable span before they stopped in a shallow arroyo where raspberries that had ripened some time before now hung dried out on the stalk if they had not yet fallen to the ground. They had all stopped to drink from a trickling stream that meandered through the winding gully, but here, the buck separated himself from the remaining does. Ceptke indicated that they should go after the three does as there would be a greater chance of getting one of them rather than to follow a solitary animal. Quitkwa, however, felt that they were only likely to get one animal in either case and that the buck appeared to be much larger than any of the does. Ceptke agreed to go along with him, but he also let the Minnecou know that they were making a mistake.

The two hunters followed the buck's trail up the embankment and across a long level meadow. The trail led them up a slowly rising ascent on what appeared to be a long ridge, running from north to south, and then descended down a very steep hill and into a rocky valley where a narrow, but gushing river had carved several long gorges through the soft stone of the valley floor. Here, they lost all trace of the buck's trail as it vanished in the broad areas of exposed ledge, effectively leading them well away from his harem and onto an indistinct trail. Quitkwa searched frantically for a hoof print or a snapped branch along the edges of the exposed limestone, and after long and tedious scrutiny, found the point at which the buck had leapt into a swath of ferns that remained relatively intact, making it difficult to discern that a large animal had passed that way. Ceptke looked surprised that the Minnecou would have found such a clever escape route, but again indicated that he would follow, and shook his head, knowing that they were never going to catch up with him. Quitkwa proudly took up the chase once again and followed the deep hoof prints through a stretch of soft mud to the edge of another area of exposed rock, even larger than the first.

"This buck is very strange or desperate," Quitkwa whispered. "Pronghorn always avoid mud." The Paccu shrugged at the unintelligible muttering.

Ceptke admired the buck's apparent intention to divert them from the does and then delay them for as long as possible. Quitkwa, nevertheless, once again began a thorough search along the perimeter of the ledge for some sign as to which way the buck had chosen to shake his pursuers. But this area of exposed limestone was criss-crossed with many smaller tributaries and diversions of the main stream that made the area difficult to maneuver. It would have been relatively simple for the antelope to walk along the center of any one of these long rivulets without leaving any trace of its passing; they were virtually free of any sand or debris that would suggest disturbance. Quitkwa's hopes soon began to fade, and he became increasingly irritated at the Paccu who wouldn't even attempt to help him. Ceptke was instead poking around in the pools and holes of the strange rivulets, totally ignoring the buck they were supposed to be hunting.

Quitkwa watched incredulously as Ceptke dove into one of the pools that had carved deeply into the huge limestone deposit. He couldn't believe that the Paccu was so certain of the antelope's escape that he would pick this moment to go swimming. Besides, there was still time to pick up the trail of the does. Quitkwa resumed his search, but soon gained a sense that something was wrong here. The Paccu had never resurfaced. He ran to the edge of the pool where he had last seen him, but there was no sign of him anywhere. The bottom of the pool was perfectly clear, yet Quitkwa could not see the Paccu. Maybe Ceptke had seen something and hidden, with no time to warn him. After looking around for some time, he detected nothing of consequence other than the disappearance of the Paccu. He laid down on the smoothed ledge and cupped his eyes to get a better look into the pool, when directly beneath him, the Paccu swam right out of the ledge of stone.

Ceptke burst through the surface, gasping for air as he babbled in Paccu. Quitkwa gave him an unintelligible look; the Paccu dove back under and once again disappeared into the side of the ledge. Quitkwa looked over the edge a little further but still couldn't see where the Paccu had gone. He walked around to the other side of the pool, but could see nothing until the Paccu emerged once again, apparently right out of the stone face of the ledge. Quitkwa dove in and Ceptke swam down the stone face of the ledge to where he pointed out a submerged opening that was as long as a man, but very shallow. It was shaped like a large mouth where it was wide enough to swim through at the center, but became increasingly narrow at the corners.

He followed the Paccu, somewhat apprehensively, through the eerie looking mouth and into the cold darkness beyond. He felt his way along the top of the submerged tunnel until he reached an abrupt end where his buoyancy thrust him through the water's surface, to an inner cavern. Ceptke called to him from a short distance away, and he swam in the direction of the voice. Between strokes, he swam face-first into a buttress of rock. As he cursed his sudden pain, he felt the Paccu's strong grip dragging him out of the water. He found himself standing on a ledge of incredible smoothness, untouched for millennium by the relentless forces of ice and sun, but ground flawlessly by the gentle flow of water over countless generations.

His eyes adjusted to the sudden darkness and he perceived several areas around him where the water took on a glow from the outside sun. Ceptke pointed out all of the different entrances to the newly discovered cavern, all four submerged. Each one faced in almost the exact directions of north, south, east and west, and the rays of underwater sunlight formed a faint cross in the still pool.

Both sensed they were standing in a powerful place amongst the countless trails they had traveled during the courses of their lives. Gazing upon the cross, they instinctively knew that this was the intersection through which all things were meant to pass. They sensed that this cross was the divine symbol for mankind, and somehow associated with all wisdom, love, sacrifice, and everything meaningful in human life. It was the pathway to the Creator. Neither wanted to leave the holy place, but they sensed an urgency in finding food and shelter for their people. They had also left their weapons alongside the pool and feared that enemies would find the bows and quivers of arrows to use against them.

Once outside, however, the area was deserted, though they sensed they were not alone. Their weapons in hand and facing downstream, the hunters simultaneously caught sight of the mysterious antelope posed majestically against the backdrop of white and gray limestone cliffs. Though the Paccus and the Minnecous traveling in this direction were by no means overladened with food, neither hunter raised his bow. The antelope had led them here. Quitkwa gave testimony that he would never hunt antelope in this territory again as long as he lived, though the only witness to this didn't understand a word of what he said. The Paccu seemed to make some kind of statement directed at the mysterious antelope as well, but both Minnecous and Paccus alike had long standing beliefs that the Creator was witness to all, and that no broken promises would ever be forgotten. They would be dealt with according to the situation. No promise, therefore, no matter who it was directed to, was broken without good reason.

By this time, the sun had lowered itself further into the afternoon sky. Their only chance of finding food for the band lay in what game they might encounter on their way back. They had taken a considerable amount of time, and while returning with a heavy burden of meat would excuse their tardiness, to come back late and empty-handed would invite anger and insults. As it was, if they went straight back to meet the other two scouts, they would arrive at an acceptable time.

They retraced the route they had taken, but curiously, while they did find some minor traces of their own steps, they no longer found any hint of the pronghorn. Even in the mud, the former hoof prints were as if they never existed. They took this as a sign that the buck was indeed sacred, and they were relieved that they hadn't been foolish enough to raise their bows against it. However, both hunters kept a keen eye out for other game to hunt in order to justify their absence.

They found several trails of deer along the way, but there was no time for stalking; they would have to run across whatever game they could hunt by chance. They tread silently, listening intently for inadvertent noises, but the first sounds they heard were the voices of Shatomi and Boaka as they held up several fat hares for the returning scouts to admire, while they laughed mercilessly at the empty-handed young hunters.

"Everyone else knew you would never catch up with that big buck," Shatomi took his first step in showing Quitkwa that humiliation walks with everyone. "Did you think that you were special?"

"I caught up with the buck, but I no longer hunt pronghorn anywhere north of the encampment at the lake," Quitkwa defended himself.

"Then you took a full afternoon to track a large buck so that you could say you no longer hunt pronghorn if you missed him?" Shatomi needled. "Did you want to find out if he would allow you to join his herd?" he laughed.

"This is no time for laughter," Quitkwa said in a plea for seriousness. "The buck led us to a holy place. The Washan should be with us so that we could show him. He would know what this place is for. It is a place in a secret cave where the only ways in are from under the water. From inside, there are four entrances where you can see the

148

sun shine through the water from the north, south, east and west. The sun shining in through the entrances makes a cross in the water. When we came out, the buck we had followed, but not seen, was standing unafraid of us, and when we came back, his tracks had disappeared," Quitkwa reported.

Shatomi noticed a change in Quitkwa's manner that was quite unexpected. Enough of a change to convince him that Quitkwa was not making excuses or telling stories. Ceptke also seemed to have a different manner about him as Shatomi guessed that he was also relating his revelation to Boaka. Shatomi glanced at the sinking sun, slung a string of rabbits over his shoulder, and pointed in the direction of the doe's carcass. "We must save these stories for the clan or they will not have enough time to set up for the night," Shatomi reminded them. "Maybe Ketanka will send out another hunting party at twilight and allow you to return to the holy place." He thought for a moment. "Do the Paccus have a Washan with them?"

"I don't know if the Paccus have a Washan at all," Quitkwa responded languidly.

"Maybe the old woman will know if there are any Paccus with us who would be worthy to speak to the spirits in a holy place," Shatomi suggested. "Go find a couple of carrying poles for the meat while I finish gutting it. These two will probably look around to find out more about the area to tell their people. On the way back, we'll look around that stream again and make sure that everything is still safe for an overnight camp."

Shatomi walked off with the string of rabbits hanging from his neck. Boaka had several more hanging off of the drawstring to his breechclout. Boaka signed to the two Minnecou that he and Ceptke would be looking about the area for a short while, just as Shatomi had suspected. He knew by the way they had been acting that they had never been in this area before and that while they were fascinated by many things, they were intent on making sure there were no unseen dangers. The Minnecou had passed this way many times before, but had never made an overnight stay in this particular section of their northern trails. Letting the Paccus check it out thoroughly could prove to be a good precaution. Both Ceptke and Boaka seemed to be highly capable scouts as well as warriors.

Shatomi lowered the doe from the maple limb and quickly slit up the belly of the drained animal with his chert knife. In a few short moments, the doe was cleaned and dressed to travel. The meat will have to be cooked thoroughly after being exposed to this weather, he thought to himself. He remembered the first time he noticed the intense humidity and a vision of the three screeching hawks blinked momentarily through his mind. From the top of the knoll, he looked around in wonder as to what had become of them. They hadn't even touched the meat they seemed to crave when the four hunters had left. He didn't hear them, but off in the distance, he spotted their large bodies perched on the tops of the highest branches in the midst of a spreading pine grove. They seemed to be silently surveying the area that he and the others had chosen as an encampment for the night. Shatomi suddenly felt a sickening feeling for these birds. He couldn't explain why, but he didn't want them anywhere around the clan or their territory; even buzzards had never repulsed him in this manner before. He caught glimpses of Ceptke and Boaka as they made their way around the area of the chosen site, and felt a desire to kill the irritating hawks as they cocked their heads back and forth, taking in every move of the two Paccu scouts.

Quitkwa noticed the strange look on Shatomi's face as he walked up with the carrying poles. "What's wrong?" he asked.

"Why are those hawks watching everything we do? I have never seen hawks act in this manner before. They usually hunt and then go back to their nests until they're hungry again, but these three are acting like crows. Stranger than crows. When animals act strange I want to kill them, just like when a bear keeps ripping into the lodges. After seeing those snakes, I don't think we should take any chances," Shatomi related his seemingly childish anxiety.

"If they bother you that much, why don't we sneak up on them while they're distracted by the Paccus. We'll need some hawk feathers to decorate our braves soon anyway. Those Snake people are sure to come after us after what you and the others did to them this morning," Quitkwa stated. "And our warriors will have many opportunities to prove their bravery."

"We didn't do anything more to them than they did to us," Shatomi defended their actions.

"Look what they did to the Paccus. I don't think the Paccus did anything to them and they surrounded the Paccu village and wiped them out," Quitkwa replied.

"We are not like the Paccus," Shatomi seemed unconcerned. "We are always moving. The Snake people will find out that the Minnecou are unlike any other people they have come across before."

It seemed strange to Quitkwa to think that the Minnecou were any different than any of the other peoples he had seen while they constantly traveled along their extensive migratory route. He knew that other tribes spoke different languages and wore different clothes. They had different customs than the Minnecou, but he had never thought of the Minnecou as being a whole different race than the local tribes they ran into from time to time. But then he realized that most of these different peoples lived in the same little village year after year. And he understood what it meant when they would say whose territory they were on as they headed north or south. Each tribe could always be found in the same area. The Minnecou had year-round villages to the south, where many of the traveling Minnecou would stay with relatives during the cold winter months, and trade and barter away their season's gathering. He wondered which ones were the real Minnecou; the ones in the villages or the ones on the trails.

The Minnecou in the villages were very different, he thought to himself. They would spend a whole spring catching the fish that ran up the river and then, after the water would empty out of their meadows, they would make thousands of small hills over whole fields and fill each hill with seeds and rotted fish. When summer came, there would be corn, pumpkins, gourds and beans growing throughout the village. These people also had a fibrous plant called cotton. They grew four different colors of it that they would weave into patterns on their family looms. At this time of the year, they were just beginning to start harvesting everything. Just before this, they spent most of their time watching it grow and keeping the birds and animals away from it. Good thing, Quitkwa thought to himself, it would be too hot to work like they do in the spring and fall at this time of the year.

Quitkwa looked up just in time to witness the angry bearing on Shatomi's face. Suddenly he realized that he had been dreaming as he drifted along behind Shatomi who was trying to sneak up on the three hawks. He had begun to shuffle his feet as he got caught up in his thoughts; enough to send the three hawks flapping northward. Quitkwa stood there foolishly hanging his head in shame. This had never happened to him before.

Shatomi pointed an angry finger back down the trail, and

trudged back to fetch the gutted antelope and the string of hares. Shatomi put Quitkwa in front so he would remember that there were eyes watching from behind, and to keep his wits about him. They put everything down once they got to the stream and investigated for quicksand, medicinal herbs, beaver dens and the like to make sure it was a worthwhile place to camp for the night. Both Shatomi and Quitkwa sniffed the water to make sure it had not become fouled in an unknown stagnant area upstream, and when both were satisfied, they went in search of the two Paccus.

They found them not too far upstream, where they were sampling blueberries. Boaka signed that they had discovered fresh buffalo dung, though they had not seen any. If they could get the whole group here without too much of a commotion, they might not spook the buffalo. Shatomi indicated that it would be best for them to remain with the meat while he and Quitkwa went back to the band to inform them of what lay ahead and where they would be camping for the night. The Minnecou scouts stealthily headed southward, towards the traveling band that had now narrowed the distance between them.

*　*　*

Quitkwa tensed as he perceived Shamira still keeping pace with the front-runners of the band. He prayed that Shatomi would not relate his daydreaming episode to the rest of the band. Washeena strove to keep up with Shamira, clasping tightly to her strong, yet delicate hand.

The two scouts went directly to the front of the band, their hands held to their mouths, signifying silent travel. Quitkwa could see the cheer in the eyes of the first people he passed as they anticipated fresh game in the area ahead. As the Wolf brothers' families, Petawahin's and his own family gathered around them, Quitkwa whispered that there were buffalo not too far ahead. The smile on Shamira's face and the look of admiration was all he needed. His shoulders went back subconsciously as he began to strut in his search for Ketanka. Shatomi happened to glance back and looked Quitkwa up and down.

"Are you awake now?"

Quitkwa's face burned in sudden anger, but he dared not defend himself for fear of releasing even more details. Shatomi muttered his teasing insult so silently that it was unlikely anyone even heard it. But Quitkwa was certain that everyone was listening and that Shatomi had purposely made a fool of him.

"Why don't you stay here and let the people know what's ahead so that they will move a little quicker. When you get close to the stream, slow them down and make sure they remain as silent as possible. I'll find Ketanka and let him know we've found a safe place for the band to stay," Shatomi said.

"We'll move quickly towards the stream, and I will keep them on the other side of the flat land while I go ahead into the valley and make sure there are no buffalo to spook," Quitkwa said with an air of importance.

Shatomi slapped him lightly on the shoulder, indicating that it was a good plan, and Quitkwa strutted back to the front of the procession with an enthusiasm that was sure to get the band moving with a quicker and lighter step.

"We must move quickly! We may be going on a hunt before we set up camp," he ordered as he approached the group containing his family, the Wolf brothers' families, Shamira and Meequaw, and an assortment of Paccus including Wanachan, the elderly Paccu woman. "When we get to a flat area at the top of the second climb, I will go ahead and make sure we don't scare the buffalo." He maneuvered himself to walk alongside Shamira. Then he bent down and scooped up Washeena, throwing her into the air and catching her as she descended with a scream and then laughter. Quitkwa put his fingers to his lips. "Shhh! We don't want to scare the buffalo do we?" The young girl shook her head in such a serious manner that Shamira was inclined to laugh, but in the back of her mind, she was irritated that men always seemed to play with the children in a manner that would make them scream, and then tell them that they were supposed to remain quiet, as if it was the child's fault for making too much noise. Quitkwa's coddling of the child, however, caused her to smile, and he took this as a sign that she welcomed his company.

"There is a stream of clear water and many berries growing along its banks where we will spend the night. We found the trails of deer and we have already gotten a doe antelope and rabbits. The two Paccu scouts are watching over them now while they wait for the rest of the band to catch up," Quitkwa confided in her as if she should be the first to know. "There is also a very holy place nearby. Me and one of the Paccus discovered it while we were trailing a buck that led us there."

"You found a holy place?" Shamira questioned. "How do you know it's a holy place?"

Quitkwa went on to describe everything he'd seen in the cavern and the mysterious events involving the antelope. Shamira's eyes widened in wonder as he related the strange details, but by the time he had finished, the whole front of the procession had stopped moving, and he was standing in the middle of a crowd, anxiously awaiting his every word. He walked rapidly away towards the north, hoping that Shatomi would not see that the band had stopped.

"We cannot afford to slow down now," he yelled out as he carried Washeena at a rapid pace, Shamira at his side. "With all of the buffalo that lie ahead, we have much more to do than just set up camp for the night." The crowd stared at him, many with pursed lips. He knew they were thinking that he was the one who had caused everyone to stop in the first place. "Besides, I'm getting hungry," he laughed. Some turned into smiles, but many lips became tighter. The Paccus gathered around Wanachan, trying to find out what the young Minnecou had said, while they simultaneously labored to keep up with the quickened pace.

Most of the clan were relieved that they had only a little further to go, after pressing northward at twice their normal pace since sunrise. They were already more than halfway to their northernmost hunting area, but the Paccus, unaccustomed to this type of rigorous travel, were beginning to lose pace with the sturdy Minnecou. Most of the clan had gotten little sleep; the Paccus had gone without. While buffalo hunts were usually exciting for both tribes, most would have preferred to rest for the night. But, when there were buffalo in the area, the hunt could not be put off because there was no way of knowing what the herd would do. Both the Minnecou and the Paccus knew from experience that to miss an opportunity like this could prove disastrous. Both tribes had spent as much as a whole season without a glimpse of the sometimes elusive herds.

The Paccus remained further north throughout the year than any other tribe the Minnecou had ever encountered, but they were already north of their normal summer territory and considerably north of their wintering grounds.

Every break in the forest was cloaked in yellow blossoms of goldenrod. With the last full moon, the crickets had already begun their ceaseless chorus of chirping throughout the day and night that would last until the frosts of fall. The terrain was half forested, while the rest remained open in vast meadows of diverse grasses and late summer blossoms. Most of the grass and weeds had browned on the surface, remaining green closer to the earth. The early summer flowers had disappeared, and the asters and goldenrod reigned over the meadows until they too would whither in the chilling frosts to come. The waning daylight had become suddenly apparent, and every living creature scrambled in preparation for another cold winter.

While it was still humid and as hot this far north as any other place in the Paccus' territory, the cold returned much more quickly here. They sensed that as soon as this particular wave of hot and sticky air was violently ushered out, drier, crystal blue skies would bring the first hints of autumn's chill, while further south, the warmer air would linger for a brief time. Blossoms of fireweed dressed the dark corners of meadow edges with white and purple flowers, while rose-red heather blossoms stood out in the sunlight, indicating where the ground remained wet. Dark brown cattails were sprinkled in amongst the heather and became much more dense around the perimeters, where their own greenery smothered out all else. The band of Paccus and Minnecou skirted these wetlands as they wound their way northward, but took careful notice of herbs, berries, and fur-bearing animals whose skins would provide protection from the icy winter winds. Every Minnecou clan had been stranded for an entire winter at one time or another by sudden snowstorms that could blow up even as the leaves were changing. Some of the small maple saplings had one or two red leaves on them and the thick growth of grass and weeds of early summer had thinned to the point where not much else remained other than the tough stalks of blooming goldenrod and pod-laden patches of milkweed.

The forefront of the procession soon found themselves approaching a large flat meadow and the occasional sound of shuffling feet could be heard, but only amongst those walking alongside. The field was empty. Nevertheless, the band waited at its edge while Quitkwa went ahead to where the two Paccus were waiting. They moved towards the edge of the meadow and indicated to Quitkwa that all was safe. They had not seen any buffalo as of yet, but the band was to proceed as quietly as possible until they had scouted out exactly where the buffalo were. Quitkwa waved the band ahead with one hand, while the other was held close to his mouth, signaling silence. Birds and crickets chirped hollowly in the hazy din, but the only betrayal of the band's presence was their high visibility as they toted the heavy loads on their backs.

Quitkwa and the two Paccus scouts waited for Shatomi, while the first of the weary travelers began to quietly remove the heavy loads of food, clothing and belongings, placing them on the ground around the scouts. There was still a measure of daylight left, barely enough time for a hunt, and Quitkwa became anxious for Shatomi to return with news of whether they would scout again tonight or not.

He was surprised to see the Wolf brothers appear on the far side of the meadow, and watched with envy as Mahkawan's three boys held them captive behind a clump of bushes, while Shamira ran to greet them. Then he inadvertently overheard the Wolf brothers' wives as they plotted to rid themselves of the young woman. He didn't like their plan to use Ceptke, however, and became increasingly annoyed at this development when he spotted the large Paccu and found him following Shamira's movements as well.

Soon after, Ketanka and Shatomi strolled onto the flat meadow, quietly discussing as they crossed the open stretch. When they reached the site for the overnight camp, they walked off to the side and continued their conversation for quite a while. As they were about to return to the clan, the Wolf brothers walked over and the conversation resumed once again. Quitkwa looked at the two Paccus who had the same look of impatience on their faces as he felt himself. Not being able to restrain himself any longer, he strode over to find out what was going on.

As soon as Quitkwa reached the private little council, Ketanka immediately began to question him.

"How far to the holy place from here?" Ketanka asked.

"We could get there and back before dark and still have some time to look around," Quitkwa said with certainty.

"You are sure you know how to get back to this place?" Ketanka asked. Quitkwa nodded, visibly offended.

"I have heard stories of such a place, though long ago. But everyone who went there had a difficult time trying to find it again and I don't want anyone out there stumbling around in the dark. There is no one here who does not need rest tonight," Ketanka warned him.

"I know exactly where it is and so does Ceptke," Quitkwa stated.

"Good," Ketanka was satisfied. "You and Ceptke will bring Kwoita. He knows what to look for to tell the Washan when he returns," the chief said. "Shatomi will take Boaka with him to scout for the buffalo, and we will hunt them at dawn. It is too late to hunt them, skin them, and carry all the meat back here before darkness. We will take our chances and wait till tomorrow. The Wolf brothers, here, will take several of the Paccus back down the trail we have just traveled and make sure that none of the Snake warriors are following. When they get back, they will sleep while we hunt the buffalo and everyone prepares the meat."

"The women and old ones prepare the meat," Quitkwa protested.

"There will be no honoring ceremony after the hunt and no all day feast," Ketanka stated with resolution, ignoring Quitkwa's protests. "We will eat quickly and prepare the rest of the food for travel. By that time, the Wolf brothers and the Paccus who go with them tonight will be rested and ready to move as well." Quitkwa hung his head in disappointment as he realized that his capabilities for great hunting feats would go without ceremony tomorrow, and this being the first real hunt they will conduct with the Paccus.

"Go!" Ketanka bellowed impatiently at his son. "I want you back here before darkness."

Quitkwa retreated hastily in search of Kwoita and Ceptke so that he could get quickly out of his father's way while he was in a demanding mood. The band had relaxed and the chatter and laughter began to increase as word spread that the hunt would be delayed till daybreak, providing the scouts came back with good news. He found Kwoita at the end of the procession, just stepping onto the meadow.

"You are to come with me and Ceptke," Quitkwa addressed the old Minnecou. "We have found a very sacred place and Ketanka wants us to take you there so you can find out what it is and tell him more about it than we would know."

"You have found a sacred place?" Kwoita almost laughed aloud. "Stranger things have happened before," he said, shaking his head. "What makes you think this is a holy place?" Kwoita asked before he found himself hiking all night in search of something as common as grass in a meadow. Most often, only the Washan could pick out where a holy place was located by the way the clouds would always be in the same formation, the moss on the trees would face out from a central point instead of all being on the north side, or an infinity of other indications that would only be apparent to an extremely scrutinous observer.

Quitkwa went on to describe everything he had seen starting with their trailing of the antelope and ending where they found their own tracks as they returned, but the hoof prints they had followed into the valley were no longer present. Kwoita seemed quite impressed and Quitkwa became very proud of his discovery when he noticed Kwoita's enthusiasm in getting started to the sacred cavern.

"I'm sure we will find many more strange things about this place once we start looking. The Washan knows how to use most of these things or at least what they are for. Did you notice anything strange about the buck?" he questioned. "Any unusual markings or maybe something strange about his horns?"

"No, he looked the same as any other to me," Quitkwa said. But a vision of the strange pronghorn appeared in his mind. "There was nothing strange about the horns," he admitted, "but that buck had no dark patches...and I'm certain it had a short mane!"

"Then what you saw was a big doe," Kwoita corrected him.

"No!" Quitkwa denied. "Too big for a doe. And the horns were longer. Pronged!" Kwoita shook his head questioningly.

"There was something else strange about that pronghorn," Quitkwa muttered and then turned his eyes to the ground. Kwoita waited, but Quitkwa remained silent.

"Well?...Speak!" he said impatiently

"It wasn't anything that was different in the way he looked, but in the way we felt about hunting him," he went on. "As soon as we saw him, both of us turned our arrows away from him and I felt as though I owed this animal. I promised that I would never hunt pronghorn in this area again, and the Paccu made some kind of a promise himself because he talked at the buck in the same way I did." Kwoita could contain himself no longer.

"Let's go now," he dragged Quitkwa by the arm, "before it gets dark!" The two Minnecou raced across the meadow in a sudden burst of energy. Ceptke got up to his feet as he saw the two of them approaching at a rapid pace. Some of the other Paccus had been huddled around Ceptke as he related his experiences and were prepared to follow. But Kwoita signaled them to stay. They ignored him and picked up their provisions, ready to follow no matter what the wrinkled old Minnecou had to say. Kwoita held up three fingers and pointed to Quitkwa, Ceptke, and himself, and then gave them a hand sign that Quitkwa had never seen before. They all shook their heads; Kwoita held no authority over them.

Just then, Wanachan walked over to find out what was going on. Ketanka was already approaching from the small camp his family was setting up.

"Tell them that only three of us may go," Kwoita demanded of Wanachan. "If we go in confusion, then confusion is all we will find," he said. Kwoita showed neither anger nor emotion as Wanachan translated. The Paccus looked upon Kwoita and decided the old Minnecou may know what he is talking about. One of the Paccus smiled at the straight-faced, though funny looking old Minnecou and hesitatingly admitted that maybe it would be best to wait, at least until tomorrow.

* * *

Shamira hurriedly placed her sleeping robes and helped Tumaris and Wanashta put their food and cooking utensils away. Along with Meequaw, the four of them set up a large frame and covered it with hides to shelter them for the night. Shamira immediately noticed the change in the Wolf brothers' wives as they sought to shun and belittle her as soon as the two warriors had eaten and disappeared back across the meadow with a small group of Paccus. They deliberately chose to set the frame up in a place that would leave her sleeping on the outside edge of the temporary shelter. Other than Shamira's quickened pace, however, the two jealous wives could find no indication that she had even noticed their rudeness.

"You'll have to sleep over here. We'll need most of the room in this tiny shelter for the children and our husbands," Wanashta said gruffly as she pointed to an open edge of the canopy where Shamira would serve as a windbreak to the rest of the inhabitants. Shamira knew that the Wolf brothers would not be returning until it was time to get everyone up and about, preparing for the hunt in the morning. She looked up at Meequaw and noticed the obvious look of anger that was building up in her. She betrayed a faint smile and a barely perceptible wink.

"Oh no," Shamira declined. "I cannot make your families uncomfortable for my sake. My grandmother, though, does need shelter to keep the dampness off of her swollen joints. I would prefer to sleep under the stars tonight while the air is still warm. You know that I always sleep outside when we travel, as long as it is warm enough."

Meequaw turned her back to the two women so that they wouldn't see her delight in the way Shamira had so easily made their plans backfire on them. The two women looked worriedly at each other. They knew that when the Wolf brothers returned and found her sleeping outside of the shelter, they would be angry at them for not making Shamira feel completely welcome in whatever they had to share. Even worse, the men would seek to comfort her as well as admire her willingness to sacrifice so that others would have more.

"Now Shamira," Tumaris sought to undo the damage. "You know that the children adore you and before they tire out, you will be sleeping in amongst them as well."

"I think the boys are getting a little too old for that now," Shamira further twisted their plans. "If they wish to join me, they could always sleep out here as well," she said stubbornly.

"If you enjoy sleeping outside, then we will respect your wishes so long as you know that you are perfectly welcome to sleep with us," Wanashta said in a voice loud enough for several of the surrounding groups to hear. She looked at Tumaris and smiled as she knew that now they would not appear to be rude or ungracious to anyone. "My children will sleep inside tonight. It looks as though it may rain."

"It won't rain till tomorrow," Shamira said with an air of certainty. "And, we should all sleep out in the rain from time to time, it helps us to appreciate what we have. Isn't that what you always said, grandmother?" Meequaw nodded, though that's not what she meant by her use of this expression.

"I find little to appreciate in sickness, and there is enough to worry about with my children healthy," Wanashta said as pleasantly as possible while the people around could still overhear as they went about their chores of cooking and setting up shelters. "But if it should rain too hard, you get yourself inside here," she said as she stooped into the low shelter, making it appear as though Shamira was the cause of any friction.

"I'm going to look around," Shamira said, trying to escape

from Wanashta's manipulation.

"Be careful and don't get lost," Wanashta yelled from inside of the shelter, "Sleeping out in the rain is enough worry to give your poor old grandmother for one day."

"My granddaughter is as capable and has more sense than many of the warriors. I never have to worry about that one," Meequaw smiled.

Wanashta stuck her head out from underneath the shelter and gave a look to Tumaris. Tumaris looked away, not wanting to get involved any further. "Sleeping out in the rain shows a lot of sense," Wanashta muttered.

Shamira had picked up her weapons and was already beyond hearing when Wanashta muttered her barely audible insult. Her confidence soared as she walked away, remembering only her grandmother's words of praise.

CHAPTER 10

A swirl of confusion surrounded him as his stomach churned tumultuously with the horrible food that had been forced into him. Sequannah, still shackled to Quiktkoata's litter, glanced about in a daze. One moment, his heart would beat frantically and he would be more than aware of what was going on around him. But then he would drift off into a listless stupor, barely cognizant of the chaotic scene that had slowly befallen the entire procession. The Paccus were screaming out in terror and the booming commands of Quiktkoata pounded into his heart, shattering his numbing reveries like sudden claps of thunder.

Something deep within him caused his stomach to spasm uncontrollably, and he couldn't get a grip on the fear that surged through his entire body. Even his vision was affected, blurred and racing. Every dark corner and space between the slowly swaying branches seemed to be laced with intricate webbing. The sky above, that he knew to be gray and unbroken, crawled with symbols, though they moved so quickly he could perceive none of them clearly. The air was too thick to breathe and everywhere around him, mosquitoes and gnats pierced into his skin while he remained helplessly tied in an outstretched position. His perception was deteriorating and a tightening fear crept slowly into control as he imagined that Quiktkoata was doing this to him and the Paccus.

He saw Snake warriors taunting the panic-stricken Paccus, and a sudden anger seethed in his blood as he witnessed a horde of them single out one of the Paccus to harass. He couldn't see what they were doing, but he knew it was horrendous by the timbre of the Paccu's deranged screeching. Several of them moved on to look for another victim, where Sequannah had a clear view to the torture. The biggest Snake warrior placed his little finger on the shoulder of the Paccu causing him to scream out in sheer terror. Another dodged at him with out-stretched arms, like a bird of prey swooping in for the kill. The Paccu screamed once again and the Snake warriors fell to the ground, their eyes in tears as they lapsed into addictive fits of laughter.

Sequannah tried to comprehend what was going on, but he couldn't fathom what would cause the Paccu to scream out in agony. He seemed to have no dignity whatsoever. One of the painted warriors regained his composure and strutted up to the Paccu. He stared for a few moments as the Paccu lay trembling. Suddenly, he put his fingers into the corners of his mouth and stuck out his tongue while making a gurgling noise. The Paccu became spasmodic and flailed at the air with his arms and legs, screaming in gasps. They fell into another fit of laughter as other Snake warriors gathered around to view this particularly funny Paccu.

Sequannah suddenly found himself laughing uncontrollably. He'd never seen anything so funny in all his life, or so it seemed. He tried to see through the crowd of painted ones to find out what they would do next, but they had gathered too tightly around the screaming Paccu. Sequannah's fits of laughter heaved out of control even as he listened to the painted ones howling wildly with delight at the funny Paccus.

A sudden crash of thunder followed by the raging bellow of Quiktkoata's voice made the hair stand up on Sequannah's neck, arms and legs. His laughing stopped abruptly and so did every other noise in the stifled calamity, except for the occasional moans of the Paccus. Quiktkoata started roaring out commands once again, but before he had finished, the Paccus were screaming in terror and his men were hopelessly bound in strains of laughter. Sequannah found no reason to laugh, though, being in such close proximity to Quiktkoata. He glanced up at the cruel leader and saw him struggling to stand in his litter. His muscles seemed unusually large for a crippled man, but he obviously had no strength in his legs. Sequannah couldn't tell whether the Snake warriors were laughing at the Paccus or at Quiktkoata, and it appeared as though Quiktkoata couldn't either. He was furious.

Sequannah pondered if Quiktkoata had only recently become crippled and if his warriors had finally gotten the courage to rebel against the powerful Washan. If they defeated him, maybe he and the Paccus would be let go. It didn't seem real to him, though, and his eyes were beginning to play strange tricks on him. He dared to look up at Quiktkoata's face again and then nothing at all seemed real. The laughter of the Snake warriors echoed endlessly through his head, while a loud buzzing noise filled in the din. Quiktkoata's face was ever changing into strange distortions; sometimes glistening, and sometimes appearing to melt. The sound of crickets and cicadas seemed to be an invasion of huge, alien creatures. Everything became increasingly distorted and Sequannah began to panic. He felt his own face drooped in exhaustion and he could sense his eyes to be only half open. Strange visions danced all around him and the only thing that kept his focus on reality was remembering how the Paccus were in mortal fear of imagined pain and illusions.

He leaned his head back, staring into the infinity of squirmy etchings in the sky, and out of the corner of his eye, a sudden movement raced across the sky. It had already disappeared before he had time to see it clearly. A moment later, another whooshed directly over him. As he focused in on it, he realized it was a spear with a bundle attached to it; a strangely familiar black and white tail sprung out of the wrap as it flew overhead. The Washan! He thought to himself. The Washan has poisoned everyone with one of his magic potions. Nothing he was seeing was real at all. He had heard the men of the clan speak of the Washan's potions before. He knew he was under a powerful spell, but he also knew that all he had to do was wait for the potion to wear off. But, then his eyes began to burn profusely, and the stench of skunk spray made him want to vomit. The Washan's potions were indeed powerful, Sequannah thought to himself, to make an imagined skunk smell so strong.

Many of the painted warriors vomited, so intensely foul was the spray. But the thought of skunks flying on spears had struck them as so funny, that after a brief moment of panic and confusion, they fell immediately into fits of laughter, struggling to breathe, and to stop the burning in their eyes. Another loud roar from Quiktkoata silenced the crowd once again, but one painted warrior lost his fear of the cruel one and laughed loudly from a hidden place in the brush. Others began to grin convulsively at the warrior's outrageous laughter, and soon almost all of the Snake warriors were choking and whimpering simultaneously as they tried desperately to control themselves. The harder they tried, however, the more difficult it became.

The scene around him became increasingly chaotic, and the constant, sadistic laughter and screaming seemed to wrench at his very being. Amongst the confusion and strange visions, he suddenly glimpsed the sober face of Petawahin, peering at him from a short distance away. Sequannah became instantly soothed and secure, even in the midst of this vast group of insane savages and captives. The Washan's face appeared directly behind his father and his heart quickened. For the first time since he had seen the evil snakes, he sensed the possibility of rescue. Evil snakes or not, he thought to himself, the Washan had powers that Quiktkoata himself would find difficult to reckon with. But the Washan tugged at Petawahin and then tried to drag him away. Petawahin fought him briefly, struggling his way towards Sequannah, but then they both glanced to the west and quickly disappeared in the underbrush. Sequannah felt suddenly crushed, as if all hope had instantly vanished. Only a small flicker of faith remained enkindled within him as he prayed that the Washan had found a better way to free him. He glanced longfully into the surrounding brush, hoping that the two Minnecou warriors would turn up within reach of him.

Suddenly, his scalp burned wildly in pain, and his head was jerked back with such force that his eyes nearly bulged out of their sockets. Quiktkoata glared down at him as he wrenched Sequannah's long crop of black hair.

"I know who you are," he growled in perfect Minnecou. "Your people will all die just like the other clan of Minnecou warriors who dared to rise up against me."

Three hawks shrieked by them, fluttering wildly around the litter; a sadistic grimace appeared on Quiktkoata's scowling countenance. "Perhaps if any survive, they will be more open to civility," he sneered, his teeth clenched tightly as his voice dropped off to a near whisper.

Thunder roared through the long and winding valley as the dark and ominous clouds to the south finally began to move. Painted Snake warriors who had remained considerably far behind the procession and hadn't eaten any of the food, infiltrated the area, their sharp and deadly spears before them as they scoured the underbrush. They had remained distant from Quiktkoata and his newly acquired slaves in order to trap any Minnecou shadows that dared follow. They gathered the laughing warriors from among the low bushes and arranged them into groups which they formed vanguards around in order to protect them. Three huge and swirling masses of thick, dark clouds moved rapidly overhead and stopped briefly while the three hawks each entered separate funnels. Sequannah could see upwards through the funnel into which one of the hawks had flown, and far in the distance, he could perceive the stars that only displayed themselves during the night. As the hawk reached a certain point into the mouth of the eerily whirring mass, bolts of lightning swirled in the hawk's wake, crackling loudly. The Paccus screamed in absolute terror as the treetops swayed violently and small branches were sucked off into the long tubes of whirring clouds. But not even the slightest breeze ever reached the ground as the strange storm quickly disappeared towards the northwest.

A group of six painted warriors struggled towards the litter with a huge and extremely hostile warrior who made them all seem adolescent in comparison. They had him bound in thick ropes and whipped viciously with their snake whips, tearing long, bloody streaks into his flesh. They kicked, punched, pulled and cursed at the powerful warrior who could easily have killed any pair of them. After a long and arduous struggle, they finally dragged him to the foot of the litter and held him for Quiktkoata to see. Sequannah turned to his side to try and make out who it was that they had captured. His heart nearly stopped as he witnessed Mokotak covered in blood; his face swollen with huge welts and his deerhide clothing torn in tatters. Two snake warriors each latched onto a thick braid of his hair while they simultaneously forced their knees into his back. Two other warriors held their copper spear points to his throat while the remaining two kept their whips at the ready. Quiktkoata pointed back at Sequannah.

"Put him in the front of the litter and tie this big one in his place. Keep your spears to his throat, and if he should weaken or stumble, your blades will continue forward," he sneered. "Remember little Minnecou," he bellowed, "that my eyes will always be on you; to look back will cause you more suffering than you could ever endure. Your life will last until there are no Minnecou left to trap. Your only purpose from now on is to act as bait," he laughed. Quiktkoata once again bellowed out for everyone to prepare to move, but Sequannah could no longer understand his language, though his low voice was as clear as the stars he had witnessed through the funnels.

It took quite some time before the sober Snake warriors could gather their stricken companions, but it was the Paccus who caused Quiktkoata to quake with impatience. They held onto anything they could get a grip on and clenched tightly in mortal fear. Without all of the Snake warriors capable of helping out, it was nearly impossible to get a whole group of Paccus to stand freely without one of them suddenly falling in an overwhelming fear, and grabbing onto a clump of bushes or a large tree root, clamping on tightly so that none of them could move. The first group of Paccus was nearly ready to be moved when one of them, in the middle of the line, fell to the ground and wrapped his legs around the trunk of a large tree. Several Snake warriors whipped and kicked as they tried to yank him away from the tree, but nothing would cause him to let go for even an instant. They pierced his throat with one of their spears, and he quickly died in a gurgling scream. This so upset the Paccus that they all fell to the ground, grasping for anything in sight and refusing to let go, even if it cost them their lives. They could neither hear nor see anything clearly amidst their constant hallucinations. The Snake warriors then knew that they had made a mistake, for Quiktkoata did not want any of them killed unless it was absolutely necessary. It had already cost him dearly for this particular expedition, and new slaves were the only commodity of any value from the poor villages of this great northern continent.

* * *

Sequannah stared languidly onto the trail ahead as the effects of the mushrooms gradually faded. He was exhausted from the experience and felt as though he could have slept for days, but the fear of Quiktkoata's eyes constantly scowling, kept him in a state of tense sleeplessness. His hair was no longer tied tautly to the top of the litter and he no longer had to walk backwards, but could see where he was stepping and what lay ahead. He felt somewhat better to have Mokotak close by, though he knew that he should never wish this on anyone. But, at the same time, he felt totally hopeless as he suspected that Mokotak would be killed before he would ever have the chance to talk to him. He might never have anyone to speak with in Minnecou again, condemned to spending the rest of his days amongst strange and cruel foreigners who would never care more for him than they would care for the dogs that haunted the edge of their villages, vying for scraps of food.

Quiktkoata focused on Sequannah, and though he held extreme contempt for this race of what he considered to be wild animals, he couldn't help but admire their muscular symmetry, their physical radiance, and their extreme cunning. He knew that his warriors would become apprehensive about trying to annihilate another clan of these shrewdly elusive warriors. They had surrounded Minnecou warriors before and worked their way in for the expected slaughter, only to find no one at the center of their focus, and several of their best warriors silently snuffed. The slippery Minnecou filtered themselves through and around every trap the Snake warriors had so meticulously set. Invariably, they would count only one or two Minnecou victims against a score of their own, and to pursue one of these clans always led to a swamp or briar tangle that would leave the Snake warriors scattered and in tatters.

Quiktkoata also knew of the futility of trying to domesticate them for slavery, for if he allowed the captured Minnecou to remain with their own kind, they would find a way to escape and come back for the others...or his Snake warriors would begin to disappear, one at a time, without a trace or a clue as to what happened to them. If he separated them, they became immediately listless and sickly looking, and would die within a change of the moon, never contributing in the slightest to the building of his empire. But eradicate them he must, for they have a penchant for assisting even tribes who are strangers to them. They would recruit any captives they could steal from Quiktkoata's slave drives and soon these would be as slippery as the Minnecou. They would stop at nothing to protect their precious migratory trails and even staged raids against Quiktkoata's city in order to remove the threat to their lands. This is the third clan of Minnecou that Quiktkoata had run into and even he himself had no idea as to how many such clans existed. No matter the cost, they had to be killed, not routed, for they would always return.

But it was always in the back of his mind that one day he would find one of these Minnecou warriors who would be adaptable enough to embrace the Snake peoples' ways, and help to teach his warriors the tactics of the fearsome Minnecou warriors. It may also be possible for such a person to help the captured Minnecou to adapt to the empire's needs as well. Eventually, those Minnecou who resisted would be either killed through the Snake warriors' newly acquired knowledge or shunned by those Minnecou who had accepted Quiktkoata's rule and protection.

Here, walking directly in front of him and tied to his litter, a perfect choice for Quiktkoata's designs occasionally stumbled, though Quiktkoata knew him to be thoroughly exhausted. He may not be well versed as of yet in Minnecou warfare, but he was probably just within that point in his life where adaptability to a completely different lifestyle could still be possible. Though very young, this Minnecou was obviously accepted as a warrior, and being raised as a Minnecou, he must have a good idea of their tactics through stories and training. Quiktkoata perceived many possibilities for this young warrior other than just bait for a Minnecou trap, but first he must succeed in breaking the young warrior's rebellious streak through alternate applications of forcible submission and coddling, depending upon the boy's behavior. It was an undertaking that could take several years to complete successfully, but then there was no way of knowing just how many of these clans roamed this beautiful continent, or if it would be possible to ever rid the land of all of them. Quiktkoata knew that it would be a practical maneuver on his part. After all, his family and ancestors had spent generations of breeding and training to finally develop hypnotic snakes, though much of their power lay in the faith of those who believed in the snakes' legendary capabilities. But, at the same time, Quiktkoata knew this to be true of his own powers. They were a combination of his faith and that of his followers; not just simply trying to believe, but actually already accepting these powers as truth.

* * *

Quiktkoata marched the procession eastward for many days with relatively few incidents to slow him down. His legs had begun to regain their strength, and he could nearly stand without holding onto anything. The Paccus fared better as well; Quiktkoata had allowed them plenty of rest and food after the strange Minnecou potion had worn off. Sequannah found himself to have more comforts than any of the Paccus, though. He was now tied to the litter by only one hand, but it was with some kind of strange metal rope which seemed to be a long line of circles that he couldn't bend to untie. He could eat by himself and the humid air had dissipated along with the strange weather he'd seen while under the influence of the Washan's potion. The cooler air had invigorated the entire procession and the insects had disappeared as well. Even the moaning of the Paccus had diminished to occasional sighs.

Sequannah had taken but a few quick glances towards the back of the procession, remembering Quiktkoata's threat of unendurable suffering, but so far, Quiktkoata had not caught him. He had to know if Mokotak was still alive. The last time he saw one of the litter attendants feeding him, Mokotak appeared to be strong and unaffected by the torturous beating the Snake warriors had dealt him.

Day after day they moved either southward or eastward and gradually the trail became clearer. Grassy areas now surrounded a well-defined path, and as they rounded each hillside, it became wider as more gravel was exposed to the elements. Smaller, well-traveled foot paths began to intersect with the trail they were now on, but clearly, they were on the main route that led to the center of Quiktkoata's empire. Down one of these small paths, Sequannah saw a group of slaves gathering reeds from a marsh and laying them out in the sun to dry. Several small, square buildings were visible in the distance, and Sequannah marveled at the perfect geometric figures of these strange wickiups. Soon they began to cross many such paths; some showed more of the various tasks that the people were performing, others left no hint as to what lay at the end of them. Sequannah heard voices coming from many different places amongst the thinning woodland, and sometimes he heard groups of people singing strange, yet beautiful chants that echoed across the valleys as the procession wound through increasingly hilly terrain.

He could see that they were coming onto a large, cleared area, as the sun shone brightly between the trees, illuminating what appeared to be an abrupt border between dense woodland and the open prairie. As they tramped down a small hill, the view opened up under the canopy of trees and Sequannah observed a large body of water out in the middle of the open area. At first, he thought it was a lake, but further along, he could see they were approaching the widest river he'd ever seen. Great wooden structures, some square, and some shaped like huge dugout canoes that he'd seen in villages, were floating in the river, tied off to massive posts that were placed in the water in rows. These posts also supported platforms where many people were walking above the water. They seemed to be made of many small trees tied side by side, with all of their branches cut off.

An odor in the air, however, immediately insulted his senses. It reminded him somewhat of the odors he had experienced in and around the small villages that his relatives maintained in the south, except that this smell was everywhere, whereas in the Minnecou villages, it only became noticeable in certain areas. Not quite as strong as a skunk, but infinitely more foul in nature, it seemed to be emanating from a narrow ditch that flowed into the great river. As they marched alongside one of the pungent channels, Sequannah saw human waste and animal offal continuously flowing to a point where it was absorbed by the great river. As he looked along the length of the shoreline, very many of these channels had been dug into the soft sand and lined with rocks. Most of them seemed to be coming from a large collection of huge square structures where more people than he'd ever imagined were moving about in a large confusing tangle of paths, seemingly unaware of the odors that nearly choked Sequannah to tears. Many of the Paccus were trying to duck their heads into the crooks of their shoulders in a futile effort to dodge the disgusting barrage of their senses. Even the Snake warriors would pinch their noses as they walked by certain areas, and this was apparently their home. But as Sequannah looked around, he noticed that most of the inhabitants of this section were dressed in tattered clothing and were sickly looking creatures for humans. Quite a number of them were wearing some kind of cloth hood that had a slot across the vicinity of their eyes, and completely covered the rest of their faces. They were filthy and smelled nearly as bad as the channels, themselves. This was no wonder, because from time to time, Sequannah would witness Snake warriors bellowing out at them and threatening with fanged whips. They would then obediently wade into these putrid channels and break up the floating rafts of refuse that threatened to block the flow, and cause the thick ooze to seep over the banks.

The people wearing hoods were treated as if they were not people at all. Many were carrying large baskets filled with animal excrement to distant fields, where a seemingly endless line of them traveled back and forth. The rest were all performing other functions where the putrid odors particularly reeked. Fires used for cooking and many other strange and unknown functions to Sequannah also seemed to weaken the very purpose of the air around them. Sequannah witnessed many wonders, but he couldn't imagine them as being important enough for all of these people to endure the poisonous gloom over the entire area.

As soon as he had left the forest, everything became bleak, suppressive and overwhelming in comparison to whatever this huge mass of people intended to get out of this arrangement. But he suspected that most of these people were being forced to endure this way of life, though he couldn't fathom why they wouldn't prefer to die trying to escape than to continue on in a life of suffering and shame.

They marched the captive Paccus and the two Minnecou onto one of the long piers that reached out into the main current of the river. Sequannah had strange sensations as he looked down between the cracks of the logs that made up the floor of the dock, and gazed upon the steadily flowing current. He felt somewhat as if he were walking sideways, although he knew himself to be walking straight. The illusion disoriented him enough to bring about a queasiness in his stomach. When they reached the end of the dock, there were many square rafts onto which the Snake warriors began to lash the first group of Paccus to ferry them across the river. Sequannah was absorbed in the careful arrangements that the Snake warriors undertook to get the new slaves tied down without incident, when he noticed the strange looks of fear on the Paccus' faces as they gazed across the river in trembling resignation.

Then he witnessed a vision that nearly stopped his heart. Like this side of the river, there were many square structures, but infinitely more in number. They extended for as far as he could see up and down the length of the riverbank, and they were so close together that they almost appeared to be one continuous structure. But, what sent the chill into his spirit was a huge and winding serpent in the midst of the city. Even lying flat against the ground, the imposing serpent's thick body was taller than the people. The mouth was wide open, and a small mound with a flowering, forked tree stood defenseless within its looming jaws. Hundreds of people crawled up and down its sides and walked along the top of its back. The head was completed and the front part of the snake was black, but the rest of the long and winding body was the color of earth. Along the top of the head and the very first part of the snake's body, a checkered pattern of yellow and black stood out strongly against the backdrop of drab, square structures, but it faded quickly into an outline that seemed oddly incomplete.

Quiktkoata's litter was loaded upon an exquisitely ornamented craft that resembled an enormous dugout canoe, with the exception that it was much wider and deeper. The bow rose high out of the water with a small platform on top, where Quiktkoata's litter was placed into perfectly fitted notches for the poles. Many Snake warriors moved the heavy craft with long handled paddles, while two warriors steered with poles from the rear of the boat. Sequannah thought he would be going along with the litter as well, but he and Mokotak were tightly shackled after they had been removed from the litter and placed on a raft with several, hand-picked Paccus from each group, most of whom were involved in one way or another with the rebellious uprising that had left several painted warriors dead. Karnack and Woltah were among this group. With Quiktkoata on his way across the river ahead of them, the Snake warriors became much more aggressive and rough with their cargo, particularly with this group.

Just like the others, Sequannah and Mokotak were lashed down in a lying position to shackles that had already been built into the raft. Their legs were first tied tightly together and then placed in an area between two studs, where they were fastened down tightly to the bottom of the raft. Their arms were tied similarly in a position directly over their heads, and their elbows and shoulders were contorted in intense pain as their arms were tied together as tightly as possible without breaking them. Their heads were placed into slots whose edges rose up to the height of the captives' ears as they lay face up on the bottom of the raft. A rope was tied tightly across their open jaws, pressing the back of their heads into the backboard in such a manner as to cause a tingling sensation across the back of their skulls. After their mouths were gagged, the Snake warriors tied another rope around the captives' elbows and drew it in until each captive's face turned red with pain. Sequannah was still young and flexible so that whereas the Paccus emitted stifled screeches through the thick lashing, Sequannah's elbows were touching and still the pain was only a mere nuisance.

One of the Snake warriors thought to tighten the lashing at his jaws to cause him similar pain, but another stopped him for fear of ripping the flesh at the corners of the boy's mouth.

Mokotak growled like a grizzly when the pressure was applied to his elbows, and the Snake warriors jumped back as a sudden surge of strength threatened to buckle the raft. One of the posts near his wrists had snapped and the two studs at his feet were bent towards him. The Snake warriors immediately put their spear points to his throat and he was forced to remain still. He was allowed, however, to remain in his loosely tied position; the painted warriors were fearful of trying to move him again. They satisfied themselves by pressing their spears to his throat as they made the relatively short journey across to Quiktkoata's city.

Upon their arrival, each captive was removed one at a time and dragged away to different destinations, beginning with Mokotak, who was led away by four massive Snake warriors who stood waiting at the dock. The rest of the captives were led away by two warriors each, including Sequannah, who took this as a sign that they no longer considered him to be a fledgling warrior. Throngs of spectators spat and cursed at the new prisoners, while children threw handfuls of dirt that caked on the saliva. Cheers rang out with every slash of the Snake warriors' whips, then the captives were taken in different directions to keep the most dangerous ones apart.

They led Sequannah along the bank of the river, next to a vast, flat plateau that was a maze of agricultural undertakings located at a safe height above the water, an area of rich and fertile bottomland that long ago was a part of the now shifted river. From here, he could see that the massive serpent was actually a huge mound of dirt, with people climbing up and down in a continual line as they carried baskets full of dirt and dumped them as directed. At the head of the snake, slaves were carrying alternate baskets of black and yellow stones to make up the checkered patterns.

Sequannah was led through the huge gardens that preceded the city, where several groups of hooded slaves were engaged in laborious details. Many of the crops had already been harvested and some captives were pulling the old stalks and plants out of the ground while others followed behind, dumping foul smelling baskets of rotted fish upon the ground. Piles of dried stalks and plants were blazing here and there, and where they had burned to ashes, many slaves were turning the ashes and rotted fish into the soil as they chopped away continuously with stone hoes.

At the far corner of one of the fields stood an immense pile of rotted fish, where several hooded captives were tied with the strange metal ropes to an outcrop of granite ledge. They were wading in amongst the slimy and putrefied fish and filling baskets which they would then carry to the outside of the smelly mountain of rot, placing them in rows for the long lines of unhooded slaves to carry into the fields. Groups of unhooded captives came up the bank from time to time with long nets full of squirming catfish, carp and eels, some of which were sorted out to clean and then dry on racks; the smaller ones were tossed into the rotting pile along with the scraps of offal from the gutted fish.

The two Snake warriors brought Sequannah to a small wooden structure where they ripped off his deerskin shirt. They covered him with a rough, hooded garment that draped over his arms and tied at the waist with a short cord, woven through the coarse material. They fitted him with a long and heavy chain to a collar that was assembled from two metal pieces held together by pins that the Snake warriors roughly hammered flat as they held him by the hair to an anvil. The sharp blows caused bruises to his neck that would be tender for several weeks, teaching him not to strain against the collar. Once the bruises healed, if the captive began to strain at his collar to loosen the pins, a few quick raps would make the area tender once again and would be repeated until the captive learned not to try to escape.

The two Snake warriors then unexpectedly tore off the hood of the garment and led Sequannah to the granite ledge where the other end of the long chain was hammered to one of the loops embedded in the granite. He was the only one of this group to be left unhooded, and as he looked around, he realized that this would probably be the best area for any intruders to infiltrate the foreground of the heavily guarded city. He was left purposely exposed and now he realized that Quiktkoata fully intended to use him as bait to capture or kill any Minnecou relatives that dared to attempt his rescue. The two Snake warriors placed a stack of empty baskets next to the fish pile and shoved the top one in Sequannah's hands. They then each grabbed a handful of hair and an ankle and threw him face first into the slimy heap. They laughed heartily and sadistically as they cracked their fanged whips and shouted out only two words in a strangely accented Minnecou

174

tongue: "Fuull baskette."

Sequannah found that he couldn't keep a steady footing in the slimy and sliding mass, although the hooded slaves who were also working the pile seemed to have no trouble at all in maneuvering themselves to any point they chose. Even when he fell, the slippery ooze would slide through and underneath his hands as he tried desperately to pick himself up. The Snake warriors stood by, solemnly watching, though occasionally turning to laugh to themselves. After some time, Sequannah had still not managed to find a way to stay afoot, let alone get even one tiny fish into the basket. The Snake warriors began to grow impatient. They wouldn't walk in amongst the pile to demonstrate as they were not sure of their own success, but they cracked their whips and screamed what Sequannah took to be insults and mockery. When he finally got his footing, the guards cheered and laughed at the young Minnecou as they encouraged him to move in the direction of his basket, now quite some distance away as a result of his constant stumbling.

Sequannah couldn't understand how the other slaves managed to stay afoot. Whereas he was covered in a slimy film and spotted with fish blood, their tunics were dry, and only their bare legs were immersed up to their knees. They moved quickly and confidently through the shifting mass and when one of them fell, all of the slaves laughed heartily. Even the guards would laugh. Sequannah took three steps with relative ease, and as he approached the basket, he deliberately fell into the slimy ooze. As he stood up, he could hear the sound of laughter coming from the other slaves working the pile. But the guards didn't find the same amusement with Sequannah's actions and one of their whips cracked loudly within a whisker of his ear. "Fuull baskette," the demand was repeated.

Sequannah pressed the basket into the pile and began to quickly fill it with the surrounding refuse, but when the basket was completely filled, he didn't stop. He kicked more fish at the basket until it was no longer visible. Both Snake warriors lashed out at him and he dove into the slimy heap and swam through to the center. The guards tried desperately to reach him, but he would hide behind one of the other slaves no matter where they tried to maneuver themselves. The shorter guard seized the long chain and dragged the choking Minnecou out of the pile. He grabbed Sequannah by the hair and immediately let go; the disgusting slime left his hand covered with

175

hundreds of tiny fish scales. He then satisfied himself with an unhindered kicking spree at the rebellious Minnecou. The larger guard pressed another basket into his grip and they both forced him into the pile again.

Sequannah crushed the basket and then tore it apart, and he was jerked down once again by the iron chain and dragged, choking his way through the rotted fish. The shorter one grabbed the chain near to Sequannah's neck and dragged him over to the granite ledge where both warriors lashed him down to the sun-heated stone, face first in an out-stretched position, and began to viciously whip at him. They didn't want to kill him, but he had to learn that rebellion was neither tolerable nor possible. Sequannah, however, would not prove to be a quick learner, for he would rather die than let himself be used for the sacrifice of other Minnecou, never mind the miserable existence that promised to be his future.

Sequannah spent the remainder of the afternoon pinioned to the granite ledge in the hot sun, though at this time of the year, it wasn't as intolerable as it would have been in midsummer. The slave guards occasionally wandered over and gave him a sharp kick–though they appeared to be forceful, he knew they were holding back. Sequannah, however, had had enough punishment and didn't dare provoke them any further.

When the sun sat on the horizon, the hooded slaves were ordered off the fish pile and herded over to the square structure. A group of people without chains had arranged bowls of food in a line for the hooded slaves to eat. The two guards removed Sequannah's lashings so that he could sit upright, but they shortened his chain by anchoring it down to another pin in the granite so that he wouldn't even be able to stand, and definitely not get food for himself. The two guards then went down and made certain that all of the food was eaten before they ordered the group of hooded slaves into the wooden structure and then walked off towards the city. Sequannah was left on the granite ledge. He didn't mind being separated from the other slaves, because they couldn't speak his language, nor he theirs, but he could still smell the food that had already been eaten, even over the stench of rotting fish. He could nearly taste the ground corn and the meat that was simmered in it. A kind of pudding had been made from one of the strange vegetables they grew and he wondered if its taste would be as sweet as its smell.

The sun sank below the furthest hills; painted rafts of orange, black and lavender floated listlessly over the horizon, detached from the woes and perils of Quiktkoata's city. Sequannah sat with his arms wrapped around his legs, his chin resting on his knees, as he grappled over escape and suicide. His fingers were too weak to bend the iron circles and his sense of loyalty to the clan was too strong to allow him to survive as a lure in a trap. There was no way to warn the Minnecou if they dared to try and rescue him. Once they crossed the river, there was no escape. New guards came from the city had positioned themselves at vantage points from which they could see any intruders or escaping slaves. Through a square hole in the wooden structure, Sequannah watched the silhouettes of hooded figures peering out from time to time. He could hear their quiet talk and their sudden bursts of laughter. From a point somewhere along the top of the bank, one of the Snake warriors threw a stone that hit the wooden structure. Silence.

Darkness came nearly complete as only a sliver of moon barely illuminated the exposed dark soil of the fields, but the city remained bright with countless torches, and song and revelry lasted well into the night. Sequannah saw what he thought to be fireflies on the ground, but shortly after they lit, a tiny, yet piercing squeal seemed always to follow. He heard the faint rustling of rats through the weeds as they dragged little tidbits of food from the fish pile. A thick, cold body slithered over Sequannah's feet, its scales sliding easily and slowly over the warm human flesh. A short distance away, the snake's eyes became suddenly bright, a faint illumination cast in its foreground. In the dim light, Sequannah discerned the silhouette of a plump rat, a fishtail hanging out of his mouth, but a paralyzed terror left him helpless. The light faded rapidly and a loud screech followed. Sequannah listened as the snake struggled to fit the fat rodent between its jaws for quite some time before the rustling at his side faded rapidly away in the direction of the city.

The dark, roaming serpents were barely discernible as they shifted loosely over the slight inclines and came together in one massive stream that slowly disappeared towards the city. Every so often, Sequannah would catch sight of a faint glistening as one of the slithering creatures' scales would reflect the scant moonlight towards the smooth, granite ledge. The cricket song became increasingly louder as the river of serpents faded into the city and one of the hooded slaves from the square structure ventured out towards the ledge. The slave produced a small cloth that had been dipped in cool water and began to clean the long stripes where the Snake warriors' whips had been powerful enough to slice the flesh. Sequannah was surprised to hear the soft tones of a young woman's voice as she tried repeatedly to communicate with him. All of the slaves had been hooded, but he suspected that they were all men with the strength that would be needed to work in the fish pile.

The young woman kept reciting different words to him, but he hadn't a clue as to what she was trying to say until she said "Paccu?", and her voice took on a questioning tone. Sequannah looked up and repeated "Paccu." The young woman removed her hood and smiled broadly, prattling on in a litany of gibberish. When Sequannah didn't respond, her voice took on a questioning tone again. She pointed at him and questioned "Paccu?"

"I am Minnecou," he said proudly. "Not Paccu!"

"I speak you word also," she said with a thin accent. "But not many. Father of me teach many tongues. Only little Minnecou words. Come from very far to south, bigger village than this. Father used to be one of many Washans. Now he is Sikun. Father chief?" she questioned.

"My father is not chief," Sequannah said. "But the chief and the Washan often ask for his counsel. He is hunter, warrior and scout."

The slave girl couldn't understand Minnecou so rapidly and Sequannah repeated it slowly along with hand signs that she could barely make out in the dark.

"What is counsel?" she asked.

"Knowledge, wisdom," he tried to explain.

"I hope your father has counsel not to rescue you here," she said solemnly.

"It would not be possible," Sequannah sighed. "The Snake people only leave me here to trap my people. But my father knows many tricks to fool these stupid Snake warriors. There are just too many of them...and they have snakes and hawks for eyes to help them. It is a long way to get here and a long way to get out of their territory if they found out about him."

"Minnecou used to much travel, more than anyone," the girl said.

178

Sequannah seemed surprised that the young woman knew so much of the Minnecou ways. "To travel is different in your own territory than that of enemies."

"Minnecou have no territory," she said as a matter-of-fact.

Sequannah thought about this. "There are many small Minnecou villages to the south of here," he replied.

"Not Minnecou," the young woman stated emphatically.

"I have many relatives who live there all the time, but they are small villages. Perhaps you have not seen them. Maybe you hear of someone else," Sequannah tried to silence her contrary opinions once and for all.

"Related to Minnecou," she said. "But not real Minnecou. Minnecou travel all the time. Stay alone and avoid other tribes. Father of me know much about all peoples. Say Minnecou travel always."

"Your father does not know as much as you think he does," Sequannah retorted. "We stay in the villages every winter. We don't always travel."

"Then you are not Minnecou. Minnecou always travel. Far!" She would not give in.

"Why would I say I am what I am not?" Sequannah said irritatedly. "I am Minnecou, there is no other name for me."

"You always stay in village for winter?" she questioned.

"Whenever we can return before it snows."

"Then perhaps you are Minnecou," she agreed, "if you do not always stay in village for winter."

"What did you do to cause them to send a woman to the fish pile?" Sequannah changed the conversation.

"I choose fish pile."

"You have made a poor choice."

"Quiktkoata would not look for me here," she whispered.

"Why would Quiktkoata care about you?" he almost laughed.

"My father is Sikun, but Quiktkoata make everyone think that he is greater by always demonstrating his power. He makes big storms and has snakes and hawks to frighten the people into believing in him. He teaches them to hate the followers of my father and the other good Washans' ways. He tells them of how all the Washans speak of generosity while they enjoy all the riches they demand from the people. The Washans all got together and convinced their followers that Quiktkoata was not so powerful a Washan as he is a sower of hatred and fear. They taught them to ignore Quiktkoata. They would not trade or stay amongst them and treated those filled with greed and self-indulgence as the lowest form of human. This so angered Quiktkoata that he took all of his followers and moved north to create the greatest and richest empire ever known and take revenge one day against those who had treated he and his followers as anything less than the warriors of the Creator."

Sequannah took an interest in her story, but found it difficult to believe as well as understand. "If your father and the Washans are powerful enough to make Quiktkoata leave, why did they not wipe him out and put an end to the evil of the Snake people?"

"They did not make Quiktkoata leave. He left because there were too many followers of the Sikun. Their lack of fear and refusal to follow him caused his power to weaken. He came here in order to fulfill the prophesy of the rich and powerful empire that would rise up from the great and empty land to the north, which is here. Many miracles and feats of magic are prophesied to spring forth from a land to the north that was rich in all things but empty of people...except those that live in the poor villages...and those nomads that travel far and survive by taking only the smallest amount from the land. But it is also prophesied that no matter how powerful an empire should become, it shall always become the inheritance of those who serve, for they live in care of one another. Care for me, because I will never bring fear or mistrust to you. Care for all of the captives here, no matter how weak they seem, for they shall inherit everything. I must return to sleep now as every day is long here. My name is Tarote." She gestured for his name.

"Sequannah."

"Do not live in fear and do not choose to die," she pleaded. "Minnecou prefer to die than to live this existence. But there is always a reason for us to be here whether we know what it is or not. It may be uncomfortable, but you must try to sleep well, for every day is long here." She pulled her hood back over her head and returned to the square structure, leaving Sequannah somewhat more comfortable but quite confused.

CHAPTER 11

Paccu and Minnecou shelters sprouted upon each shallow rise of the nearly level field. Shamira tread carefully down the embankment at the edge of the meadow and waded across the shallow stream to walk along the other side, where it wasn't so steep. Upstream, she came to a small pool where many of the Paccus had found a good place to bathe themselves and their children. Shamira smiled and greeted them; they waved back, but did not smile, then casually resumed playing with and washing their young children.

Further up she found Sabatt, Petana and Kalashte, Mahkawan's three young boys, taking turns diving from a thick, oak limb situated over a deep pool in the stream. Some of the Paccu boys were diving with Mahkawan's sons, along with the solemn young Paccu she'd seen with Wanachan. He was older than the other boys, and after diving a couple of times, he climbed high into the tree, and gazed intensely into the surrounding forest. Had he been Minnecou, she would have smiled and warmed to the young boy's concern. But being Paccu, she regarded his posture as little more than arrogance.

She passed the noisy group and headed further up the quickly ascending gullies of the brook. There were many more pools and falls as the stream wound its way around and over the steadily rising ledges. She found the berries that Quitkwa had spoken of, and several thick vines with roots that were certain to bear tubers of sweet yams. Droppings of deer and moose were present within a short distance of many of the pools, and she had even found slides used by minks and otters. This was a place they could stay for the passing of a moon, if necessary, though not quite as bountiful as their destination in the foothills of the Dark Mountains.

Shamira shed her deerskin clothing and moccasins, dropping into one of the pools to bathe herself. She went straight to the bottom and swam up the middle against the current, then off to the same side where she had left her clothing. She pushed her hair back over her ears as she slipped through the surface of the water, letting her feet drift to the bottom in the gentle swirls near the bank. The sudden snap of a branch froze her movement, but set her heart to racing. She glanced slowly around, careful not to disturb the calmness of the pool. No one was in sight. At the top of the basin was a waterfall. Shamira slipped quietly beneath the surface, hugging the bottom as she struggled upstream. She nearly ran short of breath and came up sputtering beneath the shallow falls, where the water ran deep, and it was difficult to find anything to hold onto as she watched from her hidden spot.

The flow of water blurred her view, and hearing anything outside of the narrow passage was impossible. She wondered if it was wise to have come this way, especially since her clothing would be easily spotted. Through the tumbling cascade, she suddenly perceived the dark form of a large body moving slowly in the direction of her clothing. It was an animal, she was certain. The long legs were of the deer family, though she couldn't see clearly enough to be sure. It stepped over her clothing without stopping to sniff. Trotting to the stream's edge, it stopped and spread its forelegs wide to stoop for a drink. Shamira stuck her head part way into the flow of water. The buck startled. She glimpsed his pronged horns before quickly pulling her head back under the falls; a smile appeared on her face as the confused animal searched in wonder. She knew by the horns that it was an old male antelope and she wondered if this was the one Quitkwa had seen.

The buck spread its legs once again, dipping to the water's surface. Suddenly, it looked up and stared at the falls, scanning from side to side. Shamira remained perfectly still, but the pronghorn spooked, hopping up the bank and into the woods. She lurched out from under the falls and witnessed an unusual sight as the hind end of the animal cleared the top of the bank—it wasn't a buck at all; it was female. But the momentary glimpse left her uncertain. Perhaps the water had blurred her vision...or the angle of the animal's leap had caused a distortion of appearances. She swam to her clothing and quickly dressed to follow.

The deep tracks were obvious in the soft mud of the riverbank, but more difficult to distinguish as they wound their way through a stand of hickory saplings and over a series of ledges. Shamira followed them down a particularly steep slope, and found herself in the middle of a narrow, winding valley, with many inlaid rivulets carving deeply into the stone of the valley floor. Grayish-white cliffs rose and fell in a winding gorge stretching from the northwest and down towards the southeast. But the antelope's trail abruptly ended on a large, flat outcropping of water-stained ledge, and no matter where she looked, there was no trace of the animal.

The humid air thickened and the incessant rhythms of frogs and insects were eerily distorted. The cricket song became so loud that the noise of the rushing water seemed almost dwarfed in comparison; the buzzing whine of cicadas in the oppressive steam echoed through the valley in a see-saw of ever changing tones. Large black flies stood out sharply against the light gray bedrock, and bugs of every color and description crawled over the leaves and boulders of the surrounding forest floor. The mysterious antelope could have slipped away easily through this intense distraction, and through the many islands of thick laurel, crowded onto every patch of earth that had managed to settle into the empty potholes and crags of the extensive limestone deposit.

The sun perched in the crook of the jagged tops of limestone cliffs–a brilliant ball of softening red light, casting a pink hue on the facing cliffs and the surrounding treetops. Daylight was fading and she reluctantly headed back to the camp so as not to cause concern amongst the clan. She traced her way back and came across a few faint imprints of her own tracks, as she was not trying to cover her trail, but there were no longer any hoof prints. She wanted to investigate, but the sun was already in twilight. Everyone would be needed for the hunt tomorrow, so she resigned herself to the fact that the elusive pronghorn would remain a mystery. The clan would certainly not accept any more delays in their journey to the Dark Mountains.

She noted that nearly all of the blueberry bushes had been stripped clean and found a lone Paccu woman still picking at the stream's edge while everyone else had returned to their makeshift camps for the night. Shamira helped her pick the last couple of bushes and threw dozens of handfuls of berries into the Paccu woman's basket. Neither could understand the other's language, but they seemed content with each other's company. This was the first time one of them had smiled at Shamira without merely trying to be polite. Shamira admired her for working after everyone else had gone back to their campsites as she knew the Paccus to be low on food. She sensed that this young woman would stop at nothing to insure the survival of her people without having to rely on the charity of others. By the time they had picked the last bush clean, all they had established were their names: Powhantin and Shamira. But they had developed an unspoken bond between them. Shamira gestured that they should return to the meadow, but then heard the sounds of bickering voices coming from somewhere in the woods. The two women smiled and hid next to the stream to overhear what all the complaining was about. Most of it appeared to be in Minnecou, though, with only a word or two coming from Ceptke as he tried to make himself understood to Kwoita.

"Did you not tell me that it was not very far away?" Shamira heard Kwoita.

"Well yes, but we went..."

"Did you not say it was very simple to find once you have been there?"

"Me and Ceptke both..."

"I have heard enough of you and Ceptke...you and Ceptke." he repeated sarcastically. "I am an old man if you have not noticed, and I have been running all day covering his friends' sloppy trail while trying to keep up with a band that wants to run across the world in one day. After all of this, I have to follow you and Ceptke in circles until the sun sets, and then," he paused for effect, "...then we have to stop and find something for you to eat. You have shown me nothing sacred other than your worship of food."

Ceptke shrugged and smiled into Quitkwa's exasperated expression. Though he had a clue as to what the conversation was about, thankfully he had no way of becoming involved, for after Quitkwa had led them around in a few circles, he had stepped out in front to lead them with the exact same results.

"I told you, grandfather, that we probably have to find that buck antelope again and he will lead us back into the strange valley," Quitkwa said angrily.

"Yes, and now my voice is hoarse and my throat is sore from making mating calls while you search for enough food to fill your endless appetite." Kwoita returned, just as angrily.

"It would not hurt my feelings if your voice were turned into a whisper right now," Quitkwa insulted.

"The only reason it is not is because the Creator knows that you deserve the punishment of having to listen to me," Kwoita's voice rose.

Shamira sensed their conversation had come to an end and as they were heading towards the two women, but not yet in view. She grabbed the Paccu woman's hand and led her out in the open so as not to betray their eavesdropping. Shamira still had her bow draped over her shoulder as Kwoita and the younger men came into view.

"What do you need with a bow to pick berries?" Kwoita questioned his grand-daughter. "You know you shouldn't risk spooking the buffalo by wasting your time hunting small game."

"I was not hunting. I only took my bow for protection while I scouted around the stream. I met Powhantin, here, on my way back and have only helped her pick berries for a short time," she said.

"I should have sent you out with these two," Kwoita said sarcastically. "You would have seen everything in the area, but little of the wonders they have set the whole band to talking about. Perhaps you caught sight of the great buck antelope that these two story tellers have been hiding behind to excuse their poor sense of direction," he said with an air of doubt.

"Yes, yes!" she exclaimed. "A large..." she hesitated, "buck came up to one of the pools further up the stream. I followed it through the woods to a valley of white cliffs, but I lost track of it there."

Quitkwa's eyes widened as Shamira testified to the truth of the two scouts' story; a broad smirk appeared on his face as Kwoita looked in his direction. "Take us there, now!" Quitkwa demanded.

"It is too dark to find our way now," Kwoita said angrily. "Never mind trying to make our way back. If it's alright with Ketanka, we'll try again at dawn and either delay the buffalo hunt or join them later." He gestured for everyone to follow and they walked back to the meadow as the fireflies became brightly visible.

They found that a large council had been assembled with Minnecou and Paccus invited alike. They had started without Kwoita and his small group and were trying to determine what was true out of all the stories about the Snake people. While they agreed that to distance themselves from these mysterious happenings would be most desirable, most were curious as to the new mysteries of this little known area. Many disagreed as to whether they were far enough from the Snake people to consider themselves safe. While retreating to the foothills of the Dark Mountains would allow them to spot the approach of any Snake warriors on the lower plateaus, and lose any enemies with a quick retreat into the maze of endless valleys, many felt that the omens in this place were meant to keep them safe and that to continue on would prove disastrous.

After all was translated to the Paccus, Ketanka let it be known that everything will go as originally planned with one exception: Kwoita, Ceptke, Quitkwa and Shamira will continue to search for the elusive valley of white cliffs at dawn. Everyone else will go on the buffalo hunt early tomorrow morning with the obvious exception of the Wolf brothers and the Paccu warriors who would guard the trail leading to the encampment throughout the night; they would rest while the rest of the band hunted, butchered and readied everything for travel. Those who disagreed could go their own way, as long as they didn't interfere with the plans of the rest of the band.

*   *   *

Shamira returned to the small, makeshift shelter, listening to Meequaw's praises of Ketanka's ability to get the whole band of Paccus and Minnecou together and have everyone understand what was going on and what was to be done.

"If they don't like it, they can go somewhere else," Meequaw went on. "I would prefer that the Paccus go their own way and we go ours," Meequaw commented. "But they are not a foolish people. They know that if they stay with us, they are safer from the Snake people than they would be on their own."

"It is also the same with us," Shamira said. "If they decide to separate from us, not only would that make us weaker in numbers, but they could lead the Snake warriors to the rest of us. Many of them are tired and wounded. Perhaps when they recover, they may prove to be good allies."

"I find it hard to agree until I see the Wolf brothers' wives over there, watching us as if we were Paccus," Meequaw whispered. "I don't even want to stay with them. They moved your sleeping robes back to a comfortable spot, so you wouldn't sleep outside tonight."

"I'll be sleeping outside anyway...I want to wake with the first light of morning," Shamira said. "If they think that I'm only trying to cause trouble between them and their husbands, tell them that I will be gone before the Wolf brothers return. When we get to the Dark Mountains, you and I will make our own lodge, as we've always done."

"We see with the same eyes," Meequaw agreed.

*   *   *

Boaka and Shatomi moved quickly and silently ahead of the band as Ketanka led in the general direction the two scouts had last seen the herd. They communicated quite efficiently with their nearly identical sign languages, and were even beginning to use a few of the words they had learned from each other to make their simple conversations more clear. The humid air, however, was even more oppressive than the previous day, and every movement seemed a monumental task. Both were coated in a glistening sheen of sweat, and the lack of wind provided no relief. Some of the trees were beginning to change color, and they knew cooler air was imminent, but this heat was more stifling than anything they could remember. It was certain to be changed with only the most violent of weather, for at this time of year, the air was usually crisp and chilled clear.

The herd had browsed to quite a distance from the area where Boaka and Ceptke had originally found the first signs of buffalo. When Shatomi and Boaka finally located the herd in the late twilight of the previous day, it was some distance from the meadow. The band had hoped that the herd would circle around to a closer grazing area where it seemed as though the particular low valley they were following would lead them, but as everyone followed the marked trail of the two scouts, they realized that the buffalo had strayed further away instead; it would be a long haul back to the meadow.

Shatomi and Boaka skirted the opening where they had last seen the herd and paralleled their meandering course eastward. The bison herd had climbed a steep incline and filtered through the woodlands, into the bottomlands of another green valley of rich grasses. The two scouts could see that the herd browsed contentedly for a time before some calamity had caused them to do what both the Paccus and Minnecou feared most. They had stampeded down the long valley. They could have run all night before ever stopping. They could still be running even now. Worse than that, when they finally stopped, they may have split up into many smaller herds.

Most unfortunate, though, was that they had bolted towards the southeast, and for as far as the eye could see, the green meadows were torn to expose the brown dirt in the same direction. Ketanka was certainly not going to follow a herd of buffalo and lead his clan into the whips and spears of the Snake people. The two scouts doubled back towards the clans to let everyone know that the buffalo had stampeded towards the southeast. They could see the wrangling in Ketanka's eyes as he tried to think of some way that they could still get to the buffalo herd, and insure that they had at least enough food to begin the winter; they could be pinned up against the Dark Mountains for the duration. But it was too risky to head back towards the Snake people, and would be that much further to haul the meat.

The Paccus began to dissent when he announced that they would have to return empty-handed–they were very low on food. Then the Minnecou became upset when Ketanka suggested that they split up their food supplies in equal shares with the Paccus as soon as they returned to the meadow. Ketanka had to convince his own clan that it would be equally dangerous for them if any of these Paccus were captured, just because they were hungry enough to follow these buffalo into the snares of the Snake people. It would be impossible for them to cover the trail of a buffalo herd and all the Paccu and Minnecou tracks that would be mixed in, leaving a clear path to their overnight encampment and showing the Snake people where the band was headed.

Ketanka found himself at odds with both peoples, but he had to lead fairly and maintain peace between those who disagreed. It was of utmost importance that he keep the two tribes together and try to establish a lasting bond between them, but he was not so sure that the Paccus would prove to be an asset, nor was he certain that any lasting alliance was even possible. The buffalo herd had been spooked into a stampede and this proved to be an event that affected both tribes equally. If the two tribes were to become allies, Ketanka had to make sure that both sides felt that their futures were the same and their chances for survival equal. He did not keep these ideas in the back of his mind, but explained them fully to the best of his ability to everyone. They could either stick together or go their own separate ways. But no one was to be left thinking they had been deceived if they had chosen to stay.

They returned with a new feeling of camaraderie, and Ketanka had temporarily achieved his goal of keeping the two tribes together. Something in the air, however, soon began to affect the good feelings, and although they were not inclined to argue with each other, an overwhelming sense of doom settled over the trudging procession that was returning empty-handed and weaker from the oppressive heat. Most of them knew that it was probably best that they didn't find meat in this heat as it would be more gamey in taste and spoil quicker, but to come back with nothing could also be taken as a sign that they had formed an alliance that was distasteful to the Creator.

The sun still cast a sharply defined shadow through the

thickening haze, and even the leaves on the trees had wilted. A faint booming in the distant southeast suggested that relief was on the way, but it would be temporary; only a storm from the northwest would clear the air once and for all. A quickening breeze, however, began to blow strangely out of the north, yet they could all hear the storm approaching from the southeast.

They hurried their pace in order to get back in time to provide themselves with at least some shelter in their flimsy, make-shift lodges. When they came to a particularly elevated slope, they were afforded a good view in every direction, and while the wind continued to increase from the clearing skies to the north, the entire eastern and southern horizons had mounded up with a very sharply defined edge of billowing clouds, seemingly darker than the night. The sun became covered in the mid-morning sky and a jagged crown of brilliant gold outlined the face of the approaching storm. The first flash of lightning nearly blinded the bewildered band and after what seemed to be a long pause, a crack of thunder rolled over them like an unexpected wave; the ground shaking visibly in its wake. Several more quick flashes set the band to running in the direction of their hope-lessly frail shelters.

As they converged upon the meadow, Kwoita had also led his small group into the encampment. The Wolf brothers and their Paccu companions ambled about in a daze amidst the sudden commotion. Huge, billowing, black clouds poured over the meadow and in the distant southeast, three enormous funnels wound their way towards the band, throwing up dust and trees high into the air. Scattered pellets of hail began to fall, but as the darkness poured itself upon the camp, they quickly grew to fist-sized chunks of ice, thumping into the earth and trees in a deafening crush. The collapsing shelters were quickly abandoned as the Paccu and Minnecou refugees fled to the protection of thick oaks nearer to the stream. Some were knocked unconscious by the unusually large hail, and those who came to their rescue were battered in return for their compassion.

Shamira held tightly onto the trunk of a large oak and pressed herself flat against the bark to avoid the pummeling hail. She could just barely see over the embankment and onto the flat meadow where only a couple out of the many shelters were still standing. In front of the clutter of shelters, Wanashta struggled at the limp form of Tamahna as he lay unconscious. Their young daughter, Washeena, lay a short distance away, bleeding and screaming as the hail rained down on her with loud thumps. Shamira ran out, scooped up Washeena in her arms and carried her back to the safety of the large oak. The muscular form of a Paccu raced onto the meadow and picked up Tamahna to carry him off to a safer place; Wanashta ran screaming hysterically behind him, the large hail bouncing off of her, seemingly unnoticed.

A pronghorn antelope leapt through the encampment, kicking over the two standing shelters and sending the remaining inhabitants scrambling for cover. The antelope flashed by Shamira and as it soared through the air, she was shocked to discover that it was, in fact, a doe. Several members of the band shouted out for everyone to follow the animal. As they fled, stretching their deerskin shirts over their heads to deflect the hammering hail, the antelope's tracks showed clear and deep in the soft mud, and just as deep in the hard bedrock ledges that jogged throughout the hilly terrain.

They led straight into a white-cliffed valley and stopped abruptly at the edge of a deep, emerald-green pool. The hail receded as soon as they entered the valley, but a deafening roar chugged in from the southeast as treetops were ripped off behind them and the thick laurel was spread flat against the ground by the wailing wind. Ceptke dove into the pool and yelled for everyone to follow as he dragged a sputtering Tamahna under the surface. Shamira screamed over the roar of the wind to make sure Washeena understood not to try and breathe as they went under the water, then jumped into the shimmering, cold depths in search of the hidden entrance. The valley became dark as night, with only three strangely glowing columns visible as they wound their way up the valley, bouncing off the walls of the white cliffs. The pool was suddenly filled with bodies, groping for an opening in the now pitch-black pool. A faint glow on the northwest edge lured them into the mouth of the elusive cavern, and a strong current quickly pulled them to its center.

Inside, a glow from each of the four entrances created a dim light, as well as a faint cross where the rays intersected in the middle of the pool. The last of those to make it into the cavern were at a loss to comprehend the light; everything was black when they had leapt into the pool. They searched frantically for loved ones and relatives, but some were missing and left to the fate of the strange and powerful tornadoes. The group congregated on a smooth and strangely warm ledge where there was little room to stand without falling off into the water, let alone elbowing their way around to search for loved ones.

A dull roar outside became increasingly louder and the bedrock, itself, began to tremor in a sickening hum against the screaming wind.

"The water is disappearing!" Quitkwa yelled frantically.

As soon as the water dipped below the tops of the entrances, the dim light inside of the cave vanished, and a deafening whir tossed the band violently about as they held tightly onto each other in the maelstrom that had erupted from what remained of the water in the bottom of the pool. The water level rose rapidly and when the entrances were covered once again, the dim and soothing light returned and the violently spinning water became calm enough for the band to find their way back to the ledge, though they were badly bruised and battered from having been thrown against the walls of the cavern. But the lull was short-lived, and the wind started to roar again. When the walls began to quake and the water level dropped once again, they held tightly onto one another as the second tornado roared into the valley, its screeching mouth biting and sucking into the earth like a colossal upended leech, exposing the entrances once again.

They clenched each other in a death grip, waxing into a solid mass of taut human flesh like a huge boulder tossing in a whirlpool. Three times they were exposed to the power of the pillars and three times, all had endured of those who had the good fortune of making their way into the cavern. When the final assault from the violent columns of wind subsided, the band was left lying on the ledge. The pool became smooth as new ice, a throng of small birds sang cheerfully as the dawn as they fluttered next to the roof of the cavern and landed fearlessly on the humans below.

"We should learn from these small creatures of the Creator and sing our praises as well," Ketanka bellowed. And as the Minnecou sang of their thanks and praise, the Paccus joined in with their own songs, while thousands of small birds flew in circles next to the roof of the cavern with many different songs sung in unison. The light of the cross became increasingly brighter and as the water level began to drop once again, the band held tightly onto one another and sang even louder in the hopes that they would increase the Creator's strength and not expose the entrances to the evil outside. But the water level continued to drop and when it reached the tops of the entrances, a brilliant light came pouring in and the cross in the center of the pool became as a blinding and warm white light. The small birds streamed out of the entrances and a ledge was exposed that led out of the northern entrance of the cavern.

"It is a sign for us to head to the north," Kwoita exclaimed, and the band slowly filtered out of the wondrous cavern.

Once outside, the battered yet grateful survivors had to shield their eyes from the blinding light of the sun as it reflected from the white, rain-soaked ledges of brilliant limestone. The oppressive air had vanished and a chill, crisp breeze invigorated the weary band. The laurel and surrounding trees of the valley, though, had disappeared entirely. They climbed the northern cliffs of the valley and as they reached the summit, the meadow where they had previously camped came into view. The three powerful tornadoes had destroyed everything. There was no trace of any of the band's belongings or shelters, neither was there any sign of those who had not made it into the cavern. As they looked around, it became horribly apparent that neither tree, shrub, nor even blade of grass had been able to withstand the powerful grip of the whirling pillars. For as far as they could see, nothing remained but the rocks and ledges that had been torn, scraped and scattered haphazardly all the way to the horizon in every direction.

They had returned to the meadow, Ketanka thought, with the intention of splitting everything evenly amongst both the Paccus and the Minnecou. But this had now been completed without bickering, deception or ill feelings. No one had more than the clothes on their backs, and many of these garments had become so tattered, they were barely worth keeping. Ketanka could see that no one had been able to hold onto their bows and arrows or even a small knife, neither he himself. The air had become chilled and they had neither hides nor trees for shelter. They had no food or weapons and there was no sign of life all the way to the horizon. The only exit accessible to them pointed to the cold regions of the north, and this at a time when winter was approaching. Neither Paccu nor Minnecou were experienced in surviving the extremes of winter weather this far north, and were generally laden with food and hides to bring along with them on their journeys southward.

There was no decision for them to make, however. Each understood they had been saved, and were it not for the Creator, they would have met with the same fate as those that had not made it to the cavern. North was the direction they were pointed in and north was where they would go. They stumbled their way over the boulder-strewn terrain and trudged across the desolate expanse towards the foothills of the Dark Mountains. This outlying region directly north of them, was a bountiful area, and far against the horizon, the humped peaks loomed in a dark, purplish-blue cloak, suggesting they had been spared by the pillars that had eliminated all life before them.

A large wall of debris had been thrown clear to the edges of the stripped area and the band was forced to climb over a pile higher than the peaks of the black cliffs near the lake, extending completely around the now barren plateau. They found a spot where the wreckage was heaped lowest and carefully climbed over and through the entanglement of trees, mud and boulders, picking out pliable and straight branches to use for bows and spears. Once over the mass of debris, they found the trees still standing. However, they were thinned of branches and completely stripped of leaves for a great distance into the forest.

As they advanced further, the leaves had already started to change in the lower wetland areas and the cool air suggested that very soon, they should be heading back towards the villages in the south if it was possible to get by the Snake people. They were not sure, though, if they were meant to remain here for the winter or only to refit themselves with fresh food and weapons before their return southward. Ketanka felt that they should follow their instincts and return unless they were confronted with a sign to tell them otherwise. The Paccus, however, felt that to remain in one place until spring was the best way to survive–that if they gathered everything now and built lodges to withstand the cold, they would not get caught stranded on the trail.

Ketanka knew that they still had time before it would be absolutely too late to head southward. It was possible that even if they left immediately, they still could get bogged down in early snowstorms, but these were generally followed by warm spells, where the band would be in little danger of starvation or freezing to death. Ketanka led them to the stream where they usually set up camp in this area and sent all of the women off to find fish, wild onions, turtles, frogs and whatever edibles were available. He assembled the warriors and split them up into hunting parties to head out in every direction in search of meat and hides.

Ceptke and Boaka emerged as informal chiefs of the Paccus, dividing their own warriors into hunting and scouting parties. Wanachan was given charge of the Paccu women and was told by the two scouts that they would be spending the winter in this camp. If the Minnecou tried to interfere with their lodge building, she was simply not to translate any Minnecou demands or arguments in favor of leaving.

Ceptke and Boaka were in awe of their new surroundings. Come spring, they would take their warriors, find the Snake village, and then free their relatives from Quiktkoata. But they would return here. This was their new territory. There were no enemies this far north and game seemed plentiful. The only doubts they had were that once they freed the other Paccus, their alliance as chiefs might not be honored. But, after, if they were to rescue the captive Paccus and lead them back to a peaceful and bountiful land, did they not earn the right to lead their people, regardless of their blood lineage. They had learned through Wanachan that the Minnecou chose their chief by which warrior most people agreed to follow. Often enough, it did turn out to be a chief's son or brother, who would lead when the chief died, or was in sharp disagreement with the majority of the band. But just as often, the new chief had no direct blood ties to the old.

Ketanka went out with Quitkwa, Quebathe and Shatomi, while the Wolf brothers went out with their three sons in search of game. Kwoita remained close to the camp, helping the women fish the stream and find the large bullfrogs that provided little meat, but a viable source of sustenance should the hunting parties come back empty-handed, or stay on the trail for several days. The berries had already shriveled. Acorns, chestnuts and hickory nuts, however, had just begun to fall, and Paccu and Minnecou women alike gathered and spread them in the sand to dry in the sun.

Kwoita helped the Minnecou women make traps to snare trout that were swimming with the current. They tied pieces of small worms inside the funnel-shaped traps and when the trout entered, they could neither turn around nor swim backwards to free themselves. The Paccu women, under the direction of Wanachan, were digging up long and pliable roots near the bases of trees and vines, and tying them together to fashion long nets that could be cast into the stream and retrieved quickly enough to ensnare a few of the passing trout and suckers. They worked for quite some time, fashioning two such nets, while two of the Paccu women gathered nuts and herbs, searching for bullfrogs and slow moving turtles as they went along. The Paccu women moved much slower than the Minnecou. Kwoita could see that their were hearts were heavy and somewhat bitter towards his own clan. The Paccus had lost two warriors and a young girl in the confusion of the sudden storm; the Minnecou had suffered no losses.

One of the Paccu women wandered away, and Shamira heard her sobbing. Powhantin went looking for her and Shamira followed to see if she could help soothe the woman's pain. When she found Powhantin cradling the distraught woman in her arms, she sat down beside them and put a caring hand on the woman's arm, but was quickly brushed aside. Powhantin spoke soothingly as if to reassure the young mother that Shamira shared in her grief, but she turned towards Shamira and yelled at her in a sharp Paccu reprisal. Shamira stood to put a more comfortable distance between them.

"My only wish is to help comfort you through your grief," Shamira whispered softly. The distraught woman spit on the ground and threw a handful of sand at her. A flash of anger erupted within, but Shamira held herself back. "I am no help here," she said, and walked off. The Paccu woman yelled sharply at her again, but Shamira ignored her tone, though her face set hard as she waded back into the cooling stream to remove those traps that strained with snared trout.

Wanachan wandered over to the stream's edge and spoke quietly to Shamira. "Do not be angry with her, Shamira. She sees that the Minnecou have lost no one, while her relatives are either dead or in the hands of the Snake people. She thought that she had at least been able to save the life of her daughter, but when she jumped into the pool, the child panicked and kicked itself free. That was the last she saw of her. She does not feel that the Minnecou understand what any of us Paccus have been through, let alone share in her latest grief."

"My father and my only brother are gone because of your people. Sequannah has been captured and my father has followed to try and free him," Shamira said. "It was my father who rescued these very Paccus who spit and throw dirt at me for trying to help them, when they could have been still moaning under the whips of the Snake people," Shamira rebuked without raising her voice.

"I know that my people have not been very friendly," Wanachan sympathized. "And it may even seem as though they are ungrateful, but they have been through very much pain. They worry about surviving the winter moons up here with nothing to start out with. And there is much danger of being captured by the Snake people if we try to go to our winter village. Patience and understanding are sometimes rewarded very generously," Wanachan stated, "but they are also sometimes harshly punished when they are abandoned prematurely. I know how they appear to the Minnecou, but if you accepted them as if they were truly a part of your own clan, you would understand their pain, and never abandon them. They are proud people, and just like the bear or mountain lion, they are best left somewhat alone when they are wounded. We are not as weak as we appear...we were ambushed, and outnumbered as well. Come spring, the Snake people will learn that they have made a mistake."

"You have but a handful of warriors left to fight hundreds of vicious Snake warriors," Shamira softly laughed. "How can you expect to be more than even a mosquito bite to them?"

"Not all of the Paccus your father freed came this way with us. Two of them crossed the river and went far to the southwest where our sister clan lives," she whispered. "They will be here looking for us next spring if they are not already on their way to kill the Snake people before winter."

"They have enough warriors to fight the Snake people?" Shamira whispered.

"Well, maybe with your clan and if you, too, have sister clans, we may be able to free our relatives and push the Snake people out of here. There is something I see here that could help you understand...if you believe. When I was a child, a great and powerful Washan lived among us who could make a blue sky turn dark with clouds and pour rain upon the dusty earth when the corn threatened to wither on the stalk. He foretold of many things to come, most of which we have first seen, but only later, understood. He would tell us that to understand before you see is most sacred and wise. He was a very good and just man who always looked for what the Creator would want, not even considering his own desires. The Creator walked with our people always then. One night, when the Washan was sleeping, he walked from this life and into the next dream. But, during his last days, he spoke frequently of two peoples who were very different from us, one of whom would be our allies. Which ever one we chose to be our ally, the other would be banished from this land for countless generations. Our choice would determine how this land would be ruled for countless winters into the future, yet we would not be among the rulers, so we must choose wisely. I see the two very different peoples and I choose the Minnecou."

"I also see something happening here within your own clan. I can help," Wanachan looked sympathetic. "You are at a time when you have just become a woman," she stated patiently. "You will soon experience bad treatment from your own people. But do not worry, as your beauty fades with age, so will these problems."

"I do not find your conversation very comforting," Shamira said sarcastically. But, she could see that the old woman could be right in what she said, remembering how she was recently treated by the Wolf brothers' wives. However, Wanachan could also have been a witness to this incident...she did understand the Minnecou language.

"If you were homely, you would feel left out," she went on. "If you were plain, you would feel threatened by women like yourself," Wanachan went on. "So you see that everything is truly balanced. Your advantages are your disadvantages as well. Everything depends upon what is in your heart. Once this becomes clear, that is how you will be treated. Whether you have a good heart or a bad heart will soon become evident to those who are closest to you...the more you show of yours, the more you will see of theirs."

"The Paccus should see that I have a good heart," Shamira stated. "I have done nothing but try to help them and they have not shown good hearts to me."

"No," Wanachan agreed. "They have shown you hearts in pain."

Wanachan turned back to her small group of women. The Paccu woman who spat at Shamira was now gathering the hickory nuts that had fallen to the ground and removing the four-pieced shells. Though still sobbing, her anger had subsided to the point where she could return to working for the good of the tribe. The young woman looked up at Shamira who was watching from a distance, and although she couldn't find it in her heart to smile, neither did she cast an expression of ill will. Shamira could see that Wanachan was right in that they were all merely in pain, for all of the Paccus' expressions were similar to that of the grieving mother.

* * *

Kwoita watched as both groups of women gathered their fish and food in their different ways. He now remembered seeing those nets that the Paccu women had woven when he was a young boy. He couldn't fathom, however, how he came to recognize Wanachan after all these years. She was just a small child when his Minnecou clan happened to run across a tribe of mountain dwelling people. The Minnecou had gotten stranded on the cold and windy plains during a year when the winter snows came early and deep. The two different tribes worked together throughout the winter hunting the buffalo herds that had been stranded with them. The Minnecou remained with the Paccus throughout the spring and into the early summer that year, and of the few members of either tribe that learned to speak the other's language, Wanachan became their best interpreter.

Kwoita could see that Wanachan resembled her childhood features in no way except one: her large owl-like eyes. He remembered her always following him when he would go fishing and he'd try to get rid of her and her incessant talking. He would try to hunt some of the smaller creatures with his little bow, but she would always follow, asking the Minnecou word for this or that, and he never would see anything but small birds. But these small birds were always around the clans of every tribe and it was forbidden to kill any animal that would willingly and peacefully come into an encampment. Kwoita never found any game to hunt as long as this owl-eyed girl was on his trail. He would think of some of the wildest insults to rid himself of her, but they struck her as so funny, she only wanted to hear more. Kwoita enjoyed seeing the owl-eyed girl laughing and eventually he found himself creating these humorous insults wherever he went.

After all these years of not seeing her and nearly forgetting about her completely, he could not find one insult within his heart to throw at her. This was a woman who was not to be insulted, but he also sensed that she seemed to be disappointed that he didn't. Just to see her again, however, was a strange turn of events in Kwoita's eyes.

The Paccu women had barely gathered enough food to get them through the day when Wanachan drew several wide circles onto the ground, and all of the Paccu women searched for large flat stones in the stream bed. They held onto these stones with both hands and began to tear away at the earth in the center of the circles.

"You don't have quite enough food there to be in need of

a cache," Kwoita laughed. "Especially to try and fill holes that big."

"We're building lodges for the winter!" Wanachan laughed. "These holes will be dug deep enough to keep the wind out...then we will build a cover over it."

"Who said we were staying here for the winter?" Kwoita asked sarcastically.

"We have decided to stay!" Wanachan stated with a smile. "Now it is the Minnecous' turn to decide what they will do."

"The Minnecou will gather enough food to keep them alive before they make any decisions about their wintering grounds," Kwoita said knowingly.

"We already know there is plenty of food to get us through the winter, right here. Why look any further?" Wanachan exclaimed just as knowingly.

CHAPTER 12

All along the horizon to the east, Sequannah observed the jagged form of Quiktkoata's city as the first hints of dawn began to outline the flat and peaked roofs of its strange lodges. Torches were still lit, their flickering shadows steadying in the breathless dawn. Sudden sharp commands began to stir the strangely beautiful city into wakefulness. Throughout the night, he had only managed a few short naps; recurring fearful dreams entangled him in the city's trenches, dragging him along in a stream of ooze and refuse, carpeted with thick black snakes. His neck had swollen to the point where the collar now touched flesh at every point instead of hanging slightly loose. His head was a pounding fury and his surroundings became blurred with each movement.

As daylight illuminated the shadowy details of Quiktkoata's strange empire, Sequannah watched the front of a long, flat structure, where many of the Snake warriors gathered before scattering out to their various posts throughout the city and fields. The subtle tinging of an iron chain caused him to turn back towards the square structure, where the slaves of the fish pile were housed. One of the hooded slaves had crept to the granite ledge and was crawling up to Sequannah. The air was chilled and he shivered. The hooded form approached him, leaving an obvious, darkened trail through the heavy droplets of morning dew. As he suspected, when the hooded figure reached his feet, the gentle whispering of a young woman fell softly through the ringing in his burning red ears.

"You must do as you are told and obey the commands of the Snake warriors," she whispered. "They know that you will be sickly today, but if you express a willingness to try and please them with hard work, they will be much impressed and will reward you generously. I don't know why they have chosen to let you go without a hood, but they must think you more valuable than the rest of us.

"They want me to be seen. They want to kill my clan when they try to rescue me," Sequannah said blankly. "Quiktkoata wishes to eliminate the Minnecou. The longer I survive here, the more risk I put upon my people. My only honor would be to make them kill me."

"You must live, Sequannah!" her voice rose urgently. He attempted to cover her mouth, but she stepped back. She began to whisper once again: "You must live Sequannah. My father knows where I am and he will come for me when the time is right. Maybe tonight. Maybe ten sunsets from tonight, but he will come for me. We can take you with us. When he realizes that you intend to die if you do not escape, he will certainly take you along with us. None of the others here know that I am here to watch Quiktkoata. I can escape whenever I choose. I tell you because you are Minnecou and will never fit into the Snake people's ways...no matter how hard you try. You must pretend. Try to do what you are told, even more than you are told, and they will reward you and even come to trust you. They know that you are different than the others here. You could convince them that you would be loyal to them without any ties to the other slaves. I must go back to the lodge, the guards will be coming soon."

Sequannah watched as Tarote slipped quietly back to the square lodge, and knew that when the Snake warriors came out to the field, they would be able to clearly see the darkened line left in the silvery dew. As the guards approached, they picked up small stones and hurled them sharply against the square wooden structures, shocking the hooded figures into wakefulness. Sequannah thought quickly and rolled several heavy boulders towards the lodge. When they crashed into the structure he yelled loudly in Minnecou for the hooded slaves to waken. It was time for them to get into the fields. The slaves came running out of the lodge, yelling angrily at Sequannah as he sat laughing on the granite ledge. The approaching Snake warriors enjoyed seeing the enmity that the young Minnecou had caused between himself and the other slaves, and smiled approvingly as Sequannah rolled several more boulders into the side of the lodge. Sequannah smiled back, knowing that he was well on his way to gaining their trust, and had effectively disguised Tarote's glaring trail as well.

The same two Snake warriors arrived as the morning sun tipped the horizon. Hooded slaves hoisted their stacks of baskets and lined the edge of the fish pile just as the Snake warriors reached their posts. They released Sequannah from the iron hook in the granite, and one of them led him to the steaming heap, while the other fetched his stack of baskets next to the lodge. Sequannah waded into the pile and immediately fell headlong into the slime, to the jeers of all the other hooded slaves. From their laughter, he could immediately tell they were men. He heard nothing of Tarote's higher pitched voice, and if there were any other women in this miserable lot, then they must be built like men and have the voices to match.

He pressed one basket after another into the slimy muck, filling each to about three quarters. He then scooped armfuls of the small fish into the baskets until they were full. He made an obvious display of anger towards the other slaves, pretending to take this anger out on them by working twice as fast. He finished filling his stack of baskets before everyone else, even though he was last to make it onto the fish pile. Even as he filled his last basket and placed it in the array of his other full baskets, two unhooded slaves approached with two tall stacks of baskets each, and placed them at the edge of the pile. Sequannah grabbed one of the full stacks for himself, though there were at least twenty slaves working the pile. He labored feverishly to fill the baskets, and when one of the other slaves tried to take some, he yelled and screamed in his foreign tongue, refusing to let go. With each basket he filled, however, one or more of the hooded slaves would stalk over and take three or four baskets while he was busy.

The other slaves recognized immediately what he was trying to do and worked feverishly as well. Soon, the other three stacks disappeared, leaving Sequannah's empty baskets as a glaring display of unfinished work. Some of the slaves grumbled at Sequannah, but others seemed to be praising him as they took the remainder of the empties and filled them to the brim. Now there was nothing left for the slaves to do but wait for the unhooded slaves to come and pick up the full baskets and tote them out into the fields. Sequannah saw a group of them approaching, but they weren't carrying any stacks of empty baskets. The slaves of the fish pile were already well ahead in their work, and it appeared as though they would be able to rest for an even longer spell. Sequannah was extremely grateful; he was sweating profusely and couldn't discern whether this was a result of his frantic work, or a feverish symptom of infection in his swollen neck and burning head.

When the group of unhooded slaves reached the fish pile, he was surprised to find that they were not on their way to pick up the first baskets of compost, but were, in fact, bringing the morning meal out to the workers in the field. The smell of roasted corn and simmering meat made his stomach grumble with anticipation. He sniffed the air in rapture as the faintest of chill breezes carried aromas of cooked food to his fish-fouled nostrils. He knew then that he wasn't under the spell of a fever, for his appetite would have been lessened.

There seemed to be no rationing of the food, and Sequannah ate till he could no longer bear to remain in a sitting position. The other hooded slaves seemed to be laughing under their breath as Sequannah threw handful after handful of tender, simmered meat down his gullet, between gorging binges of sweet roasted corn. Sequannah noticed that the crowd was rapidly growing, then the sound of cracking whips cut sharply through the air. He looked over at the fish pile. Not only were the full baskets already on their way over the vast fields, but hundreds of empty baskets stood waiting to be filled in their place.

He waddled back to the pile along with the other hooded figures, and as he stepped into the oozing slime, he became nauseous at the foul smell that had been forced upwards through the crooks of his toes, and stirred into the fish pile's distinct atmosphere. Though everyone could smell this rotting heap from far off in the fields, and those slaves carrying baskets right under their noses were often nauseated from the foul smell, to be in the midst of the fish pile was an altogether different experience; the breath was nearly stolen away and the lungs never quite seemed to satisfy the demand for air. Long spells of leaning into the rot often caused the slaves to see a darkness closing in around them as their consciousness began to fade, and they would instinctively move outside of the pile if they had ever experienced this before.

Sequannah, however, had no form of communication with

the others, and Tarote had neglected to warn him of this extraordinarily unpleasant sensation. After a long spell of intense work, as he tried desperately to gain back the lead that the slaves had acquired before their morning meal, his stomach was in his throat and spots suddenly began to blank out his vision as he fell face first into the pile. He didn't even feel the strain of the iron collar on his tender and swollen neck as he was dragged out of the depths of muck. He awoke with his eyeballs straining from their sockets as he violently vomited upon the gray filmed fish eyes staring blankly back. When he could finally stand, the gas-filled fish at his feet burst under his weight. The sudden stench forced him even further from the pile, where he crumbled to the ground and fell into empty vomiting fits.

The shorter Snake warrior dragged Sequannah over to the anvil in the lodge, and with his iron hammer, broke one of the links in the chain at about arm's length from Sequannah's neck, then led him away from the fish pile towards the imposing structures of Quiktkoata's city. No guard was left in the shorter one's place as all of these hooded slaves were chained to the granite ledge. Were they to try and overpower the remaining Snake warrior, he need only move outside of the reach of their chains. If they slacked in their work and threatened the lone guard, he would merely sidestep them until the other guard returned. Then they would lash out violently, even fatally, at the rebellious captives and whomever they felt to be responsible.

Sequannah noted the casual and even enjoyable attitude of those unhooded slaves who tended the small fires of burning stalks and vines, then spread the ashes over the surrounding loam. Those slaves who were carrying the baskets of fish would hurriedly transport their ungainly cargo to its appointed destination, and slowly return for another load. Another group stood in a line, each with a flat stone attached to a long stick, pounding and turning the fishmeal and ashes into the dark, rich soil. This group constantly droned songs of praise, that Sequannah had only perceived to be a low humming from his place amidst the fish pile.

The short Snake warrior became almost amiable towards Sequannah, an abrupt turnabout from yesterday's demeanor. He led him through a confusing array of intersecting trails, reassuring him as they went along. Many of the structures along these paths were much larger than Sequannah had perceived them from the distant granite ledge; some four or five times the height of a man, others covering enough ground to encompass three or four encampments such as his whole clan would construct. He peered inside as he passed their wide openings, bewildered at the rich and beautiful creations adorning their inner chambers, disappointed when some of them turned out to be drab stalls with dried straw spread over the floors: sleeping quarters.

The humped back of the earthen serpent wound eerily through the collection of huge, wooden structures, and when they reached the head of the looming snake, an especially ornate building dominated the area. Blocks of stone set a short distance in front of its opening were piled on one another in such a way as to allow people to step on one, and then easily step up to the next as they climbed their way into the opening of the vast chamber. Directly in front of the opening was a flat terrace upon which three large, gilded copper cylinders with movable wooden doors were fastened securely to the stone. The doors had intricate designs engraved onto them and the tops of these cylinders were adorned with beautiful copper castings of the moon, stars, birds and snakes.

The building itself was the only one Sequannah had seen where the construction was of stone as well as wood. This must be one of the stone lodges that his grandfather had spoken of, he thought to himself. The roof of this cavernous structure was strangely rounded, its edges draped in a beautiful green and strangely molded border, where the green residue of copper rust ran down the white stone sides of the imposing structure in braided patterns. As the short Snake warrior led Sequannah past the front of the opening, a cool bank of air flowed down the steps from the entrance of the chamber, similar to chills he had experienced at the mouths of caves. Inside, the huge room was very dark in comparison to the bright sunlight outside, and Sequannah could barely see the rows of torches lining the walls of the great hall. This must be Quiktkoata's lodge, he thought to himself; his skin crawled as the cold, musty air slid over his feet. The Snake warrior paused in front of the steps and forced Sequannah to bow in submission as he himself did.

He then grabbed Sequannah with one arm and hoisted him off of the stone terrace, simultaneously throwing a loop of the chain over one of the many bars that protruded more than a hand's length over the top of the copper cylinders. When he let Sequannah down, his feet rested flat against the ground. The short guard climbed up on one of the copper support braces and hoisted the chain up to the next loop, so that when he let it down, Sequannah would have to remain on his toes to keep from choking. Sequannah reached to his throat as he was jerked upwards, but couldn't fit his fingers between the iron collar and his swollen neck. He stretched his arms overhead and grabbed onto the chain in back of his neck to relieve the pressure his own weight was putting upon his throat, and quickly the shorter warrior let him down once again. That short warrior was much stronger than he appeared, Sequannah thought to himself.

Sequannah still had his hands overhead, holding tightly onto the chain, but the Snake warrior pulled his arms down and tied them tightly behind his back so that he would have little chance of freeing himself while no one was around to watch. Sequannah observed the imposing little figure out of the corners of his eyes as he disappeared into the depths of the cavernous hall. A constant low humming in a strange and lilting chant flowed steadily out of the open chamber door; the constant rattling of seed-filled gourds turned the conversation within to muffled whisperings. Sequannah struggled to stretch as high as he could on his toes without losing balance and leaning sideways to put further strain on his collar.

Inside the door of the chamber, strange glittering of shiny yellow metal gleamed from a multitude of directions. It almost appeared as though the Snake people had captured many small pieces of the sun, holding them captive in the strangely haunted chambers. Sequannah looked up, reassuring himself that the sun wasn't any dimmer, but how would he count all of the stars at night to find out if any of those were missing?

He examined the strange cylindrical cages on the terrace, surprised to see such works of art covered in bird droppings of enormous size. A scattering of tattered feathers and many small bones littered the floors of all three cylinders. Tiny pieces of small jewelry and what appeared to be the toys of infants were encrusted into the heaps of feathers, dung and bones at the base of the copper cylinders. At his feet, he noticed what appeared to be one of the bracelets he had seen Paccu infants wearing on his march with Quiktkoata's procession. The realization that babies were sacrificed to flesh eating birds at this very place made his skin crawl.

A cold looking man suddenly appeared at the chamber opening. He slapped Sequannah with the back of his hand, muttering insults as he opened the wooden door of the cylinder. Sequannah sensed hostility in the indecipherable, yet womanly voice. His weak tap and ridiculous costume almost set Sequannah to laughing. The shimmering folds of his long black and yellow robe were bizarre, but the large bun, tightly woven at the base of his skull, was fitted with an array of long and brightly colored feathers that stood higher than an arm's length above his head. Sequannah sensed strongly that this peculiar man had a distinct dislike for him. He noticed the medicine bundle tied to the man's waistband–a Washan of the Snake people! The Snake Washan hesitated for a moment, looking Sequannah up and down. A metal knife appeared in his hand and disappeared just as quickly. He looked back and forth towards the opening, then quickly darted back inside. This man may have tried to kill him, had not the shorter guard suddenly appeared at the entrance.

The short guard watched the Snake priest until he was completely through the chamber door, and when he lifted Sequannah and his chain off of the post, a look of contempt was evident as he scowled at the disappearing black and yellow robe. He led Sequannah back down the steps and around the side of the building, towards the huge, earthen serpent. As they skirted the front of the head, Sequannah could now clearly see the yellow and black checkered pattern that began at a point between the serpent's eyes and gradually widened to the width of two men laid end to end. The squares were filled elbow deep with alternate applications of sulfur and coal. Two distinct paths issued from between the shabby looking collection of wooden structures, hidden on the far side of the serpent; one black with the dust and chunks of coal, the other laden with a trail of yellow powder. The guard led him down the black trail and Sequannah found himself staring down a gaping hole in the earth, surrounded by thick wooden beams. The warrior from the fish pile handed him over to another guard and Sequannah was led into the chilled depths of the cavern, past many black-eyed, hooded men who were filling baskets with chunks of coal while others clanged and banged against the walls with metal implements. A steady stream of unhooded slaves carried the full baskets out onto the earthen serpent.

"Another Minnecou who fears to work," the guard said, though Sequannah could barely distinguish his own tongue through the thick accent. "Quiktkoata does not learn that Minnecou are useless. Your people make more work, and never give anything back to me. I learn Minnecou tongue, teach them many things, but they do not

206

learn well. They know what I tell them, but they never listen. It is honorable to die in battle," he sneered, "but they prefer to die in chains."

"Chains?" Sequannah wondered.

He grabbed hold of one of the loops at Sequannah's throat. "Chains!" he answered gruffly. "You work and do as we tell you, then you will live. Maybe become warrior, maybe learn many things. No work, you waste away to the elements without food and water and clothes to keep you warm. Fuull baskette!" was the last thing Sequannah heard as the guard handed him the top basket from one of many stacks.

Sequannah found this to be infinitely better than standing in the fish pile, but the darkness was strangling. A black dust choked his lungs as it drifted up to the opening of the mine in a never-ending cloud. Small pieces of grit found their way into his mouth, and soon his saliva tasted like the odor of decomposed muck at the bottom of stagnant swamps. What seemed to be a blessing in comparison to the fish pile, quickly took on a torturous burden of its own, and as Sequannah tried in vain to keep the black grit out of his mouth, he became increasingly aware of the dangers and evil feelings of this deep, black hole. At times, the wooden beams would creak loudly, as if crying out in pain. The men around him would immediately fall to the ground and roll into a ball. Some would try to run, but snapped to the hard floor when they reached the end of their chains. Soon, Sequannah found himself falling to the ground whenever one of these loud creaking noises suddenly erupted, and several times he discovered the wisdom of it when he was covered with black dust, and chinks of the shiny stones rained down on his back.

Most of the moaning and creaking seemed to be coming from an area further down into the dark hole. One of the hooded slaves who was closest to the set of beams cried out in terror with even the faintest squeak. The guard would frequently crack his fanged snake whip within a hair's width of the screaming slave's neck, but to no avail. The guard would then quickly step back, removing himself from the dangerous area, while cursing the hooded slave in a language unknown to Sequannah. Sequannah filled his baskets quickly. The guards were amazed to see this young slave working like no other Minnecou before. They yelled and screamed at the basket carriers to step up their work because the filled baskets were beginning to block the passageway, then they disappeared for quite some time.

Sequannah slowed down while they were gone; he

couldn't breathe well in the dusty cavern. A stream of basket carriers suddenly flooded the passageway, and Sequannah recognized several of the Paccus that had been brought here in Quiktkoata's last raid. Among them, a familiar profile became evident in the light of the tunnel entrance. Woltah seemed to be yelling at his own people as he strutted along, carrying two baskets instead of one. Sequannah reached out and tugged on the rough cloth of Woltah's new garment. He bent down, squinting in the dim light to see who this unhooded coal digger was. He kicked a slurry of dust into Sequannah's face and voiced a low, yet guarded threat to the young Minnecou. Sequannah was taken aback, betrayed by someone he felt should have been his friend. Maybe Woltah considered it to be his fault that they had been captured by the Snake people. He may even be angry at Sequannah for filling so many baskets and making more work for his people. Sequannah could see that he was making many enemies here if that were the case, but at the same time, the guards treated him no better than any of the other slaves. He was isolated from everyone by his strange tongue and the only one in this place he could even communicate with was the Snake guard who watched over the basket fillers. One or two assistants accompanied him during the course of a day, but neither even attempted to communicate with Sequannah in the Minnecou tongue. They bellowed out their commands in the tongue of the Snake people.

When the Snake guards finally returned, all of the basket carriers were suddenly ordered out of the tunnel. Two of the strangest looking men Sequannah had ever seen forced their way into the hole, grunting and sweating heavily as they hoisted an immense wooden beam on their thick, muscular shoulders. Although all of the languages here were foreign to Sequannah, when these two cursed and kicked at the coal workers in their way, the harshest sounding tongue he had ever imagined assaulted his ears like the growling of a grizzly. Their faces were covered with hair and the scant light from the tunnel opening showed their skin to have a pinkish hue. Their hair was nearly white in comparison to any other human hair he had seen, and it hung in long, greasy strands around their bristling faces. They stopped at the place where the creaking wood was loudest and kicked the screaming slave into a dark corner. One of them pulled out a handful of iron spikes from somewhere within his strange looking clothing and began hammering away at them while the other beastly looking figure held the immense wooden beam overhead against the roof of the tunnel.

Sequannah could see the spikes being driven right into the hard oak. He couldn't believe his eyes when the other man let go, and the heavy beam remained suspended against the ceiling as if it were straining against it. He couldn't see the two support beams recessed into the sides of the cavern walls. They cursed violently and spit frequently while they worked; Sequannah witnessed their malicious nature as they tossed chunks of coal at the screaming figure in the corner. Even their laughter had a gruffness about it, coming from deep down within their fat bellies.

When they seemed satisfied with their work, they left through the opening, but quickly returned with another large beam that they carried to the end of the tunnel. They went in and out until they had brought in a substantial piles of these beams, then Sequannah heard them banging and grunting for quite some time at the bottom of the passageway. He heard them clearing the way of hooded slaves as they made their way back to the opening, and once more they returned with armloads of small, angled wooden blocks. They nailed two of these into the corners underneath the first beam they installed, and brought the remainder to the end of the passageway, where Sequannah heard them banging a while longer. They then left through the opening, their strange colored skin glistening in rivulets of rank smelling sweat.

The Snake guards returned and once again, the scraping and banging and filling of baskets resumed as a long line of waiting basket carriers streamed into the tunnel. Within a few short moments, Sequannah began to feel choked up in the coal dust again, and for the first time since the hairy-faced men had come, he realized that for a time, the air had been relatively clean. He looked up with a sigh at the long line of unhooded slaves that rapidly depleted the supply of filled baskets, and again caught a glimpse of Woltah approaching his position. He worked as fast as he could to keep ahead of the stream of basket carriers, and Woltah didn't even look in Sequannah's direction as he seemed to stumble into one of the young Minnecou's baskets, kicking its contents all over the boy. He cursed Sequannah and motioned for him to slow down, all the while looking at the Snake guard to make sure his signal hadn't been detected.

Sequannah realized that he could be working this tunnel for quite some time, and with his separation from the fish pile, he'd already lost the only friend he had come to trust. His thoughts drifted to the hooded woman. There was no hope of escape without Tarote; he was alone. The few other Paccus in the line of basket carriers either refused to look at him or didn't recognize him. None had made any attempt to make contact with him or even acknowledge that they knew who he was, though he was lashed conspicuously to Quiktkoata's litter for all to see during their long march. He slowed his pace to nearly a halt; at least he would not be an enemy to the basket carriers, but none of them seemed to notice. After he had come by to pick up the full baskets several more times, Woltah finally gave him a nod of approval when his stack of baskets became high and the full baskets were no longer keeping pace with the line. The whole line of basket carriers had gradually slowed their pace so that the Snake guards wouldn't notice, but when several Snake guards marched from the direction of the earthen serpent and began to complain to the guard in the tunnel, his two assistants returned, and the cracking of snake skins whipped the crowd of slaves back to a frantic pace.

Once the guards were placated, though, the slaves gradually slowed again, and Sequannah understood the pattern. They all worked silently together to restrain the pace as much as possible, not only to keep from exhausting themselves, but to prevent the dust from choking them. Towards the end of the day, Sequannah had become quite accustomed to the ways that the slaves had developed to keep from being worked to death, and was actually beginning to feel almost rested. The light began to fade at the entrance of the passageway and a loud cry from the Snake guard signaled the end of the day's work. A group of servants came into the tunnel where the hooded slaves were chained down, carrying clay pots full of roasted corn and meat again. Dozens of large mats were brought in for the slaves to sleep on when they finished the evening meal.

Sequannah was surprised to see Woltah at the head of this line of servants, alongside the Snake guard. After only two days here, the Snake guards were trusting and friendly with a new Paccu warrior? Woltah walked directly over to where the slave who had spent much of the day screaming was now sitting, anxiously awaiting his food. He pointed accusingly at him, and spoke to the Snake guard. The two assistants broke his chain with an iron hammer and dragged the screaming slave out by the hair. Sequannah could now see why the Snake guard kept him at his side, relieved that he had slowed down and done as Woltah had signaled him to do. But then, Woltah moved further up the line and pointed to Sequannah.

"So you are also behind the slowing down of the work today," the Snake guard sneered. "I expect this from a Minnecou. Did you think that by working only when I watched would be enough to fool me? I have many eyes to watch for me. And if you end up dead like every other Minnecou that has been through here, there is nothing I will do to help if you cannot do your work and help me."

"He told me to slow down," Sequannah pointed an accusing finger at Woltah. "I filled many baskets very quickly, but he made me go slow."

"No one tells anyone what to do here but me," the Snake guard shouted. "Every Minnecou who comes here tells me that my eyes lie to me. You are the same as the others no matter how much I was told to expect anything different from you."

The two assistants returned to the tunnel and the chains were broken; Sequannah was dragged by the length of his hair as they pulled him through a tangle of paths running between the simple wooden structures to a mounded circle. Several wooden crosses fashioned from two beams lashed tightly together, protruded from the ground. The cold iron chains pressed tightly into his skin as his ankles were bound to the base of the vertical beam. They bound his feet with ropes as well; apparently the chains weren't enough. They then slid him upwards, ignoring his screams as large splinters were forced under his skin. They tied his wrists tightly against the horizontal beam. The hint of an autumn chill was drifting over the city in the crisp and hollow twilight, and the two cruel assistants grabbed a basin of cold water and flung it over Sequannah. The sudden shock stole his breath away, stifling his constant scream.

Sequannah only became aware of his screaming when he lost his breath. He clenched his teeth to absorb the pain. At one time he would have been able to endure this type of punishment without so much as a whimper, but the demands that were placed on the slaves were just about all that a human body could endure. His feet felt frozen, and as he looked down, he could see them turning purple from the tightening of the shrinking ropes. His hands turned a reddish-purple with the weight of his body constricting the circulation. He strained to pull himself up a little further, and when he dropped back down again, the chain slid up to where it was no longer around his ankles. The pain of iron against bone subsided in welcome relief. As darkness settled in, he listened to the straining and groaning of grown men as they sought to change their bound positions, no matter how slight, so that they might relieve the pressure from some nerve known only to themselves. Amidst the low groaning, an enraged growl suddenly erupted from the far side of the mound, and although it nearly stopped Sequannah's heart, moments later he realized it was Mokotak. A loud crack issued as one of the hewn beams snapped. Sequannah felt the vibration through the wooden beam on his back as the thump of a large body reached the surface of the mound.

A clattering commotion erupted from a nearby shack. Moments later, two Snake warriors struggled out with spears and snake whips. Sequannah strained his neck to see. Mokotak was grappling with the chain that held him tightly to the vertical beam. Mokotak saw the Snake warriors scrambling towards him as he banged furiously against the remaining beam with his shoulder, but he couldn't gain enough momentum to make any effect upon the deeply rooted post. He attempted to climb the post to force the chains over the top, but the Snake warriors were upon him, whipping furiously as they forced him back to the ground with their spears. One of the spears moved towards Mokotak's throat, when a loop of rope drifted over the Snake warrior's head, jerking him violently to the ground. A hooded figure suddenly appeared from out of the faint twilight, stood on the Snake warrior's back, and pulled tightly against the rope, snuffing the life out of the fallen guard.

The other Snake warrior wheeled when he realized that his partner had been yanked to the ground, and thrust with his spear towards the hooded figure. A large hand grabbed onto his ankle and twisted violently while reeling him in. The Snake warrior let out a momentary scream over the sound of cracking bones, but was quickly muted when a large stone held in Mokotak's other hand pounded his face fatally inward. The hooded figure quickly grabbed a hammer from one of the Snake guards, and shattered one of the brittle iron links in Mokotak's chain. Mokotak limped around momentarily as his feet and legs lost the numbness that had set in so long ago. Another hooded figure appeared from out of the shadows and began to cut away at the ropes around the slaves' arms. The sound of iron against iron tinkled painfully loud in the cold, silent darkness enveloping this outcast portion of the city, yet chain after chain was shattered, despite the danger of being heard.

Sequannah held back a scream of pain when he fell forward as the ropes on his wrists were cut—the chains were still wrapped tightly around his legs. There was no time to free the slaves safely. The ropes were cut, the chains were broken, then on to the next. Those who were unable to follow at least had the opportunity to flee. Sequannah's legs had not yet suffered from the cold numbness that eventually caused the deaths of most rebels tied to the cross. The slave that had been yanked out of the mine with Sequannah screamed wildly from his perch, unwittingly covering their escape. His constant scream was expected. The others, however, had to get out of the city before the whole of the Snake warrior contingent tired of listening to the screaming fool, and decided that the other slaves had sufficiently learned the kind of punishment that was inflicted upon those who rebelled against Quiktkoata's empire.

They ran along the winding shadow of the great earthen serpent, then raced northward through the dark passages of the slaves' quarters. They waded into one of the ditches separating the fields that had been cut down close to the ground during the harvest. A whiff of the fish pile caused Sequannah to hesitate. "Mokotak! Mokotak!" he strained his whisper. "There is another slave we must free!" he pleaded.

"There is no time! We will be seen if we get out of this gully," Mokotak returned unemotionally.

"Tarote must be freed as well," he said as he crawled out of the smelly ditch.

Mokotak grabbed onto his foot. "You will come with us."

"Tarote's father is a powerful Sikun from the sacred city of stone," Sequannah pleaded. "More powerful than Quiktkoata."

"How do you know this?" Mokotak asked hurriedly.

"She is here by her own choice. There are no other women forced to work the fish pile," he insisted. "When her father comes, she will give him the information to put an end to Quiktkoata and his people."

"If she can do this, then she can find her own way out of here," Mokotak decided. "There is no way to determine if she tells you the truth."

"You can be certain that I have told the truth," a soft voice interrupted. "But you must get out of here now! Do not worry about the snakes; no one could ever see to follow them, and they search only for rats at night. Follow this ditch to the end, then stay in sight of the river as you go northward, but do not go too close—there are Snake warriors all along its length."

"You're not coming with us?" Sequannah asked incredulously.

"My father and I will remain here until it can be arranged for us to be moved north to Quiktkoata's other city, where the copper and iron are mined, and turned into weapons and objects of greed."

"Better if you returned to your home," Mokotak said. "We will help you get there. Minnecou travel fast and know many trails."

"No one is safe when a Washan like Quiktkoata is in power," she warned. "It will only be a matter of time before he will rule all of those he has not killed. My father and I must find a way to stop him. The other Washans will send whatever help they can."

"You cannot cross back over the river except for one place," Tarote warned them," and if you should choose to go back to your people, I must demand that you not attempt to cross back here. If you choose to help us, then you will not be able to contact your clansmen until we are through here, no matter the outcome, because we need this crossing place in the event that escape should become necessary. If Quiktkoata or his warriors should discover it, we shall be cut off from any outside contact. We will take you to a safe place where you can decide which way you will go. If you are still here when we head north, then you will be coming with us. Go and catch up with the others. The one with the hood is Semmida. He will lead you safely away from here. You will soon learn to feel safer with him than with your own clan."

"Who leads this war party?" Mokotak questioned. "You or your father?"

"I lead until he is familiar with everyone involved in destroying Quiktkoata's empire, and knowledgeable of how our people can gain control. Many of the Snake warriors are also with us, as well as Quiktkoata's followers. Now go or you will be caught and staked down in the fields."

"A Minnecou warrior does not live under the rule of a woman," Mokotak sneered. "Your father will have to lead if I am to follow,"

"When we need you, my father will lead, now go!" she said without a hint of becoming offended.

"Move!" Mokotak pushed Sequannah ahead. But as

Mokotak began to follow, a loop of rope drifted over his head. He turned, and the cold metal of a copper knife slipped sideways through his lips, past the line of his teeth.

"I am very capable of handling myself as a warrior," Tarote whispered through her teeth.

Mokotak bit hard into the soft metal, and yanked the knife away from her with his teeth as he jerked the rope and forced Tarote to fall into the muck at the bottom of the ditch. "We shall see," Mokotak grinned. She took this as a sign that Mokotak had in fact already made his decision to stay.

CHAPTER 13

Ketanka posed solemnly near the top of a knoll, scanning the barren plateau that had been stripped by the three raging funnels. Piles of debris formed a jumbled wall that would remain for years. The few leaves remaining on the felled trees had curled into tiny brown rattles in the stiff breeze. Outside of the devastation, the yellow leaves of autumn drifted by on northwesterly winds, scooting over the terrain as they landed within the barren stretch. Tiny clumps of green grass had begun to dot the lifeless area, but the unbroken winds had already sifted the grains of sand from the gravely surface into tiny, shifting dunes. A lone coyote caught Ketanka's attention as it meandered over the desolate landscape, sniffing into every crag and pile of leaves that had managed to gain a foothold, in search of quarry that would have little chance of escape in this open area. But sniffing was all the coyote had managed to accomplish, and as it continued to scour the terrain, Ketanka could see that it was still on an empty trail.

Since they first reached the foothills of the Dark Mountains, the moon had changed from a mere sliver to a distant pink globe in the crystal, pre-dawn sky. Both Paccu and Minnecou hunters had found more game than they had expected, and nearly everyone donned freshly tanned hides, while stores of dried meat hung on racks so plentifully, they nearly had enough food for the winter. The Paccus had dug into the ground to escape the biting cold to come, and Ketanka had persuaded the Minnecou to do the same; a prudent step in the event they were unable to return southward.

After a restless night, the chill morning air seemed to

restore the vigor he was slowly losing through lack of sleep. Nearly half a moon had gone by with no sign of Petawahin and the Washan, and Ketanka delayed moving southward without any confirmed knowledge of the Snake people. The Paccus complicated matters even further with constant talk of their huge sister clan. Ketanka realized that if the rumors were true, the small, Minnecou clan would be swallowed up in the presence of even more Paccus, and the food they had gathered in ample supplies would quickly vanish.

Something else was beginning to gnaw at him, though; if the Snake people were aware of the devastation that had visited this area, it would be a simple matter for them to skirt around the outside of the barrier of debris to hunt out any survivors of the catastrophe. The coyote was another reminder, if not a warning. A column of smoke from a small campfire could bring down hordes of eerie warriors, yet the Paccus seemed relaxed and secure. Among them, some spoke of Ketanka as merely fretful, while others secretly rumored that he wanted to move everyone again for the sole purpose of maintaining Minnecou power by removing them further from their sister clan.

As daylight flowed from the eastern horizon, Ketanka witnessed the change of seasons all around him from his position atop the largest hill, overlooking the Paccu and Minnecou encampment. Many of the surrounding trees were becoming bare as their red and golden leaves drifted away in the windy dawn, and Ketanka was all too aware of the camp's increasing visibility. The first signs of movement brought Ketanka back down the hill where he roused the camp into wakefulness with his unusually loud and bellowing voice.

"We move today!" he boomed out. "Everyone up! Prepare to move!" He sought out Tamahna and asked him to go into the valleys of the Dark Mountains and find a place for the band to make a new camp.

"We have held no council meeting," Tamahna declared. "We have lodges that are nearly finished here and still you declare that we must leave?"

"I see coyote crossing the dead land this morning, sniffing in the piles of leaves for something to eat. He hunts here because whatever he should find will have little chance for escape," he answered solemnly. "Look around you. Soon we will find ourselves in a pile of leaves with no place to escape."

Tamahna could see that the changing winds had taken off

many of the leaves overnight. It didn't take very much imagination to envision how vulnerable their camp would be when the surrounding trees were reduced to skeletons. He gathered his weapons, a parfleche of dried meat, and set out immediately after he'd spoken with his family and Mahkawan.

"Ketanka!" Wanachan complained as she hedged the heavy figure. "Why do you still insist on moving when we have already prepared to spend the winter here?"

"I speak to Minnecou, not Paccu. Your people are welcome to do as they choose," he croaked. "But I must protect my clan. I see danger here, and while there may be less game in other places, I would prefer to eat less than to wake up with a spear at my throat."

"My people have already finished building comfortable lodges for the winter," she insisted. "They are not going to abandon them just because the Minnecou were slow to start and their lodges aren't built as well. Some of the Minnecou may have to walk further to find the right materials, but that is their own fault and yours as well for waiting so long to begin preparing for the winter."

"You listen, but do not hear!" Ketanka warned. "If the Snake people come to this area, do you think they will send scouts in the middle of the dead place, where they can see that no one is there...or do you think that they would look on this side for survivors?"

"We can have our warriors watch for them at night and scout for them during the day so that we can escape easily if they should be foolish enough to try and attack us at this time of the year. But there is no need to start building new lodges until we know that these have been discovered."

"What if everything should remain calm for two moons, and then the Snake warriors should suddenly find their way into this area?" he warned again. "How will you dig into the hard ground to build new lodges then? The Snake warriors already have a village to return to, even if they cannot catch you. You will have nothing but robes to spend the frozen moons in."

"Two moons from now, there will be no Snake warriors foolish enough to be out looking for slaves," she insisted. "We will hold a council meeting, but you can be sure that the Minnecou will travel alone," she warned.

Ketanka was not so concerned with the Paccus' safety, though, as he was with that of the Minnecou. Secretly, he felt the

Minnecou would probably be better off without the Paccus; they tended to surround themselves with a false sense of security. They weren't as capable of defending themselves on the trail, or even within their own encampments, and Ketanka had hoped to improve this situation by the spring. He would much rather have been able to reach the other clans in the south, but the risk of his own clan being captured or killed could put the other clans in a position where they would have no one knowledgeable about this area, possibly hindering any escape or defense from this direction. If any of the clans were to be overtaken by the Snake people, all of the Minnecou people could be vulnerable to Quiktkoata's Snake warriors. They were now at their greatest distance from any of the other clans, and although at this point, it would be understandable that they wouldn't have any contact with the others, the fact that they have seen or heard from no one within the other clans throughout the summer, added tinder to the fires of Ketanka's fear.

"Just as you have sent messengers to your sister clan, so will we to ours," Ketanka told Wanachan. "Our best warriors should have returned by now...it is becoming clear that I will have to select from the few I have left. But to remain here could prove to be very unwise. We will leave immediately. We have ample food and have restored ourselves quickly here, but now is the time to give our thanks and move on to a safer place. Whether your people choose to remain here or come along is their own decision. But, I ask that those who wish to follow be made aware that we will not allow them to travel back and forth between the two camps–there will be no trail for Snake warriors to follow! And all Paccus as well as the Minnecou here will destroy their lodges before they leave so that wandering bands of Snake warriors will find no shelter here," he added.

"You wish for my people to continue under your leadership and destroy all of the work they have completed here as well?" Wanachan asked incredulously. "You have persuaded us to follow you this far, but I am afraid that this has come to an end...unless you can become much more persuasive than you have been with me."

"I do not try to persuade your people," he said in a low, restrained voice. "You can put the choice before them or not; we are moving today. But any of those who wish to follow are welcome as long as you make them aware of our wishes."

"I will tell them, but I do not think any of my people will

follow the Minnecou if they will be cut off from their own, much less destroy the lodges they have worked so hard to build when they could be used for storage while they are empty...or a place to return to should they tire of being bullied by the Minnecou," Wanachan said in scorn.

"The Minnecou have forced nothing upon your people," Ketanka's voice cut into her. "We will protect our clan in the best way we know, and if the Paccus wish to follow, they are welcome. But we will not welcome guests who will put us in danger," Ketanka's voice rose. "Anyone who follows must obey our wishes or they will not be allowed to stay. If you want to see what being bullied is, go visit your relatives in the Snake city!"

"You know as well as I that since we have been with the Minnecou, it has been Minnecou leads and Paccu follows," she said. "We are very grateful for having been rescued from the Snake warriors and for having the chance to heal our wounds and become a clan again, no matter how small. But from now on, the Paccus and the Minnecou will either walk side by side or they will find separate trails. I don't know how many other Minnecou clans there are or what you intend to do once you have spoken with them, but you can be sure there will be very many Paccu warriors here either very soon, or after the snow melts in spring. One day they will be here, just as we have always gone to help them. And you can be sure that they are not going to count on Ketanka to make their decisions for them! I am not here with you to speak on behalf of my people, but rather to find out what is going on. But from what the Paccus have been discussing in the last few days, I have already told you how they feel about the Minnecou."

"If you are certain that these warriors will come, then those Paccus who wish to follow and my own Minnecou will not destroy their lodges," Ketanka relented. "Your Paccu relatives will need them if they decide to come before winter. All contact between the two camps will be done with one messenger who will take a different route every time he walks between the two camps. We cannot leave a simple trail for Snake warriors to follow if they should overrun your lodges."

"Now you are talking of things that we may be willing to listen to," Wanachan said, obviously pleased that she had been able to affect this proud Minnecou's disposition.

"If any of your people come along with us and there is time before the ground freezes hard, we will build extra lodges to shelter anyone who escapes in the event that this place is attacked. If we are alone, we will take care of ourselves and the Paccus can do the same," Ketanka offered, realizing that from now on he will have to find a practical reason for the Paccus to remain as their allies other than mere protection. It had become very clear that they were on their feet again and no longer helpless refugees.

* * *

Ceptke was decided. He had watched the Minnecou girl for too long; his heart ached. Even their own women had urged him toward her. But the Minnecou warriors might not feel the same. They watched her every movement.

Twice, he had almost followed her into the forest–his instincts were overwhelming, but his sensibility warned against it. Even one of the Wolf brothers' wives hinted that Shamira liked him. Every time he glanced in Shamira's direction, the one called Wanashta would point with her chin and make eyes to suggest he follow. Once, she even spoke to him: "Shamira sees Seppy."

The dawn was gray with morning fog. Shamira had passed moments earlier; the rest of the camp was still sleeping. Ceptke climbed out of his lodge and followed her moccasin prints along the side of the stream. He knew of a pool, further down, and slipped through the forest to arrive ahead of her.

He got there just as she did, but she continued on. Again, he followed quietly behind, but this time, he wouldn't try to anticipate where she was going. She went on and on around several bends. Ceptke was amazed at how far she strayed from the camp to wash.

Suddenly, her trail disappeared. He could see which direction she'd gone, but her tracks disappeared in the thick leaves. Ceptke looked over the bank of the stream to see if she had followed a smaller tributary. But he could find no other flow. Then, he noticed that in a cove of the stream, where the water should have been calm, the surface was somewhat disturbed. The tributary she found seeped under the bank, bubbling into the stream. He slipped westward through the dense brush, and soon he heard the tumble of a small stream as it threaded through the ledges in the hills to the west.

It was no wider than his own height for most of the way. Ahead of him, he saw a deep cleft in the stone face of the ridge. The stream flowed out of it, and he knew where she'd gone. As he slipped further into the thickets, he heard a loud splash. Then he hurried into the gorge before she surfaced.

The walls were three times the height of a man, winding into an inner chamber where a thin, but loud fall, echoed off the smooth walls. Ceptke found a flat ledge where her clothes were bundled in a neat pile. He watched her bronze body, tight in the chilled water of the pool. When she turned, she focused immediately upon him, her eyes flashing hostility.

Ceptke smiled, thinking that he had merely surprised her. But her expression didn't soften. In a few quick moments, he knew he'd made a ghastly mistake. She would tell the Minnecou warriors, and there would be even further friction with the Paccus. He quickly turned, stumbling along the thin ledge. He lost his footing and hung precariously for several moments before finally losing way and crashing through the surface of the icy pool.

He came up sputtering, his eyes wide with shock from the frigid water. His clothing would be soaked all day. He heard laughter echo off the walls as a spray of water splashed over his head. When he turned, Shamira gave him a haughty look. She was no longer angry. She dove into the depths of the clear pool, her bottom breaking the surface before she disappeared. Ceptke's face was a mixture of shock and joy. He could take no more, and dove in after her.

* * *

The yellow leaves had fallen to the earth and the trees laid bare in the remote valley Ketanka had chosen to shelter the clan for the winter. Ceptke had brought along one Paccu family and two other warriors to help build extra shelters before the ground froze hard. Thin pillars of smoke sifted out of the dome-shaped covers of the mostly underground wickiups; the sun rose later each morning. A thick coat of frost covered every spot of ground with the exception of the round roofs of the submerged shelters. Every direction was laden with the humped scenes of an unending succession of bluish-purple mountains, whose tops were now crowned with the white splendor that would soon find its way into every crag and valley from here to some distant southern location left impassable till spring.

Ceptke stood poised, ready to return to the Paccu camp at the edge of the barren area, slightly more than a day's march to the southeast. The two warriors gave him messages to convey back to others in the Paccu village, most of which appeared to be jokes and insults. The Paccu family slept on in their underground lodge, out of the morning chill. Kwoita popped his head out of his own warm lodge as if he was waiting for someone else to stir before he himself would come out. But he knew the Paccu scout had planned to return today, and his instinct told him that soon the distance between the two villages would become impassable in heavy mountain snow.

Although Kwoita could speak only a very few words in the Paccu tongue, his memory of their sign language was adequate enough to communicate.

-Bring back any Minnecou who should find your camp,- he signed. -They will be looking in that area.-

Ketanka rose from his own lodge to bid the agreeable Paccu a safe journey. "Tell him to make sure that his people know there are extra lodges here if the game has gotten thin there," Ketanka asked Kwoita.

Shamira had just wakened, herself, and came out to see him off as well. She handed him a packet of dried venison along with some nuts and dried berries.

-I have plenty already,- he signed to her.

"Tell him that he may need more if it should snow and delay his journey," Shamira asked of Kwoita.

Ceptke gave her a smile and a nod of appreciation for her concern, then scrambled down the embankment and over the stream. Shamira would have gone with him if it weren't for Meequaw and the possibility of wagging tongues within the clan; she knew things would be much better if she remained with her own. But, she also knew that if Ceptke didn't return soon, she might not see him again till spring. And Quitkwa always seemed to find time to follow her around, looking for attention whenever Ceptke was away. She wished she could find a way to tell the chief's son without hurting or angering him. Quitkwa would always be just a young boy to her until long after she had begun a family of her own.

She kindled a small fire behind a makeshift lean-to that kept out the constant breeze from the prevailing winds. Slowly, the men began to gather around in the chill autumn dawn. Quitkwa stumbled out of Ketanka's lodge and found himself a comfortable corner behind the shelter where he would listen to the morning talk to find out if anyone had planned anything interesting for the day. Shatomi spoke of hunting the elusive white mountain goats before the snow on the higher peaks had become too deep, while the Wolf brothers were discussing the possibilities of finding moose or beavers in the swamps of the valley over the next ridge. Kwoita was talking with the two Paccu warriors who felt that hunting would be a welcome change from digging out more shelters. But they were talking about hunting wolverine, and discussing tactics for trapping the vicious carnivore that would sometimes wander twice the distance that a warrior could travel in the course of a day. The fur was what they were after; they could use this to keep their faces warm without any frost building up on it during the truly frigid days. Every other type of fur becomes caked with ice from breathing. The luxury of wolverine fur can become a necessity on a long hunt.

"I'll go with you," Quitkwa volunteered as Kwoita explained to the other Minnecou what he and the Paccus had planned for the day.

"Too many!" Kwoita waved him away. "I had to spend too much time just to get them to let me go along. I am almost one too many!" he said as he walked off towards his lodge to fetch some trail food and his small bow.

"Shamira!" Quitkwa turned back towards the shelter. "Shamira! You like to hunt. Come with me and we'll get plenty of wolverine furs. The Minnecou will need them. Those two Paccus will steal every shot from an old grandfather like Kwoita."

"I am old but I am not deaf," Kwoita yelled back across the camp. "I am not going to hunt, but to observe. I take my bow for protection or in case I have the good fortune of stumbling into something worth shooting, but I am still too quick even for you to steal one of my shots," he said defending his hunting prowess, while at the same time relieving any obligation to match the Paccus'.

"I cannot go today," Shamira answered in feigned lament. "I must help to gather wood for the winter before the snow falls and covers the dead and dry wood on the ground."

"Then I will go alone," he declared.

"Oh, no!" Shamira protested. "Why don't you go with Shatomi?"

"He wants to hunt for the white goats. I want to get wolverine fur for all of us," Quitkwa said.

"The Wolf brothers may need someone else along," she prodded. "Especially if they find moose."

"I am not looking for someone to let me walk behind them. I am going out to get the furs we will need," he stated.

Quitkwa left Shamira alone behind the windbreak, staring into the fire, and went to find his weapons and extra furs to wear for the day's hunt. While he would normally anticipate the day to warm up, he had no idea to what heights these wolverines would bring him. He had followed their trails before; these tireless hunters would climb straight up and then back down the highest of mountains in their relentless search for food. As he prepared to set out, he realized that Shamira was not going to send him off with the same concern she held for Ceptke. He had seen looks passed between them; looks that that gave him pain in his chest and stomach. Often, Shamira's chores seemed to take her far from the new village. Then Ceptke would be nowhere to be found.

He went back to his mother's lodge to get a few pouches of dried meat and berries. When he returned, Shamira was gone. He shrugged indifferently rather than admit defeat, then trudged over the smaller hills to the northeast.

The air remained chilled and crisp till nearly late morning before Quitkwa was able to remove some of his cumbersome garments. But this was because he was steadily climbing in elevation, rather than from colder air blowing in out of the north. Trails of deer and elk meandered the ridge lines of each successive hill, but he was looking for signs other than those presented by hooves. He found the paw prints of wolves, coyotes and those of red and gray fox, but the elusive nature of wolverines, and the difficulty in locating a fresh trail, became a disappointing trial by the middle of the afternoon.

Something in the pit of his stomach had been bothering him all morning, and oddly enough for Quitkwa, it wasn't until late in the afternoon before he realized that he hadn't even eaten any of the food he'd brought, so absorbed was his search for wolverine tracks. The jerky, though, was unsatisfying during this time of year; his appetite became insatiable as the lean months of winter approached.

A snowshoe hare inadvertently moved within Quitkwa's field of perception, and soon roasted on a small fire he'd made for heat as well as cooking in the waning afternoon. A thick, gray overcast streamed from the northwest horizon; the air became still and damp. Quitkwa stared in anticipation at the sizzling meat, when a motion in the corner of his view caused him to turn suddenly.

The distinct and strange lope of a wolverine, far down the ridge, sent Quitkwa scrambling for cover. The elusive creature had scented fresh meat. He crept to a place further up the ridge where he lay in hiding, wondering how close the wolverine would come to the burning fire. But as the animal zigzagged across the open meadows and disappeared into their hidden coves, Quitkwa grew frustrated when it was regularly passing in and out of view and then suddenly vanished. He waited and waited for the wolverine to reappear somewhere near where he had last seen it, alternately watching the burning roast and the surrounding area, in hopes that the creature would make an attempt to raid the seemingly abandoned meal. But the fresh meat turned to ashes before Quitkwa's eyes, while the wolverine failed to reappear.

Quitkwa crept slowly down to the fire to be as close as possible if he should, by chance, flush the wolverine out of the brush, but there was neither sign of the creature nor movement in any direction. His breath became visible in the chill of twilight as he picked strands of rabbit meat from the warm ashes. It was as tough as the jerky; the appearance of his quarry had only served to ruin his meal. He plodded down the hill and followed the wolverine's meandering trail through the amber-colored straw. It wound its way toward the fire, then doubled back at a point where it would have been close enough to pick up the scent of a human. Quitkwa had heard stories of how wolverines would sometimes come right out and fight a hunter for his meal, for lack of experience with the seemingly weak and defenseless humans. They would even take on grizzlies if necessary, but apparently this wolverine had experience with humans, and probably more than once. Quitkwa followed the trail with an increased vigor, hoping to find the animal's den, and perhaps even more furs.

It was nearly dark before he gave up and found a place to settle in for the night. Ketanka and the others would be upset with him for not warning that he might be gone for more than a day, but, he thought, they should expect this when a warrior goes hunting. The jerky and dried blueberries tasted better than they had earlier. He leaned back against a cold stone ledge, somewhat satisfied, then drifted off into a fitful sleep that afforded little comfort in this vast and lonely territory.

He emerged from his pile of robes early on in the next morning, but only after the first rays of sunshine had reached down to his elevation on the eastern side of this lower ridge. The sky had cleared sharply; the thin hazy clouds of the previous evening lay as a coat of fluffy snow over everything within viewing distance. Although the snow didn't even reach the top of his moccasins, the wolverine's trail was now covered. Quitkwa was nonetheless optimistic. Now he could follow the trail of any game he chose, and save even more time by cutting across whenever the path wandered. The morning sun climbed, while Quitkwa found many more rabbit and deer tracks, and the prints of small mammals and little birds, but nothing of the wolverine. Quitkwa became frustrated when the morning sun suddenly burst forth in uninterrupted warmth. Soon, the white fluff turned to a rapidly drying dew on the mostly brown grasses.

He could go on for days, nearly in sight of his quarry, yet never close the gap. Now he wished he'd gone with Shatomi or the Wolf brothers. At least he would have been able to say that the snows became too deep, or that there was nothing in the area, but he knew the wolverine to be somewhere ahead of him; he just couldn't locate the trail. If it was still hunting in a meandering pattern, it might not be far away. But if it had become spooked or decided to move into another area, he may never catch up, even if the trail became clear.

To Quitkwa's good fortune, though, the wolverine reappeared. His heart quickened as he kept pace with the elusive beast: over hills, through thickets and blowdowns, along steep winding trails, but no matter how fast he followed, the distance remained the same. His breath heaved, and his expression drew taut as he struggled to keep up. It almost seemed to be deliberately leading him, staying just out of range to avoid his arrows. The animal had definitely seen him, but made no effort to lose the human on his trail. In fact, it seemed as though it had slowed its pace to match his own.

Quitkwa followed all morning long and into the afternoon, quickening his pace in countless efforts to catch up with the luring animal, but always finding himself at the same distance. He saw the wolverine more than a dozen times, and had to stop twice to remove more robes as they descended into the lower elevations. The hills became less steep as they raced relentlessly eastward, but the peaks afforded more limited views as hunter and prey blazed their way out of the Dark Mountains.

The air from below began to emit a strange scent, foreign to anything Quitkwa had ever known. As he followed the wolverine over a particular ridge, the whole valley was engulfed in a thin haze of stagnant smoke. The burnt smell, however, was not that of wood or grass, but rather a volcanic odor. There was nothing in his view to cause such a strange phenomenon, nonetheless he followed the ridge southward in the event there were unknown dangers lurking below. Some distance away, he spotted the wolverine heading northward along the same ridge line, and though he had nearly forgotten about the animal, this reminder served to steer him north instead.

The wolverine led even further into the foul haze, then vanished. Quitkwa wavered over finding the source of the smoke, when he spotted a pile of brush some distance down the slope; possibly where the wolverine's den was located. A rustling from within told him that he'd finally cornered his quarry. Knowing this to be an extremely vicious and dangerous creature, especially when cornered, he crept slowly towards the lair, allowing a small avenue of escape where his arrows would pin the swift animal to the ground as it made a run for its life. A faint whimpering from the direction of the woodpile suggested the presence of offspring. Quitkwa crawled further down to get a better look; his bow at the ready. He saw a hint of fur, and ducked aside to avoid being seen. He knew he'd have to flush the animal out eventually, but he wanted to make sure that he'd covered every avenue of escape before he made any sudden movements. A twig caught on his clothing resulting in a sudden snap. The animal merely twitched, but neither stirred nor looked in the direction of the intrusive noise.

Quitkwa dared to move further down the slope until the animal was in full view. It was licking itself, apparently unaware of the human only steps away. It panted irregularly. Upon closer inspection, Quitkwa could see that this was not the animal he'd been following at all. It was a wolverine, but its fur was patched with sickly looking mats. The animal glanced at Quitkwa, motionless and inoffensive, staring listlessly ahead, and awaiting the final moment. A slight, moaning whimper confirmed there were no offspring in hiding, only the sounds of suffering. Further down the slope, Quitkwa caught sight of a small and winding brook, tainted red. The air was foul in this strange valley and the water as well. When he looked back, his eyes must certainly have deceived him—a pile of bones and matted fur lay where he had last seen the sickly looking animal. After hearing no sound, he ventured towards the lair and kicked the branches away. The den was empty. The carcass had withered under many moons.

He followed the stream in the direction of its source and was confronted with the strange sounds of metal, scraping and pounding against stone, over a din of hollering voices. Words as foreign as the ringing metal implements, were harsh like the growl of a grizzly. The oddest looking humans he'd ever seen stood in tyranny over a massive group of swarthy slaves, some of which he recognized from the many different, local tribes. The slaves tore feverishly into the earth in search of unknown treasure, while the husky, pink-skinned humans screamed out in their foreign tongue. Their faces were hairy; light-colored hair hung haphazardly in long greasy strands. Their arms and hands were layered in dirt and grease, the remnants of a thousand gorged meals.

Scattered throughout the area were hundreds of Snake warriors. Across the valley, many small mounds billowed thick smoke into the air as slaves shoveled black stones and wood into their openings. They poured baskets of green rocks and dirt into basins on the tops of the mounds, then watched the ore melt into a pool. Quitkwa could perceive the faint glow from his hidden position atop the ridge.

The slaves on the valley floor scraped green rocks off of the stone ledge, and loaded them into baskets. Others dug channels into the finished areas, then scorched them with an inferno of wood and coal to make the underlying ledge red hot. The small canals were then flooded with cold water, which in turn caused the ledge to crack with the sudden change, allowing the slaves to dig into the veins of copper more easily.

Quitkwa couldn't perceive the changes that had taken place here. The broad, flat area was once a natural part of the surrounding area, being made up of several large hills. But they were rendered flat through the constant tearing of earth and ledge, to the point where it now looked like an ancient valley, whose floor should be braided and criss-crossed with an equally ancient river.

Many square, wooden structures stood on the distant side of the artificial plateau. Quitkwa couldn't even guess what these were used for, other than maybe to house the many hundreds of slaves and pink-skinned humans, but there were strange activities conducted in and around some of the largest of these structures. One was a bustle of activity, with slaves running in and out carrying baskets of moist earth in, dusty dry earth back out. Some toted strange looking wooden carvings, used to cast a multitude of molds. Large ladles of molten metal hung from hooks in the center of long poles that were in turn hoisted on the shoulders of pairs of sure-footed slaves. But, every so often, Quitkwa would see one of them stumble. The splash of molten metal would cause them to scream out in pain and terror, then drop the heavy ladle to the ground where it would pop and sizzle and sometimes explode.

Several of the smaller wooden structures were involved in the same function. Dense, black smoke began to erupt from one of them, then flames appeared, quickly shooting high into the air. Dozens of slaves scrambled out, running back and forth to the soiled stream with large clay pots filled with water to throw on the fire. Far across the valley, new slaves were being driven down to the village by a party of Snake warriors. Their whips and shouting could be heard even over the tumult on the valley floor. One particularly large slave reminded him of his cousin, Mokotak. The manner in which he walked, towering proudly over everyone around him, was instantly recognizable, but then he suddenly stooped, shuffling along with a limp. The hood draped over his head concealed his identity.

Quitkwa took a few short steps towards the valley floor when two arrows whistled by his face. He quickly spun—three Snake warriors were nearly upon him, shouting for other Snake warriors to take up the chase. But the clamor surrounding the burning shack and the raucous Snake warriors driving the new slaves, caused their cries to go unheeded. Quitkwa bolted up the ridge and back towards the west. The three Snake warriors separated; one followed directly behind, while the other two scrambled to intercept him at different points along the top of the ridge. Quitkwa lost sight of the other two warriors, perceiving only the one behind him as he discreetly eyed the edge of his vision. Arrows hissed lethal threats from every direction; he became disoriented; escape had eluded him. Dozens of arrows issued through the thin branches, while sudden movements flickered everywhere in the brush; he was surrounded by many warriors. He crept to a defensible position, determined to kill the most Snake warriors before they inundated him.

It seemed he confused the Snake warriors though, for they shot at each other, leveling few arrows in his direction. He heard screams of pain as they scrambled over the top of the ridge, and he laughed to himself as the other Snake warriors killed all three of the Snake warriors who had first spotted him. He lay still in the small clump of brush cedar, listening to the Snake warriors as they tramped around in search of him; the fighting had ceased. He crouched there half smiling, yet half in fear that he would never slip away without one of these Snake warriors spotting him from some hidden place amongst the brush. The branches in front of him suddenly parted–his heart stopped in terror as the face of a Snake warrior thrust to within a hand's width of his own.

"Where is the rest of the clan?" came the familiar whisper of the Washan.

Quitkwa pointed a trembling finger westward as he collapsed to the ground in relief. "I thought you were a Snake warrior," he gasped. "Why are you wearing Snake people's clothes?"

Petawahin suddenly appeared, throwing a heap of garments from the dead Snake warriors at him. "Put these on now or you'll learn quickly," he warned.

Quitkwa threw the clothing on as Petawahin hurried him along. No other Snake warriors were near them and Quitkwa was beginning to take offense at Petawahin's pushing. "It would be easier if I could do this without running," Quitkwa complained. "I don't see any more Snake warriors around."

Petawahin pointed in the distance. A large hawk circled over the warriors and slaves in the valley. "One of the strange hawks that followed the clan," Quitkwa casually observed. "They are a nuisance to the Snake people as well," he determined.

"They are scouts for the Snake people," Petawahin was terse. "They have followed the clan?" he demanded. "Then the Snake people know where our clan is. We must warn them or they will all be killed," Petawahin became frantic.

"We did not see them after the big storm," Quitkwa tried to calm Petawahin.

"They may have been watching from a distance where you could not see them," Petawahin warned.

"No!" Quitkwa was adamant. "After the big storm, there was no place for them to hide. All of the trees and plants were torn out of the ground and blown away. Even the grasses were gone. Nothing left but sand and stone."

"Clan gone too?" Petawahin asked, his eyes cast in fear.

"Ketanka brought us to the Dark Mountains," he said. "Paccus remain in the small hills next to where the earth is now barren."

"How did the clan stay on the ground when even the trees and grasses could not," Petawahin questioned. He remembered the power he had seen in the three funnels when they raged towards the clan; his fear that Quiktkoata had concocted this mysterious power was now confirmed.

"We followed a strange antelope to a valley of white cliffs where we hid in a cavern...under the water."

"A valley of white cliffs? A mysterious antelope?" the Washan questioned. "You must bring me to this valley. You remember where it is?" he spoke more in demand than question.

"I know where it is," Quitkwa replied hesitantly. "But if I try to find it, there will be nothing there."

"Then you know nothing," Petawahin sneered.

"He knows that the mystery is with us," the Washan declared. "No one will ever find the valley of white cliffs unless the antelope takes them there. The Creator protects us or the clan would no longer be. If you could have shown me this valley, it would have been just another valley...just good fortune on the part of the clan. The Creator has much for us to do but we must do things in the Creator's way, not just in the way that would be best for us, or we will be abandoned to the wolves."

"We must protect the clan," Petawahin tried to clarify the Washan's words.

"We must protect the clan, the Paccus and even the Snake people if that's what the Creator shows us. We will have no protection unless we do what is best for all," the Washan said with finality.

"I will not protect those who would kill my family," Petawahin said indignantly. "Only fools protect their enemies!"

"Most enemies are only a very few," the Washan said. "The rest are the same as you. They only protect themselves and their families. Quiktkoata and his closest followers are your true enemies. We must help those who would do better without him, and those who only live under his rule out of fear. They must know that we are not their true enemy."

"Perhaps we should build them a new village while they hunt our clans down like dogs?" Petawahin said sarcastically. "You know they can't survive without their huge village."

"We must find a way to rid them of Quiktkoata and let their people rule the city they have built," the Washan became irritated.

"You have seen how well guarded Quiktkoata's city is," Petawahin said incredulously. "We could not even get in without being seen by their warriors, or those ugly snakes. We had to stay hidden under the leaves to avoid being seen by the hawks."

"We may find a way into their city through this smelly place," the Washan suggested. "They always send warriors and slaves back and forth between here and the city. We may be able to disguise ourselves as slaves and Snake warriors bringing back the metal weapons and ornaments that Quiktkoata never seems to have enough of."

"Sequannah and Mokotak were brought to this place during the night," Petawahin said. "We should find them and free them, and then get out of here quickly. Anything else we decide to do can be done later, after we know we are all safe."

"I have already told you that the Creator has chosen us to become involved," the Washan warned Petawahin. "If we think only of our own, it will either fail or it will never last. We will be abandoned and left to the wolves. Every path we choose will leave a trail of blood and sorrow until there are no more Minnecou left to roam the trails of our grandfathers. All will be forgotten and replaced with these smelly camps for as far as the eyes can see and the feet can run. We must sacrifice for what we know to be good and lasting or there will be nothing."

"You know the language of the Snake warriors," Petawahin ignored his words. "You said they speak like the people of the stone villages. With these clothes, we could walk among them until we find Sequannah and Mokotak. Then we could lead them out in the night. Once the clan is back together, the Snake people will never get close to the Minnecou again. We know their tricks and their secrets."

"The Snake people, the Paccus, the white ones, the Minnecou...we are all as one body no matter how difficult it is to see," the Washan feigned patience with Petawahin. "Our own eyes cannot look at themselves; they must look elsewhere in order to perceive themselves.

If you walk on the ice for too long, your foot will have no

feeling for you and soon it will become black and feverish. Will you not cut this off in order to save the rest of the body? When you cut this off, will you not protect all of the body, especially that which was closest to the blackness and fever? So it is with Quiktkoata and his people."

Petawahin perceived that no matter what words he stood on, the Washan would kick them out from under him. He didn't like these Snake people, and perhaps the Washan was right. Maybe they should find a way to take the power away from Quiktkoata, instead of hiding from them.

"Quitkwa," Petawahin suddenly turned to him. "How far to where the clan is now if we hurry?"

"Maybe two days if we run," Quitkwa estimated.

"How many Paccus are there at their camp?" Petawahin asked.

"It is difficult to say," Quitkwa answered. "Some Paccus came from their sister clan and many more were supposed to follow. Whether they have gotten there, I cannot say."

"How far to where the Paccus are camped?" Petawahin kept demanding more information.

"From the clan's camp it is about a day's walk. From here it is probably the same distance as the clan; two days run," Quitkwa determined.

"Ketanka does not intend to head south at this time of the year, does he?" Petawahin continued.

"We dug lodges into the ground to stay for the winter, and built more for the Paccus if there is not enough room at the Paccu camp," Quitkwa answered.

"Quitkwa, you return to the Paccu's now, and find the old woman. Find out how many warriors they have ready to fight and bring them to where the clan is staying. Tell Ketanka that I will wait here with the Washan for five sunsets, and try to get Sequannah and Mokotak freed from the Snake warriors. We will find weakness in these strange people. Before dawn of the sixth sunrise, you will return to the bottom of this ridge, where you will be out of sight of the Snake warriors. Ask Ketanka to send as many warriors as he can with the Paccu warriors, and we will find a way to destroy this village," Petawahin ordered. Quitkwa looked to the Washan, but the Washan stared solemnly through him, neither agreeing nor disagreeing with

Petawahin. Petawahin may have twisted the meaning of his words to obtain more support in the event that Sequannah and Mokotak could not be reached. In either case, however, there would be warriors here to confront the Snake people. "Go!" Petawahin demanded. "And don't let the hawks see you. Hide in the leaves when you hear their call, and keep your eyes to the sky and hills. Make sure the others hide well when you return or there will be an army of Snake warriors waiting to ambush you."

The snap of a branch caused the three warriors to spin northward, then freeze their movements. A white headed eagle flew swiftly away through a cloak of soft white pine. Quitkwa and Petawahin looked to the Washan. "Not evil," he assured them.

Quitkwa disappeared swiftly and silently over the ridge to the west; Petawahin was amazed that he hadn't mentioned food. The Washan maneuvered himself back up the eastern side of the ridge to watch the village; Petawahin followed. The large hawk was soaring down the valley, occasionally screeching. It hadn't seen anything amiss; it would have been screeching incessantly and much louder as it flew in tight circles over its enemy. The great hawk suddenly dove, knocked a small child down with its beak, then seized the kicking bundle in its claws. The fierce raptor soared slowly down the valley in the direction of Quiktkoata's city, its treasure securely grasped. A woman ran screaming and crying from one of the wooden structures, but everyone ignored her pleas as if nothing had happened.

"We must bury the dead Snake warriors while the hawk has not seen them," the Washan whispered.

"And then we will hide till nightfall," Petawahin added.

"No!" the Washan declared. "If we wait till nightfall, the Snake warriors will not be able to see us...they will speak to us...and demand answers. If we go now, they can see that we are Snake warriors and we will only have to give their sign and keep distance between us."

"You know their language from the stone city?" Petawahin questioned.

"I know the language of Quiktkoata and the Snake people, but these warriors speak in a different accent which I cannot always imitate," the Washan returned. "But even if I know their language, you don't."

The two Minnecou hid the dead bodies of the Snake

warriors carefully so that the wind would not inadvertently blow the leaves off of them. Then they headed down into the valley, several paces apart. They crossed over the red muck that once was a clear running stream, and stood at the edge of the large open area separating them from the village on the valley floor. The Washan turned slowly from time to time, scanning the horizon, and pretending to signal another Snake warrior hidden at the top of the ridge; they had killed three of them. Petawahin imitated the Washan, while keeping a vigilant eye for his son and Mokotak. They remained in these positions until all of the slaves were led off the ledge at sunset.

Snake warriors began to filter out of the surrounding forest and down onto the valley floor, as a large contingent began to form near one of the wooden structures. Petawahin and the Washan were still in plain view and waiting for an opportunity to find their way into the village, when the contingent suddenly began to move in their direction. They glanced at each other, knowing they had only moments to decide whether they should run, or stay in their positions, hoping that the Snake warriors would pass without incident. As the party drew closer and closer, Petawahin realized that while they were each debating whether to stay or run, the time had already passed for them to escape. Even if they had made an attempt, they would not necessarily have been successful, and would also have alerted the whole valley that there were enemies among them, making it impossible to rescue Sequannah and Mokotak. As the contingent approached even closer, many of the warriors began to focus on the two Minnecou garbed in Snake warrior's clothing. They both sensed something was expected of them. They looked at each other once again, desperately wishing that the other would remember what it was, as the yipping party of Snake warriors moved within lance throwing distance of the hopelessly outnumbered Minnecou.

CHAPTER 14

Mokotak and Sequannah followed Semmida along the length of the ditch for some time before they turned abruptly northeastward and out of the cleared fields surrounding Quiktkoata's city. The new moon provided little light and the three figures were virtually invisible as they slipped quietly into the forest. A mist rose from the fields as the air chilled sharply; autumn was nearly upon them.

"Why are we being taken in a different direction than the others?" Mokotak wondered aloud to Sequannah.

"They are too fearful of Quiktkoata to be of any help to us," a thickly accented Minnecou tongue returned from the hooded figure. "Quick! We are in danger. If any Snake warriors see us, they must be killed before we can return to the others, or they will follow us and tell of our location."

He led them along a jagged path, steadily rising as it traced the perimeter of a series of hills. At a certain point, they climbed straight up and perched quietly under a small overhang. From here they could see Quiktkoata's city as it became quickly illuminated with hundreds of torches. Snake warriors scoured the myriad alley ways, overturning everything in their paths in a frantic search. The three fugitives listened to the faint yelling and screaming of those leading the hundreds of Snake warriors in the distant night. Soon, all of the fields were covered with wandering torches, roaming along the perimeter of the forest for clues as to where the bold slaves had made their escape. Though they couldn't see clearly, the three escapees knew that, by now, the fields were swarming with thick, black serpents, while Snake warriors tried desperately to keep up under flickering torch lights.

A clatter from up the path clutched Sequannah's heart; his ears thumping in terror. Mokotak tensed. Dozens of Snake warriors suddenly rushed beneath them. The faint tinkling of metal implements forewarned their approach. They raced through the forest, down towards the fields, to intercept whatever had disrupted Quiktkoata's city. Moments after the noisy shadows disappeared, the voice from under the hood whispered frantically. "Move! Now!"

Semmida ran swiftly; the two Minnecou could barely keep up. Ahead of them, they heard the ting of metal once again, yet the hooded figure prodded them along in the direction of the oncoming Snake warriors. "Quickly! Move!"

He led them to the edge of a dizzying cliff, leaped out, and caught onto a swaying and flimsy treetop, then rapidly descended its length. "Jump!" he whispered loudly. "Jump or die!"

Sequannah looked up at Mokotak, his face in a doubtful frown. Mokotak scooped him up by the hair and a handful of garment, and tossed him out onto the treetop. He bounced off several branches until his arm hooked over a small, bending limb. No sooner did he grab the branch when the whole tree shook violently under the weight of Mokotak, as he clawed desperately to stop his fall. Sequannah nearly lost his grip as Mokotak swept past him, bouncing down the tree. When Mokotak finally clasped onto a branch capable of holding his weight, they could hear the Snake warriors approaching the edge of the cliff, towards the sound of the snapping branches. They clung silently to the tree as the Snake warriors strained to see through the dense pine boughs for any movement below. Sequannah's hands were covered with sticky pine sap, and the pains from his scrapes began to burn. He wasn't in as much pain as Mokotak, he thought to himself, yet not even the slightest of groans erupted from beneath him. Two arrows whistled through the branches. The Snake warriors leaned far over the edge, searching for movement, when one of them slipped. Another grabbed onto his foot and several others strained and grunted until they finally pulled the petrified warrior back over the top of the cliff. They lingered for several more moments, but still there was only silence below them. After letting several more arrows loose, they abruptly turned back towards the path, convinced that perhaps the noise had come from a different direction.

The two Minnecou climbed cautiously down the tall pine until they reached the rocky ground where Semmida had been waiting for some time. "Follow slowly if you must, but do not stumble over the rocks. In some places they will cause a slide. Any Snake warriors nearby will know where to find us. If you run, you will break an ankle or a leg, so move slowly. The Snake warriors will not come this way unless they are certain we are here."

It was a difficult and arduous task to even crawl over the rugged terrain in virtual darkness, especially when they crossed so close to the Snake warriors. Both Minnecou were tempted to run when they heard war parties close by. But even when they moved slowly, they nearly lost their balance several times. Small pebbles rolled under their feet, almost causing them to slip into crags barely wide enough for a leg, yet deep enough to fall suddenly up to the hip. The snake warriors' torches seemed bright enough to illuminate them as they crossed the wide and open area, but by crouching slowly, they never were seen. The sound of running water murmured ahead as they approached a narrow, rushing stream in the middle of the rocky maze.

"Wait here!" Semmida ordered them.

Mokotak and Sequannah crouched between the jagged rocks as they waited for the figure to return. "Will we stay with these people and fight Quiktkoata, or return to the clan?" Sequannah whispered.

"If it is possible for us to return, as they have said, then let us learn how these people plan to fight Quiktkoata, and what they want from us. If it does not seem wise, we will go back to the clan...or the Minnecou villages in the south. The clan must be halfway there by now. But, you can see as well as I that if Quiktkoata is not stopped now, it will be even more difficult later. The Paccus are not the only ones to be wiped out by the Snake people. There are whole nations that are now slaves in Quiktkoata's city, and many of them seem to like it. The Minnecou would never be so foolish as to enjoy living in such filth under the whips of strangers, no matter how much food they give us or how warm they keep us in their strange square lodges."

"I lived in the villages before; even at your age I was still working in the village of our relatives in the south. My mother always lived there, and all of her relatives before her, but my father was brother to Ketanka; always moved with the clans. I know how to live their ways...they work together, to keep the villages strong, the food plentiful, and the people happy. But I will not work to make Quiktkoata stronger. I will live like my father. I knew him like you knew your mother; I was very young when he was killed. I only saw him when the clan returned in winter. I wanted to go with him.

He was killed during my fifth winter, then I had to wait till I was your age before Ketanka would take me with the clan. I know how to work the fields and I know how to work the clay, but to move with the clan is my choice. It is the choice of my blood because it always tells me what is best to do. If we do not defeat Quiktkoata, we will all be forced to live in the villages, whether they are Quiktkoata's or our own. I choose to move because it is my blood. You will choose the same because you know no other life." Mokotak told more to Sequannah than he had ever heard him tell anyone.

Sequannah had only been vaguely aware that Mokotak had not always been with the Minnecou. He considered the strength of Mokotak, then considered his own strength; both his mother and father always traveled with the clan. His view of the villages was one

238

of curiosity about their strange ways and customs, but never a desire to stay. The Minnecou trails always led to a new scene upon which to gaze; a new herd of buffalo to hunt; a new enemy or a new ally; a new river or a new mountain to look beyond for the means to keep the clan going. But to live in a village would be to live like the very old...those who asked the clan to move on without them; they would stay in one place with a supply of food as they waited for their final days to pass.

Sequannah was young, and his feet were restless for distant trails. His whole body told him always to move. Every barrier held treasure for him and his people just beyond. If Semmida had a way to rid the area of Quiktkoata without risking the lives of the clan, he would be willing to stay and sacrifice his own life alongside strangers.

"Follow me!" the hooded one called. Mokotak and Sequannah followed the voice, the sound of rushing water always to their left. They clambered over the rocks, to a place where the hooded figure pulled three round floats out of a deep crag. They were crafts, constructed of several round hoops with hides stretched across them, and a larger hoop on top whose sides were connected to the lower hoop and sealed with pitch. The lower part was filled with air and sealed with stitching and more pitch. "Go slowly with these and learn to maneuver them and keep your balance. They move silently through the water and the Snake warriors will not be able to see us because they sit so low...so don't move suddenly. If you fall out, you may be sucked into one of the holes at the bottom of the river. These are very dangerous because they are wide enough for you to fall into, but too small to fit through on the other end. The power of the water will hold you there until it crushes you through to the other side, where of course you will be dead."

Semmida climbed into his first so that he would be ahead of them to show them where to stop. Mokotak grabbed his and jumped into it from the steep bank, nearly going right through the bottom. He wobbledaround precariously for several moments before regaining his balance. Sequannah quickly jumped into his own before Mokotak drifted out of reach. But he didn't land quite right in the gloomy darkness, and the hoop went straight up on edge, tossing Sequannah off of its side. Mokotak heard the splash and tried desperately to maneuver to where he could grab him. Sequannah suddenly surfaced, sputtering as he gripped the side of Mokotak's craft, while his own raft drifted out of sight.

"Don't let go!" Sequannah tried to keep his voice low. "I can feel the water pulling me down." He held tightly onto one of Mokotak's hands while his other arm flailed desperately at the craft.

"Be careful!" Mokotak warned. "You're going to put both of us in the water!" Sequannah continued to kick and flail.

"Stop, or I'll let go of you," Mokotak warned him again.

"I'm being sucked down to the bottom," Sequannah gurgled.

They drifted around a small bend and Semmida grabbed onto Sequannah as well. "Here is your raft," he said quietly. "You'll be able to get into it easier over here." The craft had drifted to where he had been waiting for the two Minnecou.

"He nearly got sucked down into one of the holes," Mokotak breathed a sigh of relief.

"I don't know exactly where the holes are because it is very dark," Semmida laughed, "but they are not here. This I know. There are only two of them, but I thought it best to warn you anyway."

Sequannah guessed at the expression on Mokotak's face in the darkness, and smiled, knowing that Mokotak would really have wanted him to witness this. Mokotak, however, said nothing in regard to the incident. He was interested in moving out of danger from the Snake warriors. "How far to where we are going from here?" he inquired. Sequannah got into the circular craft and floated alongside the two men.

"It will take us all night to paddle in darkness, but it is only a short distance from the stream's edge once we reach there. There will be plenty of food when we arrive and you will be able to rest for as long as you need. There is much to do, though, once you are rested. By the time the moon is full again, there will be no time for any sleep. Take advantage and rest until then, because after that, if you choose to join us, we will be in among the Snake people again," the rebel explained, throwing his hood back.

"Why do you help us to escape if you intend for us to go back there again?" Mokotak demanded. "Why didn't you just tell us of your plans and hide us some place in the city?"

"We had to get you both out of there because you were tied to the crosses. When the Sikun's daughter was informed, she demanded that your friend be freed. When they tie you to the cross, that is it. If you live, they give you one more day to work for them...if you show no promise or they don't like you, they tie you to the cross again and throw water on you until the ropes shrink...tight enough to make your hands and feet turn black. Then they let you rot there until they need the cross for someone else. Tarote learned that the High Priest has an unusual dislike for this boy through messages from her spies. He very rarely even acknowledges the new captives Quiktkoata brings in, let alone try to kill them. No doubt, Quiktkoata has plans for your friend that anger the High Priest."

"Who is this High Priest trying to kill me?" Sequannah said in disbelief that anyone in Quiktkoata's city would have reason to single him out.

"He is the one in the long black and gold robe who approached you in front of the great hall," Semmida answered. "He would have found a way to kill you without Quiktkoata ever finding out. Everyone knows of his ability to hide things from Quiktkoata, though no one else inside the city can manage to hide anything. When you realize the power of the High Priest, you will be thankful that we were able to rescue you."

"You may have escaped without our help anyway, but that is very doubtful. The way this one snapped that cross will really give them something to wonder about, though. Tarote will be very glad to have you with us. If you had gone any way but the way I have taken you, or the way the other slaves were taken, both of you would have been killed."

"The girl," Mokotak questioned. "Who is this girl who claims to be the daughter of a great Sikun. She is a powerful warrior for a woman, but she could not lead against the Snake people. She says her father will lead but he is a Washan. Washans cannot kill."

"Her father is powerful, but probably not in the way you think of power," the rebel answered.

"You mean he knows the mysterious powers," Mokotak said knowingly.

"He has mysterious power; more than Quiktkoata. But that is for Washans who only want other people to be in awe of them. He will tell you that the only way to gain the true power is to accept that the weakest and most humble are worthy to be served by their ruler. He teaches that those who would perform feats such as no normal man could perform, and then demand to be served, are using trickery. If too many people believe in their power, and they themselves believe, then the power can become real through faith. That is what has happened with Quiktkoata. The Sikun warned his followers, but they stood by their fear and Quiktkoata's power has soared."

"I have seen the power of the snakes," Sequannah said. "There is a power in them that is real. I could not move or even see. I felt like I was a snake that did not know how to move. How could this be trickery if I have never seen or heard of such snakes before?"

"It is as I have said," the man answered. "Quiktkoata and his ancestors from many generations before have bred these snakes for hundreds of years. With their faith and the faith of those who have followed and feared them, the snakes now have the true power. But it is not lasting. Once you understand that the power in the snakes is no greater than the power that the Creator has hidden within you, then you can overcome them."

"Then, these snakes hold no power over you?" Sequannah asked.

"Well, I don't intend to go looking for the snakes to test myself. Even if I had beaten them before, I wouldn't go looking for them because it is very difficult to overcome their power until you have done it several times. If you're not quick enough, you'll find yourself tied to the cross."

"We should continue downstream now, though, if you've gotten better at balancing these craft," he addressed the two Minnecou. "It would be best if we could finish our journey before daylight." The three warriors paddled off with only the stars to illuminate their way.

* * *

Quiktkoata had not been seen in the city since he had returned with the latest group of slaves, though his anger could be felt throughout the empire. His slave guards increased everyone's workload, running about in a nervous frenzy, desperate to appease the cruel one's mood. He had taken to wandering the catacombs located under the great hall, where his snakes bred and wintered. Most of the snakes were dormant by day, hidden in the deepest recesses of the catacombs. At night, they still roamed the empire, consuming the constant replenishment of scavenging rats, and terrorizing any slaves wandering loosely. Often, these snakes would lie at the foot of the crosses on moonless nights, staring at the suffering slaves with their glowing eyes, as if they knew enough to revel in the terror they instilled in these doomed captives whose nightmares would only cease after death. One snake roamed the empire day and night, never resting nor even eating; a snake with a yellow and black checkered stripe down its back: the "eyes" of Quiktkoata. It was often wandering among the catacombs with the cruel one. Sometimes it would become as rigid as wood, and Quiktkoata would use it for his staff, its tongue still darting in and out. It was never known to have inflicted wounds on anyone, but those who were foolish enough to step on it, or deliberately injure it, were greeted with a loud and screaming hiss. Shortly thereafter, the perpetrator would be put to death in the most vile manner. The crueler the punishment, the more pleased was Quiktkoata.

A tall and slender figure had entered the great hall, his black and gold robe fluttering behind as he found his way to the cold, stone steps leading down to the seemingly endless levels of chambers that had been hollowed deep into the earth. When Quiktkoata had first brought his people here, they searched for many days for a small mound, built upon the earth, near to the wide and muddy river. One of the few times Raestar had ever seen Quiktkoata laugh was when they had found this small hill and set the Snake warriors to digging. Shortly thereafter, they uncovered a stone monument with a serpent recessed into it, its yellow and black stripe checkered in shining gold and black onyx. They dug down to the base of the monument where they found an enormous stone slab, resting on top of the soft bedrock below. Quiktkoata instructed them in how to build an elaborate rigging to remove the stone slab. Once removed, the warriors found more dirt and were ordered to remove this as well. They dug down to three times the height of a man, where the dirt began to pour into a side chamber. Quiktkoata sent them down with torches, ordering them to investigate. They roamed the catacombs for only a very short time when they came rushing back to the opening, clambering over one another as they tried desperately to climb up the monument and out into the light of day.

Quiktkoata laughed deep bellowing laughs as each soldier came scrambling over the edge of the dug hole, their faces distorted in terror. They had gone through several of the dark chambers, adorned with strange stones and mosaic tiles, creating strange illusions on the floors of these rooms. When they came to a certain room, they could see their torches reflected endlessly in every direction, and from every corner of this ancient catacomb, thousands of black snakes came oozing through the cracks in the walls and floors; some tiny and wriggling, while others were huge, thick and black, swaying their heads back and forth as they loomed closer and closer. They had seen Quiktkoata's snakes before, but never in such appalling numbers, and never in such an enclosed area without the presence of Quiktkoata. The huge and glowing golden eyes radiated evil and terror; one of the warriors slumped lifelessly to the floor of the chamber. The others bolted in panic, jumping on and over the hissing floor, desperate to find their way back to the opening. Quiktkoata laughed hardest when one of his bravest warriors came screaming out of the earth.

He ordered them to build the great hall over the entrance. Everyone joined in with the warriors so as to appear to be working with all of their heart in the quest of building Quiktkoata's new empire. The promise of great wealth and power drove them even harder, for his empire would eventually cover the earth in every direction, beginning from the great hall, and spreading outward. Their children for generations into the future would share in the power and glory of Quiktkoata's empire, and those who chose not to follow would do their bidding, or be eliminated from the earth. The prophesies had always attested to the coming of a huge and powerful empire on this northern continent, and Quiktkoata sensed that the time to begin was now, for he knew himself to be the father of a new kind of people; those who would rule the lower humans just as the lower humans rule the animals. Quiktkoata's empire would rule all living things, and the earth itself would be changed to his liking. His followers and relatives would inherit his power and empire, and all of their subsequent generations would walk the earth with might and glory, ruling every tribe, nation and land on earth.

Raestar descended the steps leading down to the catacombs, and walked unhesitatingly through the maze of haunting chambers, in search of the master. Raestar knew the way, even in total darkness, for sometimes it was best to travel blindly through Quiktkoata's chambers. Especially if he was in a foul mood, for there was no telling what form of beast or vision one might encounter in this colossal underground honeycomb. He carried a torch with him today, however, for Quiktkoata had summoned him after many days of silence...this meant Quiktkoata had finally resolved whatever it was that had weighed so heavily upon him. The three hawks fluttered past him, and from their flight, he could tell where Quiktkoata was now located. He climbed down several levels and found his way to three chambers where he could see infinitely in every direction, each of these a certain distance and direction apart from one another. The third such room led into a great cathedral hall a short distance away. Hundreds of snake heads swerved suddenly in his direction as he entered the hall, swaying hypnotically as he approached. Raestar tensed visibly for a moment, shook off the serpents' spell, then casually walked up to Quiktkoata.

"I pray there is good news for us all," Raestar inquired of his unexpected summons.

"Instruct the Washans to prepare plans for running and securing the empire while half of the warriors are gone. All of the slaves will pack food, weapons and shelters for the warriors to travel, and it will be ready by sunrise in two days. Prepare the white ones to travel as well; I'll not leave them under your watch with all of the warriors that will be gone. They will also help to fight and send terror into the hearts of the Paccus and Minnecou who have never seen such creatures before," Quiktkoata spoke unemotionally.

"It is rather late in the year for gathering new slaves," Raestar noted. "I trust that a new and glorious project has been planned for your grateful followers."

"Neither you nor any of your faithless Washans are yet worthy to question me!" he thundered at the shrinking High Priest. "And you will not be worthy until I allow it. Come into these chambers while I am away and there will be no way to conceal your acts— your bones will litter these floors, and your screams of terror will still echo here when I return. I will haunt you even in the next life as a lesson to the others if you dare to defy me."

Raestar had seen the wall of strange stones' power in the chamber he now occupied with Quiktkoata, though he no longer dared to look at them in Quiktkoata's presence. Quiktkoata had deduced Raestar's ability to manipulate their power, no matter how little his comprehension. Raestar had gazed upon the stones once and pictures of the city of Teyotewakan drifted before him, somewhere between himself and the stone. The scenes were moving as in real life and he almost felt as if he was there, though no one in the scene appeared to be aware of him. Another stone brought scenes of a large and flat, barren plateau, but there was no sign of life in any direction, and the air was becoming so thin as to suffocate him. When he came out of his strange daze, Quiktkoata stood before him, his powerful grip on Raestar's throat. "Do not ever have dreams of coming down here when I am gone," Quiktkoata had threatened him, "And never let your eyes drift to these stones unless I instruct you to do so. I will decide who will inherit my power, and because I choose you as High Priest does not mean that you will even be considered as my successor. Remember, that in order to inherit anything of this empire, you must also be alive. Only those who follow me faithfully will not find their end prematurely." Quiktkoata never allowed him to enter the chambers in his absence after this, and Raestar had not yet found the courage.

"My watchful eyes have discovered a new Paccu village near an area where I have wreaked devastation upon our enemies. They cannot possibly be survivors, but distant relatives to the Paccu slaves we have just permitted to enter our glorious empire at the lowest levels," Quiktkoata informed the High Priest. "They come from many directions, in small groups, to a new village, where the Paccus are building many underground lodges to house the incoming bands. At least one Minnecou was among them, and it is in the best interest of the empire to surround and capture them in the event that the Minnecou has poisoned their spirits against us."

"Perhaps they have heard word of the coming of your glory and come forth to pay tribute to the empire that rules all," Raestar said respectfully. "The power of the coming empire is known in the prophesies of all peoples."

"The are too ignorant and poor to comprehend the wealth and knowledge that is being placed before them," Quiktkoata emitted in a low and steady voice. "Like nearly all the others before them, they must first be made to suffer before they can enter into the empire and share in our great power. But those who take longest to accept the new glory, shall receive the smallest share, and those who refuse shall be eliminated, for order must extend throughout every pathway and trail, and the empire shall expand infinitely and eternally. Those who have had the wisdom to follow me here are on the path to true glory and they shall become the heart, will and spirit of all things in this universe of disarray. My own ancestors have planted the most powerful seed ever known to this world and I am here to bring this seedling to maturity. Each successor to my empire shall find his garden even more easy to maintain. For as in any garden, where snakes will eliminate the enemies of fruition, so shall it be within my own empire. Our strength and reason shall spread to the source and destiny of every breeze and gale, with perpetual harvests of the fruits of this most powerful seed. Many generations from now, when the earth is full and bursting with the fruits of our glorious empire, there will come a time when it shall become necessary to find pathways to other worlds, where this garden shall spread even further, and the whole universe will learn the glory of our empire. I entrust you to maintain this garden, while I am away clearing new fields and plowing the weeds underfoot," his tone changed to one of encouragement. "Go and make preparations for the spiritual and physical needs of our powerful warriors so that they may travel with the necessary comforts and resolve." With just a few words of encouragement, Quiktkoata always accomplished his desires without ever even getting into the details of what he expected. Their fear was enough to prevent them from being neglectful. Even now, the High Priest would ask no further questions of Quiktkoata, but instead go immediately about his task, attending to every possible detail involved in sending out a massive war party that could end up snowbound in some remote place for the entire winter.

As Raestar ascended the stairwell leading out of the catacombs, he passed by several of Quiktkoata's most important warriors, waiting patiently for the information they'll need to plan their initial attacks and find safe routes to bring their new captives back. They bowed their deepest respects to the High Priest as he drifted through the entrance to the stairwell; no one but this man had the nerves of metal that were imperative to even step foot in Quiktkoata's terror-filled chambers. The sounds of flapping wings and a low, powerful hiss erupted deep within the entrails of the earth, from the far reaches of Quiktkoata's catacombs; the powerful warriors tensed as the tyrannical Snake leader came forth to spread his countenance upon the empire. They followed him faithfully as well as fearfully to a large chamber in the upper reaches of the great hall, where two large wooden doors were closed, then bolted securely behind them.

* * *

The citizens of Quiktkoata's city worked at a frantic pace, abandoning their normal labors to prepare every item imaginable for the enormous horde of warriors who would sacrifice to protect the western reaches of the empire. Never had they seen the Snake warriors preparing for battle at such a late time in the season, with the onslaught of winter expected so soon. Many large contingents poured into the city daily, streaming from the constantly expanding horizons of the new and glorious empire. Slaves were busy everywhere preparing goods for travel. They unloaded an unending succession of rafts and barges that were at the same time bringing in the harvests and trade goods from the various tribal villages that now fell under Quiktkoata's domination. There were whisperings in the city that a plague of renegades was gathering somewhere in the outlands in an impossible attempt to assault the powerful new empire. Others told of a new tribe that had wandered into the western hills; Quiktkoata wanted to absorb them quickly into the empire to spare them the suffering of another brutal winter. Still others spoke of rumors that the Minnecou had banded into one nation, and were preparing to harass the glorious people of Quiktkoata's empire.

Quiktkoata's original followers occupied a wealthy, secluded area at the center of the city, where men and women walked the streets and alleyways in fine and beautifully colored feathers, cloth and fur garments. They wore strings of pearls and breastplates of abalone. Men and women alike wore long spooled earrings made of copper and inlaid with precious stones. Splendid gardens and commons were lined with flowers, bushes and trees of all descriptions, taken in from various places throughout the new territory. Many beautiful and rare flowers were brought in from the very remote wetland areas, while common shrubs like flowering laurels and rhododendrons were planted and cultivated in various arrangements throughout the central part of the city. The trees were mainly in the form of saplings, though some were fully matured; nearly all of the flora within the locale was uprooted and slash-burned so that Quiktkoata's empire could begin setting order to the chaotic flows of nature.

Especially gifted artists and craftsmen were allowed to sell their wares in special markets located in convenient areas throughout the gardens. The aroma of fine food constantly wafted through the air from the plentiful dining halls that were constantly preparing food for the elite followers. They would dine at their leisure, any time of night or day.

All other citizens of the city were forbidden beyond the walls and entrances to this exclusive paradise, with the exception of those who were selected and entrusted to maintain the grounds and buildings, and those many workers who were endowed with artistic gifts. They were still hard at work with the completion of this sanctuary–a reward to the men and women who had the wisdom to follow their glorious, though terrifying leader, out of the suppression of Teyotewakan and into the wilds of the northern continent. They had worked long and hard to get this empire started with Quiktkoata and now they had earned a life of wealth and power. Their only responsibilities were to oversee the welfare of the slaves and the planning of further extensions of the city. The new slaves now carried out all forms of the physical work that the inner circle had merely begun. The more each slave contributed to the expansion of the empire, the closer he moved to the inner circle.

There were now promises that all of the new villages that had accepted Quiktkoata's rule would be equipped with such sanctuaries, to be filled with those slaves in Quiktkoata's city who showed promise and loyalty to the empire. The slaves were cutting each others' throats through betrayals and accusations so that they might have the opportunity to leave the fields, mines and fish piles, and enter into the sanctuaries of the countless villages that were rapidly falling under Quiktkoata's dominion. They hungered for the knowledge and ability to run the countless operations involved in the success of the empire with the greatest efficiency. Some worked hard and honestly, for this was their nature, while others schemed constantly and ruthlessly. They knew this to be what would attract Quiktkoata's recognition. The white ones were small in numbers, but they were given their own section of the city as well, and many of the new captive women were brought into their section to keep them complacent.

The white men designed and constructed most of the square lodges within the empire. They were given their own command of a large group of slaves, to instruct in the art of building and laying out foundations. These slaves were also used to perform particularly dangerous tasks as well as all of the menial labor. Although their section of the city was open to all within the empire, few would venture into their quarters unless it was absolutely necessary. The whiteskins would grab any woman they chose from groups of passers-by, beating the men to a pulp if they so much as looked upset about the situation. At night, their section of the city was always ablaze with torches until well into the early morning hours, with strange and loud singing, screaming and violent fights. Quiktkoata often gazed upon their section of the city during their loud and violent nights, wondering how he could instill their ferocity into his own warriors–without the resistance and disloyalty these strange creatures tended to display. Regardless of how he enjoyed their ferocity, a legion of his most fierce warriors, equipped with the new metal weapons, would be sent in from time to time to quell the boisterousness, and to remind them of his absolute authority. Within a short time, the torches would be doused and a peaceful quiet would befall the city.

A fear of these bearded ones still lingered, though, from when Quiktkoata had first conquered them in the mines to the north. He had sent dozens of war parties against them, but their fierce resistance drew terror into the hearts of the Snake soldiers, because they would attack brutally and savagely with strange weapons of metal that had never before been seen. Quiktkoata knew that these were not merely resistors–they were savagely aggressive on a level he hadn't quite anticipated. They seemed to love the many battles that Quiktkoata launched against them, whipping themselves into such a frenzy as to foam at the mouth and scream in wild laughter as they killed ruthlessly and were killed themselves. Many of them were still used in the running of the copper mines, but the majority of them were brought down to the city because they were the only people Quiktkoata had conquered who were capable of working with stone as well as wood. It took a full year for Quiktkoata to finally claim victory over them, and then he had to torture and punish them for many more moons before he could get them to carry out even the slightest of his demands.

Eventually he got them involved in the project of building the great hall, and though Quiktkoata's original followers had only managed to begin the foundation for the structure during all of this time, these hairy-faced people constructed the walls and dome at such a furious pace that Quiktkoata elected to give them their own section of the city, apart from the other slaves. They delighted in the stone work that made the other slaves wince, and seemed to be in awe of the plans Quiktkoata had placed before them. They had only known of simple villages and elusive nomadic tribes on this continent, but to see such engineering skills coming from anywhere in this uncivilized and savage land was an unexpected marvel.

* * *

The captive slaves were scattered everywhere throughout the city, many still in chains and many covered from head to toe in thick, rough-cloth garments. A small amount of the slaves were kept hooded at all times to prevent harm from the spiteful and vengeful Snake warriors. While some of these hooded figures merely had the types of faces that would invoke hatred, ridicule and sadistic torture from the Snake warriors, others were actually disguised because they had been particularly fearsome resistors within their tribes who had killed many Snake warriors. If discovered, they could well have been murdered by vengeful comrades of the fallen Snake warriors. While Quiktkoata wasn't truly interested in the welfare of resistors, he would always respect the fiercest warriors, and take the time to break them of the loyalties they held for their own people. It wasn't difficult. Not even a shred of them existed outside of the empire. It was clear to the whole tribe that they would no longer function as anything but part of the Snake community. Eventually, many of these would be absorbed into one of the Snake warrior contingents, with the exception of those Minnecou warriors who had been captured; thus far, none had become even remotely loyal or trustworthy.

The smallest portion of the hooded slaves were concealed for the purpose of hiding their identities from enemy spies that Quiktkoata knew to be laced throughout the empire. Through careful manipulation, he was often able to spread misinformation into the intelligence of his enemies. Occasionally, some of the hooded slaves were spies under the direct orders of Quiktkoata himself. They would watch the Snake warriors as well as hooded slaves who were suspected rebels. Attack from the self-righteous empire of Teyotewakan seemed inevitable, and Quiktkoata knew there was an underground network passing information along to the south. Yet, even his mystical snake could not detect those involved.

* * *

Sabanote was led in chains to the fish pile. Tarote glanced

up briefly from her basket to survey the new captive who would suffer the misfortune of being assigned to the fish pile. The large Snake guard and the shorter one brutally hammered the iron collar around his neck and each grabbed an arm and a leg, tossing him face-first into the slimy mountain, and laughing sadistically as he struggled to gain a foothold in the slippery mass. Tarote had witnessed the same scene when the Minnecou boy was taken to the fish pile, and this exact duplicate of events immediately raised suspicion. It wasn't the Snake warriors' action that caused her concern, but the new captive himself. He became suddenly bold and resistant to the guards' demands. He destroyed the basket he was handed, and was beaten brutally for his brashness. Only once had she seen this type of behavior in the fish pile, and that was when Sequannah was brought in. Virtually every other slave brought here had a mortal fear of the Snake warriors, and would obey every command to avoid the inevitable death or insanity that followed if the captive continued to resist conformity to the Snake empire's demands. The new captive's ravings were in the Minnecou tongue. After having listened to a true Minnecou, however, she detected a different accent in this slave's tongue. While it was a possibility that he could have come from a different clan than Sequannah, suspicions also arose out of the fact that he was hooded. She knew Sequannah to be trustworthy. He was left unhooded to lure other Minnecou into the empire and to their deaths. Mokotak, huge and extremely conspicuous, was also left unhooded, even though he could easily have been detected, regardless of disguise. Something deep within her told her that this man was not of the same breed, yet his physical attributes and his absolute resolve were a match for those of the Minnecou.

The Snake warriors would have shortened his chain and restricted him to the ledge had the sky not been overcast and the heat more intense, but as it was, they continued to jerk him out, and then toss him back in until he finally obeyed their commands and took to slowly filling the baskets. When the food came around that evening, he was fed just as the rest for he had worked most of the time he was there. But later, if his pace did not improve, he would be left hungry at the end of the day and fed only in the mornings until he kept pace with the others. When the Snake warriors left, and the slaves were confined to the sleeping shack, the new captive kept to himself and huddled into a corner of the square lodge. One of the last slaves to enter the structure looked menacingly into the corner nearest the door, where the new captive sat cross-legged, his knees drawn up to his chin. He growled out an unintelligible complaint, then kicked the new captive deeper into the corner. When the Minnecou suddenly sprang upon the aggressor, the seasoned slave of the fish pile had anticipated this reaction, pulled the new captive's hooded face into the butt of his knee, then promptly tossed him out the door.

The Minnecou quickly shook off the unexpected attack, and rushed back into the door which was simultaneously slammed in his face. He ran around to the side of the square structure to one of the holes that served as a window, and found these to be closed up as well. He kicked furiously at the building, pounding against the sides with his long chains in a desperate effort to draw the arrogant slave out, and avenge the unexpected and unwarranted assault that was dealt him, but several Snake warriors descended upon him. The alleged Minnecou kicked and flailed furiously until he was chained down to the granite ledge in an outstretched position.

"Those who don't get along with their fellow workers cannot be allowed to sleep with them," one of the guards shouted in a thickly accented Minnecou tongue, pressing the palm of his hand into the captive's throat. "I am told to make you learn to work. Again I am cursed with another Minnecou. I should kill you rather then allow another Minnecou the chance to escape. Because of your people I must now work within this stench. There will be no more chances, nor even punishment on the cross. If you do not work, or you do not obey anything that you are commanded to do, expect nothing less than death."

The new captive relaxed his strain against the shackles and closed his eyes, the only part of him that was visible to the glowering Snake warriors. They left him in frustrated defeat on the granite ledge. Towards the middle of the night, the air became quite chilled. When he lifted his head, he could see smoke drifting out of the square structure that housed the other slaves. They had lit a small fire in the pit that was central to the structure to keep themselves warm, while he was left out in the chilled, damp air of the night that filtered upwards from the river. He waited and waited, certain that one of the slaves in the shack would come to comfort him, as they had comforted the Minnecou boy several nights before, and then he would learn their secrets and find out if they were truly involved in the escape of the two Minnecou. As the night wore on and dawn was imminent, he stirred from one of his few naps, staring hopefully towards the small shack, waiting for the slaves to come to him. But as the sky brightened and several rocks rammed sharply against the slaves' quarters, he was shocked into wakefulness and a sense of dread overwhelmed him. His ploy was fruitless. His neck had swollen to the edges of the iron collar; when the Snake warriors unshackled his chains and jerked him to a standing position, his head pounded in fury, feverish. But there was nothing he could do to extract himself from this situation. Quiktkoata had given him strict orders under the penalty of death. No one was to know that a spy was sent in among them, not even the Snake warriors, for they were under suspicion as well. How the young Minnecou had survived such an ordeal suddenly became a marvel to him. The strength of these warriors sent a terror through him almost as powerful as that of Quiktkoata when he realized what kind of human beings were said to be terrorizing the empire—especially after hearing of how the large Minnecou had managed to snap the heavy wooden beams of the cross, and knowing what the young Minnecou, who was little more than a boy, had survived without complaint.

Everyone was thrown into the pile; their stacks of baskets lined up at the edge. They filled them quickly to have everything ready for the other slaves who would be carrying them out to the fields. Sabanote worked to the best of his ability, but the Snake warriors maintained their animosity, and he feared he was in for much more retribution than the previous day. He knew that if he at least made his best attempt at trying to obey their commands, they would not kill him, but they would punish him endlessly if he didn't do his share of the work, regardless of his physical condition. His head reeled with each movement, and the collar was beginning to cut off his wind from the swelling of the bruises. A small amount of relief came when the baskets were full and they awaited their morning meal. But the smell of the approaching food suddenly caused his stomach to turn. He retched horribly, while the other slaves ignored him, complacently picking at their morning nourishment. The collar tightened dangerously with each heave—he became dreadfully aware that he may lose consciousness—but the retching stopped and a relief and calmness began to return. He heard the soft, sweet voice of Tarote as she comforted and encouraged those slaves around her, and he remembered the gentle tone of those that he and the rest of Quiktkoata's followers regarded as enemies. These same people who were supposed to have been oppressing Quiktkoata and his followers from achieving their true potential, had achieved much higher abilities through their capacity to endure the suffering of hardships as well as excess.

A sudden allure and comfort found in the voice of Tarote caused him to adore this woman, despite the fact that she had ignored all of his suffering thus far. Perhaps she was already well aware that he had been planted there as a spy. Whether he tried to endure these hardships, or admitted to the Snake guards that he was a spy, he would find death in either instance. The Snake guards were behind the shack, loathe to hear even the chatter of slaves as they slopped down their morning meal. Sabanote took the opportunity to drag himself to Tarote's feet.

"Listen to me closely," he beckoned with his feeble voice. "I am a spy for Quiktkoata. I know that you do not trust me and with good reason. You are probably already aware that I am not Minnecou, but I beg you to listen to me for I have nothing to lose. I can see now that I will die here no matter the outcome, except with the grace of your mercy. I cannot endure the illness and infection that has overtaken me as long as I am sentenced to stay here in this filth and torture. Neither can I take refuge with the Snake guards, for Quiktkoata would put me to death if I am discovered. You can see that I have only death and your mercy as my fate. Sometimes it takes the push of death to bring a confused man to his senses. I beg you to have pity on me."

"I am but a poor slave girl who has been separated from her family," she answered meekly. "But perhaps it would be best if we helped the spy of Quiktkoata, for there's no telling what type of punishment will befall us for your death," she eluded his implications.

Sabanote fell back with a sense of relief; perhaps he would be spared after all. The Snake guards came back from behind the slave shack and began to unshackle Sabanote. A panic came over him as he realized that perhaps he had confided in the wrong slave. Perhaps Quiktkoata had sent other spies into the fish pile to test his loyalty. But they unshackled the other slaves as well.

"Good fortune for all the slaves on the fish pile," the Snake guard announced. "Today you will all be going to the city to help the warriors prepare for the trail." The slaves smiled with cheers of delight. Sabanote sat brooding, knowing that Quiktkoata was well aware that he wouldn't be working the fish pile for long.

CHAPTER 15

Ceptke's brow wrinkled in confusion as the Minnecou warrior picked his way over the jumbled mass at the perimeter of the barren area. He had seen Quitkwa when he left the Minnecou several days earlier. His sudden appearance alarmed the Paccu warrior– Ketanka had made it clear that he wanted as little travel as possible between the two groups so that if the Paccu encampment was discovered by the Snake people, the Minnecou would not be endangered as well. Curiously, though, Quitkwa approached from an easterly direction, when he should have been coming from the northwest. He must have gotten lost, then had to double back, Ceptke thought to himself.

"Hide your food!" Ceptke laughed. "Here comes a Minnecou who could wipe out our winter stores by himself!"

Many Paccu warriors gaped at the Minnecou who had acquired such an odd reputation for himself, considering his slender form. Quitkwa shrank under the glaring eyes of such an imposing gathering, his superior demeanor evaporating with each step into the mass of Paccu warriors, most of whom appeared much more formidable than any of the other Paccus he'd seen. But, he knew he had to maintain absolute strength; their assessment of him would have much to do with their reaction to his message. And this he carried out flawlessly, for the Minnecou fear was nearly invisible to an outsider. A fearless Minnecou exuded an imposing countenance, but Quitkwa was somewhat daunted in this large gathering of ogling Paccus, and appeared instead, merely a staunch warrior.

Ceptke stepped out to welcome him. Quitkwa flashed the scout's signal that he was bearing a message of importance. Ceptke immediately sent for Wanachan, offering some of the food Quitkwa had scented during the last part of his journey. The Paccus who had previously been with the Minnecou, welcomed him with broad smiles and a sense of genuine friendship that Quitkwa had not anticipated, especially with the scowls they so often wore when they were traveling with the Minnecou. Even the women seemed to take a sudden liking to him, and many of the new Paccu women seemed eager for Quitkwa to notice them. These new Paccu warriors, however, seemed much more powerful and stern. If not for the greetings of the Paccus he'd already known, it would have seemed like an enemy camp.

He devoured the mound of mushed maize that had been set upon the wood of the campfire in just the right place to cook it through without burning the outer crust of the huge biscuit. A ladle of venison stew had a taste similar that of Minnecou cooking: none of the hot or spicy herbs that most of the village tribes were adamant about. The broth had a more meaty flavor, accented with leeks and wild garlic. Quitkwa finished his food hurriedly, then waited patiently for Wanachan to appear. A strange feeling came over him, though, as he sat in this foreign camp. While he was cramming his meal rapidly down to his gullet, the Paccu strangers watched curiously, faint smiles softening their stern faces. After he was through, however, their expressions seemed to drift from eagerness and great expectation, then slowly to a questioning gaze. These are stranger than the first Paccus, Quitkwa thought.

Wanachan zigzagged through the maze of domes that now covered the village, scolding the following children to wait at a distance. She would interpret the Minnecou's message for the mass of Paccus that had surrounded the slender, though muscular young warrior.

"Quitkwa!" she greeted him. "We are happy to have you with us this day. What important message do you carry to your Paccu friends?" The Paccus seemed more amiable, now that they were amongst their relatives and once again part of a village.

"I bring the word of a scout about a village of much importance to the Snake people where many Paccus are now captive. Our Washan and one of our scouts, even now, are searching for weakness within the strange village. They send me to learn if a war party will come from this new Paccu village, and from Ketanka as well. There is need for many warriors as we will have to defeat this Snake village in order to free our people. But we will have to be cautious. They have many scouts and spies guarding the smoky village..."

Wanachan waved him to silence so she could translate before she'd forgotten what he said. The Paccu warriors listened intently as the first words were translated, then began to whoop and holler wildly when they heard news of their captive relatives.

"I have told them that you come in search of warriors to fight and defeat a Snake village where Paccus are being held. As you can see, they are anxious to take revenge against the Snake people," Wanachan gazed proudly upon the gathering war party.

Ceptke demanded to know the location of the village and how far away it was. Wanachan translated Ceptke's demands. Quitkwa pointed towards the northeast, then back to the northwest.

"Three days of fast trails will bring us to the Minnecou camp, and to the valley where we will meet our Washan and one of our warriors." Quitkwa shortened his message so that Wanachan could translate accurately.

Quitkwa had more to tell, but Wanachan rapidly translated Ceptke's response: "Our warriors will be prepared to leave today and we will meet the Minnecou near this Snake village if you tell us the way."

"I was told to take all warriors to Ketanka's camp, where we would make plans to get everyone close to the Snake village without being discovered," Quitkwa countered, concerned that he wouldn't be able to convince them to follow Petawahin's plans.

"It is our people who are held prisoner at this village and it is our fight," Ceptke informed Quitkwa. "The Minnecou have been very brave in helping us to escape, and they are welcome to fight alongside us, but we have many more warriors than you and we will defeat the Snake warriors to free our relatives."

"There are Minnecou captives there," Quitkwa pointed out the concerns his own clan would have.

"There cannot be many," Ceptke reasoned. "And we will treat them as if they are our own," he promised.

"Our Washan and one of our bravest warriors look for weakness within the village, while I have come to gather war parties to fight the Snake people. We must meet with them before any attack will be possible, at dawn in three days. It would be best if we arrived in the night so we could prepare to attack at first light." Quitkwa was growing frustrated at these short translations.

"Would it not be quicker if went directly there, instead of going high into the mountains and then crossing over the many hills and valleys that would steal the strength of our warriors?" Ceptke questioned as the Paccu warriors began to grow loud and restless.

"There are many dangers that the Paccus are not aware of that could warn the Snake people of our approach. A brave Minnecou warrior has told me of how to bring the fighting warriors there secretly," Quitkwa was steadfast.

"Who is this great warrior you speak so highly of that we should follow his every command?" Ceptke inquired arrogantly.

"He is Petawahin, the warrior who freed you and many of the other Paccus here from the Snake warriors after they destroyed your village," Quitkwa said confidently.

"He is the one who's son was captured with Woltah," Ceptke observed.

"Yes," Quitkwa acknowledged. "He is certain that both his son and Mokotak, the tall warrior, are also at this strange village. They were seen with a group of Snake warriors that went from Quiktkoata's city up to the smoky village."

"We cannot allow this to change what is best for us...and what would be best for all," Ceptke declared. "We will go directly from here as soon as we are prepared. The more information you can give us as to where their scouts are and how best to avoid them, the more likely it is that we will arrive undetected."

Quitkwa had Wanachan translate the information regarding the strange hawks, the groups of Snake warriors scattered throughout the surrounding hills, the activities he had seen in the smoky village, and about the strange, hairy-faced humans. The new Paccu warriors reacted with suspicion and disbelief. Ceptke assured them that they had better learn to accept the strange activities and powers of the Snake people as fact, or they would put the whole war party in danger.

"We stand against the powers spoken of in the old stories that have been handed down from those who came before us," he warned them. "Let us have faith in the powers of our own ancestors and pray that the Creator will give us the strength to remove the evil of the Snake people. All warriors who love their relatives and have certain faith in the Creator of all things, will prepare for the path of war, and be ready to move at sunset; we cannot wait till dawn. All those who stay behind may remain here or follow Quitkwa to the Minnecou camp. There are many Paccu warriors there as well. Know that you will be among your own as well as the gracious Minnecou who have become our greatest allies. Let us call upon the Creator for his power in our warriors!"

A loud and eerie combination of screeching and whooping suddenly erupted all around Quitkwa. His skin crawled and the hair stood out on the back of his neck as he found himself screeching and whooping uncontrollably, though he hadn't understood any of the words Ceptke had spoken. The deafening screeches, whooping and trilling became successively louder and more intense than Quitkwa could ever have imagined; his own voice contained such enormous power that he couldn't even begin to fathom its source. The Paccu men and women alike stood planted to the earth, their faces bulging with the force of faith and cries for the Creator. The whole of the earth around them was inundated with the force of their deafening howls; the ground tremored; small and insignificant clouds that dotted the sky overhead spilled their moisture and enraptured them with a strength they had never realized. They were rewarded a hundredfold for their faith, and each stepped with radiance and a sense of purpose that only the ancients could have known.

Quitkwa was amazed at the power that Ceptke's words had unleashed. He stood dumbfounded at the obvious high regard that the Paccus held for this smiling warrior who had no more power than he to find the white-cliffed valley; who had no more prowess in hunting and scouting. But his power to evoke the faith of his followers had completely eluded Quitkwa, for only with a strong faith in their purpose could they surmount the multitude of obstacles that stood before them. Only this faith could open the trails that lay beyond their imaginations. Quitkwa felt power in this faith.

Wanachan appeared before him with another bowl of stew and a large maize biscuit which Quitkwa accepted with great appreciation, then proceeded to toss into his gullet as if his mouth were an unnecessary component of his digestive system; a mere hatch that enforced controls upon his appetite. Those warriors who had been racing to prepare themselves for battle, now stopped to watch the Minnecou eat; their faces cast in broad smiles. Quitkwa was baffled with their strange looks of anticipation.

"Take your time with that food!" Wanachan nagged. "It will be some time before those who are to follow you will be ready."

"Follow me?" Quitkwa blurted out through a mouthful of mush. "I am going back to the Minnecou camp!" he asserted.

"Yes, and certain ones will be following so they can be under the protection of the Minnecou and the many Paccu warriors there," she informed him.

"What protection?" he laughed, "There are ten times as many warriors here as there are Minnecou and Paccus combined in

Ketanka's camp."

"Not anymore," Wanachan advised him. "Another group of Paccu warriors as large as this one went up there yesterday with Boaka. There were not enough winter lodges for everyone here."

"I cannot lead these people into the Minnecou camp," Quitkwa swallowed hard. "Only one messenger can travel between the two camps. If I have to lead a large group there, it will leave a trail that a blind man could follow."

"There is already a trail there from yesterday," she said. "If this concerns you, then you can cover the trails of yesterday as you go. We have accepted the Minnecou as our brothers and sisters, and our warriors will afford them the same protection as we would our own. It is only right that the Minnecou should do the same for us. It is what is best for all!"

Quitkwa suddenly had a revelation of the Washan who would give him no advice as to Petawahin's plans. What now stood out clearly were the words he had just heard and those that the Washan had spoken to Petawahin: "We must do what is best for all." And he remembered clearly enough of what the Washan warned would happen if this was neglected.

*　*　*

Quitkwa wondered nervously about Ketanka's reaction to his fumbling of Petawahin's plans. But, there was some solace in the fact that neither Ketanka nor any of the others had even heard of these plans, and therefore nothing had truly been discussed or agreed upon. His every step towards the new Minnecou encampment wallowed in uncertainty as some fifty Paccu women and children followed closely behind, while a dozen Paccu warriors tried to conceal both their trail and that of the previous day. Quitkwa had no idea as to how well they were achieving this objective. Petawahin's plan required such crucial timing that he couldn't go back and check on them.

They climbed higher and higher as they crossed several successive ridges through unseen gaps and hidden gorges. The sun was fading quickly and many wondered as to whether it was wise to have left so late in the day when they could have waited till sunrise. But Quitkwa was leaving immediately, and they had a choice of finding the Minnecou village on their own, or following someone who was familiar with the pathways through the maze of gaps and valleys that would eventually lead them to their destination. They sensed an urgency as well in the necessity for Quitkwa to bring his message as quickly as possible to the hundred or so warriors who were camped at Ketanka's village. The Minnecou forces were considered to be insignificant. However, their particular talents and knowledge would be essential in the effectiveness of the Paccus' attack.

"Where will we camp?" Wanachan demanded of Quitkwa. "Everyone complains that it will be too late to even begin looking for a good place. Soon it will be dark up here in the shadows of the mountains.

"We will travel all night," Quitkwa answered sharply.

"We have not prepared for this," she said somewhat surprised at his answer. "You are so worried about concealing our trails; how do you propose to cover them in darkness?"

"You know as well as I that your people could not disguise the trail of a mouse, let alone that of a group this size!" he answered snidely. "I taught them very little about concealing a trail so that it would at least look as though they had tried. Anyone following may have some difficulty, but they would pick up what they need here and there, and when they get to the point where we had to travel in darkness, they will see our trail very plainly and think that we feel secure with what we have done."

"Wouldn't it have been better to cover the trail properly in the first place?" Wanachan interrupted him.

"It would be impossible to cover both our trail and that of your warriors who came through here yesterday while we are traveling in darkness," he returned.

"If you had planned a place for us to camp for the night..." Wanachan again interrupted.

"If we do not get to the Minnecou village very quickly, how will our warriors meet Ceptke's warriors at the Snake village?" Quitkwa had questions of his own. "If we try to camp overnight or even attempt to conceal all of our tracks, how will we make it to the other warriors before dawn?" He paused to allow her reply, but there was none. "We will move throughout the night, as quickly as we can, so that by daybreak we will reach the ridge just before the camp. Then we will walk in a line along the side of the ridge so that Ketanka's scouts will have a very clear view of us. This way, Ketanka will know of our coming long before we get there and we can double back on a well concealed path to go directly into the village. I will take one or two of the Paccus who are with us now, and in the morning light, we can conceal the path that your warriors took yesterday that leads directly into the camp. This way, anyone who tries to follow our trail, will walk along the same ridge as we will tomorrow and be in plain view long before they find their way to the camp, giving everyone time to flee or stand and fight, depending on what we see across the ridge." The Minnecou had learned this trick from moose who would often travel in a wide circle at the end of a day's wandering and then settle down at a point near to the beginning of the circle, where they could see whatever would attempt to stalk them. Then, when those following the moose's tracks were at the furthest point away in the wide circle, the moose would make its escape.

"I guess you are right, Quitkwa," Wanachan admitted. "There's no telling what you Minnecou have in mind, but I should have known by now that the Minnecou always have a plan, no matter how confused they look."

Quitkwa was well aware that every Minnecou always had a plan and for the first time realized that not all people were like this. But, he did take exception to the notion that Minnecou appeared to be confused.

Wanachan wandered back among the rest of the Paccus and informed them that they would be traveling throughout the night. The warriors in the rear immediately stopped covering the trail when they heard of Quitkwa's insults, but darkness was already upon them.

The group became weary as they trudged towards the heart of the Dark Mountains, for even though they would only be crossing two ridges into the range, the elevations were considerably high and the slopes became increasingly steeper. A half moon provided some light as they picked their way across the expansive valleys; had it been overcast or the moon been new, it would have taken much longer. To climb the steep slope presented little more problem than the extra effort, but to climb back down the other side, they had to zigzag their way to the bottom to avoid slipping and falling.

At the top of the second ridge, a small amount of snow had accumulated to a depth over their ankles. Their tracks were highly visible, probably even from a distance, Quitkwa surmised. There were no trees and very little brush at the top of the ridge, and some of the

Paccus became concerned that anyone following would be able to see their trail from a considerable distance and therefore find a shorter route to the Minnecou camp.

"This snow will be gone after the sun rises," Quitkwa dismissed their fears. "What is most important is that we get to the village quickly." Quitkwa then pointed straight down into the valley to show them the fastest route. The snow had fallen after the other Paccus had passed through yesterday, and their trail now lay hidden under the white blanket. Often, the billowy, gray clouds that pass overhead and pose no threat to the lowlands, spawn sudden squalls when they drift into the side of a particularly high ridge. Even in fair weather, the chance of snow is not always remote.

Wanachan was translating many opinions to Quitkwa from the Paccu warriors who had spent more than half of their lives on the side of one mountain or another. "Some warriors say that while the snow will probably melt by sundown tomorrow, our trail will be the first area to melt and will be visible from the first ridge we crossed. They say we should trample a large area so it will appear as just a warm spot on the mountain, or a place where the snow was blown away. Also, some do not like the trail you have chosen. They say it is too steep for this kind of snow."

Quitkwa stopped to consider their concerns. "Which way would be best?" he asked Wanachan to translate. They pointed southward along the length of the ridge. "That would take too long," Quitkwa said stubbornly. "It would be best if we went straight down, and then north along the side of the ridge, where we will be in plain view of the camp," Quitkwa persisted. "I will go this way. If you choose to go the long way, that is up to you, but I must get to camp."

Quitkwa proceeded down the west side of the ridge as the first hint of dawn began to lighten the eastern horizon. When he turned to see who was following, he became angry to see that those who were still within his view had set themselves about the task of trampling down the snow in a broad area around their trail. Some were looking down at Quitkwa from time to time as he began his descent, but none had followed, even when he was halfway to the edge of the snow line and hadn't slipped at all. He looked back once again and took heart in the fact that some of the Paccus had begun to follow the steep trail he'd laid out for them. When he got to a point about three-quarters of the way to the end of the snow, he slipped and slid for several paces, where he grabbed onto a small shrub to keep from continuing down indefinitely. The other Paccus stopped where they were.

"It is okay!" Quitkwa yelled up to them. "Just be careful. You can see where I began to slide before you get there." Quitkwa now noticed that the bulk of the group had already headed southward, choosing their own path. Only a few of the Paccus were now following his trail. He picked his way down a little further, and slipped again down the steep slope, scraping and bumping as he tried desperately to find something to grab onto to halt his fall. He plowed into a large boulder and smashed his face and shoulder; a large bump in the middle of the run had caused him to turn completely around. When he tried to stop against it with his feet, he succeeded only in making his fall head first.

The snow on top of the ridge had been of a powdery type, but what Quitkwa had failed to realize was that as they descended the ridge, the air became warmer, causing the snow to fall in a wetter form, and consequentially, much more slippery. He was now soaking wet and badly bruised.

He looked up to see how far the Paccus had gotten and Wanachan called down to ask if he was alright. "Yes!" he answered. "Just bruises. But look, I'm almost to the end of the snow!" Wanachan waved to him and the last he saw of his followers were their backsides as they trudged their way back to the others up the ridge. "Don't forget," he yelled after Wanachan. "Make sure everyone walks along the ridge for a good distance so the scouts will see them." She waved her hand again to show that she heard, but didn't turn around to face him, demonstrating that she no longer accepted him as one to follow.

"You are all ruled by fear," he insulted. "A crowd of nervous jays!" he muttered to himself. But after taking no more than three steps in the ice and slush, he found himself bouncing and bumping down the rest of the ridge to where he came to rest, legs astraddle one of the first conifers at the edge of the tree line, his groin in painful agony.

He rolled around in pain, looking back to see if any of the Paccus had seen, or would attempt to come to his aid. But they were no longer in view. From this point forth, however, he would be able to hold onto the trees through the rest of the snow. Within a short time, he would be at the point on the ridge where he had wanted the rest of the Paccus to travel a northward, parading themselves before the remote, Minnecou camp. The Paccus had chosen a path much safer than the route Quitkwa had chosen. But this would delay them till as late as mid-morning. Quitkwa understood their apprehension at following him, for the way was very steep and looked much more treacherous than it actually was. They would most likely have suffered bumps and bruises as he did, but he was disgusted by their unwillingness to sacrifice for the good of the whole. If he had not taken this route, the information he was carrying could have been held up at a time when it could be crucial for the fighting warriors to be already on their way.

Quitkwa picked his way down the slope to a point where he unexpectedly caught sight of an obvious and recent trail. It led directly across the area he intended to lead the Paccus. It couldn't be possible for them to have already been through here, Quitkwa thought to himself. Upon closer examination, though, he found the trail to be at least a day old; there were a few snowflakes that had not yet melted on top of the obvious tracks. Quitkwa wondered as to whether the Minnecou had spotted them first as they came over the ridge and sent them this way, or if Boaka had the presence of mind to deliberately lead them in this direction to protect the secluded camp. There were no Minnecou tracks present to give him a clue, but then the Minnecou were always conscious of what they left behind; they traveled through many territories, some friendly, though most unsettled and scattered with different peoples.

He blazed his own well-concealed path in a direct line to the Minnecou village, and arrived out of breath, anxious to speak with his father. The scene around him was infinitely different than what he had left five days previous. Paccus were everywhere, hauling bundles of food, furs. They carried branches from nearby trees to erect over the many holes that had been dug into the ground, but not yet covered. Armloads of hay, hauled from distant meadows, would be banked up against the lodges to protect them from the bitter winter winds. At the center stood Ketanka's huge lodge, low to the ground like all the others, but much larger in diameter. Quitkwa felt proud to see that Ketanka's foresight to place his lodge at the center and build it large enough for council meetings, granted him the natural right to dominate the camp, for Boaka and many other important and powerful looking Paccus had chosen this exact spot to congregate and direct the affairs of the sprawling village. Many of the Paccus already displayed their respect for the hulking Minnecou chief who seemed to control his own people with a word or a nod. Kwoita was always on hand to translate what little he knew of the Paccu language to the chief. As Quitkwa approached, Kwoita was using sign language unfamiliar to most Minnecou, causing the important Paccus who had gathered around Ketanka to burst out in uncontrollable laughter, while the huge Minnecou stood firmly before them, the faint trace of a smile betraying the pride he took in his wit.

"Here comes the one who forgets his family when he steps out of the camp," Ketanka suddenly thundered. The Paccus' heads spun around to see what had brought about his sudden change in tone, invoking the wrath of this croaking giant. "Is this a time to abandon your people without telling them how long you will be away?" he roared. "Five suns the whole camp knows not whether you are dead or alive, and you come back empty-handed as well."

"I return with messages from Petawahin and the Washan...Snake village to the east of here," Quitkwa rapidly blurted.

Ketanka's eyebrows raised slightly and he turned to Kwoita with a wave of his hand. "Gather all Minnecou warriors and tell them to meet here immediately. Have Boaka gather the most important Paccu warriors and invite them to sit with the council."

"The important Paccus are right here!" Kwoita reminded him. "Boaka is hunting with Shatomi again."

"Send someone for them then!" he answered quickly. "I will invite these Paccus after I have talked to Quitkwa and our own warriors." The Paccus looked on, aware that something of importance was taking place, but unsure of whether it pertained to them. Since their arrival on the previous day, they had been involved mostly in serious conversations with the Minnecou chief through Kwoita and Shatomi's rough translations. Their last bits of conversation had just become more casual. The Paccus had begun to settle down and work on plans to prepare themselves for the winter. During the brief time they had been here since their arrival from the south, they had come to think that any war parties would be delayed until spring. The winter would be best utilized by establishing hunting camps towards the east, where the Snake people came from. Later they could be used as hideouts from the Snake people if they couldn't attack their villages. They would raid at night, instead. At the same time, small parties could be sent to locate Snake villages that housed captive Paccus and scout out their strengths and weaknesses.

But, as Minnecou warriors began to pour in from places throughout the village, and some of the hunting parties began to return so that Minnecous could attend an obviously private council, the Paccu began to talk among themselves. The young Minnecou warrior who had so recently returned blurted out but a brief message, and the whole Minnecou clan became entrenched in a flurry of activity. This same Minnecou was immediately brought to what they had come to think of as the Minnecou council lodge, and was talking with the heavy chief for some time as increasing numbers of warriors filtered in from the field. When the Paccu leaders saw Kwoita returning to the council lodge, they surrounded him and asked through sign language if there was something happening that they should know about. Kwoita told them that the young Minnecou scout was now in council with Ketanka and his warriors. When they had learned what information was brought by the chief's son, the Paccus would be informed.

The Paccus had a sense that they were being excluded from something very important, but their lack of ability to communicate with the Minnecou became a stumbling block when Kwoita continued on past them and climbed down into Ketanka's lodge. Many Paccus gathered around the lodge, and Ketanka became aware of a threatening and obviously irritated crowd encircling his council. In his concern over Quitkwa's unexpected message, he had neglected to consider that the Paccus were now the overwhelming majority in this encampment. He had become accustomed to having all important information relayed to the Minnecou council first, and then to others. But when Kwoita informed him that an irritated crowd had begun to assemble around the council lodge, he sent him back to invite several of the Paccu leaders to sit on the council.

By the looks on their faces as they filled the empty spaces in the council lodge, Ketanka could see that his neglect was an obvious blunder. A strained atmosphere now permeated the sacred council meeting; Ketanka was hesitant to light the council pipe as he waited to see if Shatomi and Boaka would return from their hunt.

The two hunters, however, were just now approaching the council lodge, and were suddenly descended upon by the Paccu crowd. "Boaka!" they called. "What is all this about?"

"Snake village to the east," he yelled out. A deafening war whoop erupted outside of the council lodge. The Paccu leaders in Ketanka's lodge didn't appear too pleased that those outside of the council lodge had apparently learned of the message before them.

Shatomi and Boaka climbed down into the lodge and took up places in back of Ketanka, the only area left where there was room for them to sit. The most important Paccu warrior from the south sat directly across from the Minnecou chief with those of lesser importance furthest away from him, towards the sides of the circle in descending order. Ketanka lit the strangely figured pipe with the long nosed-beast. The warriors assumed an attitude of trust within their small circle, and the outside commotion became non-existent; truth and knowledge were about to be exposed to all. When the pipe returned to Ketanka, he put it away and looked upon the gathering.

"Important news comes from the place of the rising sun," Ketanka began, and then hesitated so Kwoita could translate as best he could with his fragmented memory of their sign language. "My son, who is honorable as both scout and warrior among our people, brings messages from our warriors as well as your own. An important Snake village two days to the east of here holds Paccu and Minnecou captives. One of our warriors gains knowledge for us to destroy this foul smelling boil upon the flesh of our Earth Mother. Many of your warrior brothers, those you have just left, are now moving in secrecy toward our enemies, and they request the aid of Paccu and Minnecou warriors to battle the evil people who have enslaved and murdered our relatives. I know that it has been thought best to wait until after the pains of winter have passed, and the grasses become green once again. I realize that it would be much more practical for us to wait until we have more knowledge of their strengths and weaknesses...and also the locations and powers of their war parties.

But I also know from many years of experience with Petawahin that when he calls for a war party, we will have all knowledge necessary to defeat our enemy. To determine the depth of truth in my words, consider that your great warriors, Ceptke and Boaka, along with many other of your Paccu relatives, were freed from the grasp of our common enemy through the hands of Petawahin...and he brought them back to the safety of our clan, the enemy unable to follow."

Boaka testified to the capabilities of Petawahin, though he had seen little of this powerful warrior since he had first walked among the Minnecou.

"I must stay and provide Minnecou women and children with safety and protection, as well as those Paccu women and children who wish to stay behind. A large group of Paccu women and children and old men, along with several of your warriors, should be coming into view across the valley very soon...they have abandoned the village near the desolate area. The camp we are in must remain full, and some warriors will have to stay among us to provide protection in the event that Snake war parties should come to this area. It may also be necessary to send out many hunting parties to provide food in the event that our battle with the enemy is not entirely successful. Our warriors must have a place to return to, especially if the cold north winds of winter have already begun to paint the earth white. I regret that I cannot join in the battle to destroy the evil village, but my warriors and my son will carry the tomahawks of death to the throats of our enemies, and support your brave warriors to the end. From this day forth, though we are two different peoples, we will walk the earth as brothers and our justice will be the same...death to those who would enslave and murder our kinsmen for the purposes of continuing their evil. We will treat them with the same endearment they have shown us and since neither of us need slaves in order that we may live as human beings, that only leaves death for their punishment." Ketanka paused to let his feelings sink in.

Boaka took advantage of this pause and maneuvered himself to the side of the Paccu leader, across from Ketanka. He spoke briefly with him and the powerful looking Paccu turned to Kwoita with a barrage of sign language, giving him a lengthy message to relay to Ketanka.

"I understand that you have a Washan who is also away from your clan. Our Washan is now getting very old and can no longer endure the cold winters up here in the snows of the north, so we were forced to leave him behind with the rest of our clan of which this large war party you see before you is only a small part. We will accept your Washan as our spiritual guide as all Washans' knowledge comes from the same source. However, our Washan warns that to kill those who refuse to arm themselves and fight against our warriors would invite long-lasting evil spirits to dwell amongst our people."

"While it would seem to be a weakness on our part and an invitation for our enemy to avenge their dead when they become strong once again, to take up an evil enemy's ways is to eventually become them. This is not tolerable among the Paccus as we are a peaceful people. Our warriors are as strong and capable as any, but for many generations, our Washans have taught us that to sow hatred and cause for vengeance among any human beings will bring a never-ending harvest of ill will among our children."

Ketanka was taken aback by the powerful looking Paccu's unexpected comments. While he did consider the Paccus' stand as a possible weakness, especially where the Snake people are concerned, he could also see the logic and wisdom behind their Washan's views. But, knowing how the Snake people had slaughtered those Paccus who had resisted them, his views of what would eventually happen to Minnecou and Paccu clans who refused to meet their enemy with equal force troubled him.

"And if the Snake people continue to murder and enslave our relatives regardless of whether they resist or try to flee, will you continue to follow your Washan's principles and allow these evil people to exist while your own clans disappear from the face of the earth?" Ketanka tried to soften any steadfastness with which Paccus may hold onto these views.

"Our warriors...even our children, women and old men, have already determined that to flee or abandon this land is not tolerable," the Paccu answered. "Therefore, any Paccu that the Snake people encounter will be resisting and not fleeing. Any Paccus that are attacked or enslaved by the Snake warriors or anyone else will be their lifelong enemies until they abandon their desires to rule the Paccu nation. There will be no gain for any enemy to try and enslave our people for their own profit, there will only be misery and disappointment for them. They will have to risk their own lives and those of their warriors in order to engage us, but there will never be any lasting gain from it for them, instead, we will become a curse on their people until they learn to stay away," the Paccu said resolutely.

"As chief of the Minnecou, I praise your words and those of your Washan," Ketanka concurred with the Paccu's assessment. "And I hope that the Minnecou here have learned something from their Paccu brothers. The Minnecou have always felt similar to this, as many times throughout our travels, back to the beginning of the earth, enemies have tried to change our ways and we have always resisted. We have always resisted because this is our blood. The blood of our people flows different than the blood of others and is of a different substance because that is what the Creator has given to us. Not only will we accept the Paccu way, but we will embrace it, for it is already the spirit of our nation. We may never live in the same way as the Paccus," he pointed out. "But of the same spirit, I am certain we are guided."

"Now we must set about the task of choosing who shall go to battle and who shall stay," Ketanka determined. "Many plans and preparations must be made and they must be made very quickly, for there is little time and our warriors must run like antelope to meet their brothers and destroy the evil."

"There are warriors with the Paccu women and children who are on their way here now," Quitkwa pointed out to his father. "They will be tired from their overnight journey already, while all of the warriors here are still fresh. There are enough of them to accomplish what you need here."

The Paccu leader nodded his agreement with Quitkwa's observation and Ketanka accepted the arrangement, retaining Kwoita and Quebathe, as they would be needed to insure that Minnecou needs would be met. Ketanka had Quitkwa inform the Paccus as to the dangers they would meet on the trail, the terrain they would traverse, and the supplies they would need in order to reach their destination with as much strength as possible. Paccus and Minnecou alike offered suggestions as well as their own personal strategies involving battle, moving war parties over long distances quickly, and hiding from the enemy so as to be able to strike with force as well as surprise.

When everything had been decided, though admittedly in haste, the warriors filed out of the lodge and confronted a throng of Minnecou and Paccu warriors, women and children. Everyone had gathered around the council lodge, anxiously awaiting word from their leaders on what they were to do. The Paccu leader stood at the highest point and yelled out brief messages that were not translated to the Minnecou but were answered in unison by the entire throng. The Minnecou didn't even know the meanings of the words they suddenly found themselves screaming at the tops of their lungs. After the last of these messages was relayed through the Paccu leader, an enormous war whoop erupted among the crowd and the Minnecou were simultaneously surprised and exhilarated by the sudden power in their voices. When the strange and overwhelming power suddenly released its hold on the crowd, an echo was heard coming from the southeast to which the village turned in unison. A long line of Paccus could be plainly seen on the distant side of the ridge across the valley, jumping and whooping with the same fanaticism of those in the camp.

CHAPTER 16

Semmida, Sequannah and Mokotak arrived at their destination in the chilled pre-dawn hours. Heavy droplets of cold morning dew clung to every branch, bush and blade of grass. Their hands and feet were numb from the crisp, cold morning air and from the icy water in the bottoms of their flimsy crafts. But the Minnecou recognized this autumn cold snap as a preparation rather than a discomfort. They were very cold for the moment, but when the icy winds of winter raged around them, even then they would not feel as cold. Their very blood will have taken on a new form.

Semmida led them through the thick brush to a small opening in the side of a huge mound. The Minnecou would have taken this to be just another hill, but it was too perfect in dimension; there were no irregularities. It was cloaked in tall trees and thick undergrowth, but careful observation revealed that it was definitely an unnatural occurrence. There were no rocks or boulders of any description except one irregularly shaped overhang, under which a small opening led into the center of the mound. Even this bit of ledge was difficult to perceive through the tangle of trees, shrubs and evergreen laurels that would conceal the opening even after the leaves had fallen.

Semmida beckoned them to follow him through the narrow opening, then quickly disappeared into the earth. Sequannah slipped through easily, but Mokotak had a difficult time trying to fit his shoulders through the cramped and twisting entrance. As his feet cleared the outside of the opening, he found himself hopelessly contorted, and though he could still fit through, his twisted position allowed him no leverage. Sequannah had to pull him through.

Although the outside of this mysterious mound appeared to be a massive pile of soil, the passageway to its inner depths was completely encased in walls of solid rock. Once inside, a small chamber presented itself. Against the far side were stone walls, laid down many years before for the purposes of defending the entrance against intruders. Behind the bulwarks, three warriors hid in the shadows; bows at the ready, arrows to drawstrings.

Semmida led the two Minnecou through several small passageways and into a large chamber. The ceiling was etched in scrolls of limestone that appeared to have been hand-sculpted by the most patient of artists. Above the layer of limestone, Sequannah perceived many cracks in the stone lining up in perfect squares. Blocks of stone had been cut, then laid in a continuous arch throughout the length of the passageway. It had to have been done in ancient times for the many thin stalactites to have formed. The top of the chamber was barely out of Mokotak's reach; its sides arched far out to where the ceiling tapered to meet the floor in shadow. It was actually an enlarged area of a continuing passageway, but served as a main chamber where tables of stone held baskets and pouches of food and fruit. A shallow stream trickled off to one side of the chamber, then disappeared deeper into the earth down a water filled passageway. Stockpiles of pure, white quartz and shiny, black obsidian were heaped near one of the tables where an ancient man with silver, braided hair sat patiently chipping at a large nodule of obsidian. Several women were butchering a deer and hanging strips of meat to dry on a rack over a smoldering fire. The smoke swirled around the chamber, then whisked off through small holes and finger-width cracks near the highest point of the ceiling. The old man nodded, quietly showing his acceptance of the two new warriors, but quickly turned his attention back to flaking the razor-sharp material.

The two Minnecou noticed there were many places laid out for people to sleep, perhaps as many as a hundred, but there were only five women and an old man in the chamber. Sequannah wondered why there were so many beds in a cave, especially since they were all set up in rows with stone dividers carved out into the floor, their bottoms lined with matted cattail fluff.

"There are many people here with you?" Sequannah questioned.

"There are some here now, but in the coming moons we will fill this chamber with many warriors," Semmida answered.

"These are the sleeping places of all your warriors?" he questioned further.

"There are more places than this cave, but these are set up for when the time comes for our warriors to come up from the south. We use the square holes for sleeping, but that is not what they were originally used for. There once was an ancient city here that is now gone. The mound that covers this place was not here then. If you looked at it before you came into the cave, you would have seen that the mound sits next to a stream at the lowest point of the land. Long ago, the people who lived and farmed outside of the city could look down upon all of these square holes and see the shadows cast by the sun. By looking at the shadows from east to west, they could tell exactly when the sun passed the middle of the day. By watching the shadows from north to south, they knew exactly how much had gone by of each season so they would know when to plant, and when the long winter would be over. Follow me," he invited them. They went to the far end of the passageway, the strange holes carved into the floor for the entire distance on either side of them. At the end of the chamber, the passageway dropped off sharply, and in back of the rows on either side was a large stone plug that could be lifted and manipulated into almost any position through the leverage of a long and sturdy pole attached to the plug by means of a short length of chain.

"They used to fill those square holes with water, but for what purpose we haven't yet discovered," he told them. "Go and look at the bottoms of the pits; each one is connected by a small hole at the bottom so that they all fill evenly. You have seen the small stream running at the side of the passageway?" he questioned. "There are gutters carved in from it so that they could divert the water into the beds, but now the stream runs too low to ever get water in there again. Look! The stream is now lower than the beds."

The two Minnecou could see that he was telling the truth, but they were amazed at the amount of work that the ancient ones found so necessary.

"There used to be another stream on that side of the chamber, but that no longer flows," he went on. "Now the beds on this side will always remain dry."

"Then that is where we will sleep," Mokotak cut in, and walked off towards the most comfortable one he could find, too tired to listen to this strange man who had suddenly become much too talkative for him. He fell into one of the pits and drifted immediately off into a deep and exhausted sleep.

"Perhaps you should rest as well," Semmida suggested. "You must be tired."

"I am," Sequannah admitted weakly. "But this place is strange. I cannot sleep." Semmida paused in thought for a moment.

"These chambers used to be part of a city long ago," Semmida spoke to distract and comfort the young Minnecou. "Perhaps even before the Minnecou roamed the area of earth around us here." Sequannah knew this not to be true because it was common knowledge that the Minnecou had roamed this area of earth since the Creator had first made it.

"This is only the very beginning of the cave. The rest extends far below the earth. Hundreds of chambers exist below us, and many more than that, used for different purposes. The people used to live here inside the earth during the time when the sun was too hot. Everything outside became scorched and barren; the ancient people began to live in here. Look at the end of this chamber and you will find many passageways in many directions. In every chamber, you will hear the sound of flowing water, but if you follow the chamber where it is loudest, it will always lead to the river. From here, the passageway will lead you under the river and out onto the other side. If you choose not to follow us, you can return to your people that way."

"The Sikun thinks that Quiktkoata's city lies over another city, similar to this one, but not connected to the caves in this one. The city Quiktkoata had chosen to build over was said to be one of infinite mystery—one of evil and strange power; a curse for all time."

"Then why did you allow him to build there?" Sequannah asked. "Why did you not eliminate him and his followers and then destroy the place of mystery so that no one could ever return there?"

"We did not know of these places until recently. We kept Quiktkoata and his followers from holding any power in Teyotewakan because he turned the people against each other. The city of the Creator was built many years ago so that all of the different peoples could send their Washans to become learned in the ways of the Creator. For many generations, there were no fights among the different peoples, nor even among themselves, because there was a common knowledge to solve all problems. A Washan was always selected from each clan and sent to Teyotewakan to learn the laws of fairness, and to find the wisdom in their own clans' ways so that all would understand the needs and ways of each other. The city was built to serve the Creator and thereby bring peace and prosperity to all."

"Quiktkoata's ancestors were once the most powerful of all tribes far to the south and controlled the land from the seas in the east, all the way to the ocean in the west. They spread fear and unrest among the different clans to keep their control over them, always convincing each clan that their neighboring clan was responsible for any problems. Then they would pledge that as the most powerful clan, they would protect them from further injustice as long as they would protect Quiktkoata's ancestral clan from enemy uprisings. They were expected to accomplish this by warning Quiktkoata's ancestors and giving them the food and wares that they would not have the time to prepare, themselves, as they watched the countryside and kept the peace. In this way, Quiktkoata's ancestors always remained the most powerful nation for many years. But the Washans knew what was going on. They would meet secretly and share their medicinal knowledge and their spiritual wisdom, and through these meetings, they learned that most of the anger between their clans was caused by Quiktkoata's ancestors. They were protecting nothing but their own control over everything. Each year they would cause more and more trouble between the clans so that there would be murders and even battles between them. Then they would demand even more payment to protect the clans from each other. They had all of the clans convinced that they would destroy each other without 'their' warriors to control the peace."

"But the Washans began to meet in larger groups, without the knowledge of Quiktkoata's ancient relatives, and among them they convinced their clans to restrain their anger for their neighbors and instead look for the involvement of 'the peacekeepers' as the cause of the problems. Quiktkoata's ancient clan did not know what was going on, but they did realize that they were losing control over all of the tribes and many were refusing to pay for protection because their enemies were no longer hostile. Quiktkoata's ancestors then unleashed a reign of terror by catching poisonous snakes and releasing them near certain villages. They discovered that the tribes had become peaceful through the efforts of their Washans, so they blamed certain Washans for the curse of the snakes and tried to renew the anger between them. But the Washans held onto their trust, and one among them by the name of Skan rose up against Quiktkoata's ancestors, and told them they were no longer welcome in their village. Quiktkoata's ancient relatives then committed a series of murders through careful manipulation of their snakes, and blamed everything on Skan."

"Skan, however, was a Sikun, devoted to the Creator. He

continued with his message of peace and refused to allow 'the Snake people' to step onto the grounds of his city. At the same time, he welcomed all of the other clans into his poor village and gave them food and drink, regardless of how little his own people had, and the other clans' hostility towards them. After a while, the other clans began to accept Skan once again, though he was nearly banished by his own people for wasting their precious food on clans who had been indignant towards them for so long. But after the initial acceptance of Skan back into the group of Washans, his power grew very quickly and the Snake people were turned away from all of the villages. Skan preached the ways of the Creator to the Washans, and they, in turn, taught their clans. They worked and planned together to build a large temple to show their respect and love for the Creator, who had brought them out of the fear of Quiktkoata's ancestors and spread peace among the poor clans. All of the clans became much more prosperous without the demands of the Snake people and Teyotewakan grew to an enormous city where Washans learned the just ways of the Creator. People from all over the land came to humble themselves before the Creator, who had delivered them from so many generations of fear and hatred."

"But Quiktkoata's ancestors had not changed at all," he went on, "though they were much poorer and had lost nearly all of their influence among the tribes of the lands. They tried desperately to regain their power by using their snakes once again. They bred stranger and stranger snakes; some with eyes that glowed in the night, others with strange patterns on their skins, and still others that could dance and perform simple tasks. They bred the poison out of their snakes because too many of their own people were getting killed, but still, they managed to spread much fear throughout the population through the use of these unusual creatures. They began to question the Washans' motives and say that the Washans had a life of luxury without any work, while the people spent their days dragging huge stones to build the city larger and larger. They spread stories that the Creator was a myth, and that the Washans had made up the story so that they could rule the world and have all of the clans as their slaves."

"Many of the clansmen listened to Quiktkoata's ancestors, but most did not because they knew them not to be trustworthy. The Washans knew that as long as the Snake leaders lived, they would always find new ways to try and destroy the peace in Teyotewakan. After much arguing, they finally decided that they would have to kill them in order to save the rest of the Snake people, or eventually they would lead them into war against the city."

"But the Snake people learned of their plan, and in one day, all of the Snake people deserted Teyotewakan and headed far to the north. They had knowledge of an ancient city where strange people lived long ago. It took them many years to find it, and when they did, most of it was buried. They spent even more years digging it out, but they overpowered the tribes of the area, and forced them to do most of the work. Quiktkoata's ancestors found many strange powers lurking within the endless chambers underneath their newly claimed city, and though few could face these powers and still remain sane after their experience, those who did became powerful Washans."

"But they were not satisfied, nor would they be until they had gained back their influence over all of the clans in the south once again. Those who were able to survive the catacombs under the strange city began to raise and breed newer and more powerful snakes in the strange chambers. Quiktkoata's relatives wore a certain musk that these snakes were repelled from, but they never let this secret slip into the hands of the clansmen from Teyotewakan. This is known from some of the legends of the Snake people. They were not seen anywhere near Teyotewakan for many generations and the people had begun to think that they were only an old myth. Grandmothers used to warn the children to watch out for the Snake people—even the children would laugh.

"Many, many years later, a beaten and poor looking nation straggled into Teyotewakan from somewhere out of the north. They claimed to be a wandering tribe, looking for a great city that, according to their legends, would allow them to become closer to the Creator. But these people had several snakes with them as well, though none of them seemed to have the mysterious powers that were spoken of in the legends. They also wore many bracelets and rings with emblems of snakes and hawks. Some of the clansmen of Teyotewakan thought that these were the descendants of the Snake people. They heard stories that they were beaten by nomadic tribes to the north and were exiled out of their homeland; that they were refugees, not travelers looking for a place to settle. For many generations, they were always treated with suspicion and held back from any positions of authority within Teyotewakan until one rose up among them by the name of Quiktkoata. He spoke out openly against the clans who suppressed them, and spread discontent among the clans who had accepted them by spreading rumors of the injustice that prevailed throughout Teyotewakan. Of course, they were not true, but they were spoken in such a manner as to always question the authority of those Washans who ruled Teyotewakan. Soon, every decision made by the Washans was greeted with suspicion and the clans were beginning to fall apart. This is when Quiktkoata and his followers were shunned by the good clansmen, and Quiktkoata heard rumors that the Washans had plans to kill him. He left the city before he even found out if the rumors were true, claiming that any who followed would become the heirs of the earth in the greatest empire of all the ages. The prophesies spoke of such an empire in the vast continent to the north, and many people from all of the different clans chose to follow Quiktkoata."

"Six summers ago, when Quiktkoata's exodus from Teyotewakan first began, the Sikun sent spies along to find out their true destination. Many people from throughout the villages abandoned their ancestral homelands and followed Quiktkoata's lures to wealth and power, most of them from the poorer farms that could not produce much corn or anything else. Those craftsmen who had any ability chose to follow Quiktkoata only because the majority of their relatives had gone. But the Sikun planted many spies in among the exodus, for it seemed as though no matter how far Quiktkoata and his relatives were removed from Teyotewakan, they always maintained some form of influence, and they were very likely to return as well. The Sikun was concerned about the possibility that one day Quiktkoata would return with much power, for the purposes of reclaiming Teyotewakan for his relatives once again. Their rule of terror and deceit could not be allowed into the city of the Creator, ever. Teyotewakan was built out of respect and trust of the Creator. It is the center of our lives and from it comes the wisdom to live among all clans in peace and understanding. Quiktkoata's only interest in the city is its power and wealth. He tried to manipulate all of the trade—from the craftsmen's pottery to the farmers' corn—so that he could have more control over the decisions within the city and could have more clansmen to work off their indebtedness to him. Now it is feared that if he is successful in his new empire, he will eventually rule everything that falls within his grasp. There will be no end to his and his followers' desires, and there will be no satisfaction for them even if they reach the ends of the earth. The Sikun says that even then, they will find a way to go beyond."

Semmida looked over to Sequannah, expecting him to be

sleeping, for though he was trying to give the Minnecou an idea of what was taking place, he really didn't expect the Minnecou to comprehend. He was more or less trying to put some perspective and order to the ways of the Snake people in his own mind. "You are a nomad," he spoke softly. "You don't even understand half of what I speak of. But then, your way of life is of equal mystery us. It is said that a Minnecou could walk from here to Teyotewakan and back in the same footsteps, remembering every mountain, hill, river and stream, and having a clear recollection of every horizon. But to understand the ways of village life must be confusing to you, and even more so in the ways of Teyotewakan."

"I have been to the villages in the south," Sequannah informed Semmida. "We travel through many villages and see their ways, but to move is the way of our blood. We trade with them and we see how they plant their gardens and fish their rivers empty. We see how they hunt out all of their game until they can only eat their vegetables and the few fish they can catch, unless we bring them dried meat from the trails of our never ending village. They move their villages a little each year, but we always know where to find them because the smell travels far. Our village is everything that exists between the strange villages. You will know when you are in our village because you will smell only the flowers, trees, the animals and the wind. The grass stands untrampled, and every distant trail for the village people is a haven to us, where the spirit of the Creator whispers the secrets of all living things."

"We swim with the fish in the rivers and we roam with the buffalo on the plains. We run with the rabbit in the thickets and we crawl with the turtle in the mud. Grandfathers have told us of towers and structures where villagers place their pride, but the Creator always reclaims these things for they are borrowed from him. Grandfathers have taught us that all things human are built of words and hunger, but only the trails of the Creator go on forever. And when these trails become choked off with the dusty paths of villages, and their smell wilts the strongest of flowers, the Creator will turn the earth over upon them and a new set of trails will unfold. And so we follow always the trails of the Creator, for they are the only things that will last, and only that which will always be is best for us to follow."

"The Sikun will enjoy your conversation," Semmida looked at the young warrior with admiration. "Not only do you endure the trials that a grown man could easily fail, but you have a knowledge of your peoples' ways that would be admirable for even a Washan. Rest, as your friend has wisely chosen to do. Sleep until you are restless with energy and do the same tomorrow. Soon we will be among the Snake people again, and we will do their work by day as well as our own by night. Eat if you are hungry now, but you must sleep and rest." Sequannah laid in the soft cattail down of one of the pits, then drifted off into heavy slumber.

* * *

Mokotak awoke after what seemed to be a brief nap, but was actually longer than an average night's sleep. He heard the sounds of talking and laughter from both men and women; a group of people were chanting and dancing at the far end of the cavern. He lifted himself out of his sleeping place and saw that a great crowd had assembled around a large and noisily crackling fire. Mokotak stood to climb out of the pit, but his muscles tightened into near spasms. He had been worked heavily in the mines and then bound for some time on the cross; his whole body was rigid and sore to the bones. He felt as if he was still bound. When he climbed out of the shallow hole, his back tensed in further spasm, but he walked down the rows of square holes in search of Sequannah, slowly working his muscles loose. Many of the square pits were occupied with sleeping bodies, but Sequannah was nowhere to be found.

Mokotak doubled his way back towards the crowd of dancing people, where most of the pits seemed to be empty, and found Sequannah sleeping soundly in the midst of the boisterous group, in the pit closest to them.

"Wake up!" he shook the young warrior. "Why do you choose to sleep in this noisy place?"

"There was no one here when I went to sleep," he answered groggily. "But they are still not as loud as your snoring was."

"Get up!" he urged Sequannah once again. "We'll find Semmida and see what's going on here."

"They're dancing!" Sequannah said incredulously and then closed his eyes again. Mokotak reached down into the pit and grabbed the back of Sequannah's breechclout, hoisting him out bodily. Sequannah found himself shocked into wakefulness, then realized his disrespect towards Mokotak. "Forgive me, Mokotak," Sequannah apologized, "I speak rudely in my sleep."

"Come, let's go to the outside. There's no way to tell if it's day or night in here." They maneuvered their way to the other end of the long chamber and back to the narrow passageway. Once inside the smaller chamber, they surprised the three warriors guarding the entrance, who immediately wheeled and turned their bows on the two Minnecou. Mokotak flashed them a sign, showing that he was an ally and not an enemy, but they refused to turn their bows away, threatening to shoot if they didn't return immediately to the main cavern. Mokotak took a step forward and one of the warriors released an arrow in warning that passed between Mokotak's head and shoulder. The other two stepped closer and pointed their arrows into his face at full draw. Mokotak looked toward the entrance, but not a hint of outside light showed through. He couldn't remember if daylight had been visible from this point the first time he was here. He determined that it must be nightfall or close to it, for in full sunlight, there should have been at least a hint of light.

In a darkened corner, Sequannah perceived two glowing objects slowly swaying, and pointed to them. A low hiss erupted from the dark recess and the three warriors turned immediately, releasing their arrows into the blackness. A loud hiss echoed throughout the chamber and the glowing orbs disappeared. One of the warriors grabbed an unlit torch and knocked frantically with a piece of flint and a piece of pyrite to produce a spark large enough to ignite the oil-soaked cattail. The chamber became instantly brilliant as the torch finally caught. They scrambled to the dark corner where they had first seen the snake, and found the thick black carcass lying on the chamber floor, its eyes shut tight. One of the warriors forced one of the eyes open and it appeared to glow, even in the light. Its tail swerved back and forth, though the creature was dead. An arrow had penetrated the head and run lengthwise for some distance before protruding through the thick scales of the viper's skin.

One of the warriors glared at the two Minnecou, waving them back to the larger chamber. Their motion had caused the snake to investigate, and had the warriors not killed it, thousands of them could be on their way here shortly. Sequannah and Mokotak realized they had made a mistake and turned back to the large cavern, feeling somewhat childish at what was probably only viewed as an ignorant error by these strange warriors.

As they entered the main chamber, they were met by Semmida and several others who had gone in search of them. "I learned that you left the cavern, and before you found yourselves in conflict with the guards, I had hoped to find you. I see that they have turned you back graciously," Semmida said. Sequannah and Mokotak glanced at each other, but said nothing. "Follow us," Semmida beckoned them. "The Sikun has come among us and is interested in meeting those of the many different tribes here in the land of the north." The two Minnecou looked around, and recognized that three of the members of Semmida's party were Paccus. Several more were from different villages that fell along the Minnecous' trails, while still others were strange and foreign.

He led them to the other side of the cavern, where the fire crackled, and the strange people from Teyotewakan danced to their deeply accented singing. From here they went through several small holes and passageways that had been carved through the floor in ancient times by the underground stream, now reduced to a trickle. Several small creatures fluttered by their heads as they negotiated the narrow tunnels and low ceilings. Semmida led them into another medium-sized chamber, smaller than the one where the square pits were located, but much larger than the chamber where the three guards watched over the entrance. At its center stood a tall, older man. His hair was somewhat gray and his stomach was no longer flat and lean. Two chirping sparrows perched on his shoulders, while others fluttered gleefully around his head. Torches on the cavern walls lit the area sufficiently for visitors to see his face. His hair had been braided into one strand that came directly out of the top of his head, and was tossed to the left side where it ended at the level of his hip. Sequannah thought bats had been fluttering by him in the darkness of the tunnels, but now realized they were sparrows. The man smiled and greeted the group with several unintelligible words, in the middle of which fell the Minnecou word for greeting. One of his teeth was half broken off and his expression was either one of slow intelligence of profound peace; his new visitors couldn't tell which, but in either case he appeared almost foolish.

"This is the Sikun who will lead us in battle?" Mokotak sneered sarcastically as he whispered secretively to Sequannah.

The two Minnecou waited patiently as the Sikun spoke at

great length to the three Paccus, none of whom were recognizable to the Minnecou. Elements of their clothing and their tongue told of their ancestry. When the Paccus left, Mokotak and Sequannah pushed forward in anticipation of hearing what the Sikun had to say, but Semmida urged them back, introducing one of the other guests to the Sikun, instead. Mokotak paced in and out of the entrance as the conversation began to go on much longer than he expected, even longer than the one with the three Paccus. When the strange guest passed Mokotak outside of the cavern entrance, he hurried back in, expecting to be able to finally have his counsel with the Sikun, but already there was another guest. Sequannah began to pace along with Mokotak, in and out of the cavern entrance. Semmida stormed over to them when their irritated whispering threatened to disrupt the conversations of the Sikun.

"I realize that you are Minnecou and that it is difficult for you to stay in one place, but you are insulting the Sikun," he warned. "Look at the others. They wait patiently for their turn. They do not pace; they do not whisper; they do not wear a look of anger. Come back in here and sit quietly. Watch the movements of the Sikun and study his manner if you cannot understand his conversation, for everything about him will speak to you if you listen."

"When will we be talking to the Sikun?" Sequannah asked, a hint of impatience thinly masked in his tone.

"You will be last," Semmida informed them. "The Sikun judges what his guests need and then gives them what he thinks is best. I think he has decided that the Minnecou need a lesson in patience." Mokotak's and Sequannah's faces immediately soured.

"No one treats a Minnecou in this manner," Mokotak snarled. "Especially when we are here to help your cause. We did not need your help to escape from Quiktkoata."

"I only said that I think the Sikun may be testing your patience because I have seen him do this before," Semmida acquiesced. "But the Sikun has many reasons for what he does that are not always apparent. In either case, it will not hurt you to be patient." The two Minnecou warriors were somewhat appeased, but though they waited quietly as the Sikun spoke with the rest of his guests, they could not change the scowls on their faces.

After the last guest had left, Sequannah and Mokotak felt relieved that they would finally be able to speak with this Sikun. Then they could decide whether they would stay and help these strange people or return to the clan. Both Minnecou felt as though they were wasting their time and that they would be returning to the Minnecou clan as soon as their audience with the Sikun had concluded; this Sikun had impressed them little with his fluttering sparrows–the only mystery to dispel his almost foolish appearance.

"Greetings to my Minnecou warriors," he addressed them, as if they had already enlisted in his aid. "I am Teokahannah. Some call me Sikun, but I do not give myself this name."

"I'm told that you have slept well, perhaps too well for Minnecou warriors. Your feet are already restless for the trail. But if you are to join us in defeating Quiktkoata, you must learn to be patient...as if you were hunting a sly fox. Everything must fall at a certain time, even if it becomes necessary to wait for moons for what would seem to be only a minor stumbling block. You must learn to respect your enemies as you would your own family, for even as you attack and slay them, there must be compassion to bring them among us when the struggle has ceased, and to put enmity forever behind until even their survivors have lost the taste for revenge."

"It has become well known throughout this land that the Minnecou have proved to be Quiktkoata's most feared enemy. But they have also become the object of his wrath. No one knows, other than the Minnecou themselves, just how many clans roam this great land. But it is the hope of all the villages and slaves who have fallen under Quiktkoata's domination that they are as plentiful as the buffalo in spring. It saddens us to hear that two clans have been destroyed, even though the cost to Quiktkoata was great." The two Minnecou warriors looked distressed and unbelieving.

"Who tells you that two clans have been destroyed?" Mokotak demanded. Ketanka's Minnecou had not been in contact with any of the other clans since the previous winter, and even now it was probably too late to begin their return southward; the leaves had already changed and were falling to the ground to blanket the forest floor for winter. For the first time since any Minnecou could remember, it appeared as though the great gathering of the clans during the coldest moons of winter would be a very bleak affair. On rare occasions, one of the clans would become stranded in an early snow, but messengers would always be sent ahead to hear news from the great gathering and to bring back messages to those who would not be able to make it to the southern villages before spring. This year, it appeared as though two of the clans would no longer be heard from.

"It is well known that at least two Minnecou clans had been hunted down during the spring and summer moons," the Sikun informed them. "Many of Quiktkoata's warriors had been killed, not only by attacks from the Minnecou, but from dangers that the Minnecou led them to. Quiktkoata had lost many of his snakes as well. Very few of the snakes were ever lost when he attacked the small villages, but the Minnecou seemed always to find a weakness with Quiktkoata's snakes and warriors, even though they could not take them on directly. Quiktkoata managed to capture a handful of each of the Minnecou clans. He brought them back to his city to make slaves of them and to find out the secrets of their warriors. But most of them were killed to keep the slaves of the entire city from rebelling. Your Minnecou relatives always created great unrest. Some of them refused to work or eat or even sleep, and died shortly from their own refusal to live in Quiktkoata's empire. It is said, however, that some of them escaped, though no one has heard from them...and they may have been murdered by Quiktkoata's spies."

"Why didn't your people help them if you knew they were going to die here?" Sequannah demanded.

"As I have told you, there are many spies sent among the people from Quiktkoata himself, and to bring them among us would have been a great risk."

"Then why do you bring us here?" Mokotak questioned.

"We are now nearly ready. The addition of two Minnecou warriors could be of great advantage to us, even if it is a danger as well. Now that you are already here, that risk is small. The only question that remains is your loyalty, of which at this point there is probably very little. If your eyes have been open, you have noticed the stench of Quiktkoata's city, and the destruction he wreaks upon your sacred lands. He has been here now for six summers, and already, even the Minnecou can no longer follow their ancient trails. Quiktkoata seeks to control everything–his followers inherit whatever he conquers. He is jealous of our city and he tried to control that too, but our people know that to build a city as great as ours can only be done in respect to the Creator. Quiktkoata's city is of his own doing and for his own purposes. It is not an offering to the Creator and he receives no blessing in return. His Washans are no more trustworthy than

Quiktkoata himself and they are all self-serving, building their own empires of power within Quiktkoata's, but never serving the Creator to bring happiness to the people."

"They do not realize that the true master is the one who is best able to serve his people. Those who rule through fear and terror will never last. They are not trustworthy and can find no one trustworthy to serve under them. Those who rule through greed and selfishness will always be seen for what they are. Those who are tempted to follow will be the first to be scattered like the leaves of a dead tree. Its branches will snap under the wind's strong spirit; the stump will rot and wither for all to see. Even so, they will plant more bad seed and grow more trees, spreading decay wherever they go until nothing remains but a vision of withering stumps. If we allow them to spread too far, then they will be replaced with the wind-blown sand, for they desecrate the Earth Mother's skin and their scar will be forever visible."

"We must understand that we are but a force that is to groom the Earth Mother in the name of the Creator. We must give back whatever we reap from the earth in order that our children and theirs will have no debts to repay. And if we should give back more than we take, then our children will live in great bounty, but the wisdom must always be harvested as well as the bounty for there will be more children, but the same harvest. We are like the beaver who dams up a small creek and creates a new world for the fish and the frogs and the birds of the air to use to their advantage. Such is our worth when we clear a small meadow where the animals can find fresh grass and tender shoots, where birds can find worms and berries, and a safe place to nest while we plant our humble gardens. The Creator pours forth a multitude of herbs and berries in return for our hard work. Such is our treasure when we bring water to a barren area and the earth becomes green once again. We heal the Earth Mother and her scars no longer spread.

"These principles work as well when we apply them to our brothers and sisters. If we can clear a small meadow in their forests of confusion and plant but a humble garden, they too will have a harvest for their children. And if we can bring the spiritual water into their deserts, they too will become full of life once again and their scars will not spread so wide and deep. Quiktkoata and his followers are like a swarm of locusts who strip the fields of every leaf and blade of grass, leaving a desert behind them. We must set the fields ablaze wherever they take hold and make sure that they are destroyed, or they will consume everything in whatever direction the wind should blow them. The Earth Mother is a garden where our spirits can take root...and grow into the kind of beings that the Creator would approve of for their eternal journeys afterwards. Quiktkoata and his followers would foul the very earth and poison this precious womb of spirits to serve his needs before those of the Creator's."

"If we do not stop him, the Creator will find a way. But then, the good will be lost along with the evil, for his anger is equal for those who allow the evil. The Earth Mother is a gem amongst all worlds. Even the stars shine down on her in constant vigil when Father Sun takes his rest each night. We are the guardians of our Earth Mother and we must constantly groom her and guard against foul plagues such as Quiktkoata's greed for wealth and power." The Sikun detected that Mokotak understood much of what he said and deduced that he was not a true Minnecou, though probably was at heart. Sequannah, however, seemed puzzled, though he politely listened to the strange images that the Sikun used to portray life on the back of the Earth Mother. He had no idea as to the images of the greening of deserts, and the benefits of gardens and those things that bloomed along with them. His people never tended to them; only those who lived in the villages far to the south. By the time the Minnecou returned there each season, the fields lay barren in preparation for the next year.

"Do not fret, young warrior, even if you know nothing of the things I speak of, for your people are not a plague upon the Earth Mother. Your people live in balance and do not attempt to take more than the Earth Mother has to give. Everywhere you go, the land regenerates itself behind you. Your people groom the Earth Mother in a way that no other can, for they are no longer capable. You do not deplete the herds and you take no animal as an enemy, but as a fellow creature. The Creator looks favorably upon you for this. In all areas where people do not scratch the Earth Mother's skin and dig in for comfort, the Creator prefers your kind to roam, and though the animals know you as their predators as well as their friends, they prefer you to all others, and the Creator perceives this. Your people are masters as well for they are best able to serve their world and haven't the slightest desire to abuse it. You have seen the ugliness of Quiktkoata's empire and I tell you now that if we do not put an end to it and bring forth the spiritual water to replenish the desert he is creating, it will spread to the ends of the earth. There is no way of knowing if the Creator will ever allow the desert to bloom again. Our people are rooted in the huge gardens to the south and to there will they return. If you and your people will help us to eliminate Quiktkoata, we will return to our gardens and leave this entire land to the Minnecou and like peoples until only those gardens that the Creator approves of can take root here. I can tell you that the Minnecou will be rewarded for many, many generations; longer than Quiktkoata's terror will remain in your legends. Some small villages will remain, but they will be the trading places and the allies of the Minnecou, for the Creator looks favorably upon those children of his who are different, yet remain on peaceful terms. Pledge your help and enlist the aid of your people and this land will be yours to live as you always have. Entrust yourselves to the Paccus and learn to share peacefully with them and you will be more than blessed by the Creator of all things."

"And if the Paccus prove to be treacherous and selfish?" Mokotak countered. "If they choose not to honor peace between us or if they decide to live according to the ways of Quiktkoata?"

"You may have these problems with your own people as well as the Paccus," the Sikun warned them.

"There will never be Minnecou who will choose the paths of Quiktkoata," Mokotak stated; Sequannah concurred.

"There is always a way to lure anyone into the snares of Quiktkoata's ways. Quiktkoata takes you for his enemy and seeks to eliminate you, for he sees only small bands that rarely even show themselves to their enemies. But when Quiktkoata is gone and his followers are still expanding his empire, they may try to remain on friendly terms with those Minnecou who have eluded them. Eventually, the Minnecou will accept their peace and then fall into adopting some of their ways. In time, the Minnecou will also change in a manner that will keep them from being what they are now, forever. While it is true that the Paccus are more adaptable to Quiktkoata's ways, you can see that it is also possible for your own, and this I warn you about most earnestly," the Sikun became grave. "Maintain the peace between the Paccus and the Minnecou forever, for if you don't, the Minnecou will become divided more and more. There will be some who will maintain their friendship with the Paccus while others are at war with them. The Paccus will experience this, too, and there will be arguments within your own nations, as well as with those you take to be your enemies. When this happens, you will leave another opening for those like Quiktkoata to set down roots once again, for they will use you against each other until the Minnecou and the Paccus will be divided, and therefore weak. Once this happens, there will be too many generations living under their rule to even remember life as you know it now, and there will never be a return to the ways of the true Minnecou."

"With the Minnecou and your people together, we can defeat the Paccus as well as Quiktkoata," Mokotak surmised. "Then there will be no risk of Quiktkoata's kind ever returning."

"I will tell you this once, for that is all that is necessary. The Creator wishes that all peoples be allowed to exist and that they learn to maintain the peace between them. As each of you would look upon his own children, so does the Creator see each nation, each tribe, and each clan. Quiktkoata and his followers will never truly accept those who are not the same as they, and they will always seek to dominate and maintain weakness within all peoples but their own. They do not accept even the Earth Mother, and prefer to change everything to please their own eye with an ever-increasing perversion that is as infinite as the stars. As you maintain a balance with the creatures of the earth and with the Creator himself, so must you maintain a balance with all other peoples."

"If you should choose to join us, soon we will enter certain areas of Quiktkoata's city that will be made known to you when the time comes...and only if you pledge loyalty to us until Quiktkoata and his followers have been eliminated. If you choose to return to your clan and remain distant from our cause, we cannot inform you of any of our plans. There are many spies in Quiktkoata's alliance and they would stop at nothing if they had the slightest suspicion that you have knowledge of us. There is a good possibility that we could succeed in our plan without any help from the Minnecou, but I tell you that without your help and without your influence among the nations, there is no guarantee that you will have a place among the peoples when all is said and done. And I tell you that although the Paccus are our allies, not all of them can be trusted. Some of them are eager for wealth and power, especially when they can see no hope of ever defeating the Snake warriors. They will come to feel that the only hope for their people is to join Quiktkoata rather than face his wrath. But he will divide them and they do not realize that they will no longer be a people again, except when the Snake people seek a reason to deny them. With your help, and with the help of your clans, it is almost certain that Quiktkoata will fall in time, for the Snake people must be kept on the trail to defeat them. The Minnecou know how to do this. If they remain inside the city, there will be little opportunity to weaken them. As you would for your own clan, you must pledge to protect and fight for the cause of our warriors with your lives, for unless each and everyone of us is sworn together to sacrifice ourselves for the good of all, there will be a weakness among us. Do I have at least two Minnecou to count among our victorious warriors."

"I will pledge my blood to the Sikun," Sequannah immediately accepted.

"You will pledge your blood to the Creator," the Sikun corrected him. "And only if it is called upon you to do so. Do not forget that you are but a very young warrior, and you look for battle to prove your worth. But this is neither for honor nor power; it is for the survival of the good peoples and the protection of the Earth Mother. Your life may not even be noted or remembered, for we work in secrecy. Your loyalty to us can only be in the interest of fairness for all of the Creator's good people. Your reward will fall upon the generations beyond, who will live in peace and bounty. But do not feel as though you sacrifice alone, for they too must always do the same to insure their next generation and those to follow. The Creator likes to see his Minnecou roam the plains and forests, just as he likes to see his children of the villages enjoying the bounties of their gardens and the fruits of their crafts. But it is also these children who must grow to suffer and sacrifice to maintain their clans. Do not take offense to my calling you children, for we are all children in the eyes of the Creator."

"I, also pledge my life for my clan and for those of the villages," Mokotak said boldly. "I have lived two lives and see good in both," he declared with nearly as little hesitation as Sequannah.

"I feel as though there are many more than two Minnecou among us already," the Sikun said. "Be patient and rest while you can. Listen closely to Semmida. There will be cause for much bravery very soon and then there will be need for strong loyalty to hold what we have taken. I told you that the Minnecou must draw the Snake warriors out in order to make them vulnerable, but what I have not told you is that this has already been done. The Paccus and the Minnecou together have caused Quiktkoata to gather a massive war party, and they will be leaving soon to pursue the great gathering of Paccus and Minnecou that is growing to the west of here. Quiktkoata is not yet aware that Minnecou are involved as of yet, but when he does discover this, he will not tell his warriors, for they may cower in fear."

CHAPTER 17

Semmida slipped out of the cavern, leading several dozen warriors, women and children into the cool, night air. Most of the party, including two Minnecou warriors, donned the coarse, hooded tunics of Quiktkoata's lowest form of slave, while ten of the largest warriors were garbed in the thick, leather armor of Snake warriors. They crossed directly over the stream at a place where the water spread wide and shallow. Sequannah admired their calmness, considering the dangers involved with bringing two children among them so as not to make the assemblage appear unnatural. But Semmida had not taken any chances, choosing two young children who were not yet capable of speech. The rebels disguised as Snake warriors were well versed. They were supposedly bringing in a group of slaves from a village far to the east where a small copper mine had been stripped clean. The superior Snake warrior from the area had sent this group of experienced miners to work in the copper pits to the north of Quiktkoata's city, where they would be of much more value. Semmida also had several warriors who could recite the history and value of each slave to any of Quiktkoata's warriors who should inquire.

A salmon moon rose slowly to paleness as they reached the top of a low hill. Great ghosts of sparse, billowing clouds drifted slowly before the full globe of the rising moon, their bodies a deep shadowy gray, while misty edges glowed iridescent through the creamy lunar beam. A series of ridges stood brightly over the shadows of their valleys. Semmida's war party transversed them diagonally, towards the heart of Quiktkoata's city. A nervous silence slowly descended upon the group as they drove deeper into the Snake peoples' domain, interrupted occasionally by the sharp yells of Semmida's guards who took turns prodding and taunting the column to make their movement appear natural. Traveling under the brightness of the full moon lent further credibility to the group; most Snake contingents would not transport slaves in total darkness for fear of injuring or losing some of their stock.

Past the third ridge from the cavern, they crossed a flat and bushy meadow; the clanging of metal implements suddenly erupted everywhere around them. A large party of Snake warriors, on their way to gather in the city with Quiktkoata's massing army, had caught sight of Semmida's caravan in the bright moonlight. Semmida and his disguised Snake warriors drew back tensely in the shock of ambush. He quickly regained his composure and rasped angrily at his warriors for not keeping the slaves in order, a ploy to quell suspicion. Several high ranking Snake warriors surrounded Semmida, and harangued him for his negligence in not sending scouts ahead to protect the drive. Meanwhile, their own warriors had intruded into the slaves, poking them with the butt ends of their spears in sadistic jest.

The rebels instinctively surrounded the two Minnecou; these two were unaware of how to act as proper slaves. If they were asked to speak, their Minnecou accents would be detected. Several of the hooded figures tugged on Mokotak's rough clothing to force him down to their level, where his height wouldn't be conspicuous in the tight herd of captives. They were well aware of the stories that had been circulating among the Snake people about the huge and power-ful Minnecou. They could only hope that no one in the great city would recognize the tall warrior as they passed through the heart of the em-pire, seeking passage on one of the many ferries that crossed the great river to the trails that led to the copper fields far to the north. Any alternate route around the many Snake guards scattered throughout the empire would prove to be much more risky and time-consuming than to take the direct route. Moreover, they needed a legitimate en-trance into the well-guarded mining village.

The Snake warriors taunted the guards under Semmida's authority as well as the slaves, for they found no one they recognized and determined them to be conscripts, probably from the same stock as the slaves themselves; local tribesmen who had turned against their own people in order to find a comfortable place in Quiktkoata's em-pire. Although most Snake warriors had done this themselves, they tended to find those who had recently deserted their people to be most undesirable. Until they proved themselves as capable warriors in Quiktkoata's legions, they would be viewed as traitors to their own people, and of little more stature than the slaves themselves.

But the Snake contingent had an urgency of their own to fulfill. There was an army amassing in Quiktkoata's city that would dwarf anything previous, and their presence was demanded immediately. It was late in the year and the Snake warriors had already deduced that a slave hunt was not the likely cause for such an undertaking. There was already talk that there would be no snakes—they would perish in an early winter storm. Many thought Quiktkoata demanded such a massive war party to make up for the loss of their most dangerous advantage: Quiktkoata's evil brood of snakes. But others began to think there must have been a great uprising in the west, for everyone knew that to be their destination. They knew that the Paccus had come from that direction, and that a scattering of Minnecou were frequently seen there. But this didn't appear to them as a serious threat to the empire, unless the Paccus were only a small part of a much larger and more powerful nation than was previously suspected. Or, worse than that, if the rumors that the Minnecou who migrate throughout the empire, but are rarely seen, really are only a small part of a large and distant nation that would seek to avenge the destruction of two of her clans. Despite the wide wanderings of the Minnecou and their infamy throughout the region, little was known of them among the many tribes, except within those small villages far to the south where they gathered during the winter months with certain villagers they called relatives. But even these people knew little of Minnecou ways on the trail, or where they went during the other three seasons. There was some intermingling among the Minnecou and their village "relatives", but marriages were few and usually short-lived, or seasonal at best. All other tribes, including the Snake people who had recently returned after an absence of several generations, were never really sure if these Minnecou had actually come from some distant nation; nor were they certain just how many of them there were.

"Get those filthy slaves moving!" Semmida screamed at his guards; the Snake chiefs seemed satisfied with the group's legitimacy. "And keep them closer together when they have no chains," he demanded in order to placate the Snake superiors' complaints. "Two of you scout ahead like I told you, there's no need for you back here when we have plenty of warriors to guard against escapes. Lucky for us that we ran into our own warriors instead of a hostile group of rebels. And when you two scouts come back here," he screamed at two of his men, "make your accounts brief and get right back on the trail...if you linger around here again, you'll be thrown in with the slaves, and I'll see to it that you spend a long time in chains; in the fish piles if I can arrange it." The two scouts ran as if in terror of Semmida's powerful voice, while the slaves marched briskly towards the north-west to the prodding of the butt ends of the guards' spears. The Snake chiefs were suddenly impressed with this obviously powerful warrior. Semmida saluted them in an almost insolent manner, showing obvious disdain for their interference, then trailed after his party without even asking their permission to continue. After he had left, the Snake contingent's superiors were left wondering who they had crossed, for they themselves became suddenly fearful of this man. It was not what he said that bothered them, but the manner of authority in which he spoke. A warrior of his capacity, who would not be going with Quiktkoata, could only be left behind for one reason; to watch Raestar. Quiktkoata would leave only one of his most powerful and dangerous warriors behind for this purpose, and Semmida manipulated them flaw-lessly by letting them know that he was taking these slaves all the way to the copper fields. He left it to them to deduce that he would not be going with Quiktkoata's army.

As soon as Semmida knew they were gone, he spoke softly to the group: "We must make all the appearances of a true slave drive," he told them. "There will be no silence when we travel, it must always be broken with the foolish demands that the Snake warrior guards use to satisfy their sadistic natures. I want to hear moaning and begging from the slaves, and keep those two Minnecou surrounded at all times. Mokotak, if I see you standing tall once more, I'll have the guards whip you for real. There's no way for us to make it through the city with a giant like you standing so proudly. You are supposed to be a humble slave. Stay down and limp with every step from now on, even if you think there's no one watching. If you do this all the time now, you will not have to think about it when we get to the city. If they do see how large you are, you must appear lame, or you'll find yourself in one of their war parties. And soon we will have spies all around us—the warriors we have just encountered will want to be aware of our movements."

Mokotak was angry enough to throttle Semmida for his verbal affront, but Semmida seemed undaunted by Mokotak's size and strength, and Mokotak knew him to be in the right. The group stumbled their way throughout the night towards Quiktkoata's mysterious city. In the semi-darkness, Semmida's prediction proved to be accurate, though only he and his two advance scouts, along with the two Minnecou were actually aware of the watchful eyes. Towards dawn, when the party approached the imposing city, the spies conveniently disappeared with the first hint of light, apparently satisfied that the slave drive was in fact carrying out everything Semmida had suggested to their superiors.

As Semmida's small group drew closer to the bizarre metropolis, strange calls of exotic birds intermingled with the cheerful song of the native wild birds. The Snake guards wandered in and out of the huge buildings, gathering their gear and taking in their morning meals. The devoted were already on their way to the great hall, where they would chant and pray in their eerie songs for the better part of the morning, and then return during the evening and resume their dirges until long after sunset. Certain slaves were bringing in rich foods to the elite section of the city, while others were filling their stalls in the commons so the wealthy followers of Quiktkoata could haggle over the most magnificent of goods from throughout the empire.

The air had become very chilled and damp just before dawn, and the moon had shown only faintly before it set. Gray clouds streamed down from the north, yet there was little more than a stir on the ground. The sun would not show its brilliant face this day. Distant mountains to the north were white with the first snow of the season.

The river was heavily backed up with rafts and barges of every description, and although the city itself seemed to be just beginning to stir, it was obvious that the activity down at the waterfront had continued throughout the night. "This is good," Semmida spoke quietly. "There will be many empty barges and there will not be a long wait for a ferry to the other side of the river." But as he looked over to the main walkway in and out of the city, he saw hundreds of bundles and litters lined up in the street, ready to be moved. The huge buildings that housed the Snake warriors were rapidly becoming very active, and they were not going out to the shacks to waken the slaves for their day's work.

"But something disturbs me here," he warned. And when he saw many hundreds of warriors suddenly begin to gather along the main walkway, he knew that it was not going to be so easy to get across the river without first risking a long wait in the city. The warriors were all in full war armor, painted in all of their bare-skinned areas with jagged lines of black and yellow, like a gigantic mass of angry bees. From the distance between Semmida and the amassing army, they almost sounded like an irritated hive, but the war whoops that had begun sparsely with the first illumination of the eastern sky were now becoming much more frequent, and louder, giving the city a much more hostile intensity. There were no slaves in the fields and there were probably none in the mines. Every slave in the city had been herded down to the wharves, engaged in a massive effort to unload all of the barges that had come in filled to the brim from throughout all of the villages along the river in Quiktkoata's empire. Everything was being hoarded into the warehouses. Then barges were pulled up to the end of the main walkway, where they would be loaded with the warriors' gear and supplies for ferrying across the river. Out of the backsides of the warehouses, bundles that had been prepared inside were immediately carted off to the main walkway and then loaded onto the barges.

Across the river, Semmida witnessed a huge store of supplies that had already been ferried to the other side. "They must have had every slave in the empire here for several days to bring so much into those warehouses, sort out what would be needed for travel, and then ferry everything to the other side of the river," Semmida whispered, pointing at the enormous cache on the other side of the river. Apparently, the warehouses on that side of the river were not quite capable of handling such a heavy workload, though they seemed to be working at full capacity as well. Semmida wished they could find a place to hide until all of the soldiers had been ferried across the river, and many of the barges would be free, but there was too much risk involved. They may already have been seen by someone from the city, or by guards posted throughout the area. Spies had also been following them during the night. Trying to remain hidden for at least one whole day at close proximity to such a tense and hostile army as Quiktkoata's could prove to be an impossibility in itself. Just being discovered at such a time could cause Semmida and those warriors he had chosen as Snake warriors to be taken for cowards and deserters, and then executed. The slaves would be tortured to their deaths for collusion with the guards, and this would be exactly what the cruel one would use to whip all of his forces into a frenzy; to see the blood of those who would defy Quiktkoata and his omnipotent warriors.

There was no choice for Semmida but to lead his small group of warriors directly into the city, and down to the waterfront, to seek passage across the great river. If there were no barges available, then he would offer his slaves and men to help in the effort. But this could prove too distasteful for the Minnecou, Semmida thought to himself, for they must have deduced that Quiktkoata would put every effort into finding the Minnecou clan that had become a thorn in his foot. If Sequannah and Mokotak helped the slaves at the wharves, they would be lending a hand in the deaths of their own tribesmen. "This could be very dangerous," Semmida muttered to his two scouts. "Why Teokehannah burdens us with these two Minnecou is a question that has been asked by each of us more than once. I question his decisions often, and usually his actions are guided by some hidden wisdom. But this time, the wisdom is too well hidden. This time I question if there is any wisdom at all. I am the only one who can even speak to them."

With much yelling and cracking of whips, Semmida and his small party moved toward the wharves of the city, a move that could prove to be their last. The Snake guards at the wharves didn't send anyone to question or accept them into the city as they made their approach, which suggested to Semmida that they were already aware of the small party of thirty-two slaves and ten guards. Perhaps spies during the night had reported them to Quiktkoata's chief warriors. On the other hand, spies could have been implanted within the group that Semmida now led, or even among those who remained at the cavern. It was a risky venture from beginning to finish, and at every turn there was the possibility of walking into a trap, or being betrayed by one of those he led. A nervous gesture, a conversation with the wrong person, the possibility of the Minnecou being recognized or asked to speak; any one of these could doom them all.

Semmida and his followers were more than half-way across the long open area that preceded the city, and still no one had come to investigate them. A distant clatter behind them caused some of the guards to turn. Hundreds of Snake warriors emerged from the bushy area where this same small party had just paused to assess their situation. Semmida's first instinct was that he was now surrounded and hopelessly outnumbered. Perhaps these same warriors had lain hidden in the brush, listening to their conversation. Even if they had seen the small party pause and not heard their whisperings, there may be cause for suspicion. Twice he had been surprised by the sudden emergence of one of Quiktkoata's contingents. Such large groups of warriors, traveling silently enough to catch him unaware, despite the fact that they all carried metal implements that could clang and clatter with even the slightest of movements, was causing even Semmida to become slightly unnerved. If he had stayed in the brush for just a few more moments, they would have been seen spying on the city with their group of slaves. Whether they had actually been seen or not was still a question in Semmida's mind. There was, however, no hope of escape at this point.

Semmida swaggered towards the wharves, two advance scouts at his sides, while the group of slaves was being herded along at a properly aloof distance. The two scouts walked in complete confidence, the scowls on their faces suggesting that they would easily out-fight and out-maneuver any of Quiktkoata's average warriors. Semmida's guards appeared to be completely engrossed in their work, hounding their subjects and maneuvering them with the finesse of a finely tuned pack of wolves, keeping their quarry surrounded and singling out any who dared to stray. Semmida breathed a sigh of relief when the contingent headed towards the city instead of following them straight to the river's edge.

Many small, square buildings preceded the wharf area, and Semmida now walked some distance ahead of his group, though the two scouts would turn back from time to time to make sure that they always fell within their line of vision. Many well-worn pathways wended their way between the hundreds of shacks that housed the workers of the barges while the unloading took place. Semmida knew that the widest of these paths would lead either to the wharves or the center of the city, depending on which direction was taken. One well-worn path led to neither of these two principle destinations, but led instead to that section of the city where the hairy humans dwelled. Apparently, many of the barge workers had found their way into the company of these hairy-faced creatures, who would offer them strange brews for a price. This whole section of city would laugh and fight their way through the night until they fell in numbing stupors. With what little they understood of each other, they most often found themselves learning each others' words for ships and barges and anything that related to working on the water. Many of these workers now lay in their doorways, or along the sides of paths, their sweat giving off a peculiarly foul odor, their unconscious states unfettered by the extraordinary amount of activity surrounding them.

Semmida walked slowly towards the wharf where most of the Snake warriors seemed to be getting their orders, and where there seemed to be warriors of high rank running the whole affair. He walked slowly so that when he arrived at the dock, his whole party would be right behind him and in plain view. He observed everything around him, scrutinizing even the most minor of operations. The high ranking warriors on the dock began to cast suspicious and sidelong glances as he made his way slowly toward them. He stood for several moments, looking around and talking and pointing with his two scouts. Then without warning, he turned and stormed up to the dock and strode into the midst of Quiktkoata's chiefs.

"Why is this packing and loading still going on!" he screamed at them. "Was this not supposed to be finished by dawn! Is it your intention to pack our warriors in with the cargo like lice when they cross the river today. This should have been completed before nightfall yesterday–the sun already shines brightly once again and still you lag behind. Do you expect the great and honorable warriors of Quiktkoata's legions to cross with the provisions? What kind of honor is this to send out our soldiers. If you are not finished with these menial chores before the sun is halfway up the morning sky, I'll speak to Quiktkoata, himself, and you will all be out there working with these slaves," he screamed with a distasteful slant.

"Where do you come from and by whose authority do you dare threaten us with your howling?" a warrior of obvious high rank glared at Semmida. Semmida's two scouts immediately grabbed him by the arms and doubled him over whereby Semmida brought his knee brutally into the man's face.

"If you want more authority I would be more than pleased to demonstrate," Semmida hissed calmly through his teeth. He grabbed the man by the hair and threw him to the floor of the dock. "Where is my barge?" he began to scream once again. "How am I to bring these slaves across and up to the mines if you fools cannot even have a barge ready to keep this empire moving?"

"There will be barges ready soon," the man stammered from the floor of the dock, waving his men off. A bustle of activity and screaming erupted as several dozen hooded slaves were herded onto the barges that were presently docked at the wharf, and began to frantically toss the bundles back onto the decking.

"What is this foolishness?" Semmida boomed out at them once again. The man with the bloodied face and lips looked up in wonderment as to how this powerful chief could be placated. "I order you to finish this work and you move backwards! Have them throw that stuff back onto the barge and bring me an empty one. Are your skulls filled with dog shit?" Semmida would stay right on top of them until they were desperate to get rid of him. They assumed he was from some distant outpost of the empire and feared that he would now be posted in the city if they could not find a way to send him quickly off to the mines. Quiktkoata must be well aware of this man, they knew, and as long as he was around, the work would double at the docks. They preferred that this be the case at the copper mines instead, where a man like this would be distant from them for long periods of time; hopefully years.

But as Semmida looked out the corner of his eye, he suddenly wished that he had let them finish unloading so that they could get out of there quickly. Mokotak, still hunched over, was urinating all over the bundles that lay beside the dock. Sequannah was going through another set of bundles, stuffing whatever he could get his hands on under his tunic. Semmida tapped one of his scouts in the ankle with his foot and glared desperately in the direction of the two Minnecou. Both scouts slid discreetly over to them and the bloodied man began to shift his attention. Semmida immediately lumbered over to the high ranking warrior and reached down to give him a hand, bringing him to his feet in an attempt to distract him from the activities of the Minnecou.

"You must stay on your feet, warrior," Semmida consoled him in a rough manner. "I expect from this point on you will be prepared and never let this happen to you again, no matter how much another warrior out-ranks you. I had no trouble in removing your authority, instantly, and that is something you can never let go of, my friend. Prepare the men around you for just such an instance—there is no telling when it could happen again, or what the purpose behind it might be. I could have been leading a band of rebels, for all you know!" Semmida shifted his demeanor.

Another group of slaves had suddenly been herded into the dock area, and the stray Minnecou became indiscernible in the crowd. The two scouts came back to Semmida's side and reported that the other group of slaves they had been waiting for had now arrived.

Semmida looked questioningly at them for an instant and then, realizing that the warrior he'd just humiliated was wondering as well, put his arm around the man's shoulder as if he were an old friend. "How many barges can you have ready for us quickly? There is much work to be done in the copper mines if all these warriors should need more weapons sent out to them. Quiktkoata demands much copper for trade with the great cities to the south as well and when he returns, that copper had better be ready." The man gave Semmida an understanding smile, and once again swaggered down the deck, screaming at his underlings. They in turn screamed at the slaves to get the barges loaded quickly so that more empty barges could be brought in.

Sequannah felt uneasy with the large group of slaves that had suddenly been herded in with them. What would happen if when they were separated once again, and they put him in the wrong group by mistake? If he spoke the few words he had learned, not only would he be whipped for his arrogance, but his Minnecou accent would most certainly be detected. He shifted in the crowd to make sure that he was among those he had originally come with, and when he turned around, he came face to face with the short guard who had been so cruel to him at the fish pile. The guard immediately reached over and lifted the veil on Sequannah's hood to get a look at him. Sequannah stared back, half in defiance and half in shock. "So here I find my young Minnecou friend," he laughed. "I'll wager you missed my company?" he laughed again. Sequannah sneered at him and was ready to bolt when the short guard grabbed his tunic by the scruff of the neck. "Do not fear, Sequannah. I am with you. Do you really think you would have survived the fish pile if I wasn't. You should see what we did to one of Quiktkoata's spies," he sneered, and then disappeared into the crowd. The only thing Sequannah could recall this guard ever saying before was "Fuull baskette". Yet, now he was speaking in perfect Minnecou.

Sequannah felt somewhat more at ease, but he was growing weary of being surrounded by strangers, and so many of them at that. He glanced over at Mokotak, who up until this point was in much the same mood as himself, but was now receiving small chuckles and polite admonitions for his behavior. Sequannah reached under his tunic while he was hidden inconspicuously amongst the slaves, and felt the large chunk of meat he had stolen. He worked a small piece of it off to find out what kind of animals had been slain for the Snake warriors' provisions. As he slipped it secretly into his mouth, he made a strange face under his hood, but he was distracted from his analysis by the rub of a smooth leg against his own. Sequannah attempted to secretly spit out the hard and salty lump, for it was stringy and foul tasting, but the sweet voice of a feminine slave betrayed her observations.

"My Minnecou warrior returns," she said coyly. "And he offers no meat to his sister slave?" Sequannah quickly reached into his tunic and ripped off a piece in an effort to keep this woman close to him, for he recognized Tarote's soft voice. If his attraction to her was vague at the fish pile, there was no doubt now. "You do not approve of the Snake warriors' meat?" she questioned. "I have heard that Quiktkoata had ordered all of his old and sickly llamas to be shaved and slaughtered, because they would not survive the winter. I have also heard that they salted this meat heavily to disguise the taste and odor. Of course, our group of slaves were sent to do the work, so we accidentally left the carcasses in the sun for a few days. There are going to be a lot of vengeful warriors when they return, but that will be all too late," she said with gleeful sarcasm.

"This meat is no good?" Sequannah asked her incredulously. "Then I will be sick as well."

"Don't worry too much," she laughed softly. "At least you did not swallow it."

"Then I will be okay?" he asked.

"Where you stand now, you are at risk of death at any moment; and you worry about sickness?" she questioned him sarcastically.

Sequannah recognized his danger, but he couldn't help dreading what would happen if he were indeed poisoned, for he had dealt with this experience before. To worry about death had not really occurred to him, though, until this moment; he realized that he was no longer a child, but a warrior. If he should prove to be someone's enemy, he would not merely be captured and used as a slave. Now he would be killed as a threat. He was in the midst of a very powerful and dangerous empire, and the actions he was a part of were definitely a threat, though he was not quite aware of all of the details. This thought was overwhelming and Sequannah looked to Mokotak. He then realized that Mokotak never really gave a thought as to whether he would die or not. If he agreed to go on a war party, that is what he would do. There was never even a thought of Mokotak looking for a way out, or squirming under the pressure of fear.

"If I should become sick, then we could be discovered," he thought quickly. "They will surely find out that I am a Minnecou if I am asked to explain my illness."

"All of us are going to the copper mines," Tarote told him. "All of our Snake guards are with us as well."

"The shorter one," Sequannah queried. "He is not really a Snake guard."

"He is Ondada," Tarote informed him. "And the taller one, he is from the Wistachu people. They have been with us since I first worked on the fish pile."

"They put the iron collar around my neck and nearly killed me when they pulled me out of the pile. Then they threw me back in over and over!" Sequannah reminded her.

"They could not tell if you were really Minnecou until I spoke with you. But they were very easy on you because I requested that they be. I could see that you were only just old enough to have become a warrior in any tribe. They hurt you, I know, but had you been someone like Sabanote, they would have kept you close to death the whole time. Look!" she pointed discreetly. Sequannah looked over to see a very sickly looking figure, drooping in a distant corner, ready to faint or vomit; whichever came first. The Ondada crept over to the haunted soul and screamed at him with a simultaneous flick of his whip to the spy's earlobe. "He is a spy for Quiktkoata," Tarote whispered. "He has even admitted this to us. We knew he was here to find out what happened to you and the big one. He has had too much and we know that he cannot get away. If he does, Quiktkoata will kill him for failing to get in with our rebels. He pleaded with me to let him be with us, but I pretend not to know what he speaks of. He can never be trusted because he will side with whoever has control over him, and then turn around to the other side when he sees it possible and to his advantage."

"When this many slaves are sent into the copper mines, won't their chief become suspicious?" Sequannah asked.

"They are always left alone up there," Tarote said. "They never hear anything from the city unless they do not produce enough copper. The guards up there have been there since they first began mining. They do not even know what the city looks like any more. They may have heard of a big battle coming, but they would almost expect more slaves to be sent into the mines because there would be less slaves that would have to be watched in the city if they were sent up there. Quiktkoata, also, will want more copper for weapons and trading. This is their weak spot and that is why we choose to take the mines before we attempt anything in the city. If we can cut off their copper mines, then they will have no more to make their weapons with, nor will they have this to trade in the cities to the south."

"Why do we not wait for Quiktkoata to leave with his army and then take the city?" Sequannah asked as if he were a part of a huge army.

"Do you think that the group you see before you has any chance of holding this whole city?" she asked incredulously. "We do not even have weapons as of yet."

"You spoke of many warriors, and spies everywhere," Sequannah's eyes widened.

"We have what you see before you and a few spies in the city," she stated matter-of-factly.

"Then you are crazy!" Sequannah's voice rose. Tarote quickly put her hand to his mouth to quiet him. "That would be like the Minnecou trying to take this place!" he whispered frantically. "There are thousands of warriors here. We could all be killed within a few moments. Even after Quiktkoata and his army are long gone they will leave more warriors here than we will ever be able to think of fighting!"

"If you refuse, then you end the Minnecou right now," she became angry. "I could have gone to Teyotewakan by now and been quite safe. My father could have stayed down there wandering among the villages...there would be no difference to us whether the Minnecou roam the north country or not. My father is a Sikun and when he tells you that he has a plan that will work, he tells you the truth, because he cannot speak any word but the truth. The only risk of failure is that of your faith, your patience, or your courage. Do not doubt or question, but work towards the completion of our plan. Always move in the direction of our plan, no matter how little, for even the smallest step is closer than before. But never step back. Always protect whatever you gain because whatever you have left open to lose, you have never really gained. You are but a young warrior and sometimes you feel as if you are a giant like your friend, and other times you will feel like a whimpering child." Under his hood,

Sequannah's face tensed in irritation at her insult. "But this is no matter because there is nothing but an end for your people and yourself if you do not succeed. None of you could live in one place and work as a slave. You would all die or be killed. Those of you who escape will be living alone for the rest of your lives, or recaptured by one of Quiktkoata's war parties. But you will never live as you do now. Truthfully, the Minnecou have already lost their ways because they cannot even return this year and they never will again unless you and all of us are successful."

"My clan will already be halfway down the southern trail by now," Sequannah said. "They know enough not to sacrifice the clan for Mokotak and myself."

"Your clan is up in the Dark Mountains, with no place to go but further north, away from Quiktkoata's empire," she said knowingly. "Quiktkoata will push your people until they can go nowhere but to the land of snow, and then they will perish in the icy wind, or by the weapons of his warriors. Quiktkoata will never let the Minnecou return here."

Mokotak was hobbling towards them when they realized that their situation was changing rapidly. Two empty barges had been pulled up to the wharf, and some of the slaves were already being loaded into them. Whoops and shrieks from the center of the city became suddenly louder, and a deafening roar was building from the hostile crowd and the thousands of warriors. The clang of weapons and the grunting of workers could be heard everywhere as the massive army prepared to move down to the wharves. This was very untimely in Semmida's mind; he would be directly in front of the approaching mass of warriors. Semmida's guards frantically herded all of the slaves onto the two barges. Mokotak had met with Sequannah and Tarote and dragged them up the wharf, pulling them quickly onto the boat. Semmida's guards took up positions all along the outer decks of the barges and shoved off into the mighty river. They were no more than a quarter of the way across, when the wharves became inundated with Snake warriors, waiting to be ferried. Semmida could hear several of the Snake warriors haranguing the man he had beaten on the wharf. "What kind of fool would allow slaves to cross on barges that were meant for Quiktkoata's warriors?" They took the beaten warrior and all of his underlings on the dock and threw them into the foul and muddy soup that made up the river's edge.

Semmida's guards poled the barges as fast as was humanly possible and were completely across before another empty barge was even in the process of being hauled up to the wharf. Once on the other side, Semmida took his two scouts with him and dove into another crowd of Snake warriors on the western side of the river. "Why do you stand here staring and mumbling? Are you all fools? Can't you see that those barges have to be unloaded quickly? A thousand warriors stand waiting on the other side of the river, ready to fight for the glory of our empire and all of you stand here pointing and mumbling. Get those slaves off of those rafts and bring the empty rafts back across to those wharves now! Move!" he screamed at them. "Where are my provisions?" he hollered. "I am not a fool like all of you seem to be. I'll have my party outfitted and out of the way before the first warrior even steps foot on this shore. I was intelligent enough to make preparations and send word in advance so that all of my provisions would be ready as soon as I arrived." The Snake warriors seemed to be somewhat confused at these last statements. "Where are my provisions?" he screamed. "They had better be ready!"

One of them inched forward. "I'm sure that you planned everything as you have said, but I'm afraid that with the overload of work and the great effort that is taking place here, someone must have forgotten to deliver your orders."

"Who is in authority here!" Semmida's demanding scream sent shivers down the backs of the onlooking slaves. The Snake warriors pointed to one of the hairy-faced humans, some distance down the shoreline. He was surrounded by a flock of his Snake warriors, cowering under his harsh voice and rushing to satisfy his every demand. Semmida took his two scouts and stormed up to the pink-skinned man.

"You!" he pointed to the muscular man with the long strands of greasy blond hair. "You watch us cross from one side of the river to the other and still you do not think to ready the provisions we will need when we get here? I will not hold up Quiktkoata's warriors for a hairy-faced bitch like you. Get our group outfitted and out of here before the first warrior steps foot on this side of the river or you'll be in the fish piles for the rest of your days here."

The white man glared in fury at Semmida, his face quickly turning a bright red, a growl erupting from somewhere deep in his throat. "Get out of my way!" he screamed as he threw one after another of his men to the ground who had the misfortune of standing between him and Semmida. "None of Quiktkoata's fools will ever speak to me with insolence. Grab those three skunks!" he roared as he forced his way over to them.

Semmida's two scouts quickly dashed aside every oncomer and whipped each one as they fell to the ground, while Semmida stood there defiantly, his arms folded across his chest. "Wait," he requested of his two scouts; the Snake warriors had broken off their rush; only the hairy-faced one still approached. Semmida suddenly broke into a full run towards the muscular white man and planted his heel squarely into the pit of his stomach. He then wrapped his arm around the man's thick, hairy neck and tossed him over his back. When he turned and expected to find the loud-mouthed one ready to submit, he found instead that the strange looking man was grinning and growling, simultaneously. He was shouting and cursing and foaming at the mouth, as only a rabid animal would do. He drew his knife and scrambled viciously after Semmida. The two scouts each grabbed a handful of hair and a handful of beard and tossed him face first into Semmida's waiting knee. But the rabid man just shook it off and came back screaming and cursing and foaming even more, as if they had strengthened him rather than hurt him. The two scouts went to grab him again, and he picked one of them up clear over his head and held him in a position that threatened to break the scout's back when he brought him back down on his already braced knee. The other scout quickly maneuvered himself in back of the big white man and grabbed onto his greasy locks with both hands and then forced his knee into the center of his back. The white man screamed and laughed hideously, but he let the other scout fall to the ground. Semmida strode over to the man and with one sharp blow, forced the heel of his hand into the hairy throat. He watched almost casually as the strange man's eyes glazed over and his arms fell limply to his sides. The scout who was holding him allowed him to slump to the ground, where he gurgled for several moments and then sat up, gasping for breath, but clearly subdued. Semmida breathed a sigh of relief, for this would have killed any normal man.

"Get my provisions now!" Semmida allowed no time to let the incident sink in. "This will be your fate if you don't enjoy the fish pile, unless my group is loaded and on their way before our warriors get here!" The barges across the river were nearly full and ready to start across. The Snake warriors hurriedly grabbed all manner of food and supplies and loaded them onto the backs of the slaves that had been quickly ushered off of the barges. Semmida and his party were already on their way to the copper mines when the two empty barges passed the first group of warriors at the halfway point in the river. Sequannah and Mokotak, who had witnessed the incident with the hairy-faced one, both knew that the larger Minnecou could easily have handled the white warrior himself. Sequannah felt his skinny arms and legs and desperately wished that he could grow much faster than time would allow.

Semmida's party moved quickly out of the area. From their provisions, they ate as they ran to outpace any possible contingent sent to follow them. Semmida's own guards had helped to assemble the provisions, but had picked out mostly weapons, as food and clothing were not their main concern. Shortly after they had entered into the cover of thick woods, the party halted and one of the bundles was broken open. Knives and arrows with blades of copper were handed out to the slaves as well as Semmida's guards, and bows were easily hidden under the thick, loose garments of the slaves' garb. Mokotak refused the knife and rummaged through the bundle until he produced a large tomahawk. He stared at it, slightly dissatisfied for its lack of weight, but pleased that he had at least been able to find one. Sequannah pulled out a long copper knife, its sides etched like the feathers of a wing. He also took a short bow and several arrows, tying them to the inside of his tunic. Then the group was quickly on their way. Sequannah had requested one of the heavier bundles to be placed on his own back when they had first left the west side of the river, and was now almost sorry. But he thought of what he had been always told from his father, and carried the heavier load. Though he would be weak and tired at the end of his journey, once recovered, he would be stronger. Never be afraid to wrestle with the strongest, or bear the heaviest burden, Petawahin would tell him, for strength and prowess were earned as well as inherited by the most powerful Minnecou warriors.

Semmida's guards scouted well in advance and far behind the quickly advancing party. Well over one hundred warriors dressed in hooded tunics and two dozen warriors disguised as Quiktkoata's slave drivers were a powerful force in the empty woodlands of the north. But in comparison to some of the Snake war parties they had encountered, their cause appeared to be hopeless. The warriors guarding the remote copper mines could overpower Semmida's approaching army. The rebels were nothing more than a minor threat at this point. But the mining village had many weaknesses, the greatest of which was its poor communication with the rest of Quiktkoata's empire. Quiktkoata had maintained a force large enough to keep the hairy-faced ones subdued and the slaves working. Indeed, by giving the hairy-faced ones dominion over most of the slaves, not only did the mine operate smoothly, but the white ones felt they had some stature within the empire. The Snake guards who ruled over the mines were rarely changed–the white ones would always find a way to exploit any newcomers; luring them to their strange brews, and then extorting them when their uncontrollable behavior caused them to neglect their duties.

Teokahannah knew that the same Snake warriors who had first defeated the white men at the copper mines, had been kept there ever since. It had taken so long to defeat them, that Quiktkoata found it necessary to leave this small, yet powerful group of warriors to maintain order in the mines as well as the whole northern area of the empire. Other than the white people, however, this whole area was almost uninhabited, leaving his Snake guards and slaves in near isolation. Their only contact with the empire was through the long caravans of slaves and guards who transported the finished copper ingots and casts to the waiting barges on the distant river, and then brought food and supplies to the mines on their return trip. Teokahannah had learned that the mining and the caravans had been kept totally independent of each other. Those slaves and guards who were involved in transporting the copper and other goods were never allowed into the mining area, or aboard the barges on the other end. Likewise, those slaves within the mines were never allowed outside of the village, and the guards were only out on patrols in the unpopulated hills and woodlands of the northern frontier. Occasionally, they would run across the faint trace of a Minnecou footprint, but otherwise, they were alone. Most of the Snake warriors in the north hadn't been back in Quiktkoata's city since they first left to fight the white ones. And Quiktkoata was not about to risk losing his mines under the direction of inexperienced Snake guards. Consequently, many of the slaves, guards and whites were assigned to live here permanently.

Along the route between the mines and the river, two

camps had been set up where the procession would make overnight stays. Since they could stay neither in the camps of the mines, nor in the camps near the barges, a strong incentive was maintained to keep moving until they reached one of the camps on the trail, especially when it was raining, or during the winter months when moving too slowly would cause them frostbite or a night of sleeping in dugout tunnels in the snow.

The isolation of these operations left the Sikun with a very real advantage, even if his own forces were meager in comparison. The key to everything was for Semmida to get inside of the mining camps with all of his slaves and guards, and gain the trust and respect of the village chief and his warriors.

*   *   *

Tarote came running up from well behind Semmida's quickly moving procession. She had taken charge of all the scouts while Semmida instructed the guards himself. The scouts to the rear of the party could now be seen, as they had been pulled up closer to the group of slaves.

"You will be pleased to learn that no one has followed," Tarote grinned. She no longer wore the long tunic common to the slaves, but was dressed as one of the Snake warriors' concubines; Sequannah could not keep himself from ogling her slender form and radiant beauty.

"They surrounded the big white man and laughed at him when they came across the river. They were happy to see him in shameful defeat. They did not know your name, but they were cheering for the one who had beaten the white man." Tarote could barely contain her admiration for Semmida. "Come walk ahead with me," she prodded. "We have much to plan, now that we have come this far." Sequannah looked on as he kept time with the quick pace of the slaves. Pangs of longing and jealousy crept into his heart as he realized that many years would have to pass before he would be comparable to Semmida.

CHAPTER 18

After five days marching through forest and bushy meadows of rough terrain, Semmida's party approached an open plain. They had just gotten underway in the frosty morning, when the peaks of the Dark Mountains appeared through the naked branches. By mid-morning they would be taking their first steps onto a small inlet of the vast prairie that separated the forest from the foothills of the Dark Mountains. The highest peaks in the distance were covered in a thin veil of white, confirming that the first snows had indeed fallen; the possibility of a sudden storm of drifting and blowing snow had become a real threat.

Scouts had returned the night before warning that a recently used camp had been discovered at the edge of the forest. A large number of Snake warriors had occupied the site for one or two days, then split up into several small parties. Fresh track signs revealed the use of many trails throughout the area, and certain intersections showed where small parties had met briefly, then split up again. Tarote ran swiftly into the camp, two scouts immediately behind her, and found her way to Semmida.

"Many scouts were patrolling the area ahead of us last night, but today they have gathered into a war party. They have discovered the trail we left, or they have seen us from a distance, but they are gathering to ambush us where the forest meets the prairie. They are very difficult to see because they lie flat to the ground behind a hidden ridge in the prairie," she warned. "The open lands appear flat, but when we skirted the edge of the forest, we could see them. If we stay in the woods till we get to the Dark Mountains, we can avoid them."

"But when they discover that we have eluded them, they will have more reason to hold suspicion against us," Semmida reasoned. "No, we will not go around them, but we will acknowledge their presence before they would make it known to us. We will hail them before we get within bow range so they will know that we do not move in ignorance. By the time we reach the mining camps, they will obey my every command," he said confidently.

*　*　*

Word had been passed along to the scouts and warriors that they would walk out onto the prairie, and soon after, they would halt and hail a war party waiting in ambush. Many could not wait for Semmida to show them how foolishly they had hidden and planned against a warrior who knew their every move. But neither Sequannah nor Mokotak looked upon the situation with the same anticipation.

"Tell Semmida that even if they accept his party, he will put himself among enemies for the embarrassment he causes them," Sequannah warned Tarote. He remembered the pride and arrogance that surrounded the vicious superiors of Quiktkoata's warriors. Mokotak agreed and would have told Tarote first if he had been able to put his ideas into words more quickly.

"Semmida must demonstrate his strength over them immediately, or we will all be in trouble," she countered. "Our control of this party will vanish if Semmida does not show his power over them at the very first contact. They will separate us and throw us where they will. Then Semmida will find himself in some menial position where we will not be able to organize ourselves again. They must know him as a man of power and absolute authority. What better way than to make fools of them, and remove their authority first?"

But Sequannah and Mokotak did not agree. They had served as slaves under the Snake warriors and had not fared well. Tarote had served as a slave under them, herself, but she was among allies. She had been protected from the real Snake guards.

The party of slaves was marched northward with most of Semmida's guards and scouts immediately surrounding them. Tarote patrolled ahead with only two scouts to insure that the Snake warriors in ambush would remain where they were, and not attempt to move into the forest. Close to the edge of the prairie, two advance scouts from the Snake warriors' war party waited impatiently for Semmida's contingent to come into view. They were a good distance apart and somewhat difficult to see, but Tarote crept up to a point where she could still see both of them without being detected. She saw every hand sign that passed between them:

-Any sign of them?-

-No.-

-Move further ahead.-

-Fool. We will be too far away to warn the war party.-

-They could have gone around us. Then we would be

fools!-

-If they go around, they will show themselves as enemies. Then we will hunt them down.-

Tarote waited for quite some time before they began to sign once again.

-Let's move to the top of the next hill.-

-And what if they come when we are only half way there? Who will warn the war party. They will see us if we even dare to breathe.-

-Go back to the mines—watch the smelly slaves all day. Fear has no place in the heart of a scout—the heart of a true warrior!- he exaggerated his movements.

-You should be the smelly slave I watch. Foolishness is more dangerous than fear.-

-They should have been here long ago. We should find out what happened to them before they are long gone.-

-They have probably sent out advance scouts as well. They could be watching us now.-

-You have the nerve of a rabbit- the aggressive one gestured. He was about to sign another insult when the sound of voices suddenly erupted far in front of them. Moments later, Semmida's guards came ambling over the top of the ridge, prodding their slaves along as they reveled in insult and laughter. The slaves moaned loudly, and under this cover, the two enemy scouts quickly slipped back to the war party waiting in ambush on the deceptively peaceful prairie.

"They still remain behind the rise," Tarote reported to Semmida. "I watched their hand sign and they, themselves, even deduced that if we went around them, it would only be because we had seen them and determined them to be enemies. Then they would hunt us down, sending for as much help as they needed to slaughter us."

"Teokahannah expects us to do the impossible, but even when performing the simplest of tasks, mistakes can be made," Semmida aired his doubts about the Sikun's plans. "Whatever should happen, we must all stick to our plan and our stories, for to change even one person's story could mean failure. Teokahannah says that help will be on the way even as we walk into the mining camp, but there are no promises that we will even make it that far, so how can we even begin to depend on the help that we are not already sure of?"

"If you know my father, then you know that he can speak

no untruths," Tarote said faithfully. "What he tells you is of absolute certainty. He has accepted and given himself as servant to the Creator, and knows in his heart that all things necessary will be provided. Failure walks with fear, and lack of faith. My father tells you that you can hold us together and keep our faith stronger than even an army of Snake warriors could tarnish...you must believe him, for he tells no lies."

"He should lead us himself," Semmida began to lose hope once again. "He has much more faith in his plan than I."

"For all of this time you praise his words, and suddenly you find reason to doubt?" she questioned as if speaking to a fool. "How do you think you came this far without even one necessary change in his strategy? It may be very simple, but that even makes it easier to follow. And you know he would lead us himself, but he is sworn as servant to the Creator and cannot speak untruths. Our plan will require many untruths to be spoken, but the real truth must always shine brightly in our hearts. You know that even out here, it is possible that someone could recognize him, and how could he lead us into the slave camps if he is a slave. No, it is you he chose to lead us and it is you who will do so," she demanded. "Remember what he told you...until you get into the mining camp, you are a Snake guard in charge of important slaves and will be treated with no less respect than any other Snake commander. There is nothing else you need to know or think of...you are only performing your duties. If anyone in your party should become fearful, whip them as the Snake war chiefs would, for this will give your party the true appearance of a slave drive. Even if anger and resentment should arise, have no fear, for this is the way Snake people live and rule."

"Then you will feel no resentment if I tell you to wear slave clothes and travel with them from this point forward," Semmida sneered. "And even if you do, it will be all that much better for appearances. Do not forget that you are as likely to be recognized as your father."

Tarote donned her slaves' garments once again, which she fully intended to do, but the manner in which she was so aloofly ordered piqued her anger.

*   *   *

"Walk out onto the prairie and scout ahead of us," Semmida ordered the two scouts he had summoned. "It does not matter if you walk directly into the war party or off to either side, just choose the path that would lead us to the mining camp most quickly. If you see the war party before they see you, hail them. Tell what kind of slaves we have here. If they should see you first, make sure there is always an avenue of escape, and that they are aware of it. Do not step onto that prairie until you are sure you have passed no scouts that they have hidden on the forest edge to prevent your escape. This is not to be used for your escape for any reason, but only to let them know that you are not fools. You are to be intercepted by them, no matter what threat they present. If you do not, remember that your greatest threat is back here with me. Whatever doubts you have about the size or success of this war party, understand one thing—no matter how fierce or calm these next few days should become, the Sikun will prevail and I shall be his war chief. A thousand Snake warriors are less of a threat to you than we are should cowardice enter into you."

* * *

Semmida marched several paces from the edge of the forest, then turned to observe his party being hastily prodded along. His two scouts suddenly appeared from behind a rise in the prairie, signaled that everything was clear ahead, then vanished behind the rise. Semmida immediately halted the procession—three more scouts came out from the woods to confer with him. One of them walked straight out to the top of the rise, where he found the enemy war party, every bow trained on him, waiting in ambush.

"My chief sends you his greetings," the scout called out. "But he is impatient to perform the important work that Quiktkoata has sent him to do here. We bring new mining slaves to your village. He asks that you release his two scouts and either assist us in getting to the mines as quickly as possible or go on about your affairs. Otherwise, there will be battle between Quiktkoata's own war parties. He also instructed me to tell you not to have any doubts but that Quiktkoata would side with him in any dispute, no matter how trivial. He has with him the Snake empire's best and most knowledgeable mining slaves and at Quiktkoata's request is here to double the production of copper before the next moon in order to supply Quiktkoata's army while they engage in battle to the west."

"Who are you to come here and announce secrets to a war party that you cannot even be sure is truly of the Snake people?" the war chief from the mining village sneered. "We could have disguised ourselves as Snake warriors and then you would have been telling Quiktkoata's plans."

"There is no secret about this battle," the scout countered nervously. "It is known throughout the empire that Quiktkoata has assembled the largest army ever and that at this very moment has already begun the journey west with more than one thousand warriors."

"If so many warriors have been sent to battle, why were none of ours included as well?" the Snake war chief sneered.

"A man of your position must certainly be aware that the supplies for battle must always be protected and ready to reinforce the warriors in the field. Surely Quiktkoata would not entrust this task to fools. Our chief has come to bring these slaves to the mines and ready all of the warriors here in the event that they should be needed as reinforcements," the scout relayed Semmida's message.

"Who could we be fighting to require this many warriors, an empire of Minnecou warriors?" the war chief sneered. "They are only small clans."

"Minnecou and Paccu," the scout returned.

"Paccu!" the war chief laughed. "Of what consequence are Paccus? We have just received several of these new Paccus in the mines...I see no difference between these and any other slaves. They are weak!"

"They are many and they are gathering to attack instead of scattering to hide," the scout answered once again.

"Do they plan to attack here...or in the city?" the war chief joked, incredulous.

"My chief gives me only the information I have already told you," the scout returned, laughing at the war chief's attempt at humor. "He will inform all of your chiefs after he gets these slaves to the mines."

The war chief brought his party to their feet with a wave of his hand, then walked to the top of the rise where he hailed Semmida with a more intricate movement. Semmida merely nodded and summoned his party out of the woods. The war chief seemed somewhat insulted or suspicious of Semmida's response, but then quickly brushed it off.

Mokotak stooped over and walked with a well pronounced limp as enemy Snake warriors surrounded the rebels, outnumbering Semmida's guards by more than two to one. The war chief sent runners back to the mining village to warn them to double the guards on the new Paccus. His own warriors would escort the group of slaves across the prairie and towards the foothills of the Dark Mountains.

The rebels marched toward the enemy's camp. Semmida's credibility and that of his warriors would determine whether they would begin their operations or be put to death. Mokotak tried to imagine Sequannah's fear, for he himself was unsure if it would be possible to escape should Semmida fail. But he dared not try to speak to him, for with this many Snake warriors around, every move was watched and scrutinized for possible punishment. Between Tarote's group and Semmida's, there were now more than sixty slaves bound for the copper mines. However, with their escort of the Snake war party, there were more guards than slaves, laughing and cursing as they prodded the procession along.

The war chief immediately sought out Semmida to calculate his strengths, and extract what information he could about the sudden changes that the northern part of the empire was about to undergo. "Your messenger seemed to imply that you would engage us in battle if we detained you even in the slightest," he launched into Semmida, though he kept his tone prudently cordial. "Surely you must know that even a fool would recognize this as a bluff. My war party outnumbers your guards by more than two to one and even now, you can see that I have you surrounded. If you look even more closely, you will see that certain of my warriors do not take their eyes off of me, but await a certain movement of my hand, that perhaps they may be allowed the pleasure of slicing your party up as an offering to the sacred hawks. It has been very quiet here...my men salivate for battle. If you truly represent Quiktkoata's interests, I will warn you not to even think of repeating this type of message inside the mining camp, for they would not hesitate to engage you immediately, knowing that Quiktkoata would ultimately pardon their actions and merely send another party out in your stead."

"If you should find reason to test my warriors," Semmida glowered, "you will regrettably find that my messenger relayed anything but a bluff on my behalf. These warriors are the most powerful in the empire. Only a small handful of superior warriors accompanies Quiktkoata to battle. The slaves you see before you cannot be replaced as simply as you seem to think, and that is why Quiktkoata has given me such a powerful force to protect them. I assure you with the full voice of my authority that were you to outnumber me ten to one, you would fall amongst the slaughtered. Whether you are truly of the Snake empire or not, it is your war party that is now surrounded, and I needn't move a hand nor blink an eye to engage you—my warriors are trained to obey the mere sense of my desires."

"So long as you are intent on reaching the mines, I have no need to challenge your insane bluffs," the war chief sneered into the face of Semmida. "You do my work for me, for this is where I would have herded your foolish little group. And I warn you not to expect any greater respect once you reach the mines. The chiefs there will listen to no one unless Quiktkoata himself commands them personally. If I were not responsible for bringing all intruders to the council in as close to a living condition as possible, you would now be feeding the crows with your lifeless bodies. Save your threats for the council or we will beat you all senseless and drag you to the mines!" he hissed.

Semmida wasn't even looking at the war chief, but was instead looking in back of and around him, nodding his head in negative gestures. The war chief looked away briefly to see what had distracted Semmida. Several bows were pointed at him with their arrows notched and their blades lined up with his heart from every direction. One of the war chief's men moved quickly to attack one of Semmida's bowmen from the rear, but the bowman swept his foot in back of him and leveled the warrior without ever even turning to see his attacker. Indeed, the arrow notched in his bow never strayed from the path of its intended target. A hatchet pierced the downed warrior's throat and pinned him, gurgling, to the ground. Several more enemy warriors made sudden moves, and were promptly leveled from many directions, though no others were greeted with hatchets. The war chief raised his hand, commanding all of his warriors to remain motionless, as every bowman was still trained on his heart and hadn't wavered their aim in the least.

Semmida scanned the crowd and each bowman dropped his aim as Semmida's gaze reached him. Semmida purposefully avoided two of his most intense looking warriors whose aims remained steadfast. "Shall we proceed?" Semmida questioned the war chief. He nodded in agreement, and nervously glanced at his feet. The two remaining arrows were returned to their quivers, and the entire party resumed their journey towards the foothills of the Dark Mountains. The war chief's warriors had oddly lost their fervor in whipping and snarling the slaves along; the entire procession walked quietly westward, the only sounds being those of dry grass stalks bouncing off the toes of the many moccasins. It was an eerie feeling for many of the Snake empire's warriors. A large eagle circled gracefully overhead, then slowly disappeared into the southwestern horizon.

* * *

Petawahin looked questioningly towards the Washan as the group of Snake warriors swerved suddenly in their direction. There was no escape, for many others came out of the hills as their relief came for the twilight hours. The Washan noticed nothing special that these warriors did, except that a few of them went up and spoke to the commander of the large group now going out to the fields. He slung his bow over his shoulder, dropping his lance so it hung loosely from his side. Then he simply walked towards the guards' quarters closest to them. Petawahin followed. They were unaware that all that was expected of them was to return to the village, eat, then rest before they would return to the hills the following morning.

The Washan led Petawahin to the rear of a line where they each picked up a large clay pot and waited their turn for several ladles of a thick and meaty stew. One of the other Snake warriors approached Petawahin and looked him up and down. "So you are one of these big warriors that comes to improve our production," he sneered. "You come with the new mining slaves?"

"He doesn't understand your talk," the Washan cut in, trying his best to disguise his Minnecou accent. "He comes from the eastern part of the empire."

"He does not look Ondada to me," the Snake warrior's jaw tensed.

"Further east," the Washan thought quickly. "The new tribe from far to the east. They are very strong warriors; very quick."

"The further east we have gone, we have always found the new nations to be weaker than those before them," he said incredulously. "But of what value are warriors who travel amongst us from one end of the empire to the other without ever bothering to learn how to speak?" the Snake warrior stepped threateningly towards Petawahin.

Petawahin didn't understand any of the conversation, but he did recognize the Snake guard's menacing advances, and quickly dropped to the ground as he swept his stocky leg under the warrior, leveling him. Instantly, he maneuvered the side of his foot into the guard's throat, thrusting the point of his lance into the guard's open and gasping mouth, though not far enough to cut.

The Washan, shocked at Petawahin's sudden and bold attack, struggled to regain his composure. "As I've already told you, they're strong and very quick," the Washan managed to state calmly, then clutched at Petawahin to tear him away from the Snake warrior. The Washan yelled at Petawahin to distract him from continuing on this course, but not in recognizable Minnecou tones.

"He is just now beginning to understand our language, but he knows very little," the Washan apologized for Petawahin's sudden attack. "He understands your actions better than your words, and that is how he chose to defend himself. I should have anticipated this. He always becomes angry until after he has eaten." The Washan quickly corralled Petawahin back into line.

There was much chatter about the sudden altercation. Some Snake guards expressed suspicions about the two new warriors, while others praised Petawahin's swift attack and wily maneuvers. They especially liked the way he pinned the arrogant Snake guard in such a hopeless position. Many of them had to endure the taunts and accusations of this same guard, and were secretly satisfied at seeing him leveled so quickly. Some of the hairy-faced ones who had witnessed the scuffle from a distance were openly cheering the new warrior; they, too, held contempt for the arrogant guard. He often claimed to be the nephew of Quiktkoata and therefore superior. But everyone knew that he was not even related to the original Snake people, and that he belonged to one of the tribes that was subdued early on in Quiktkoata's quest to build his empire. Quiktkoata's advances into the northern continent had only begun six years previous, and while Quiktkoata had indeed taken this particular guard's aunt into his harem for a time, she was quickly discarded and the arrogant warrior was left without any true connections to the royalty of the empire.

The arrogant guard jumped to his feet after Petawahin was some distance away and shouted to the surrounding guards. "No man treats our warriors in this manner. Beat him!" he demanded. But they waved him off, laughing. "You will laugh until you all find yourselves as slaves to these newcomers. We have been here since the beginning. We were the only ones who could defeat the hairy-faced ones. You will see yourselves groveling before those who cannot even speak our words. Go on and laugh, fools!" He stormed off to the village chief's quarters to air his complaints. Many Snake guards continued to scoff, but many could see the possibility of truth in his words as well, for they themselves had displaced the armies who had been defeated and scattered by the pink-skinned ones when Quiktkoata first fought to establish this territory.

The Washan felt secure in the fact that no one had even mentioned the possibility of them being spies. Nevertheless, he dragged Petawahin off in another direction, where they would be a little more discreet. A short distance away stood a group of new slaves, quietly awaiting their fates as many guards surrounded them, curiously facing outward in a manner of protection, rather than inward to guard and prevent escapes. A particularly fierce looking chief came from the direction of the mining village's largest buildings, several powerful scouts trailing behind. They gathered their slaves, and quickly marched towards the smoldering furnaces and dusty pits.

Petawahin suddenly latched onto the Washan's arm. "Sequannah!" he whispered. "And there is Mokotak, limping." The Washan looked briefly and nodded, though both were covered as well as hooded in slaves' garments. "Let us finish our food. We'll get closer later," the Washan cautioned. "We do not want to raise suspicion." Petawahin didn't take his eyes off the group as he poured the contents of the clay pot into his gullet.

"Done!" he stated, though the Washan had barely begun to eat. "Well at least walk back and return these pots with me before we try to find a way to get closer."

The new group of slaves, along with their Snake guards, were separated from the rest of the camp. Approach was impossible in an inconspicuous manner. The Washan noted that several Snake guards from the village watched the movements of the entire group from a distance. Into the forest on the eastern side of the mining camp, stood another group of observers, high atop a hill.

One of the slaves was taken from Semmida's group, and brought out into the open. From beneath her tunic, she produced two long copper rods, each bent at a ninety degree angle. She held them in such a manner that with her fists held straight out in front of her, the rods pointed upwards and then bent towards the direction she began to walk.

Several of Semmida's warriors guarded Tarote, though more to witness her curious powers than to prevent her escape. Semmida was walking backwards in front of her, awaiting the exact moment that her magic would come to bear. They walked very slowly, almost to the center of the camp, when suddenly the two rods turned sideways from their forward positions. The slave's hands began to shake and her whole body trembled, then she collapsed to the ground in exhaustion. The village Snake guards who had been observing from a distance, moved closer to where the slave had collapsed, chattering back and forth as they meandered along, pretending not to notice. Even the guards atop the hill had shifted to about halfway down, openly shading their eyes to get a clearer view.

Petawahin and the Washan stood next to a small shack, where slaves of the mining camp were regularly bringing back old molds and fetching new ones. They pretended not to be paying too much attention to the new group, but keeping more of an eye on the comings and goings of the slaves near their pretended post.

Two of Semmida's scouts lifted the collapsed slave to her feet, and dragged her back to the edge of the village. This time, though, they started from a point on the southern end of the camp instead of the eastern side. Again, Tarote held the rods out, and pointing straight ahead of her, walked slowly towards the center of the village. She had barely moved, when suddenly, she collapsed once again in a trembling heap. The guards jerked her to her feet and brought her outside of the camp, where she was forced to repeat the procedure from a further distance. She took but one step and the rods turned immediately. This time, the guards each grabbed an arm and dragged her out into the forest, where they propped her up and pointed the rods straight ahead, giving her a slight shove in the direction of the mining camp. She walked for about twenty paces, right to the edge of the forest, and then no more than two steps unto the cleared part of the village, when the rods once again turned to the right and left of her, and she collapsed to the ground, too weak to move.

Semmida waved to his guards. All of his slaves were quickly herded to the center of the mining camp. Whips lashed the air, as the slaves set about digging a massive ditch. Semmida selected a dozen of the slaves and two of the guards. "Follow me!" he ordered, leading them to the base of one of the large and burning furnaces. "Dig a trench from here to where the others are digging their trench." He then took another group to a furnace on the southern end of the village and began the same process. This furnace, however, was run-down and abandoned, so he set another crew to dismantling the copper encrusted heap in order to rebuild it from the point where it was salvageable.

Tarote wielded a large stick to mark out a ditch, right through the center of the mining camp, and about the width of two men laid end to end. She then traced several more ditches throughout the village. The slaves would dig feverishly through the dirt and old tailings until they hit bedrock. Then they could span outward along the length of each ditch. Semmida traced smaller ditches from the furnaces to the main ditch, where the copper was supposed to be found. Then he set up smaller crews to ready the buildings to be moved that lay in the paths of the ditches.

Bakwanote, chief of the mining village, could permit their takeover no longer, and stormed down with several other chiefs and a small party of warriors. He glanced about, his jaws clenched, stalking from one operation to another, speechless, until he reached the point where Semmida supervised the moving of a small shack.

"What kind of foolishness do you intend to carry out here?" he demanded. "I accepted your authority from Quiktkoata as legitimate. I allowed you to come into my camp to find what areas you could for improvement. But I did not tell you to dig up the entire camp and tear all of the buildings down."

"We have located the main vein of copper and now we must uncover it, so that our good workers can mine it," Semmida replied calmly.

"Good workers!" the chief screamed. "These are slaves here. Slaves are not good workers. They move only by the grace of the Snake's tail," he said, referring to the guards' whips. "And I have already seen that your guards whips are only good for fanning the air."

"What should they be whipping?" Semmida replied

innocently.

"The slaves, you fool!" Bakwanote was inflamed.

"We do not do that any more," Semmida answered matter-of-factly. "Not where Quiktkoata would be able to find out about it. Nowhere in the city do guards still whip slaves. We wouldn't want to harm Quiktkoata's precious workers," he said sarcastically. "I was as skeptical as you at first, but later I found out that their work nearly doubled, and there were many less bodies to bury each week. I am quite surprised, however, that nothing has changed up here. I'm glad to see that someone has the courage and good sense to resist certain of Quiktkoata's unnecessary 'improvements.' There are many years ahead to finish the work of the empire. Why should our warriors and guards be denied their pleasure and their rights for the sake of a bunch of foolish slaves?" A look of sadistic joy came over Semmida's face. "Hear me!" he decreed in a loud voice to his warriors. "Our gracious host tells me that up here, in this northernmost post of the empire, we can go back to the old ways. So let the whips fall where they may!" Great cheers and whoops erupted from everywhere among Semmida's warriors. Semmida had a difficult time trying to quiet the obvious glee of his men, but he had to warn them. "But outside of the mining camp, we must observe the new rules, for there will be people watching. And we'll also have to go back to serving them the good food," he said angrily. Many hints of dissent came from the crowd until one of Semmida's warriors cried out: "We will stay here forever." Loud cheers once again burst forth among echoes of the warrior's statement.

"My men were leery of coming here," Semmida confided to the chief. "But your operation, up here, seems to have given them new spirit. I can see already that things will work out very well here. Even if the slaves' work seems to be substandard at first, I can always have my warriors let up on them for a time, but you are the first chief who truly understands that the empire's guards must have something to interest them in their work as well. As you can see, they are eager to get this project going now."

"Well you had better keep their eagerness alive," Bakwanote sneered. "And you'll have to do it by the new rules. Sometimes new rules and regulations take longer to be implemented this far from the city, and if you intend to double production here, I suggest that you follow the rules that Quiktkoata has set forth."

"But I have already told my..." Semmida began to plead.

"I am not interested in the dilemma you have placed your-self in," the mining chief said smugly. "I'm sure, however, that Quiktkoata will take an interest in your loyalties to the new regulations. Especially after I have sent a message to the city that will include the manner in which you have blundered in here and practically demanded power over the whole camp, when you are perfectly aware that I outrank you. Immensely!"

The mining chief's rank was only one step above Semmida's, though, and being in different areas of the empire, the authority was actually questionable as to who was above who.

"Quiktkoata himself has informed me that no one shall outrank me on this matter," Semmida contradicted the mining chief's assertions. "He asked only that I stick as closely as possible to using the proper channels. If you continue to stand in my way here," Semmida threatened, "I'll have words of my own sent to Quiktkoata, and you'll find yourself ranked among the lowest of the guards here!" Semmida remarked arrogantly, though casually.

"Why do you move this building here when it is obviously not in the way of your foolish ditch!" the mining chief quickly changed the subject, until he could get more information on this powerful henchman of Quiktkoata's.

"We will only move it back but a short distance," Semmida became suddenly accommodating. "Our new method of burning produces quite an intense heat, which I'm sure that you will take great interest in," he said, trying to appeal to the mining chief's pursuit in the operations of the mine.

"You can be certain of that!" Bakwanote warned, then marched back to the mine's headquarters with his men. He stopped suddenly, however, and turned back on Semmida. "There is one other thing that I have taken an interest in as well," he paused for a moment. "Who is that woman slave with the copper rods? She looks familiar."

Semmida took no chances. "I think you are well aware of who she is!" he said coolly.

"And you trust her as the focus of all your plans here?" the mining chief could barely contain his laughter.

"I happen to know of her love for snakes," Semmida replied casually.

"Followers of the Sikun detest our precious snakes," the mining chief said questioningly.

"Oh no!" Semmida mocked the Sikun's rebels. "This one adores our little cousins. Bring the girl," he demanded of his scouts. After some moments, two scouts returned, dragging Tarote by the arms and hair, her hood having been yanked down in back of her. "Crawl for the respectable chief," Semmida leered.

Tarote's face immediately began to contort, her chest heaving as she tried to fight off Semmida's command. "Crawl!" he screamed. She immediately fell to the ground and began to writhe uncontrollably in the dust, her tongue darting in and out, hisses erupting from deep within her."

"Who did this to her? Quiktkoata?" the chief looked on incredulously.

"I have taught her to love our little cousins myself," Semmida bragged to the commander. "But there is a good purpose for having her known here as well!"

The mining chief was no longer interested in Semmida's display of power, especially where it diminished his. He departed with his lower chiefs to the sanctity of his headquarters, for as long as that would remain to be the case.

* * *

Petawahin and the Washan observed from their post near the small shack. The sun dipped below the horizon and the air became chilled enough to make their breath visible. They had barely noticed the hooded slaves that had been shuffling past them, pretending to rummage around in the small building, and keeping an eye on these strange, new guards, posted where none had ever been posted before. Petawahin and the Washan had no idea that one of these slaves was a spy for Bakwanote, and that he was listening to their conversation whenever they would whisper to one another. But they conversed in a foreign tongue, and though it raised suspicion, he was unable to decipher their observations.

By the time the sun had completely set and the mackerel skies of twilight provided the only light, the Washan noticed that they were no longer inconspicuous. "Up on the hill in the forest, a Snake warrior watches our every move. Do not look at him; I have already seen him and that is enough. Another is watching from the top of one of the big lodges. He pretends to be watching the slaves as they come back for their meal, but he watches us more than them."

Petawahin had been consumed with the comings and goings of two slaves he believed to be Sequannah and Mokotak, and trying to find a weakness in the guards who watched over their group. He could find none, however. These were much greater warriors than the others in the village. This he could tell by the manner in which they carried their weapons. They weren't sloppy and grumbling, but rather lean and hard-faced. Petawahin had also been watching the slaves who had been coming in and out of the small shack. They all seemed to go to a tall, hooded slave when they returned to their work, signaling him with an almost imperceptible glance and nod; all except for one, who didn't even look at the big slave. Petawahin also noticed that there was no wildlife anywhere throughout the mining village except for a couple of small sparrows that tittered in the brown grass near the big slave. The manner in which he walked told Petawahin that this was a man who was probably too old to do the work he was doing, but he carried on, regardless of whether the guards were watching him or not. Curiously, though, the two sparrows would sometimes try to land on the old slave's head and shoulders. He would immediately shoo them away as discreetly as possible.

"We should move to a place where these spies will no longer find us so interesting," the Washan whispered to Petawahin.

"We must, very soon."

"I'm glad you agree," the Washan said. "Where would you suggest we go?"

"I don't know," Petawahin said, almost perplexed. "Let's stay here until these slaves go to eat. At least we will look as if we had been watching them until they were done."

Petawahin resumed his vigil on Sequannah and Mokotak, while the Washan kept his wits on the spies. They barely noticed when the old slave came struggling up to the shack, an impossible load of huge wooden molds stacked upon his outstretched arms. He fell at their feet. "Quick! Kick me!" he whispered in Minnecou. "Kick me as if your life depended on it, for that is where the truth lies."

Petawahin wound up and booted him in the posterior, and the old slave let out a loud groan and many apologies. But in between the apologies he quickly whispered. "Scream at me. Show no mercy." Petawahin and the Washan both began to scream at him and kick him in a manner that rolled him over and over. "How dare you speak to us in that manner! We'll give you what you've been asking for," the Washan laughed.

"Now pick me up and tear my hood off," the old slave whispered. "Stop kicking, and do as I say or you will be wearing these hoods yourselves," he whispered impatiently.

The two Minnecou followed his instructions regardless of whether he was a spy or a slave, for this is how they saw the slaves being treated in any event.

"Bring me to the chief who has just brought in the new slaves. I am the fugitive he seeks," the foolish looking old man instructed them. But Petawahin and the Washan were uncertain as of just what to do. They would be strangers to whomever they would bring this prisoner.

"You are not guards from this mining camp. Every slave and Snake warrior here knows that," he whispered very quickly. "And you are not with the new group of slaves and guards, for I know them all as you would know your sisters and brothers. Take me to them, and Semmida, their chief, will put you in with his warriors. He will take me as prisoner to please the chiefs of this village, but I assure you that he will treat me well."

"Why would we care that you are treated well?" Petawahin retorted, defending any action he should decide to take.

"You are Minnecou. Two of your clansmen are with that new group of slaves, as I am sure you are well aware," the old man surprised them with his knowledge. "They know me as Teokahannah...and they will capture me for reasons other than what the chief of the mining village might think. Take me there quickly, before the mining chief's warriors become involved here!"

The two Minnecou dragged him off, and threw him to the ground at Semmida's feet. "We have a prisoner here for you," the Washan announced, his Minnecou accent undetectable. Snake guards throughout the mining camp watched with interest as to what this new chief wanted with an old slave.

Semmida's scouts immediately surrounded the old man, nearly piercing him with the points of their spears.

"The Sikun! The Sikun now lies at my feet with no chance for escape," Semmida shouted, in obvious pleasure. "My patience has been rewarded–the old fool is mine." Petawahin and the Washan looked on in confusion, wondering what they had done. The Minnecou Washan had no idea that he had just turned over one of the greatest Washans ever to have lived. He had heard there was a Sikun, but had never made the long trek to the holy city. He couldn't have known who he was. He was shocked at what he'd inadvertently done, but immediately relieved himself of guilt, for this is what the old man had requested.

"These two warriors shall receive the highest honors and rewards from their courage and their ability to capture the Sikun," Semmida announced. "But do not envy these very capable warriors," he said of Petawahin and the Washan, "for now they will guard the Sikun, and be responsible to prevent his escape until we can get him to Quiktkoata." He turned to the two Minnecou. "Should he escape, you had better follow," he warned. "Your punishment will be death."

CHAPTER 19

Quitkwa felt a power he had never known, walking among the Paccu leaders in the fading afternoon. Several knives were tucked under his tunic and inside his moccasins. He gripped the wood of his bow, his other hand ready to string an arrow whenever needed. Kwoita translated for Quitkwa as he pointed out directions to the fierce looking leader of the Paccus. Boaka and another Paccu were sent out to the right and ahead of the group. The Wolf brothers scouted slightly to the left as they departed from Ketanka's nearly abandoned village. Several of the women also went along as warriors, including Shamira and some of the Paccu women. Ketanka had objected to this at first, not knowing what Petawahin's intentions would have been. But he couldn't force her to stay after the Paccus allowed several of their women to go. This was especially true, since most of the Minnecou who were in direct danger from the Snake people were of her own family.

The Paccu men carried long lances and atlatls as well as their bows, while the women carried only bows and knives. Shamira used her old hunting bow and took some of the arrows from a large cache that Kwoita had been making for more than a moon; the arrows she had up until now were only for game.

The war party's intention was to catch up with Ceptke and his warriors, so they could edge up to the western ridge of the strange village in force. But, Ceptke was nearly a full day ahead of them. Quitkwa, however, couldn't tell if it would still be possible to overtake them, or if they would have to find their trail and then try to catch up with them.

By mid-morning they were still moving at a very rapid pace. The powerful looking Paccu chief suddenly stopped, asking for Quitkwa. Kwoita translated for the Paccu leader.

"Minnecou," he addressed Quitkwa, "You have spoken of strange hawks that scout for the Snake people."

Quitkwa glanced at the sky to see what the Paccu had noticed. "Yes, it is true," he said. "But most times you will hear them before you see them...if you're quiet enough."

The Paccu turned quickly, pointing to a distant creature at the edge of the forest, calmly watching as the quickly moving column wound its way over the hilly terrain. "Do they also have eagles?"

When several warriors turned to look, the eagle immediately fluttered out of the tall yellow straw. The powerful raptor then flapped hurriedly up to a great height where it soared northward and out of sight.

"I have not heard of eagles among them," Quitkwa shrugged.

"Put us on a path that will take us directly to the village of the Snake people," he ordered. "If we arrive before the others, we will wait for them. If not, perhaps they will wait for us."

"That may put us too close to the village too soon. There will be a greater chance that the Snake people's scouts will see us if we are there for too long," Quitkwa warned.

"What if they see Ceptke and his warriors?" the Paccu returned. "If we are not there to help, they could all be killed."

"There may be a place to hide Ceptke's war party, but we will never be able to hide ours as well."

"There is always a place," the Paccu retorted. "But we must change direction. If we are to believe what you tell us about hawks, then the same could be true of eagles. You will take us to the Snake village now!" he ordered.

Quitkwa was inclined to resist the Paccu's demands, but he was unsure of the eagle's powers as well. "Tell him that perhaps it would be best to go directly to the village," Quitkwa demanded of Kwoita, "But we will send scouts well in advance of our party to find a place where we can remain hidden, even if it has to be some distance from the village."

"Of course," the Paccu muttered to his warriors. "Does this young buck think us as foolish as he?" His men sniggered at the Paccu leader's impatience with the arrogant young Minnecou. Kwoita didn't translate the Paccu's remarks. Quitkwa would learn soon enough.

They moved swiftly and silently over the endless series of hills, constantly maneuvering themselves along the twisting shadows of bare trees and rocky ravines, and occasionally crossing open areas for short distances. Quitkwa moved well ahead of the war party, working back and forth between the two sets of advance scouts, telling them which way to go, where to look for possible ambushes or enemy scouts, and which directions would provide the easiest travel. But, after a full morning of this, Quitkwa suddenly remained with the Wolf brothers for a much longer period of time. Too long, in fact, for Tamahna.

Quitkwa!" Tamahna could bear no more. "I know you are very concerned about everyone's safety, and you look for the trail that will not steal our strength. But after all the years the Wolf brothers scout for you and the rest of the clan, do you not think we have learned enough to scout for a war party yet. Do you think that you have suddenly acquired more knowledge as a scout in your two winters as a warrior?" he snapped. "Go bother the other scouts for a while, or better than that, go back and see where the war party is. You can check on Shamira. I know that will keep you occupied."

Tamahna let it slip that he was aware of Quitkwa's feelings for her, but worse than that, he said it in a manner that made it appear to be common knowledge. Quitkwa's diligent manner suddenly drained from him; even his proud frame weakened in posture. He trudged off as if he'd suddenly remembered a task of greater importance. Tamahna sensed this was not the truth–he looked like a man who had no place to go. But Tamahna knew that to have pity for the young warrior would only invite more of what he'd already endured, so he let the arrogant warrior go his own way, knowing that he wouldn't return unless he absolutely had to. But, what he didn't know was that Quitkwa had already been shunned by the Paccu scouts. He'd begun to feel vaguely uncomfortable among the war party as well. And there was definitely no warmth emanating from Shamira.

Quitkwa wandered along between the two sets of scouts

and the war party, not caring to mingle with either. In spite of feeling rejected, though, he kept his ears and eyes open, determined to work alone. He moped along, kicking up sods of mud, but soon he heard the sound of shuffling footsteps behind him. He turned quickly. There was no one to be seen. As he turned back, he glimpsed a towering figure out of the corner of his eye. Immediately, he drew a knife from under his tunic. Quicker that the shift of an eye, he held the knife to the stranger's throat, but the stranger didn't flinch.

"You may be quick on your feet, but you'll never be quicker than my knife. Speak!" Quitkwa demanded. "Who are you?"

The tall figure was clad from head to moccasins in a coarse, hooded tunic. He lifted both hands to pull back his hood. Quitkwa gazed upon the strange man's face; the almost silly grin confused him. He couldn't tell if he had captured a fool, or if the smile was one that he had sometimes seen on the Washan; one of wisdom that few understood. One of his teeth was broken off flat across so that only a short stub protruded from his gum. Two sparrows suddenly darted out of the bushes and landed on his shoulders.

"Why does a gifted young warrior like yourself walk alone among so many?" the stranger said softly.

"I hold the knife," Quitkwa pressed the point against the stranger's throat. "Only my questions will be answered." The knife suddenly slipped out of Quitkwa's grip. He dove for it. But when he tried to pick it up, there was no way to get a firm grip on it. It slid through his fingers as if coated in bear grease. No matter how many times he tried, he couldn't get a firm enough grip to lift it off the ground. The stranger, however, remained standing, patiently waiting for the stubborn warrior to give up, especially since he was affording no threat.

"I asked you why you walk alone among so many," the strange man repeated to the young warrior.

"I speak to no one unless they walk among us," Quitkwa stated obstinately.

"Perhaps some of my allies could convince you that I am not an enemy to those who rise up against Quiktkoata." The two sparrows suddenly darted over to Quitkwa, flying in tight circles above his head, like a living halo. Their high pitched song and chirping brought visions from the not-too-distant past, where he and his clan and several Paccus were emerging from a cave that had protected them

334

from three deadly twisters. From behind the banks of a hidden gully, an antelope with a huge rack suddenly appeared. It nearly brushed Quitkwa as it dashed by, and with a final leap before it disappeared from view, he could clearly see that the prong-horned creature was actually a doe. The Sikun repeated his inquiry.

"Because I am young!" Quitkwa said irritably. "They would rather I be alone so that they will not have to listen to warriors younger than themselves. Because I am young, they think I have no wisdom."

"Perhaps they are right," the stranger said.

"They are not right," Quitkwa said angrily. "I am the only one who has been this way before. I know where the Snake people will hide because I searched for such places on my way back. I know where the laurels and evergreens lie thickest, where we can hide from their hawk scouts in the sky. I know the passes to avoid, where we will not be able to see our enemies until it is too late. And, I know where we are to meet the others when we reach the Snake village."

"I know of another warrior who walked alone for many years," the stranger said. "He was very proud when he was your age too. And he had much reason to be. He was a very powerful warrior. But things were not quite as easy for him as they are for you. He was brought up in a small farming village, unaccustomed to the ways of the wanderer. There were no scouts among his people; not even warriors—only potters and farmers. He was fatherless even before he reached five winters, so he learned to defend his mother's gardens as a child. Of course, he was too small to fight off enemies warriors, so he became very clever in the tricks he would use. He would dig deep holes like a rabbit's den and then cover them up so that a man would fall into them and twist his leg. He left ropes lying around that would trip the raiders up. He would hide under the pumpkin leaves when he heard the slightest crack of a twig, or the rustle of leaves, and with his hollow tube and darts of poison, he would hit one of the raiders, and they would fall down helpless and screaming. The others would flee in panic, for they never could find where the darts came from."

"But this young boy wanted no part of farming, for his father had the wanderers' blood and this was passed on to him. His uncle fascinated the young boy with his stories of faraway places and exciting adventures when he would return each winter for trading among the villagers. But the boy's mother needed him and would not let him go with his uncle. After many years of pleading with his mother and uncle to let him travel with the clan, they finally let him go when he reached the warrior's age."

"Like you, he was full of a certain knowledge, but was young. His first year on the trail, he spent more time telling his teachers what they should do instead of hearing what they would teach him. They tired of this very quickly, and he began to feel they were jealous because he was such a great warrior and he was much younger than them. He resented their jealousy, but he would not go back to the village for he had the wanderers' blood. Instead, he walked alone among the people. Even though he grew to love the wanderers, he remained alone because he felt they were always jealous, and would never listen to him. He took out his anger on any intruders that would try to prey on his clan and he became a very dangerous warrior. No other people would even dare to sneak up on a Minnecou clan, for most who did, never returned. Perhaps you know of this man. His uncle is still a very powerful and well-known Minnecou chieftain by the name of Ketanka."

"That is my father!" Quitkwa exclaimed. "Mokotak is the one you speak of. But he does not hold anger against us. He has just always preferred to hunt and scout alone."

"Maybe that is the way it is now," Teokahannah explained, "But I speak of how this came about. This is what lies in front of you now. You will find yourself with no desire to join in with the games of the clan. You will find yourself hunting alone and fighting alone. I can tell you the wisdom, but it is up to you whether you use it or not...few people use wisdom they do not understand through their own experience.

"It is better to let others give you the power they entrust to you, than to seek a more powerful position and have them cast you down. It is better to have knowledge and advice always ready than to have it always spoken, for it is an insult when it is not asked for and a treasure when it is needed."

"You are a Washan," Quitkwa said without disdain, but without respect as well. "Your words are familiar."

"The words are to bring about what is sacred and lasting, as is the Washan's life. All that is not sacred will not last."

"Then we can never be sacred, for we will all die; even you," the young Minnecou pointed out the futility of the Washan's ways.

"Our spirits cannot die, as many believe, they live on in love or hate, whichever you choose. But you should always be aware of what each of these brings to you. Joy, love, suffering and pain; each one teaches you about the other. You must have each of these things, not just those you would choose, if your spirit is to last forever. Otherwise, you would exist as a stone, always being ground down until you are a part of something else. But your body gives you all of these things and that is the gift from the Creator. We are but the seeds of eternal flowers and this Earth is a garden. In order to exist in the eternal, the spirit must have feeling. The joys, loves, sufferings and pains that you experience in this lifetime become the essence of your spirit, so try always to find the best way to view these things because this is how you will be, forever."

"But this is no time for chatter, for many flowers will never bloom if we do not hurry," Teokahannah warned. "There are no Snake warriors between here and the village, for the present, for they are keeping a close eye on the comings and goings of a new group of slaves in the mining village. But soon, they will fear for their safety and will send scouts into the surrounding hills to search for your war parties. By the time you reach the area of the strange village, the skies will be heavy with clouds. I must tell you that your Washan and his accompanying warrior will never be able to get out of the village to tell you of their plans, so this is what you must do. Your scouts will see the Snake peoples' scouts first, but you will find no place to hide this war party and the other Paccu war party. Lead them to the woods on the eastern side of the village, and you will find a stand of oak and poplars where the leaves have fallen thickly over the ground. All of you must eat every bit of food you have brought along with you and then bury yourselves under the leaves. By this time, it will begin to snow, and the snow will fall heavy. You must stay hidden under the snow and leaves for the rest of this day and until dawn of the next. After the snow has been falling for some time, when you think that it must be night time, clear the leaves in front of your eyes so that you can see the snow above, and then clear a hole through the snow until you can see the sky. When the sky begins to lighten at dawn, all of you must dig yourselves out and prepare for battle. When you see the great walls of fire in the middle of the village, attack the eastern half of the village, for there will be many allies of ours already there. Make sure that your war party and scouts do everything just as I have told you."

"But no one will listen to me," Quitkwa reminded the Sikun. "And you yourself have said that I should wait until I am invited to lead."

"By tomorrow morning, you will have caught up with the other Paccu war party," the Sikun's eyes twinkled. "I have already spoken with one they call Ceptke. He just may extend an invitation to you. In the meantime, try to remain humble," he laughed to himself, and then quickly shuffled out of view. Quitkwa tried to follow the old Washan, but as soon as he lost sight of him, he could find neither a trace of his trail nor a glimpse of his dusty, brown robe. The same eagle that the Paccu leader had spotted, screeched out as it passed between Quitkwa and the sun, then drifted off in an easterly direction.

The sky remained cloudless, but even the subtlest of breezes no longer stirred. Quitkwa watched the animals and the sky for any changes that might hint of an approaching storm as he resumed his lonely travel. He ached for proof of the strange Washan's words. If no storm came, then he would know he had been tricked, and would know how to tell the others of his encounter with the strange Washan.

*   *   *

Ketanka was suddenly jostled from his sound sleep. "Something is wrong!" Melonak stared wide-eyed at the Minnecou chief.

Moments later, the top of his lodge was shaken furiously. A shower of spruce needles rained on the chief and his family.

"Ketanka!" the chief recognized the tone of Shatomi's frantic voice. "The strange hawks appear!" Ketanka jumped out from under his robes and scrambled through the top of the lodge.

"Are you sure they are the hawks of the Snake people?" he questioned Shatomi.

"Too big to be anything else," Shatomi confirmed his sighting. "Bigger than any of the eagles we've seen up here."

"Have they discovered the camp?" Ketanka tried to assess the situation. Shatomi shrugged. Ketanka knew that they must certainly have followed the trail of the many Paccu warriors that had passed through here in the last few days. But whether they had followed them all the way to the camp would mean all the difference, for if they hadn't, it would be possible to deceive even the sharp eyes of a hawk. Shatomi led the chief to a small notch in the ledge overlooking the temporary camp, and pointed to where he had seen the two hawks circling over the distant ridge. There was nothing in view, and the two warriors searched the skies. A muted screech from the east caused them to turn suddenly back to where Shatomi had indicated he had first seen them. Moments later, two enormous birds breached the top of the distant ridge, perching atop a couple of great red pines. The branches bowed deeply under their weight, then sprung back to a stable level. They looked like small brown bears, perhaps a couple of grizzly cubs, from a distance.

"Let's get back to the camp!" Ketanka muttered. They crawled to keep out of the strange hawks' view.

"Everyone, back to your lodges," Ketanka ordered as he returned to find the camp quickly stirring. "But pick up anything that may give away our presence." Wanachan translated the chief's orders to the few Paccus that had roused, then turned grouchily to the chief with her half-shut morning eyes.

"What is it?" she croaked, clearing her voice at the same time.

"The hawks of the Snake people are nearby," Ketanka said in a restrained voice. "I need two of your quickest warriors."

She shouted out two names. Ketanka threw a stick at her. "Keep your voice low," he warned. She looked back indignantly, yet fearful that perhaps she had been careless in her drowsy state. "Go and get Quebathe," he ordered Shatomi. Moments later, Quebathe and Shatomi stood before Ketanka, along with Wanachan and two Paccu warriors.

"Wanachan," Ketanka whispered, "Tell these two fine warriors that we need them to make a diversion for the hawks to follow. He pointed to a snow covered peak, far to the north, barely visible between the lower, dark hilltops between the camp and the distant mountain. "Tell your two warriors to run as fast as the wind in the direction of that white mountain. When they are as close as they can get without climbing it, have them search for a place that would be a good place to camp. Tell them to assemble circles of sticks to resemble lodges, and then make several small campfires with visible smoke before they hurry back here. If they are seen by the hawks at any time, they are not to return here, but they will go eastward instead, and catch up with the war party. Shatomi, you and Quebathe will go far to the west and do the same, but be careful not to be seen by the hawks or any of the Snake people, for then you will not be able to return. If you are seen, go northward first and then go east. We need both of you and the two Paccu warriors back here with us, so stay out of sight of anything, even the animals of the forest. But if you are spotted, go east and catch up with the war parties. Tell them of the Snake warriors and whatever else you learn."

* * *

Three Paccu warriors, Mahkawan's oldest son, Sabatt and Ketanka lay hidden in the crags of the ledge just above the village, watching the two hawks as they perched motionless in the trees on the distant ridge to the east. Nearly half the morning passed in silence as the five observers watched the eastern horizon. Neither of the hawks had moved, nor had any other movement been seen. Shatomi and Quebathe, as well as the two Paccu runners, were well on their way to the distant peaks.

One of the three Paccu scouts slipped over to Ketanka and Sabatt. Pointing to the southern end of the ridge, the Paccu grunted for Ketanka to observe. But Ketanka could see nothing, nor could Sabatt. Ketanka looked at the Paccu questioningly, but the Paccu pointed again and held his hand up, signaling for them to keep looking. Suddenly, a lone figure popped out of an unseen hollow and began to run along the length of the ridge top. Another followed a short distance behind, and two more came into view. The two hawks suddenly lifted off their perches and began gliding in wide circles, advancing a little further northward with each sweep. The onlookers from the Minnecou camp could soon make out scores of such figures, appearing out of nowhere. They would run for short bursts, and then vanish into bushes or behind boulders. Soon, the entire eastern ridge was overtaken with the same type of maneuvering warriors for as far as the eyes could see. Ketanka began to grow restless. There were too many of them. Even if half of those Snake warriors were to attack Ketanka's now nearly abandoned camp, the Minnecou and Paccus combined would be slaughtered.

By the time the sun had reached midday, more and more

of these warriors were making their way along the top of the ridge, traveling singly and several paces apart. The hawks had swept out of view and Ketanka was becoming anxious as to whether the two Paccu runners had reached the closest snowcapped peak to the north and completed their tasks there. Twice, he thought he saw small wisps of smoke in the northern distance, but it was too far away to be certain. The hawks hadn't circled back yet, so he knew the Snake warriors still hadn't discovered that they'd been paraded along the ridge, in full view of the camp. Sabatt suddenly grabbed Ketanka's arm, pointing to the southern end of the ridge. Snake warriors were pouring over the top of it. No longer were they running and ducking, but now they strode shoulder to shoulder. Hundreds of them covered the top of the ridge. Ketanka had never imagined himself being this close to so many enemy warriors. He couldn't feel more remorse for not moving his people earlier, but he had never seen a war party of this size. If they tried to run now, they may be seen more easily by the hawks, but they still may be able to escape deeper into the Dark Mountains at a faster pace than the Snake warriors could advance upon them. But how would the Paccus fare? Would they be able to keep up with the Minnecou in full flight? Where do these mountains end? What will they do when there is no place further to go? These questions didn't tug at him for very long. He ordered Sabatt and the two Paccu scouts to abandon the ridge.

"Wanachan!" Ketanka called, voice restrained. "We must flee now. Tell your people to flee westward in pairs. Tell them to take as much food and clothing as they can carry and head westward, keeping out of sight. If we have still not been discovered by the time we make it to the next ridge west of here, then we will band together again. If the Snake people should see us and begin pursuit, then we will all choose different directions and split them up. At least some of us will get away, and we will have stalled them. They knew of all the Minnecou and Paccus gathering here. They seek to destroy us once and for all."

Wanachan told her people of Ketanka's plans, but they didn't follow them completely. They split up into groups of three and four, according to families and relatives, instead of pairs. Ketanka had little to say; the Minnecou did very much the same. In fact, the Minnecou had one of the largest groups when Wanashta and her daughter Washeena went along with Tumaris and her three sons: Sabatt,

Petana and Kalashte. Although the groups were larger than Ketanka thought prudent, they were family, and with those closest to them. This would give them more strength–they would fight to the death to defend each other. Ketanka piled more food and clothing on each as they prepared to flee.

"We will leave them nothing!" he demanded. "If you cannot carry it far, then bury it somewhere where it will not be found, and you will not be seen."

When everyone was ready, there were twelve separate parties, none of which contained only two. Even Ketanka had three in his party with Melonak and Quetatsu. Twelve trails was enough to confuse any war party. They scrambled over the top of the ridge at the camp, one party at a time, staying close to the evergreens and boulders to keep out of view. There were many tears as they trembled in fear, hoping that none of them would fall under the keen eyes of the hawks, or run into the Snake warriors' scouting parties. There would be little chance of escaping war parties of a hundred or more warriors each.

Ketanka was the last to leave with his wife and son. There were still no Snake warriors approaching the encampment, and the hawks had not yet returned from the trail that doubled back. He gazed at the distant eastern ridge, in awe of the numbers of Snake warriors continuously pouring over it. If that is what his Minnecou warriors and the Paccus were up against in the strange village to the east, then they have surely marched to their deaths. Unless, he thought to himself, all of their warriors have come seeking battle with us at the same time we have sent warriors to their village. There would still be a chance for the Minnecou and the Paccus to defeat the village. But they would have to get out before these warriors returned, or they would be crushed.

The Paccu and Minnecou refugees reassembled on the next ridge west of the encampment. No one saw any of the hawks or the Snake warriors' scouts. Ketanka herded everyone just over the top of the crest, where they lay in watch, waiting to see what would become of their abandoned village.

The shadows grew long and the trees darkened as the colorful sunset began to fade. Still, no Snake warriors found the abandoned camp. High thin clouds streaked the sky, and the chilling air promised snow before dawn. A half moon rose as the sun set, the iridescent ring surrounding it confirmed the refugees' intuition of snow. In the valley below, a sudden blink of movement flickered between the buff-colored boulders. Ketanka held up his hand for silence. A short time later, another movement trained everyone's eyes on the valley floor.

"There are two of them," Tumaris whispered to the chief.

"I see only one," Ketanka corrected her.

"How could you miss that one?" she said pointing to a figure walking openly among the brush and boulders. Ketanka studied the second figure for some time.

"That is Quebathe!" he said with obvious irritation. "What is he doing out there? Sabatt! Sabatt! Come here quickly!"

"I'm here. What can I do?" Sabatt beamed proudly.

"Go down there and tell that old fool to keep under cover. There are thousands of Snake warriors over the next rise and he walks on the path of ceremony." Ketanka wished that Sequannah or Quitkwa were around. Sabatt was not yet a warrior.

Sabatt scrambled stealthily down the hillside and quickly caught up with the ambling warrior.

"Old fool!" he laughed.

"Sabatt!" Quebathe was stunned. "Since when do you call your elders by the name of old fool?" he said in his soft-spoken voice.

"I do not call you old fool," Sabatt teased. "It is Ketanka who gives you this name. There are thousands of Snake warriors over the next rise and you do not even attempt to conceal your movements?"

"We saw them. They're gone now," he stated matter-of-factly. "Went east. What are you doing over here?"

"Everyone abandoned the camp to avoid the Snake warriors," Sabatt responded. "Everyone's on top of the ridge over there," he pointed to the western hills.

"Went east," Quebathe repeated calmly. "All Snake warrior went east. Better tell them to get down from there and go back to the camp. Might snow tonight." The old warrior turned and resumed his slow shuffle back to the village.

* * *

Ketanka stumbled into the camp, huffing from the strain of clambering up the steep ridge. Shatomi had lit a fire for the returning group. Quebathe had gone around to each of the lodges and lit their small home fires. Shatomi was covering the stockpile of firewood when Ketanka strode up to him.

"What are you doing here with these fires?" Ketanka asked incredulously. "There are thousands of enemy warriors around!"

"They're gone," Shatomi said simply.

"All of them?" Ketanka questioned.

"There are about a hundred that went north to see about the fires those two Paccus made, but the rest all went east in a big hurry."

"They know of our war parties," Ketanka thought aloud. "But where do you think these hundred Snake warriors are going to go once they find out they'd been tricked."

"No need to worry," Quebathe shuffled over and broke into the conversation. "We went where you told us and we lit even bigger fires over there," he said in his soft voice, pointing to the west. Ketanka looked westward and noticed an orange glow in the northwestern sky.

"Looks like you set half a mountain on fire," Ketanka's voice began to rise in anger.

"They're sure to see that," Quebathe stated calmly. "Good thing it's going to snow tonight." He shuffled back to his lodge before Ketanka could respond, leaving Shatomi to explain. Ketanka shook his head. There was nothing to be done about it now.

"You had better sleep well," Ketanka addressed Shatomi. "Because long before daylight, you're going to make sure those Snake warriors went west, even if you have to make another fire. I want them lost in these mountains because tomorrow we will all be on the war path. There is no choice. We have to do what we can to keep the Snake warriors from getting to their village and slaughtering the war parties we have just sent there. We have to distract them until we can get word to the village."

"They are moving fast," Shatomi warned. "We may never catch up to them after it begins to snow."

"We'll catch them," Ketanka stated with conviction.

* * *

Semmida grew apprehensive as a new group of slaves, a

344

mixture of Paccus and Ondada, were herded towards the mining village. The ditches were completed, and the old furnaces repaired. Mokotak and Sequannah, along with the rest of the rebel slaves, were filling the bottoms of the ditches with bundles of small sticks. Behind them, more hooded rebels threw larger sticks and logs over the first layer. Another group piled coal along the top of the ditches to be pushed in when the fires were throwing off sufficient heat.

"Sequannah, Mokotak, come with me and stay with a larger group of us where we can hide you," Tarote whispered to the two Minnecou. "A new group of slaves comes to the village."

"It will be difficult for all of us," Sabanote suddenly wandered over and cut into the conversation. "The war chief of the Snake warriors already knows of how brutally these slaves were treated on their journey here. They have been watching them all day. Bakwanote has sent someone to bring the chief of these new slaves to his quarters for questioning about us. They know Semmida was lying to them about the 'new rules' for slaves. Even now, they have herded all the strange, pink-skinned ones together. Look around and you will find none of them. They are afraid that if there is trouble, the strange ones will flee."

"How do you know this?" Tarote questioned him.

"I am a scout. Now I scout for you," Sabanote insisted.

"Why would you scout for us when it is obvious that we will most likely be slaughtered right here in this camp. We all know that you are loyal only to those who are stronger. Why should we have any reason to trust you. Why should we even allow you to live when there will never be a way to be sure of your loyalty?" Tarote hissed at the deceitful spy.

"Because no matter where I should turn in the Snake empire or what I should become, there will always be a reason for Quiktkoata to put me to death. Whether it be for failing in my mission to expose your group of rebels, or for allowing you to come all the way to the mining village without warning Bakwanote, even if I expose you now and have you all killed, Quiktkoata will sooner or later find reason to question my loyalty. And now that I am truly aware of the workings of this empire, I see that no matter if I had done everything to Quiktkoata's satisfaction, he or someone else in power could always find reason to rid this world of me. So, you see, it is no longer a question of who trusts me in this world, my fate lies in whom I decide to trust. If it makes you feel more comfortable, I can tell you that there are many warriors surrounding this village right now that are not of the Snake empire."

"How can I be sure that what you tell me is true?" Tarote questioned him further.

"You can ask your father when he returns," the spy answered.

"My father has not left, he is under the protection of Semmida's guards."

"Your father is not among us at this moment," Sabanote responded.

"The Sikun would never allow a snake like you to be aware of his movements," Tarote's cynicism grew.

"Teokahannah is much more capable of seeing my spirit than his daughter is," Sabanote countered. "He knows I have contacts among the Snake warriors here as well."

"And how do you know their information is reliable?" Tarote asked.

"I am not asking information of them, I am giving them the information that Teokahannah wants them to have," Sabanote told her.

"And what have you told them so far?" she asked.

"I have told them of the Minnecou and Paccu warriors that approach the village," he answered calmly.

"And you ask to be trusted?" she became angry.

"Teokahannah wanted me to do this so that they would have to send many warriors out of the village. That way, they would not have enough warriors here to overtake us until the others returned. See for yourself," he stated. The two Minnecou looked to the west where they could plainly see three groups of scouts climbing into the hills, and two very long columns of warriors at quite a distance behind them. None of the strange speaking light-haired people were anywhere in sight.

"It seems as though there is some truth to what he says," Sequannah said to Tarote.

"Nevertheless, you keep your information to yourself!" Tarote warned the young Minnecou. She turned to Sabanote. "We will accept your information and we will let time show the truth of your words. In the meantime, you will learn nothing from us. If you are truly loyal to us, you'll be willing to earn our trust of you." Sabanote bowed and returned to his work of throwing logs into the ditches. "Follow me, quickly!" Tarote led the two Minnecou into a crowd of slaves, and set them to filling baskets with copper ore that would be fed into the reservoirs atop the furnaces. The skies had been clouding up all day, and now a thick and even ceiling of pure gray extended from horizon to horizon. Occasionally, Tarote caught a glimpse of single snowflakes when she faced the dark background of the mountains to the north, east and west. Perhaps when the snowflakes became a little thicker, the Minnecou would be even harder to spot in the crowd of slaves, and many of the Snake warriors would retreat to drier quarters.

* * *

The furnaces were filled with layers of small twigs, logs and coal. Soon all of the ditches would be prepared; the intense heating process that was required to crack the bedrock would be set. Snowflakes and ice pellets fell in swirls as the sky became darker and darker. Bakwanote had ordered the new group of slaves to work among the rebels to help complete the work before the snow became too intense. Sequannah and Mokotak stooped close to the ground as they rummaged through the mixture of snow and green ore that now filled their baskets. They turned away each time a strange slave worked their way closer to them; most went away when they could find no conversation.

"What did you get us into?" Mokotak questioned the young Minnecou when no other slaves were around and the snow was thick upon them. "Sooner or later we will fight to our deaths here and that is all we will do–die."

"You are too big for these weak warriors to even attempt fighting," Sequannah told him. "It is I who has something to worry about." Mokotak hung his head, then whispered to the younger Minnecou.

"When the time is right, stand behind me and I will clear a path that will lead us out of here," Mokotak stood bravely before the young Minnecou.

"When the time is right, I will stand beside you and fight until no more enemies stand before us. We will toss off these slaves' clothes and show these Snake warriors what they have to face when Minnecou see them as enemy," Sequannah said obstinately. Both Minnecous suddenly noticed that a strange Snake warrior was standing nearby, observing them. They immediately stopped their conversation and went busily about their work.

The Snake warrior continued to watch. Sequannah looked up after a long while, and glimpsed a familiar face before he quickly looked back to his work. The Snake warrior continued his hardened stare in their direction and Sequannah looked up again at the imposing figure. This time, however, he immediately recognized the Snake warrior. Woltah leaned back, staring at the two Minnecou, a mischievous sneer upon his face. He nodded in acknowledgment, then casually walked off in the direction of Bakwanote's headquarters.

"Let's find Semmida and tell him what has happened," Mokotak grabbed Sequannah by the arm and raced off towards Semmida's shack.

* * *

Raestar walked down the long corridor of the great hall, his robes flowing behind him. Two guards stood at the top of the stairwell that led to the catacombs.

"You cannot pass here," they warned Raestar.

Raestar put an arm around each of them as if they had suddenly become very close friends of his, but with one quick push, he was into the stairwell, dragging the two guards down with him in a toppling heap. As they landed at the entrance to the catacombs, the hiss of an infinity of snakes blasted through the door in a rush of foul smelling wind. An inhuman howl bellowed from deep within the earth, terrifying the two guards. They immediately ran back up the stairs and watched helplessly as Raestar walked calmly into the foul wind of the screaming and hissing chamber.

The pitch darkness of the catacombs began to glow dimly as thousands upon thousands of wriggling snakes poured into the entrance. Each of their eyes cast distinctive glows; some were mere pinpoints of light, while larger specimens displayed glowing orbs as large as fists. Raestar walked calmly and boldly amongst them, even stepping over great squirming heaps that brought his head close to the top of the chamber. He ignored their deafening hisses and continued through the thickest of them. Millions of snakes rushed to the entrance of the great catacombs and blocked the passage completely with their thick bodies, preventing the flow of fresh air from entering the chamber. The two guards fled the great hall at the sight of the mass of vicious snakes jammed into the entrance. Raestar had gotten past them, but now they were sure he would suffocate somewhere deep within the earth if he hadn't already been consumed by one of the massive serpents.

Raestar, however, was certain of the pure evil within him, and adapted to the foul air of the chambers as if they were fragrant currents of a fresh spring breeze. He felt his way along the walls of the catacombs until he reached a room with walls as smooth as new ice. Here he found a torch to which he struck a spark, illuminating the small chamber. The torch reflected infinitely between the perfectly aligned walls, and he could see thousands of images of himself holding the torch. One wall, however, showed a slight curve in the images; at its corner he found a crack to slide through. Following the corridors in certain directions, he found his way to two more such rooms. In the floor of the third room was a mosaic which pointed in the direction of the cathedral chamber. Raestar wound his way down a long and spiraling corridor that took him to the bottom level of the catacombs. The floor, itself, was hot to the touch. With his torch illuminating the cathedral chamber, several rings of serpents suddenly sprang to his face, gnawing into his powerful spirit with their slow hypnotic swaying. The spell barely began to take effect when he shook it off and walked over to the strange stones embedded in the ancient wall. Quiktkoata's sacred altar stood before him and he knew just where to look to find a special crystal he had seen Quiktkoata use to help him manipulate the stones. But inside the tiny leather pouch, he found nothing but the skeleton of a small snake.

He searched through a bag he held at his side and pulled out a crystal similar to the one he had seen Quiktkoata use, but his was smaller. The strange crystal was in the shape of a thin cylinder with a green outer layer and a ruby core. Raestar had certain warriors looking for one of these up in the copper mines, but had no luck in finding any. Finally, one of the slaves that had been captured far to the east was carrying several of these with him, and one of the Snake guards just happened to notice him trying to hide them. Raestar paid a handsome sum to the warrior, but he did manage to get the largest of the crystals. He hoped this would enable him to gain more control when trying to manipulate the strange stones.

Raestar pointed the crystal at one of the square stones, a deep, clear-blue crystal as large as a man's head. Immediately, he found himself on the floor of a valley, a ring of mountains surrounding him. He stood in the center of a large medicine wheel where the spokes radiated out in every direction to a circle of stone. He saw no one here and tried to manipulate his crystal in the manner he had seen Quiktkoata. He held it in his right hand and drew small circles above his head. Though it took a while and he kept sliding back and forth, eventually he ended up back in the cathedral chamber. He tried several more stones, but they led to barren landscapes, jungles and swamps. Finally he tried a round boulder of translucent pink. A swirl of snow clouded his vision, but he could see many figures walking through the blinding white haze. He could feel neither the snow nor the cold, but he soon recognized the litter that carried Quiktkoata, his army marching alongside. He laughed to himself, for he knew that he had not given them nearly enough supplies to sustain themselves should they become bogged down for any length of time. One of Quiktkoata's hawks suddenly swooped by Raestar, but it didn't appear to notice him. Raestar rose even further and hid behind a low cloud. Directly in the path of Quiktkoata's advancing warriors lay a small party of Paccus and Minnecou, waiting in ambush. Raestar watched in amusement at the ridiculously small war party as the first of Quiktkoata's scouts walked right by without even noticing them.

Two of Quiktkoata's hawks drifted underneath him, screeching as they glided along. The small war party suddenly disappeared into the snow and the hawks glided over them without noticing as well. When the whole war party had just about passed, long after Quiktkoata's litter was gone, the small war party suddenly sprang out of the snow. Several more warriors appeared from underneath thick stands of fir. Raestar witnessed dozens of arrows suddenly loosed into the straggling Snake warriors. One particularly heavy warrior mowed down Snake warriors with his tomahawk as quickly as they stepped beyond the hidden ambush. Forty Snake warriors lay bleeding in the snow as the small war party skirted swiftly to the north, then raced well ahead of the Snake army in an easterly direction. Though there were many areas to ambush the Snake army once again, the small war party continued to move well eastward of the advancing army. Raestar watched in wonder as Quiktkoata's army suddenly became a scrambling mess. A third hawk circled far in back of the Snake army, screeching wildly at the bloody scene below, and small scouting parties fanned out everywhere from the main body of warriors, searching for their enemies. Their attackers, however, were gone.

Raestar waved his crystal rapidly and found himself back in the cathedral room. Pointing his crystal at an enormous stone of transparent yellow, he found himself drifting over the mining village. Smoke was pouring out of the village in the light snow, and many of the buildings were ablaze. One group of warriors held another large group of warriors at spear point as they surrounded their captives. The light-haired ones streamed out of the village and into the surrounding mountains, as thick billows of smoke clouded Raestar's vision of any further happenings in the village. He waved his crystal slowly to try and descend into the village, but he only rose higher and higher until he could no longer make anything out between the clouds below him. He waved his crystal and found himself back in the cathedral room. He knew that Quiktkoata was in serious trouble with his inadequate supplies and the vicious Minnecou chief who seemed to have no trouble in outwitting Quiktkoata's scouts and hawks. Now he had Quiktkoata right where he wanted him. Quiktkoata would be back to the city for sure, for he hadn't the supplies to winter a thousand warriors. But he would not be coming into the city. Raestar had control. He had control of the magic stones and therefore of the empire. Quiktkoata's army would be kept just outside of the city, where they would be in perfect position to defend the empire should these mad Minnecou and Paccus try to foolishly overtake the city of the Serpent. But this is as close as they would ever get to the power again.

CHAPTER 20

Ceptke watched from high on a fir-cloaked hill, several warriors surrounding him. They were just north of the mining village with a somewhat distant view of the activities below. Two scouts had gone closer to the village and returned to the Paccu war leader.

"There are many slaves in the mining village and many Snake warriors, but I cannot tell which is our ally," one of the scouts reported.

"When the strange Washan came yesterday, he spoke of a large group of slaves and Snake warriors who would be working in the eastern half of the village. I told you to watch these men for that reason. Were they doing anything different than the rest of the mining camp?" Ceptke had to question the scouts more intensely than usual, for he had sent them out with little information in the event they were captured.

"From here, you can see that the camp is divided in half by a ditch through the center of the village. Many smaller ditches connect to the large one, and hundreds of slaves fill them with wood and black stones."

"Another group gathers on the western end of the village. Their scouts left the village and came into the hills. That is why we left. Many other Snake warriors stay behind, but they will be following their scouts—they have provisions with them," the scout said.

"They grow restless," Ceptke thought aloud. "As the strange Washan has said, they come into the hills looking for us. This confirms his words. Teokahannah was not merely a fool sent to distract us. We must find the other war party and warn them of the Snake warriors. The one they call Quitkwa already knows of them, but he will find no warriors to follow him. Send three scouts to find the other war party," he told one of his fierce looking war chiefs. "We will wait here for as long as we can, and then we will move to the hills on the eastern side of the village. Make sure they know where we are going. From here, you can see the stand of oak and poplar on the ridge. Their branches are empty, but you will recognize the bark."

He sent the first two scouts back down to the village. Tiny snowflakes began to drift in the imperceptible currents, then disappear altogether. "The snow will soon become thick in the air," he told the scouts who had just returned. "Look for thick pines and hide yourselves under them, where you will have protection from the storm but can still see the village. As soon as you see anyone try to set fire to the wood in those ditches, come and wake us out of the snow on the ridge of oak and poplar." The two scouts stealthily made their way towards the village, while three more sought the other war party.

Ceptke climbed down from the hill, leaving two guards behind to watch, while he and the others went down to begin the anxious wait for Quitkwa's war party to catch up. No sooner did they settle in, when the three scouts came scrambling back over the ridge.

Ceptke immediately spread his war party out in a long defensive line.

One of the scouts signed to them that there was no danger, then Boaka appeared at the top of the ridge, along with another Paccu scout. Boaka stood before Ceptke before the other scouts could join the group. "Snake warriors searching through the hills," he warned the Paccu war chief. "There is time to find a good place to hide if you go east."

"We already know of such a place," Ceptke spoke. "But you must return quickly to your war party and seek out Quitkwa. He will know where to take you and what to do when you get there."

"Quitkwa?" Boaka asked, questioning Ceptke's competence.

"Yes, Quitkwa!" he answered anxiously. "A powerful Washan speaks of Quitkwa to bring the two war parties together. Move quickly!"

"Do you want us to meet you in the hills east of the village?" Boaka let him know that they could move ahead if it were necessary.

"No!" Ceptke said stubbornly. "If your war party should run into the Snake warriors we must be around to help. Your war party could destroy them, but we must make sure that no Snake warriors can return to warn those in the village and tell of our whereabouts. We will wait here for you."

* * *

Shatomi set out in the dark hours of early morning and sought the highest peak to find where the Snake warriors had drifted to during the night. The full moon didn't show where the Snake warriors went until shortly before dawn, when they were foolish enough to light a small campfire. Another wisp of smoke appeared far to the west, where the mountain he and Quebathe had set ablaze was still smoldering. The sky was gray and the wind whistled atop the mountain he had chosen for his lookout. He watched for movements of the Snake warriors after they had doused the small fire. The dim morning light gave away their whereabouts. Snow was beginning to swirl down the steep mountain trails when Shatomi headed back to the camp. By the time he reached Ketanka's lodge, the ground was fully covered.

"The spirit of the Dark Mountains draws them deeper into

confusion," Shatomi reported to the waiting chief. "Some head further west, while others search to the north. They should be building themselves shelter from the snow," he laughed. "This storm will not be over soon and the drifts will pile high."

"Then we should prepare ourselves well to travel," Ketanka said solemnly.

"It will not be just a little snow," Shatomi warned. "And we might do better to stay here and keep ourselves rested until the storm is over and the Snake warriors are worn down."

"No," Ketanka looked to the floor of the lodge, shaking his head. "They know where they are going and they will get there to save their own lives and to annihilate our war parties. This Snake warrior chief is not foolish. Once he gets them to the village, every one of his warriors will see that they must destroy our warriors or they will die in the cold. A thousand warriors fighting for their lives, and whatever warriors they already have in the village, will provide no chance for our relatives. They will kill them all. We must hold them back until we can get far ahead of them and warn our war parties. To stay here now, we would only have a greater distance to catch them...and in deeper snow. No! We must prepare well now and leave this morning. Even if we stay here, the Snake warriors will be back in the spring to kill all of us, too. The time to fight is now, any later and it will already be over. Even if some of us cannot see, the final battle already stands before us. We will go forth and fight rather than lay down and die. Do you agree?"

"Yes," Shatomi answered slowly, for he knew many would die. "It is better to die fighting than to be killed hiding."

"Good!" Ketanka croaked. "Because there is no time for council. We'll get the warriors prepared for battle. The women and children should be prepared as warriors, too; they are the biggest part of our war party. I'll speak to the Paccu woman. Their choices walk with ours. They will fight, or as you say, die in hiding."

It took longer than Ketanka wished to prepare the small war party for travel. Their faces were filled with fear, for what chance would a party of mostly women and children have against the greatest enemy they had ever known.

Quebathe, however, had prepared nothing. "I will stay behind with the youngest and the elderly. It saddens me, but I can tell you truthfully that I will become a burden to you before you catch up to the great Snake warrior party."

"We may never return," Ketanka warned him. "The women and children who stay behind with you may become stranded here."

"When the weather is better, we will move south until we reach the villages of our relatives near the great river," Quebathe said, his head hung low.

"There may be no villages for you to return to, either," Ketanka said sadly.

"Just as there is no choice but to fight for you, my only choice is to stay," Quebathe lamented. "I am no longer the strong warrior I used to be. I have grown weak and slow. For me to climb over mountains in the snow will hold you back. You will never catch up to the Snake warriors. And Meequaw...would you drag an old woman to her death? A woman who has spent most of her years raising the orphan children of the clans. My wife, Shahte, she is the same as me. Of what help would she be to you? What will you do with your son, Quetatsu, in the middle of a battle? Washeena, what will you do with her? Sabatt may be of some use to you, but what of Petana and Kalashte?"

"I have always left the choice to each of you," Ketanka told the old warrior. "But I would not say to anyone "stay behind", when you know this is a fight for our way of life, forever...when our paths will all be beaten down by Snake people, and our choice will be to live as them or lay down and die. I have known you all of my years, and I know that you do not choose to stay out of fear of the Snake people or fear for your life. You see that you have become too old and there is nothing you can do about this. This is the way of things, so do not hang your head in shame. I will let all people decide for themselves, except Quetatsu; him I will leave with you and Shahte now that you will stay behind."

"I will teach him to be a warrior who is good for this earth," the gentle old warrior promised the chief.

"You answer the prayers I hold for my son and perhaps for rest of the clan. And some of the Paccus...they have brought children along as well. Meequaw will now have someone to stay with. She will not have to walk to a snowy grave. For you, it is this path you have chosen that is brave," Ketanka eyes were piercing.

"Those of you who know in your hearts that you will not

add great force to our war party, or will hold us back in any way, must look at yourselves and see if you should remain with Quebathe. I will tell no one to stay behind, and each person's decision will be honored as if it were decided by council. It is no shame to stay. Remember that if our war parties should fail, we intend to fight to our deaths. Those who stay behind may be the only seeds to grace the winds and remind the earth of the great clans."

Ketanka tried to convince Wanachan that the war party knew enough of each others' language to get along without her, but she wouldn't hear of it, for she knew her Paccu relatives would never get their words across with any effect. She left all of the children behind, with the exception of Kampote Uli, the serious one. "He will look after me better than I would trust any other warrior," she said proudly. The young man's expression remained solemn.

Sabatt walked proudly to his younger brothers, bidding them farewell. Tumaris had begged them to stay, encouraging only Sabatt to join the war party. She went with the war party, herself, because she was good with a knife and a bow, and could feed and care for the sick and wounded if necessary. Shatomi's son was also left with Quebathe, as well as his niece, whose mother had chosen to go with the war party.

The Paccus, however, were still not prepared, and Ketanka grew anxious enough to see what was holding them up. He found them hurriedly bending loops of ash, lacing thongs of rawhide across them.

"There is no time to prepare yourselves any further," he warned them. "The time to go is now."

"They are not preparing for themselves," Wanachan responded. "They already have their own. They make these for your people."

"We are already prepared," Ketanka bellowed.

"Soon, these will gain you much more time than you will save by leaving now," she said patiently. "It is much quicker to walk on top of the snow than through it when it becomes deep."

"It will be my people's problem," he said anxiously.

"We are all together," she corrected him.

* * *

Semmida took the two Minnecou into a mound he had chosen as his council lodge, its sides and roof covered with sods of growing grass. None of the village chief's messengers or guards had been in to see Semmida all day. It made him uneasy that they should suddenly change. Perhaps the village chief had discovered that Semmida and his party were not what they seemed. Now that one of the Snake guards had recognized the two Minnecou, there would be no doubt in the village chief's mind. But their work has been completed, even as the snow piles up outside. They are now set to carry out their attack upon the mining village no matter what should happen. They wait only for the storm to end. Then they can attack with the help of those war parties gathering outside of the village. There was no need to hand the two Minnecou over to Bakwanote.

"Put these two under guard with Teokahannah," he ordered one of his scouts. This would stall the village chief at least until the storm has cleared, he thought to himself.

Semmida gathered his warriors, explaining the final details of their dawn attack to immediately secure the eastern half of the village. They would then attack the western half which would be divided into four very rough and irregular sections, each of which would be surrounded by ditches of high flames. Each section would burn only for a certain amount of time and the ditches were set up so that only one section of the western half of the village would be accessible at a time; the others would be isolated in flames.

"We will start the furnaces during the night, and their vats will be filled with molten copper by dawn," he told them. "The village chief will be watching everything, to finally see our new way of mining. I think he may learn a little more than he would care to."

Moments later, three Snake guards burst into Semmida's lodge. One of them walked straight up to him.

"There are two Minnecou among your slaves. Bakwanote wants them now. This man can identify them," he said rapidly, not allowing Semmida to interrupt. Woltah stepped arrogantly forward.

"Yes," Semmida said calmly. "We have found them and they are being questioned at this very moment." Then he turned back to his men, suggesting that he had more important things to attend to.

The Snake guard pounded his fist hard on a table in the center of the lodge, screaming at Semmida. "The chief demands these two Minnecou now, and I will accept no alternative. Bakwanote demands them and I will enforce his demands," the Snake guard threatened Semmida.

Semmida immediately drew a long metal knife from his tunic and pressed its point into the Snake guard's throat, forcing him to lie back upon the table. "Tell your chief that he will get them when I am through questioning them, and no sooner. Whether there will be anything left of them when I'm through or not is difficult to say, but I will place the corpses on his lap myself if that is all that is left. And tell him to be ready for our demonstration in the morning because we intend to go ahead with our work regardless of snow. The fires will burn and the stone at the bottom of those ditches will be as red as the setting sun on a hot summer day. You tell him and his fools to be there and watch closely. I may not be here to repeat it for him again."

The Snake guard quickly retreated from Semmida's knife. Semmida's warriors had shrunk Woltah back to the entrance with their piercing stares and threatening spears. The three Snake guards fled from the lodge where they had unexpectedly provoked much more than they could handle. Semmida trusted that the incident would not be brought up until the following day, after the demonstration.

* * *

Sequannah and Mokotak were led to a small shack, where the Sikun was being held under heavy guard. The entrance was opened and the two Minnecou were thrown in bodily. Teokahannah sat cross-legged in the corner furthest from the entrance, quietly heaving with laughter at the sight of his guards trying to throw Mokotak.

"What did you do to get thrown in with Quiktkoata's worst enemy?" he smiled. "What event brings two Minnecou emissaries as my allies in captivity?" Sequannah witnessed sparrows and finches hopping among the wooden beams near the roof of the small shack.

"One of the Snake warriors recognizes us," Mokotak mumbled in his deep voice. "The one they call Woltah. He is a Paccu, but he is a traitor."

"Three, four moons ago, he had not even known of the Snake peoples' ways," Sequannah added. "Already he chooses their path, and they choose him."

"This is not unusual," the Sikun spoke softly. "The trails that Snake people follow have crossed the paths of most clans and tribes even before the Snake people were heard of, but now they have an empire and a place where these trails can lead to their own kind of honor. An honor that is distant from the sacred ways of the Creator. They do not acknowledge the powers and forces of the true Creator, where they would be forced to stand humbled. Instead, they create their own worlds and try to remove themselves from the natural way of things. They do not understand that they are the deer in the herd as well as the birds in the flock, who will turn in unison, compelled by forces they cannot see. They are the eagle soaring proudly above in search of meat, as well as the bison who grazes below. They are the beaver who builds dams and creates worlds for other living things, as well as the wolverine who tears them apart in search of his own needs. They are the bees who build complex colonies and suckle life's honey, as well as the flies who dwell anywhere and live off the dung of the earth. They do not see that they are cousin to all living things. They do not understand that they are already heir to the highest place among Earth Mother's creatures, because they do not see that the highest honor is to serve, rather than rule. The more you are able to serve the world and its creatures around you, the more it will serve you. The more you demand from it without return, the uglier it will become until it decides to rid itself of you. Such is the man called Woltah, you speak of. He follows a path that appears real to him, but it ends in the desert. We have all walked these trails at one time or another, but only fools and evil ones will follow them to their ends. This is what we must stop before they would have us all on the same trail–the trail that leads to their own honor and their own empires. The further they distance themselves from the natural world, the more they isolate themselves from the Creator, for they are one in the same."

"And we will put an end to their ways tomorrow," Sequannah said confidently. "Everything we have planned is ready, and there is nothing they can do to stop it."

"Tomorrow, we only begin the struggle, for until then, everything we have done will have been done in secrecy and with little struggle," the Sikun corrected him. "Your determination pleases me, but the true struggle only begins tomorrow. We can only serve to the best of our abilities and hope that it is enough."

"You do not know that we will win?" Sequannah became anxious. "Won't we beat them if we do as you have said?"

"If everything works perfectly," Teokahannah said, "Then

we will have won the ability to fight them. But, to win the victory over them, we must have the ability to endure the struggle until the end, for once it is started, the end will surely come for one of us. Whether it is us or them depends on who has the most faith and power behind what they are struggling for. It depends upon what lies here," he said pointing to his heart, "And here," he said pointing to his head.

Sequannah felt suddenly abandoned. Mokotak shook his head, laughing inaudibly. "Semmida, Tarote and you have all said that we have been chosen by the Creator to fight the Snake people and that the Creator chooses us to win. You have led us down a false trail," he said angrily, casting a hostile glance at Mokotak for mocking his naiveté. "You have tricked us into fighting for something you want. It has nothing to do with us. What is it that you want?" Sequannah spoke in anger. "Is it that you want your daughter back? Is it that you want Quiktkoata to fight the Minnecou and the Paccus and Ondadas and all the other peoples before they fight your own?"

Mokotak's face suddenly contorted in question as well. The Sikun shook his head and smiled in almost the same manner that Mokotak had done earlier, only now Mokotak had a wild look about him; the look of a cornered wolf.

"The Creator has indeed chosen us, but we must choose him as well. We choose him when we follow both what is in our hearts and in our minds, for where these two come together and we know it is right, this is where the Creator speaks to us. This is the part of us that is closest to him. And we must trust in him and all others who trust in this way, for this is how the Creator has made us, and this is how we gain the power of the Creator behind us. This is how as warriors we can move as graceful as the herd, and as clever as the wolf pack. We can do this because we all know what is needed together. You must have faith and trust, Sequannah. I thought that you were well suited for this struggle, but now I see that even the slightest of doubts can turn you away. You can both stay here with me if you wish. Semmida and his warriors can fight alone. Your relatives, the ones who come with the one they call Quitkwa, I believe, they can save you. They will get your freedom for you and for the rest of your clan as well. Maybe even a Paccu will rescue you, there is no way to be sure if enough Minnecou will survive because there are so few of them...and they may have doubts like the two I have with me now. It is too difficult to say, but I am sure that one way or another, someone will come to rescue you."

"How do you know Quitkwa?" Mokotak asked in his deep voice.

"Quitkwa?"

"Yes, Quitkwa," Mokotak said. "You said his name."

"Did you not know that there are warriors in the hills here to help us. Did Semmida not tell you and Sabanote as well?"

"Yes," the two Minnecou said in unison. "But..."

"They are with Quitkwa," the Sikun said in his sometimes comical accent. "Quitkwa, now there is a warrior who has great faith. To bring all those warriors back here so quickly." The two Minnecou looked at each other incredulously. "He will be remembered as one of the..."

"We have as much faith as Quitkwa," Sequannah interrupted.

"You do. You do?" Teokahannah looked as though he was struggling to weigh Sequannah's statement fairly. "I suppose we may find out tomorrow, but for now I must rest. I'm too old to be up here in the cold. I haven't seen snow since I was a child, and after all the years that I waited to see it again, I find that I don't miss it so much. Perhaps if I was born rolling in it...I'm tired. Wake me when the fighting begins," he yawned and was snoring before he even finished rolling over. Sequannah and Mokotak glared at the Sikun's back. They had been insulted, and had only each other to bring their angers upon.

* * *

Shamira had managed to clear the leaves from in front of her face; the snow, above, fell in clumps, stinging her eyes as the flakes melted into them. She managed to pack the light and fluffy snow around the edges of the hole she had created to see outside of her buried position. Her hands and feet had been warm when she first roused from her sleep, but now they were numb and burning. Her body began to shiver as it did when she first buried herself in the leaves, desperately trying to sleep through the cold storm. It was not the kind of frigid winter night when everyone would have frozen stiff and slept on forever, but it was close enough where they would all remember the pain and suffering. At arm's length, Shamira's numb hand extended just above the white blanket that covered her and the rest of the war party.

As the time slowly passed, the snow at the top of the hole changed from grayish black to a light blue. She wished she was sitting by the warm fires of her lodge, where only a few days ago, she had been comforting Meequaw for the oncoming winter; where she had been reasonably comfortable herself.

Her heart trembled when she thought of the events that were to pass with the coming dawn. By the change in the color of the snow, she knew that the time that she and many others had feared, as well as longed for, was now here. It seemed like a moment they had awaited for many years, when in actuality, they were aware of its coming for only the last few moons.

She thought of Ceptke. Her heart trembled even as much as it had for her own life, and those of her clan. She had only seen Ceptke in brief glimpses on their journey here, and she was not even sure that he was aware of her, or even if he cared. He was too busy with his scouts and warriors, making plans and trying to get everyone covered as thoroughly and quickly as possible. Everyone was full to the point of bursting, and even their jaws were sore from trying to eat all of the food and jerky they'd brought. Shamira had been quite surprised to see nearly everyone from her war party hinging on Quitkwa's every word as they prepared themselves to weather the first winter storm, and for a battle like none other after the following dawn. Strangely, he seemed as powerful as Ketanka. But soon, he grew arrogant, and it was plain that his commands were becoming increasingly foolish. It was almost as if the Creator, himself, had spoke through him, then suddenly quit.

"There will be no more food until we are standing victorious over the Snake peoples' village," she remembered Quitkwa saying to the fierce Paccu leaders. "The Creator has stored plenty of food for us in the mining village and we must scourge the village of his enemies before we can eat of his food. The Sikun has told me this himself." But later, he spoke of honoring ceremonies, and of how he was to dance alone before 'smaller chiefs' could join in. He, and to a lesser degree, Ceptke, would run the strange village until they were ready to attack the Snake peoples' big city to the south. The war parties began to laugh at him, then ignore him until he buried himself in the leaves to get away from everyone. He was so angry, he couldn't sleep, and never even felt the cold.

Shamira suddenly felt a tug on her foot, coming from

beneath the snow. She felt above herself, searching for the foot she was to tug when the time was ready, and after finding the cold and ice-covered moccasin, she woke the person above her and got to her feet. The snow had fallen deep during the night, over her knees. But the sky was laden with small patches of blue, and to the east, she could see the red and orange glow as the first rays of sunrise outlined the heavy gray and drifting clouds. To the west, she could plainly see the village they were to attack. When they had arrived the previous day, the snow fell so heavily that the village wasn't even visible, but now she could see everything clearly. The western sky was rimmed with its own eerie red and orange glow. Huge flames raced high into the air from the village below, and small explosions popped in the distance, as the snow-filled ditches were suddenly filled with molten metal and quickly burning wood and coal and chunks of sulfur. Hundreds of tiny figures were fleeing and scattering in every direction, some of them fully ablaze. She could hear the din of piercing cries and screaming, mounting up from the valley floor. But from this distance, it didn't seem quite real to her until she heard the words "Move! Move!" and she found herself in a stampede of warriors. Cries and screams erupted all around her—not of fear and pain, but of confidence and power. She ran screaming and flailing her knife into the air. The war party ran wild-eyed towards the strange village.

It was difficult going; the snow bogged down what needed to be a lightning attack. Halfway down the steep hillside, a clearing wind blew in from the northwest, and they ran straight into a bank of smoke and steam, fanned at them from the burning ditches and buildings. The stench was horrible: fumes of sulfur and coal, burning shacks, hides, food stores and flesh. Screams of terror, pain and threat came from every direction. Snake warriors were everywhere. Ceptke's war party formed a great mob, pulling every passing Snake warrior to its core, then moving on in search of more. The Minnecou war party stayed close to the Paccus, searching every building, and driving small groups of Snake warriors into Ceptke's howling mass. A massive group of Snake warriors suddenly appeared through the smoky haze, halting. Two warriors came forward from the group, and Shamira suddenly recognized Petawahin and the Washan, though they were covered in blood and streaked black from the burning buildings. Shamira ran to her father. Another large group of Snake warriors suddenly appeared from behind one of the larger burning buildings. Every bow within the Minnecou and Paccu war parties was already drawn, and several arrows flew before the Washan could place himself in the middle of the two opposing forces, screaming for everyone to stop. From the midst of the Snake warriors, two slaves were thrust forward, who then threw back their hoods. Sequannah thrust a long copper blade high in the air while his giant companion stood silently at his side.

"Do not fight with these warriors," Sequannah screamed out. "They fight for the Sikun." Semmida stepped out and cast off his hard leather Snake warrior's armor. Though these would serve to deflect glancing arrows, they were stiff and cumbersome, and caused confusion as to who was the enemy and who was not.

"Remove the Snake warriors clothing," Semmida yelled. "From this point on, no warrior of the true Creator will ever wear the shields of the Snake people. We have taken this section of the village." All of his warriors stripped down of the armored clothing and followed him to a building where hundreds of slaves' tunics were stored. Several Snake warriors were found hiding there. Those who cursed and tried to flee were killed. Those who surrendered were stripped down and handed slaves' garments. Twelve of them had surrendered, while three tried to flee. The twelve were led to Semmida's lodge, where they were left under the watch of the Sikun and several guards. Kwoita had finally made it into the village; he couldn't keep up with the younger warriors and was already showing signs of frostbite from the stormy night. Teokahannah pulled him into the safety of Semmida's lodge.

"Quickly!" Semmida yelled to the four war parties. "Band together at the southern end of the largest ditch. As soon as the flames die down, we must invade that section of the village and do the same as we have done here. Conserve your weapons and your energy–we must do this three more times and we will need every one of us. There may be some slaves to join in with us from each section, but we will not know whether they are truly slaves or Snake warriors in disguise– the Snake warriors may kill all of the slaves to protect themselves. Take your bows and we will shoot onto their buildings to set them ablaze. We must get them all out in the open and we must do it quickly before we have another section opened.

Shamira ran over to fight alongside her father. The Wolf brothers joined them as well. Shamira grabbed onto her father and held him tight. "We will win. Now that I see you still alive and still strong, this village will fall." Sequannah and Mokotak also came to fight alongside their own kinsmen as well as Quitkwa. He had no desire to lead whatsoever, and felt suddenly relieved that he was no longer in the company of so many Paccus.

Semmida arranged the various war parties at strategic points, and they inflicted a hail of flaming arrows upon the wooden structures, setting them ablaze. It took much longer than they had anticipated because the roofs were covered in snow. They learned quickly to shoot at the base of the buildings, but this was difficult as well because the Snake warriors kept tossing buckets of water from the inside and dousing the flames before they got out of control. By the time the southern end of the ditch had begun to burn itself down and Semmida could lead his men across, they had only set half of the buildings on fire. Semmida led the charge and took his men over the burning ditch even before the flames extinguished. The closest buildings were heavily damaged and Snake warriors were just beginning to run from the openings to avoid suffocating in the thick, black smoke.

"Kill all of them," Semmida ordered his warriors. The Snake warriors were dodging out of the burning buildings one by one, and Semmida's warriors rained arrows down on them. "Only one arrow at a time," he screamed at his men. "Don't throw all of your arrows away."

Some of the men began to complain that Semmida should have them taken as prisoners instead of killing them. "They are blinded from the smoke and cannot even see their enemy. It is a slaughter for us to kill them like this."

"How do you propose that we triumph over the rest of this village if we are all busy guarding prisoners," he said. "You cannot guard more prisoners than you have of warriors and still be able to continue in the battle. We must fight and kill until there are no more to resist us. Then we will take prisoners. If you are worried about fairness, then go and attack the buildings that are not burning. I'm sure you'll return here very quickly." No sooner had these words escaped Semmida's lips when arrows began to rain down on them from every direction. Some were coming from the buildings that were still intact, but others were being fired from across the burning ditches in other sections of the village. The village chief was on one of the rooftops, shouting out orders. Petawahin sent an arrow in his direction, but he was so distant that the arrow merely fell onto the rooftop. Semmida sent his men crawling up to the remaining buildings and setting them ablaze before the fires ran too low in the ditches. Snake warriors in the other sections of the village began to set up great barrages along the burning ditches, stationing warriors behind them to combat Semmida and his forces as soon as they tried to breach the flames.

Mokotak noticed that along one section of ditch, behind one of the buildings, several Snake warriors were plowing the snow with wide boards, dousing the flames of coal and wood. They would cross the ditch and come to the aid of their isolated comrades.

The Minnecou immediately responded with a hail of swift arrows. Many Snake warriors fell dead, and the rest scattered. But soon, they were all back plowing the snow into the ditches once again. More and more Snake warriors made their way to the ditches, and the Minnecou were beginning to exhaust all of their arrows. Sequannah ran to get help from Semmida, but he was still bogged down, trying to take the final buildings in the second section.

Sequannah hurried back to his own clan's battle, hoping they hadn't already been overrun. When he finally trudged his way back through the deep snow, Mokotak was out on the other side of the ditch, swinging his hatchet and taking Snake warriors down one by one. Arrows protruded from his shoulder and calf, but he hadn't even noticed. The Wolf brothers jabbed at the crowd of Snake warriors with their spears while Shamira and two Paccu women thinned them with arrows. Sequannah shot one arrow after another as he stood out in the open and at close range to the constantly building force of Snake warriors. No matter how many went down, there were always more coming. The Snake people continued to kick and plow snow into the ditches while Mokotak pummeled them. A large force was gathering some distance away, ready to overrun the small group of Minnecou. As soon as the fire was extinguished they would have access to the section where Semmida was trying desperately to win control. Petawahin jumped in alongside the Wolf brothers and shot directly into the Snake warriors as he tried to provide cover for his kinsmen.

"Get out! Get out!" Petawahin screamed. "We have no chance of stopping them. Many of them have gathered to overrun us." A large army of Snake warriors suddenly came into focus; the Minnecou realized that there was no way to stop them. Either flee or die.

At the same moment, the strange, hairy-faced ones burst

forth from one of the buildings in the third section of the village and ran to the burning ditch nearest to the woods. They began, as well, to plow snow onto the flames, and the mass of Snake warriors made a quick change of plans to prevent the light-skinned ones' escape.

The Minnecou renewed their attack on the small group of Snake warriors that were trying to breach the burning ditch, and soon these warriors were all killed, unaware that their reinforcements had been diverted.

Sequannah, Shamira and the two Paccu women began to set fire to the buildings in the third section of the village, but they were soon pinned back against the burning ditches by a roving band of enemy Snake warriors. Most of the buildings were abandoned—the Snake warriors were out fighting in the open, after seeing what had happened in the second section. Quitkwa suddenly appeared and began shooting at the Snake warriors from behind. Mokotak and the Wolf brothers quickly joined in. By the time Petawahin and the Washan were there, the Snake warriors held their hands high in the air.

They were shocked to find that they'd been taken by only ten Minnecou warriors, three of them women. The whole group of forty Snake warriors moved to pick up their weapons again, but each was quickly and accurately pierced with an arrow as they dared to move. They thought they had been surrounded and outnumbered; the anger in their faces showed their disgust for surrendering.

Despite the fact that they had no weapons and the Snake warriors were attacking them full force, the hairy-faced ones fought off the Snake warriors as best they could with boards and clubs, and soon breached the ditch that led to their freedom. Many other white-skinned warriors burst forth from another building, joining their kindred in a mass escape. Sequannah watched all of the hairy-faced ones running up the hills, a band of Snake warriors at their heels, as Bakwanote stood on a rooftop screaming for his warriors to come back. But they couldn't hear him, and no messengers would ever reach them in time. Backwanote howled as the Snake warriors disappeared over the top of the hill, leaving the third section of the village nearly abandoned.

He was in a rage at the turn of events and there was nothing he could do about it. He had waited for Semmida's demonstration just so he could rid himself of the shifty spy that Quiktkoata had supposedly sent to aid the mining village. But before he and his men had even stirred from their sleep, Semmida had set the entire village to flames and was now systematically routing the Snake warrior forces at every turn. The chief was relieved to see that the hairy-faced ones had chosen to flee instead of joining in with Semmida's forces; he knew they wouldn't defend the village if a large enough attack was launched against it. But now he had to decide whether to flee himself, or try to defend the final section of the village from Semmida's unscathed warriors. Though the rebel forces had only just begun to enter the third section of the village, the chief had already conceded this area; most of the defending forces were somewhere up in the hills, chasing the hairy-faced ones. Most of the slaves of the mining village were housed here as well. All of those slaves who were not put to death as soon as the rebellion began would increase Semmida's forces.

He considered surrender. But this would be viewed as rebellion by Quiktkoata. He and his men would be slaughtered among the rebels as soon as Quiktkoata caught up with them, and as far as he could see, Semmida's warriors may have enough force to overtake the mining village. In fact it seemed imminent, but they would never be able to stand up to Quiktkoata. Either way, the chief could see that he and his forces were doomed...unless by some miracle, they could muster enough strength to scatter Semmida's warriors. But as each moment passed, the possibility of striking any kind of effective blow against the rebels became increasingly remote. He would die fighting, along with his closest warriors.

CHAPTER 21

Ketanka, Shatomi and two Paccu warriors lay flat in the deep snow. Hidden beneath frosted branches of bushy white pine, they watched the massive Snake warrior army slowly advancing in an easterly direction through the wet and heavy snow. Their perch upon one of the highest peaks in the eastern range of the Dark Mountains gave them a clear view of Quiktkoata's ominous forces.

Banded closely together, and trudging along the same trampled path, no longer were scores of scouts scattered ahead of the huge army. No longer were there any stragglers to ambush, as Ketanka and his little band had so effectively accomplished the previous afternoon. While the four of them lay inconspicuously near the mountain's summit, the rest of their party remained hidden in the crags of the valley below. Ketanka knew that his war party could easily outdistance the Snake warriors with the new snowshoes the Paccus had made. But he would take no chances with the strange hawks that were constantly soaring overhead. They could alert Snake warriors anywhere, even in the village.

They had heard the moaning and complaining of the Snake warriors as they passed by their ambush yesterday afternoon. Their moccasins had ripped open during the long, arduous trek, and wet snow bunched around their feet as they tried desperately to keep pace with the rest of the column. Many were sick and vomiting as if they had eaten bad food. Others looked faint with hunger. Ketanka knew this by the way they gazed longfully into the forest, with an eye for game rather than enemy warriors. As soon as the hawks drifted back to the column, Ketanka jumped to his feet and readjusted his snowshoes.

"We do not even suffer wet feet, never mind the slow travel that the Snake warriors must endure," Ketanka praised the new innovation of the Paccus. "But even with this advantage we must move quickly to the east and locate the strange village."

The Paccus pointed eastward, giving the hand sign for fire. Ketanka witnessed a thin haze drifting between the distant peaks, but even as he watched, clearing winds disturbed the air. The source of the haze became undetectable.

"By the end of this day, we'll locate the village if they continue to burn," Ketanka croaked. "We must convince our war parties to leave while our feet are still better than those of the Snake warriors. By the time those Snake warriors reach the village, many of them will be hopping on one foot."

They quickly shuffled down the steep slope on their clumsy showshoes, then set their small war party to the trail. Ketanka thought briefly about staging another raid on Quiktkoata's beleaguered army, to hold them back even longer. Knowing that his small party could easily outrun the Snake warriors with their new snowshoes, this fresh bed of snow could leave a trail that would take many Snake warriors far from the main war party, and reduce Quiktkoata's initial battle strength. But he dismissed the idea when he considered how much time it might take to reach the village, and how long it would be before all of the war parties could be moved to a safe distance from Quiktkoata and his warriors. So far, he had lost no one to the enemy, and there were no injured. Better to leave them alone, he thought to himself.

Ketanka led his party eastward, seeking out the older forests and thick evergreens to avoid being spotted by the hawks. Even without them as a threat, however, he would have taken the same steps, for the sun reflected blindingly off of the fresh snow, and Wanachan had told him of an old Paccu saying: "You must be in the shadows to see in the shadows."

Sabatt guarded his mother and Wanashta in much the same manner as Kampote Uli watched after Wanachan, but they soon tired of his stoic demeanor and constant hounding.

"Sabatt!" Tumaris spouted irritably. "Change your face! If you have to act like that little Paccu, go find someone else to irritate, but stop following our every move as if we are helpless. Just because Wanachan has that sour-faced little pup hounding her every step doesn't mean that we would want the same. Get out of here! Go with Shatomi where you will learn what a warrior and scout needs to know."

Sabatt was embarrassed, but then realized they were telling him that he was no longer a child to be following his mother around. It was time for him to become a warrior and a provider. He had quickly adopted to the skills of snowshoeing, and Shatomi, having overheard the conversation behind him, waited for the young warrior to catch up.

"An old warrior changes trails yesterday," he spoke to the boy, "and the Creator has already brought us a new one to take his place. I have watched you grow for several winters, Sabatt, and I see that you are a good human. Watch, listen and care for the people. These are the things to do to become a good warrior and provider for the clan. Many warriors think that bravery makes them powerful, but I will tell you something. Bravery and foolishness are very close to being the same. If your act works, they will call you brave...if not, they will call you fool. The best thing for a warrior to do is to learn what he can from every scout, hunter and warrior. Learn from the Washan as well. Do, for the clan, what you are best at, and like to do most. Even if you are not very good at what you like to do, if you like it, you will become good. It is always best to think about the clan first, and then yourself, before you act. But I am sure that before this day is over, you will learn that there is not always time. Nevertheless, I think you will become a good warrior. Keep your eyes open and look behind you as well as ahead. Wherever you cannot see well, watch that there is no movement. If anything moves, stop and take cover, and move cautiously to find out what has moved. At some point today or tomorrow, we will meet up with our enemy. What is most important is that we see them first."

"With these snowshoes, we can outrun them if they surprise us," Sabatt smiled confidently.

"Ketanka will lead us directly to the village, because there is no time to be wasted," he warned the fledgling warrior. "No matter what enemy stands before us, he will look for a way through them. There will be no moving back."

Sabatt appeared undaunted at Shatomi's assessment of their chief. He felt confident in the strength of Ketanka's resolve, and there were no decisions to make. They would be moving eastward no matter what.

The clearing winds slowly faded into gentle, but cold breezes. With what little sound their snowshoes made, and the lack of whispering winds, their communication became sparse; reduced to hand signals. Twice, they heard the screeching of Quiktkoata's hawks, echoing off the walls of winding canyons that led away from the higher elevations of the Dark Mountains. They halted under the cover of snow laden boughs until the hawks' screeching faded in the distance. When they resumed their hurried march, they were acutely aware of their trail sign, avoiding any open areas where the large snowshoe prints might be visible from above.

The huge, puffy clouds that had alternately curtained and exposed the blinding reflection of bright mountain sun, now lay gathered near the eastern horizon. Their eyes hurt, constricting into aching squints. Most had their hoods draped low, to shadow the piercing brightness.

"It is a slow journey from tree to tree, and from bush to bush," Sabatt heard Shatomi whisper to Ketanka. "We have not heard the voices of hawks for some time. Perhaps it would be a good time to make some distance in the open, before we end up at this village at the same time Quiktkoata arrives."

"You tell me my own thoughts," Ketanka croaked softly. "But I do not want us to be caught in the open when we reach the end of this valley. Enemies could attack us from both sides, and we will have no place to run. Take Sabatt far ahead with you, and see that we are not a parade to ambush. If all is clear, shake the snow from a heavy pine, at a place where you can see us. Come back if you find sign of enemy warriors, but stay in the shadows. We will follow your trail, and watch for your signal."

Shatomi grabbed Sabatt by the arm. "Come with me, warrior," he whispered. "Now you will learn to be swift and alert among enemies." Sabatt followed eagerly, nearly outrunning Shatomi as they dodged in and out of the shrubs and trees, and along the shadows of the south canyon walls. Partridge and pheasant fluttered suddenly at their feet, causing Sabatt to jump sideways from the false attacks. A leaf drifting in the wind froze him in his tracks, for fear of Quiktkoata's hawks. Soon he began to fall behind Shatomi's lead; his chest began to heave. But Shatomi didn't look back.

Sabatt ran harder, right up to Shatomi's heels, the awkward snowshoes barely strapped to his feet. He breathed a sigh of relief when Shatomi stopped to adjust his own straps. But Shatomi's fingers were nimble, and he was gone before Sabatt had even started to adjust his second shoe. He took the time to tie his knots tight. Perhaps the next time they stopped, he would not have to adjust his.

Luckily, Sabatt had Shatomi's tracks to follow. The experienced warrior was nearly out of sight, and Sabatt was still working up to find his pace. "What do I do if I come across an enemy now?" Sabatt thought to himself. "I am not a strong warrior like Shatomi." He reached to his side and pulled an arrow from his quiver. He strung it to his bow with much difficulty as he followed Shatomi's tracks under low branches, and over rocky piles of rubble at the base of the canyon walls. "I will get at least one shot," he thought to himself.

Shatomi's tracks led up a small incline. Sabatt forced himself forward, even as he strained uphill. At the top of the rise, a wide view was opening before him. It appeared as though the trail went steeply down hill. He pushed even harder to catch up with Shatomi, for he imagined him to be far ahead. Just as he got over the top, he found himself poised at the edge of a precipitous ledge. He turned sideways and put one foot in front to stop himself. But, there was no solid ground under the snow, and he sailed through the air, landing on top of Shatomi. Shatomi shook him off, and rose to his feet. A trickle of blood traced the contour of his ear as he pointed to Sabatt's feet. The webs of one of his snowshoes had ripped, and the wooden rim encircled his knee.

Shatomi quickly scanned the area. "Fix the webbing on your shoes," he ordered. "I'll signal the others and let them know that it is safe to this point. Be ready to move when I get back or I'll find someone else to scout with me."

Sabatt knew that seasoned warriors were always strict with the younger ones, but it was necessary. He was honored to be scouting with Shatomi. Normally, only seasoned scouts would be sent out on a real war party.

Desperately, he tried to stretch the rawhide from the rim of the shoe so that it would be long enough to tie small knots. By the time he had them all tied, it was somewhat misshapen. The sound of voices, then yelling, set his heart to palpitating. He ripped the other snowshoe off, and quickly scrambled back over the top of the ledge.

Shatomi was just coming back when he saw Sabatt crouched beneath a small pine, peering into the valley. Instantly, he sensed something was wrong and crept up to him. Before he even reached him, he heard screaming, yelling and cursing in a foreign tongue. Then he witnessed one of the strangest sights he'd ever seen. Dozens of pink-skinned, hairy-faced humans were pouring over the hill. They wore many metal implements that hung shining from their clothing. Some had shiny metal caps on their heads, in the shape of pointed domes. They were cursing and screaming and foaming at the mouth. But for all their vicious looks, it appeared as though everything about them was only ornamental, for they were stopping to break off branches to use as clubs. Someone was obviously chasing them, but instead of being fearful, they appeared to enjoy it, as they searched desperately for any kind of weapon they could find in the forest.

Shatomi wanted to send Sabatt back to warn Ketanka, but he still hadn't put his snowshoes back on again. "Stay! I will warn the war party. Get those shoes back on, and if they come this way, get back to the others immediately."

Sabatt quickly put his snowshoes on as Shatomi disappeared up the valley, all the while keeping an eye on the strange looking humans in their path. Many of them broke off sharp sticks and ran back up the ridge they had just come from. Sabatt watched in awe as they laid themselves down at the foot of a short ledge, while another group gathered at the bottom of the hill. Everything became quiet for a few brief moments, then suddenly, the top of the ridge was covered with bow-wielding Snake warriors. Not a sound preceded them—they just suddenly and eerily appeared. The white humans began to laugh and curse, trying to goad them into a fight, heedless of the fact that they had only sticks to defend themselves against the well crafted bows of the Snake warriors.

Chilling war cries suddenly erupted, as the Snake warriors charged down the hill. When they jumped over a certain ledge, the hairy-faced ones pierced the running bodies from where they lay waiting in ambush. The Snake warriors began to fall over one another, and the strange ones who had massed at the bottom of the ridge launched their countercharge at the stumbling Snake warriors. Sabatt had never seen anything quite like these people before; they seemed to relish the battle they were engaged in, even though they were certain to lose. Another group of Snake warriors appeared at the top of the ridge, calmly and systematically picking off the hairy-faced ones with their well-aimed arrows. Sabatt ran back, bumping into Shatomi on the way.

"The Snake warriors are slaughtering the strange looking ones, even though they have no weapons to defend themselves. If they are enemy to the Snake warriors, perhaps they will be friends to us," Sabatt tried to communicate to Shatomi.

"I saw some strange looking warriors in Quiktkoata's war party, yesterday. I think they were like these, but they were too far away to tell. Perhaps they had been captured, and are Quiktkoata's enemies," Shatomi guessed. Ketanka suddenly appeared from out of the brush. "What is it?" he croaked.

"Fighting ahead! Between Snake warriors and some strange looking humans, if that's what they are," Shatomi shrugged. Ketanka ran ahead; Sabatt and Shatomi followed. They watched from the ledge as the battle went back and forth in the distance.

"We could easily get around them," Ketanka deduced. "But these Snake warriors are obviously going to win because those dog-faced ones have no weapons. Then we will have more Snake warriors to worry about. Sabatt! Go back and get the others. Tell them to be prepared to fight. We will have a plan by the time they get here."

Ketanka barely had time to assess the situation before

Sabatt returned with the rest of the war party. "Wanachan, have the Paccu warriors climb the south wall of the canyon and slip over the top, out of view. They will follow the canyon eastward. When they reach the end, they will circle wide to the south, and come up in back of the ridge where the Snake warriors are now fighting. Tell them to follow in the Snake warriors' own footsteps and surprise them from the rear. Tell them that the Minnecou will climb the north wall of the canyon and go down to the ridge where they are now fighting. We will attack them from the side as they charge down the hill after the hairy-faced ones. When they find out where we are, that's when I want your warriors to attack. That will confuse them enough that those hairy-faced ones will be able to attack and kill them where they hide. Tell your Paccu warriors to hurry. We will wait as long as we can for them to get in back of the ridge, but once the Snake warriors charge down the hill again, we must attack. We do not have enough warriors to hold them for long. If your warriors do not get there in time, we will be dead. You and your warriors will be on your own."

"What if the hairy-faced ones should try to run and escape instead of fight the Snake warriors?" Wanachan asked hurriedly.

"We must kill the Snake warriors with or without them," Ketanka said blandly. "They have no meaning to us. Now go! Quickly!"

The war party split in two as they deftly scrambled over opposite walls of the canyon. Shatomi led the way with Sabatt at his heels. Ketanka forced his massive frame over the jagged and snow-covered ledge, while Melonak ran beside him. Wanashta and Tumaris ran quietly behind the heaving chief as they followed the trail of Sabatt and Shatomi. Ketanka's face didn't reveal his concern. The three women saw only resolve and quickness of action. They didn't even stop to think of the impossibility of his plan. Neither had they thought about the fact that as three women, they were half of Ketanka's warriors, along with a boy of twelve. They saw his determination and lack of fear, and became the same as he.

Shatomi crept to within a river's width of the battle. Sabatt jumped in beside him, where they lay hidden behind a moss-covered boulder.

"Stay here and don't move till I return," Shatomi ordered. "String an arrow to your bow, and keep your knife in your teeth. The Snake warriors may come through here to try and attack the hairy-faced ones from the side as well."

Shatomi ran back to meet the others. They were close behind, and Ketanka had regained the wind he'd lost climbing the canyon wall. In no time, they had crept up close to Sabatt, where Shatomi had already found a place for them to hide, and a safe route to get them there. Shatomi moved back ahead with Sabatt, who stayed hidden while he was away, not even daring to look upon the battle, for fear of being seen. Ketanka crept up beside them, to get a better view of the fighting.

"The Snake warriors have retreated back up the ridge," he noted. "They have advantage in fighting from a distance...the strange ones have no arrows or good spears to throw. If they are smart, they will take cover and wait until the Snake warriors grow weary and attack."

Most of them had managed to find a hole to jump in, or a boulder or stump to duck behind, but some of them remained deliberately out in the open, just barely within range of the Snake warriors' bows. "They are crazy," Ketanka muttered.

One at a time, they would stand up and parade back and forth in front of the Snake warriors; sometimes running, sometimes walking in jerky, unpredictable steps. They moved rapidly, dropping to the ground just as hails of arrows whistled over their heads. But the whole time, they were laughing and cursing.

One stood up, snarling viciously at the Snake warriors. He performed a strange dance that brought him from a standing step, and sometimes straight to the ground, and then back up again. The arrows would sail in his direction, but always they would miss. His movements were sometimes jerky and sometimes graceful, but every time an arrow was let loose, the dancer vanished. It was as if he knew the exact moment that the Snake warriors would release their arrows, but he would be instantly gone. He didn't even appear to be watching them. And every time an arrow flew and missed, rounds of coarse and hideous laughter would erupt from somewhere among the snow-covered terrain.

They sang peculiar songs that also seemed to evoke much laughter and yelling. Ketanka and his little party sat amused from behind their hiding spots, as the hairy-faced ones seemed more at a celebration than in the middle of a battle. Two of them carried a large container, as big as a man's chest. Ketanka noticed several of these strange warriors crawling over to the container to fetch a drink, then slipping back to their hiding spots. Soon, the bawdy laughter would erupt from the direction they had crawled.

The Snake warriors soon realized they were wasting all of their arrows, and being made fools of as well. Several of them were sent down the hill; they kept close to the ground. The Minnecou braced themselves as the Snake warriors unwittingly crept directly toward them. Shatomi nearly let his arrow fly, when the Snake warriors suddenly stopped, then ducked out of sight. "They've seen us!" Shatomi whispered to Ketanka.

Ketanka nodded, then signaled the women to prepare for attack. Several more Snake warriors moved silently down the ridge in the knee-deep snow, following in the same path as the others. Each of the Minnecou had an arrow trained on a Snake warrior. Ketanka made sure that each of them was aiming at a different one by signaling which enemy they would make as their target. Once again Shatomi was just ready to release his arrow when a sudden movement caught his eye. The first set of Snake warriors crawled away from the Minnecou, back in the direction of the hairy-faced ones. The second set now ducked out of sight in the same area that the others had disappeared. If they followed the others, the Minnecou would have a great advantage.

The second set of Snake warriors suddenly came into view as they crawled with their backs to Ketanka's war party, hiding behind the first Snake warriors. The last one to get there turned on his side, and shot an arrow into a tree at the top of the ridge. The Snake warriors at the top suddenly began wailing and whooping, and charged in full force down the ridge. Halfway down, they each let go of an arrow, then slung their bows over their heads, their lances thrust before them. They outnumbered the strange ones by more than two to one, and their weapons were far superior to sticks and clubs. With the surprise ambush they had in store for this battle, it was clear that the fighting would end quickly.

The white warriors quickly gathered, issuing a counter-charge that led them snarling into the faces of the oncoming Snake warriors. They were about to clash right in front of the two sets of hidden Snake warriors, when the main force of Snake warriors suddenly stopped. The hidden Snake warriors jumped to their feet, drawing their bows no more than a few steps from the pink-skinned ones, who were now out in the open. The five Snake warriors in the rear suddenly cried out in pain, and fell writhing and screaming to the ground. When the other five turned, the last thing they saw was a group of Minnecou tribesmen, their bows drawn to the fullest. Their unconscious screams accompanied them into the cold snow.

Melonak and the two women began immediately shooting into the crowd of lance wielding Snake warriors before even Ketanka and Shatomi had turned to confront them. The hairy-faced ones stared dumbfounded as the attacking force of Snake warriors fumbled with their bows. The Minnecou war party rapidly picked them off, then ran for cover once the Snake party recovered.

Sabatt hit three Snake warriors before a barrage of arrows rained down on the Minnecou. Ketanka fell backwards into the snow with arrows in his chest and legs. The Snake warriors charged down-hill at the Minnecou, ignoring the white warriors running for cover. Shatomi and the two Minnecou women hid behind trees and continued to shoot into the advancing mob of Snake warriors. Tumaris took an arrow in the leg. When she reached down to it, another sliced into her shoulder and knocked her to the ground. Wanashta hit two advancing Snake warriors as they tried to move in on Shatomi. Sabatt fled into the woods; there was nothing near for him to duck under. He watched Ketanka's chest heaving up and down. Though he was still alive and breathing, his body jerked in spasms every time he exhaled. Sabatt looked anxiously to the top of the hills, praying for the Paccus to come to their rescue. But no one came as the main body of Snake warriors sought to snuff out the only remaining relatives he had in the war party. Several Snake warriors were moving towards Ketanka to watch him suffer, and inflict more pain. Sabatt slipped around the bottom of the ridge and quickly climbed up to where he'd last seen the hairy-faced ones. Behind every tree, stump and boulder, the strange looking ones lied in wait, their hands gripped tightly around crude and useless weapons. They nearly attacked him as he raced by, but they saw that he wasn't a Snake warrior. Suddenly, he was scooped off his feet and thrown behind a ledge.

"Stay down!" Shatomi shouted.

He and Shatomi were in a pile of the white ones. Shatomi stood, loosening arrows as quickly as he could string them to the bow. They looked at him in sympathy for what was happening to his friends, but they were angry for giving their position away and drawing the enemy towards them. He pierced four Snake warriors before they realized what was going on. They scattered briefly, then gathered once again, charging in his direction. Sabatt stood beside him, and let his own arrow fly. Past the Snake warriors, he could see the Minnecou, bleeding in the snow.

"Stand up and fight," he screamed at the strange ones. They didn't understand what he said, but when they peeked over the top of the ledge, fifty warriors were charging directly at them, some wielding lances, while others sent a rain of arrows. They glowered at Sabbat and Shatomi, but the Minnecou stood up fully, and rapidly notched one arrow after another, stinging into the fury of the Snake warriors. All of the hairy-faced ones who had been watching the brave young Minnecou from their hiding spots, suddenly charged up the hill to meet the Snake warriors. The half dozen men along the ledge with them began to laugh and cheer wildly as they jumped to their feet and threw their spears into the oncoming Snake warriors. They picked up the arrows that had been shot at them so they could use them as knives.

A chilling scream erupted along the top of the ridge, and arrows began streaming down the hill into the large group of Snake warriors. Many of them fell dead, while others tripped over their comrades. Sabatt shot his last arrow into the crowd of Snake warriors, but he couldn't tell if it was his own arrow that struck the warrior he had in his aim. They scattered into the woods. The white ones took bows, arrows and lances from the fallen Snake warriors, and set out after fleeing stragglers. They hunted them down and killed every one.

The Paccus came into view shortly after their first barrage of arrows, and split up into two groups to chase down the largest parties of Snake warriors.

Sabatt and Shatomi ran to their relatives, hoping they were still alive, and not seriously wounded. Ketanka was breathing, but he wasn't conscious. Melonak sat beside him, sobbing and massaging his cold hands. Shatomi tried to shake him into consciousness, but the old chief chanted in a feeble croak, then lapsed into spasm.

Wanashta crawled out from in back of a tree, reaching for Tumaris. "Help me move her!" she cried. "She will be trampled!"

Shatomi stumbled to his feet. Sabatt ran over to where his mother lay stricken. They dragged her by her hands and propped her against a tree. She was cold and unresponsive. Her face was gray and her head hung limply from her shoulders. Shatomi grabbed a handful of snow and pressed it into her face. Soon, her lifeless limbs began flailing as she gasped for air, screaming at her attacker.

"She fainted," Shatomi smiled. "See, she had no mortal wounds." Sabatt grabbed a mound of snow and headed for Ketanka, but Shatomi stopped him. "No. It will not work."

"He will die!" Sabatt strained.

"He will if you try that. We must get him to warmth, but we cannot do that until we remove the arrows, the same for your mother," he warned. "We must stop their bleeding before we bring them to warmth, because that will make them bleed more. Ketanka may be bleeding inside. If that is true, we cannot stop that, and he will die anyway. We will do what we can quickly, and then we must go on to the village."

Wanachan wandered over to where the Minnecou chief lay fallen. She stood over Ketanka, shaking her head as if she knew he'd reached the end of his travels. The three arrows in his legs would probably cripple him. But the arrow in his chest is what distressed her. Melonak looked hopefully towards the strange Paccu woman.

"Our Washan could heal him if he was here," she said. "You are medicine woman for your people. You are the only one who can save him. We are one people now. Save him for his family and his clan!" she cried.

Clearly, she was a medicine woman, and expected to heal the wounded. But the arrow had not gone through, and there was no way to determine just how deep it had impacted Ketanka's flesh. Trying to push it through could destroy a vital organ. Yet, pulling on the arrow could rip one out, with the barbs of the projectile's point. She could see that it was very close to the top of his lungs, as well as near to the heart and the vital arteries that surrounded it. One tug or shove in the wrong direction would end his life in a matter of moments.

"I must remove the arrow in his chest first," Wanachan looked dourly upon the chief's grieving wife. "But it is very dangerous. The Snake people's points are broad and flat. It is almost certain that he will die as soon as I try to move the arrow, but his death is just as certain if I do not...and he will die in suffering. The longer I wait, the weaker he will become. And the less chance he will have of recovering, even if I can remove the arrow successfully. He is your husband. I leave the decision to you."

"Maybe he can live with the arrow in him," Sabatt said hopefully. "There is a warrior in one of our clans who has had an arrow in him since before I was even born."

"His hands are turning blue and probably his feet as well," Wanachan shook her head. "The blood is not moving strong enough and he is not breathing enough air. He cannot live for long like this."

Wanashta supported an ashen-faced and limping Tumaris, who was determined to make her way to the stricken chief. Shatomi and Wanachan both explained the situation to the two women.

"Pull out the arrow," Tumaris said weakly. "He will not wake up if you don't. He will not be able to sing his death song. I have seen this before."

Melonak refused to look away from her husband, or make a decision as to whether Wanachan should act or not.

"He has sung," Sabatt said. "But I do not know if it was his death song."

"Pull it out anyway," Tumaris was stubborn. "We must help him die or live—not just watch."

"Pull it out," Shatomi agreed. Wanashta merely nodded.

Melonak tore herself away from Ketanka's heaving body, sobbing through her tears, "Do it!"

Wanachan cut into Ketanka's tunic to expose the area around the wound. She probed his back, opposite the wound, feeling for the point of the arrow. Nothing. She pulled slightly on the arrow to see if it was lodged in bone or flesh. It was as if it had been shot into wood. She breathed a sigh of relief. "This is good," she announced, "It stuck in bone. He will bleed heavily when I remove the arrow, but I think his heart is only bruised. She gripped both hands around the shaft, giving a quick and yanking tug. Ketanka's eyes opened up wide in pain and fear, as if he had just woken from a horrendous nightmare, but Wanachan had not the strength to hold on—the arrow slipped through her hands as if she was trying to pull a branch straight out of a tree. Ketanka's torso heaved upwards as she pulled, but fell back to the ground in spasms when she let go. His eyes rolled back in his head as his body jerked uncontrollably in the snow.

Melonak screamed as Shatomi and Sabatt tried desperately to hold the convulsing body down so Wanachan could try again. Wanashta grabbed onto the shaft of the arrow along with the Paccu medicine woman, and together with one great heave, they yanked the arrow out of the chief's tightly clenched chest. Wanachan first looked at the arrowhead to make sure it hadn't broken, and that nothing further remained in the chief's body. She then turned to the wound that seemed to be pumping the blood right out of the chief. She reached into her medicine bag and pulled out an herb-treated wad of fibers, then pressed these into the hole that had been left by the metal blade. She forced even more between his clenched jaws, while Shatomi and Sabatt continued to hold his convulsing frame.

The spasms gradually diminished as the chief lay sweating in the snow. His eyes were closed and he even began to snore, as Wanachan quickly removed the three arrows in his legs and packed the herbal treated fibers around the wounds.

The Paccus were returning along with many of the strange white humans that had helped to destroy the Snake warriors. Most of them had gathered around the two that carried the large wooden keg. They drank heartily and offered their strange beverage to the Paccus and Minnecou. Shatomi graciously accepted a mug full of the spirits, but after tasting it, he secretly poured its contents into the snow when no one was looking.

Sabatt and Wanashta helped Wanachan remove the arrows from Tumaris and pack the herb-treated fibers around the wounds. One of the white warriors came over with a mug of spirits, and poured some of it on Tumaris' wounds. Though she had only moaned and strained when Wanachan pulled out the arrows, she screamed out in pain as the alcohol touched the open wounds. Sabatt pulled his knife on the strange one, but the white man had no intention of fighting. He pointed to Wanachan's herbal medicine and then to his mug of spirits. Tumaris screamed about the burning pain, but after a few moments, it seemed to have disappeared. Wanachan knew that when a wound became infected, sometimes they would have to press hot ashes against the infection to stop it. Even that did not always work; the wound would be larger and more susceptible to further infection. But here she saw something that she had never seen before; a medicine that burns with no flame. She tasted of the medicine and quickly spit it out. Her throat was burning as well as her mouth, but when the feeling disappeared, there were no blisters or damage in her mouth or throat.

The man with the mug of spirits, whom Wanachan took to be the bearded ones' healer, went over to where Melonak was comforting Ketanka and poured some of the strange liquid on his wounds as well. Even in his deep sleep, Ketanka's body constricted with the pain. His eyes opened briefly, but after a few moments, he was once again slumbering peacefully.

The light-skinned ones gathered their gear and prepared to move on, when Shatomi tried to converse with them in sign language. They didn't understand. Shatomi used more exaggerated, yet simpler motions, to try and determine where the hairy-faced people planned to go. They pointed northward. Shatomi indicated they would leave a trail of footprints in the snow, by pointing to his own tracks. The biggest one of them, a creature with straw-colored hair and a flaming red beard, merely shrugged. Shatomi pointed to the dead Snake warriors that lay scattered all around them, and with a sweep of his arm, he indicated that he was referring to all of them. He then made a single hand print in the snow, and again made a sweep of his hand to indicate that he was referring to the Snake warriors that they had just fought. Pointing to the west, he held his arms wide and then demonstrated warriors shooting bows and throwing lances and hitting with clubs.

Once again, he pointed to the west, and then made more than thirty hand prints in the snow. He gestured towards the large group of Snake warriors they had just killed and pointed towards the single hand print. He pointed towards the west and then indicated that they were equal to the thirty hand prints. Then he pointed towards his tracks and showed that the army of warriors now approaching would follow the footprints in the snow. Shatomi turned towards the smoky eastern horizon and indicated that this was where he and his people were going, by gesturing with his chin.

The white warriors gathered together and began to discuss in their foreign tongue, while Shatomi directed the Paccu and Minnecou war party in Ketanka's stead. "Sabatt, go cut down some carrying poles. We're going to have to carry Ketanka and your mother to the strange village. I just hope that we are not walking into a losing battle there. You have seen what is behind us. We will all die if we have to spend the whole season in this snow without shelter."

"Wanachan!" Shatomi called. "Have your people show these hairy-faced creatures how to make the snowshoes. We have wasted much time here and all of us must move quickly!"

"Why should we then waste our time to show these people to make snowshoes. You cannot even be sure if they will stay with us," she said irritably.

"I can be sure that if Quiktkoata's army comes this way, they will send many warriors to follow both trails. If these strange ones have snowshoes, it will be a long time before those Snake warriors who follow them will be able to return and fight us," he stated. "If they have these shoes, no matter which direction they move in, they will be able to move quickly."

Shortly after Sabatt returned with the poles, the two Minnecou were quickly placed upon makeshift litters, and several of the Paccu warriors gathered around to help shoulder the load on the long trek to the mining village, where smoke had filled the horizon for most of the day. The sun was just beginning its descent into the western sky when the small war party was ready to leave. The hairy-faced ones marched over to the departing war party. The red-bearded one grabbed Shatomi's arm, and alongside his own, lifted them high into the air, gesturing for Shatomi to open his palm to the sky. "Together shall we struggle," he declared to the heavens. "May the Gods bring justice to those who have helped us, and then deliver us from this crude land. Guide us over mountain and sea, and let us once again step foot upon the shores from whence we first set sail."

Shatomi didn't understand a word of the white man's prayer, but he did gather that they intended to go along with his small war party—several of the loudly cheering whites hoisted the litters upon their own shoulders, marching and singing as they headed towards the village from which they had just come, clumsily tripping over their new snowshoes. What Shatomi didn't know was that they were only going back to the village to loot more food and weapons. Then they would head secretly away, following an eastern trail back to the great inland lakes of this strange continent.

CHAPTER 22

The sun glared brightly off the trampled white snow. The heaviest clouds of the early winter storm had been swept eastward along with the thinning smoke of the nearly burnt-out village. Semmida scrutinized the final area of the city to which he must lay siege. One large stone fortress which housed Bakwanote and his beleaguered army, along with several smaller stone buildings, presented a stumbling block to the invaders of Quiktkoata's mining village. Semmida surmised that the greater supplies of food, clothing and weapons were probably located within the confines of these buildings. The roofs of these structures, though made of wood, were gilded in copper, making them nearly impossible to set ablaze. The white warriors had built these lodges long ago, using copper to let the snow slide off the roofs, and to prevent enemies from burning them out.

The village chief stood upon the flat portion of the roof on the largest building, railing his taunts at Semmida and his preposterous war party of slaves and nomads.

"It is not I who is besieged here!" he laughed in the face of Semmida and his men. "We have food and shelter for the entire winter. You will all become hungry and cold, and leave this place beaten and dejected. Even then, where will you go?" he laughed even louder. "You will find no shelter for days of tramping through the cold snow, and worse than that, we have killed all the game in this area before the leaves even fell from the trees. You are beaten and you can't even comprehend it."

A hail of arrows flew in the direction of the huge stone edifice, but they barely reached the angled portion of the lichen-colored roof. Bakwanote ran back to the stairwell, but his men continued to push the snow off the roof from which they would defend their fort, should Semmida be foolish enough to attack.

Semmida gathered all of his forces. "We must attack these buildings one at a time. There may not be many Snake warriors inside some of them, but we will not even be able to capture one of them until we completely overrun the building. We may suffer many dead and injured, but we must seize these buildings one by one if we are to survive. All who are with me hold your lances high." Every lance that was available immediately pointed towards the sky, for all knew they were doomed otherwise.

The Minnecou offered to lead the charge, but Semmida refused them. "There are many windows even on the smallest building, but they are made to shoot out of and not into. My warriors are the best archers anywhere, and they must keep those windows occupied so that the rest of us can overrun these buildings."

Semmida didn't select the smallest building as his first target, but chose the most isolated instead. He didn't want his men to be fired upon from two directions while they were vulnerable in the open.

Sequannah stood fearlessly by his clan, waiting for the

gathered forces to attack. Swarms of Paccu warriors stood on either side of the Minnecou, but one group stood out. Several of the fiercest looking Paccus were assembled around a tall and smiling Paccu, who was obviously a leader within their nation. He glanced frequently in Sequannah's direction, but the young Minnecou sensed he wasn't the object of the tall warrior's search. Petawahin, Mokotak and the Washan walked away to speak with Semmida, yet the Paccu's glances didn't change direction. Perhaps I am staring, Sequannah thought to himself. He looked instead to the building they were to attack, scrutinizing the landscape. There was no cover unless they buried themselves in the snow. But while the snow was deep, it was also heavy and wet. His moccasins were already dark from the water they held to his freezing feet. To immerse themselves in this type of snow would be like jumping into the waters of a frigid lake and trying to fight their enemy through a hole in the ice. They will have to expose themselves to enemy arrows. He was smaller and younger than most of the other warriors; perhaps the enemy will consider him an unimportant target.

Sequannah let go of his thoughts and looked around at his allies, but once again, his eyes stopped at the tall Paccu, who was again looking in his direction. Ceptke winked. Sequannah's head bobbed backwards slightly, his face in a questioning frown. The Paccu turned away, shifting his way through the crowd, in the direction of the burnt-out part of the village. Sequannah felt someone brush behind him, and when he turned to see, he caught a glimpse of Shamira's doeskin dress as she disappeared among the large assemblage of warriors. He looked for some time, but he didn't see her until she reappeared in the distance, walking in the same direction he had seen the tall Paccu heading. Immediately, he understood what was going on and looked away. If his father had seen this, the battle with the Snake warriors would seem small in comparison to what would happen between the Paccus and the Minnecou.

Sequannah didn't like the idea himself, but his thoughts faded as he scanned the crowd and focused on Tarote. Whenever he saw her face, everything else was a blur. The only other face that stood out was that of Semmida's, because Tarote always seemed to watching him. Sequannah would look away when he saw this, and stare into the emptiness of the sky, or at a distant object, and then quickly change his thoughts. But this time there was no need, the Sikun suddenly broke his reverie.

"Here is my young Minnecou warrior," he spoke softly. He quickly reached out and grabbed onto the arm of another Minnecou warrior, elbowing his way through the crowd. "Quitkwa!" he said, "I am truly glad to have you two together. You are both an inspiration to Semmida's warriors, and to the younger Paccus who have come here to make a stand against the Snake village."

"Thank you," Quitkwa brushed off Teokahannah, "but I have something important to attend to," he said, anxiously staring in the direction he had witnessed both Ceptke and Shamira disappear.

"You must have received my own thoughts," he squeezed Quitkwa's arm even tighter. "The Paccus have their leaders assembled and Semmida leads his own warriors. But the Minnecou—each is a leader in his own right. It is no wonder that you know before I even ask, that you and Sequannah would do all of us a great service by arming the freed slaves of this village and leading them in battle. I know all of them personally and they have already agreed to follow you. There is little to plan. All you need do is make sure they are armed, and inspire them to follow once Semmida's warriors have the Snake warrior archers completely engaged."

"I would be honored to lead the slave peoples for you right after I attend to a most important matter," Quitkwa tried to portray himself as a stately warrior, pursuing an outside matter.

"There is little time and nothing more important than to get them organized now. Semmida will begin the assault sooner than you think. These slaves, as Sequannah can testify, have much desire in bringing about the downfall of the Snake empire. Quickly!" he guided them towards the rambling group of slaves. Quitkwa felt compelled to drop every thought except to prepare the slaves for battle.

"All of you," he shouted, strutting through the milling crowd of slaves, "pick up your weapons and gather around." Though some of them seemed to be listening, most continued to chatter among themselves and only look questioningly in his direction. "Listen to me now!" Quitkwa screamed. "There is no time for conversation. Once the attack begins, we must be prepared to step in behind the archers at the right moment."

There was a brief silence while Quitkwa screamed to get their attention, but as he spoke, they began to chatter among themselves once again.

"They do not understand our tongue," Sequannah remanded

Quitkwa. "Just walk among them and inspect their weapons. Find a place to assemble them in good order."

Quitkwa slowly arranged some of the slaves into an organized group, but he had to watch Sequannah to find out how to really inspire them. Sequannah lined up ten of them, and had them ready their lances and bows. He rolled a hoop over the snow in front of them, taking note of which slaves were most accurate with their weapons. Those who hit the center of the hoop or came closest, received praise and a smile as he led them to a certain group. Those who were less accurate were placed behind the best warriors; Sequannah wore a sympathetic expression as he explained in sign language that they would not be in the front line of battle. But always, he would take only two or three warriors out of a group of ten, and place them with the best. Sometimes only one would make it to the top group because Sequannah wanted to keep the slaves competitive.

Quitkwa soon changed his methods. His near smirk changed into a friendly smile. He had them competing fiercely and cheering wildly as one of them would hit the targets he was throwing into the air. The groups he had already selected now stood confident that the order in which they would help in the attack would be most effective. He had others run zigzagged patterns that would make them difficult targets for archers and lance throwers.

Those slaves who hadn't yet competed, gathered into a large crowd, screaming and jumping up and down in their eagerness to demonstrate their own skills. One of them came out with a long net and defied a group of three archers to hit him. He batted away their well-aimed arrows, and quickly ensnared the whole three of them with his large net, to the loud cheers of his group of slaves. But before Quitkwa and Sequannah could get through even half of them, a loud chorus of eerie whooping erupted from the Paccu war party.

Semmida's warriors began to chant and wail to the accompaniment of loud and most peculiar drumming rhythms. A group of warriors streamed out, dancing with brightly colored feathers arranged like fans around their heads. The strange feathers were nearly half the length of a man's body, and the dancers leaped and stepped as though they were in a most powerful trance. The constant jeers of the Snake warriors suddenly stopped; a tense silence emanated from the stone buildings.

Quitkwa and Sequannah hurriedly led the slaves over to

witness the bizarre affair. But they saw no more than a few moments of the strange ritual, when the dancers left, then reappeared with their weapons. Their expressions were steadfast as they made their way through the Paccus, slaves and Minnecou, to the front of the force that would attack the first stone building.

Semmida strode ahead. The Paccus erupted in another eerie tribal scream that drowned out the resumed jeering of the Snake warriors. He lined them up at a certain distance from the stone building, beckoning the rest of the war parties to fall in behind. Several arrows whizzed out of the windows of the stone building, but most fell short of Semmida and his men. Those that did reach were off target, although one of them grazed Semmida's leg. He ignored it.

Another arrow whisked past the front line of Semmida's archers, into the chest of one of the slaves. Petawahin was standing close by, and quickly covered the man's mouth to stop his screaming. They brought him to the rear to attend to his wounds.

Beside each of Semmida's warriors was a large basket of arrows from which they would take handfuls at a time to fill their shoulder-mounted quivers. As the arrows landed at Semmida's feet, he gave his archers the signal to release the arrows from their powerful bows. His own archers reached the stone buildings with ease, but the narrow windows were difficult targets; most of their arrows rattled against the stone walls. The Snake warriors moved away from the windows, then Semmida immediately called on the Paccu and Minnecou war parties to assault the building. Ceptke led his huge war party, wailing and screaming as they surged towards the building. Though they were running in irregular patterns, however, there were so many targets to choose from, the Snake warriors were merely shooting into the crowd and many wounded were falling. Mokotak led the small Minnecou party as they ran directly at one window of the building. They issued dozens of arrows to prevent the Snake warriors from getting close to the window. But the Snake warriors inside simply moved to the sides of the windows, where they could shoot anyone who got close to the building without being vulnerable themselves. Semmida's archers were useless as their targets moved back and forth from each side of the windows.

Semmida turned to Sequannah and Quitkwa as the Paccu and Minnecou war parties neared the stone building. "Attack now!" he screamed. "You must reinforce them now!"

Sequannah and Quitkwa each led their respective war parties to opposite ends of the stone building, and began their surrounding assault. The large groups of slaves nearly outnumbered the Paccu and Minnecou war parties, and with these reinforcements, it seemed inevitable that they would easily inundate the stone building that housed the tremendously outnumbered Snake warriors inside. Sequannah's group charged at the stone edifice, whooping and trilling as they unleashed hundreds of lances and arrows in their advance, but at the last moment, Sequannah heard a creaking sound and noticed something that he hadn't quite expected. The short, angled portion of the roof on the single story building suddenly lifted up, revealing dozens of Snake warriors with their bows fully drawn.

Sequannah felt the sudden trauma of impact in his shoulder as the force behind a lightning-quick arrow knocked him off balance. One of the attacking slaves at his side was hit in the throat, and fell over in his path. He tripped over the gurgling slave and the fall pushed the arrow further into his shoulder. The angled portion of the roof was shut as quickly as it was opened; Semmida's archers couldn't even shoot. As the rebels readjusted their aims to the rooftop, the other Snake warriors at the windows took several quick shots at the Paccu and Minnecou war parties, wounding and killing many. As soon as Semmida's archers turned back to the windows, the roof was opened once more, and another hail of arrows sliced into Sequannah and his group of slaves.

Sequannah couldn't see from his location, but he assumed that the same tactic was used on Quitkwa's group. He tried to crawl away, when another arrow painfully pinned his calf to the ground. Sequannah could feel the blood drain from his face as his vision began to blur and darken. He had been hit twice—the shock was knocking him unconscious. The more he fought the fainting sensation, the more nauseous he became until he vomited. His face suddenly felt hot and he pressed it into the snow. When he regained his senses and his vision no longer reeled, he tried once again to crawl away from this dangerous area, but his leg had no strength and he couldn't even push himself forward. The snow left him nothing to grab onto. Everywhere he looked, there were bleeding bodies in the snow; some motionless, some twitching, and others like his own lay moaning, with no strength to move out of fatal range.

He heard the rooftops open once again; the creaking sound

was now forever imprinted in his memory. His body tensed. He felt the arrows punching into the snow around him. He was relieved to hear the arrows of Semmida's archers cause the death screams of several Snake warriors on the rooftop. He heard one of the bodies thump to the earth before the creaking rooftop shut once again. A faint moan drifted over from the side of the stone building. Sequannah thought to himself how he and the Snake warrior were one in the same. Both lay dying in the snow.

Sequannah became aware of his own moaning, and stopped immediately. But the pain took over so that it became his only awareness. It was sometime later before he realized that he was moaning again. The rooftop must have opened once again, for now he could see that another arrow had pierced his wrist. He lifted his head. Only a handful of slaves and warriors were still attempting to seize the stone building. He mustered his strength and screamed out; his cries were but a whisper.

Moments later, he felt something tug at his body. The pain of movement shocked him into semi-consciousness once again. He woke to the pain of sharp blows to his face and realized that he was fighting one of the Paccus who was trying to drag him from the scene of the battle. The Paccu was slapping him in order to bring him to full consciousness. Sequannah held back the fight in him as soon as he realized where he was and what was going on.

The pains in his leg, wrist and calf suddenly dulled, and his strength returned as he slowly limped away with the Paccu's help. He heard the sudden crinkle of copper gilding as the roof was lifted once again. An arrow sped past him, waist high, and the Paccu picked him up bodily, running to where they would be out of range. When Sequannah reached the main body of retreating slaves and warriors, he looked back upon the building and saw scores of bodies bleeding in the snow, scattered around the impenetrable edifice. He looked around for his Minnecou relatives, and at first could see no one. But at one point in the crowd, he saw his father, Petawahin, sitting on a small platform. An old man and a young woman tugged at an arrow in his back. His powerful face stared sternly ahead as they pulled mercilessly upon the feathered shaft. Then he saw Shamira standing among a group of Paccus, consoling each other and staring into the snow at their feet. The tall one he had seen earlier was among them, but he was no longer smiling.

To his rear, Sequannah heard jeers and laughter coming from the stone buildings of the Snake warriors. They were screaming their taunts at the rebels in unison. Over and over they would repeat the same words. Most of the rebels were either slaves who understood very little of the Snake warriors' language, or nomads like the Paccus and Minnecou, who understood none. But they felt the sting of these taunts every bit as much as Semmida's warriors who understood every word.

Sequannah saw Quitkwa walking away from the slaves he had herded back away from the battle. He seemed to be looking for someone as he threaded his way among the refugees. His head was no longer held high as he roamed through the crowd in a shroud of shame and disappointment. Sequannah watched as he walked in humility, then regained his composure as he strode towards a large group that had gathered around Semmida and his humbled archers.

Quitkwa walked around the entire crowd, still obviously in search of someone, and when he stopped at a certain point, only then did Sequannah see Mokotak and the Washan. They appeared unharmed. Quitkwa spoke briefly with them, then moved on, stopping for a moment to glance in the direction of Shamira and the Paccu group surrounding Ceptke. But he continued onward, and Sequannah knew that he was looking for him. He saw him look towards the stone building once again, searching among the small drifts of snow as he moved closer. The jeers from the Snake warriors suddenly erupted, as they tried to coax him within their range. Quitkwa strung an arrow to his bow and pulled back hard to a chorus of laughter atop the copper-gilded roof. A moment later, the laughter stopped when a Snake warrior rolled off the roof with an arrow in his chest. A score of arrows returned from the stone building, and even though their arrows had emanated from a greater height, none of them reached the daring Minnecou who stood his ground. Quitkwa pulled back hard once again— the remaining Snake warriors disappeared.

Quitkwa let out a loud war whoop, and those among the rebels who had witnessed what he had done joined in. But the Snake warriors resumed their taunts; the rebels efforts were futile. Even with his wounds, Sequannah suddenly felt strong and proud to be a Minnecou after watching Quitkwa, who, like him, was among the smallest of the Minnecou warriors. Sequannah got to his feet, dizzy, then limped in the direction he'd last seen Quitkwa.

A large figure suddenly loomed in front of him. "I'll bet you thought you were dead," the Sikun laughed softly. "Here," he led him to a stump and brushed the snow off of it. "Sit. It is not becoming of a warrior to stroll about with arrows sticking out of him."

"I want to see my people," Sequannah said, his voice gaining in strength. "They must know that I am alive."

"When they find you, all the more they will appreciate you," the Sikun told him.

"Who will appreciate a warrior who does not even send one arrow upon his enemy?" Sequannah said dejectedly. "We have been beaten by the Snake warriors. We all know that if we cannot drive them out of the stone buildings, we will starve and freeze to death. Half of our warriors will have to be sacrificed just to take the small building we have just left. I want to see that my people are wise enough to leave now!" Sequannah stood again, his lack of faith in the Sikun obvious.

"Sit!" Teokahannah pushed him back onto the stump. "The healers will be here shortly to remove your arrows and dress your wounds. Then if you are still capable, you can go and find your relatives. But I will tell you this. It is very unwise to leave now. Quiktkoata is almost upon us and no one will escape. Thousands of warriors will be here soon. Those who have escaped will be his toys; like a mountain kit with a mouse. Those who stay will be the only ones saved."

"If what you tell me is true, then all of us will die, because those who stay have no chance at all. They cannot defeat the Snake warriors in the buildings. When Quiktkoata comes they will be left here out in the open to be slaughtered like fawns among wolves. I no longer find any sense in your words."

"I do not know how we can defeat those Snake warriors in the stone forts. But I know that it is what we must do. There is a means to drive them out, but we are blind to it. We must have faith that someone will see it before it is too late. Here comes someone to comfort you while you wait for the healers."

Sequannah turned, expecting to find Quitkwa behind him, but instead saw the two Wolf brothers approaching. "Mahkawan! Look! Our new warrior has taken on the spirit of the porcupine," Tamahna laughed. "We had better keep him still until the healers can come and turn him back into a human."

"He must have become angry in the battle," Mahkawan

said seriously. "See! He has only three quills left."

Sequannah tried to laugh, but the pain caused him to wince instead. "We must leave this place," he warned his clansmen. "If we don't die trying to attack the stone buildings, we will starve and freeze to death anyway."

"We all know of this," Tamahna said. "But the Washan insists that to leave will bring about our deaths. He says that Teokahannah, the Sikun has already foreseen this. Teokahannah has told everyone that Quiktkoata is already on his way here with more than a thousand Snake warriors to defeat us. He says that they left during the last full moon to defeat the Minnecou and Paccus. But how could this be true if we ourselves did not know we would be here now?"

"Quiktkoata did leave his city during the last full moon," Sequannah admitted. "And he did bring more than a thousand warriors with him...and many, many supplies. But they went to the west. Ask Mokotak."

"If it is true," Mahkawan said, "then Quiktkoata must have gone looking for us when we were in the mountains and then found out that we had come here. But we have talked to Mokotak and we have spoken to your father, and both agree that whether it is true or not about Quiktkoata and his army, it would still be foolish to remain here. Even more so if what the Sikun says is true."

"You must be in great pain," Tamahna looked sympathetically upon Sequannah. "Do not worry. We will carry you out of here if we have to. You will be a great warrior among the Minnecou," he said without expression. "Look who comes to admire their young warrior."

Sequannah glanced into the crowd and saw Petawahin, Shamira, Quitkwa and the Washan walking towards him and the Wolf brothers. A short distance behind them he could see Mokotak's head towering above the crowd, and heading in the same direction. All of them looked somewhat confused, except for Petawahin. He looked very angry. Even when he approached Sequannah he still looked furious, but when he looked down, Sequannah could see that his eyes were filling with tears. Shamira saw him and her own eyes filled as well. "Where is the healer?" Petawahin shouted angrily. "Get him here now!"

Mokotak heard from a distance and grabbed the healer who was in the middle of pulling an arrow out of an old slave. He threw him over his shoulder. The man began to protest, but when he looked down upon the huge warrior carrying him, he went limp and nearly fainted. Mokotak threw him down at Petawahin's feet.

"Take care of this warrior immediately!" Petawahin looked sternly upon the healer. "We will leave when you are done," he said. The healer didn't understand the words, but he knew the meaning, and immediately set about finding the best way to remove each arrow. Two assistants were just now coming up behind him after trying to follow Mokotak through the crowd. As they poked and pulled and tested the arrows, Sequannah heard his father and the Washan arguing, apparently a continuation of a previous argument. He heard his father say, "You speak the same words over and over, but you will no longer speak. Now you will listen because there is no one left to hear you. Our families are scattered all over the land. My son lies here bleeding, a fine warrior who may now be crippled. Instead of arguing with me here, you should be tending to him and making sure that these healers know what they are doing. My daughter chases after one of these disgusting Paccus instead of a strong Minnecou warrior. Yes, I have seen her!" Shamira walked away angrily, knowing that now was not the time to deal with her father. "We will leave at the moment Sequannah can be moved. We will gather all of our families between here and the mountains. And we will walk proudly together from now on. We will defend and fight for Minnecou and none other. I have learned. Now you must learn as well. We will gather all of the clans. Quiktkoata will run in fear when we walk before him and his cowardly warriors. Look upon them even now. True warriors would come out and fight."

"This is what I tell you," the Washan began to argue once again. "They have no honor. They do whatever it takes to defeat you and that is all. There is no shame to them. They will watch you starve and then come out to poke holes in your bloated belly so that they can laugh at the sound."

"If there was a way to get at them, I could find sense in your words," Petawahin said angrily. "But look around you. Look over at that small stone building and count the bodies in the snow. Then look to the big building where their war chief hides and see how our dead would be in piles if we tried to attack them there. Enough of your words. We will leave today!"

Petawahin walked over to where the healers were working

on Sequannah and watched for a brief time. But he couldn't bear it, and walked away with Mokotak. The Washan then came over and spoke with the healers in a strange tongue. He looked sympathetically upon Sequannah, but said nothing. Sequannah could see that his thoughts were very distant. He prepared a certain medicine and massaged it around Sequannah's wounds. It was painful at first but slowly the pain disappeared. In moments, he couldn't even feel the Washan's rubbing.

"If we leave this place, we will die and the Minnecou will be no more. Teokahannah has foreseen, and my dreams tell me the same." Sequannah didn't respond, but even if he had, the Washan merely spoke his words and left.

Sequannah looked over to where the Wolf brothers were playing with some small children in the snow. They were gathering armfuls of snow and then rolling them on the ground. Each time they rolled the ball over, more snow from the ground would stick to it and the ball would become bigger and bigger. He marveled at the things children could think of to do with commonplace things. The Wolf brothers were helping the children to push one of the snowballs that had gotten too big for them, and as a surprise, they were pushing it towards Sequannah to cheer him up. But by the time they got it over to him, it was nearly as tall as he was. They huffed and puffed, their faces straining. "If you don't get up, we're going to roll you up in this snowball," they laughed.

"You would do us all a favor if you could roll those stone buildings up in your snowball," Sequannah laughed. But then, his expression became serious; perhaps there was a use for this new discovery. He picked up his bow and notched an arrow to the string. He tried to pull back hard, but his wrist was in too much pain. Tamahna had everyone stand back. He notched an arrow to his bow and pulled back hard. When he let go, the arrow went in only up to its feathers. The snowball was nearly as hard as ice. The three of them began whooping and cheering. As Sequannah leapt to his feet, the last arrow in him was left in the healer's hand; a crowd was beginning to gather.

The sun cast its warmth upon the surface of the snow in just the right manner to make it compact. Everyone began rolling snow until they were the size of huge boulders. Even Sequannah tried to join in, but the pain made it impossible, and drained his strength as well. He was forced to step back. He limped over to one of the smoldering ditches, where many had gathered to warm themselves and dry their clothing. But, he no longer felt hopeless. He could now see hundreds of slaves and warriors rolling huge balls of snow across the open courts of the mining village. Even Semmida's warriors had joined in the enthusiasm. Sequannah tried to explain what was going on to the men who had gathered around the ditches, but he found it impossible. An old warrior suddenly appeared before him.

"Grandfather!" Sequannah said excitedly, "Did you come here alone?"

"I came here with the Wolf brothers and the others," Kwoita answered calmly.

"Where have you been then? I missed you, grandfather."

"No one waits for a grandfather when they run to the battle," Kwoita said. "As well they shouldn't. I am too old to be of any help and I am too old even to withstand the cold. The best place for me is to stand by the heat of these burning ditches. Whether we win or lose here, I have already fought too many battles for this old body to put up with another. No, I will seek what little comfort there is here until my feet are on the trail into the next world. I can find the new trail when I go on to the next world. It is you who must worry. These Snake people will trample everything and there will be no clear path to find your way to the trail of the next life. You will spend an eternity walking in circles and searching because you will no longer be able to see the true path."

"Then help me explain to these people what the others are doing," Sequannah pleaded. "They are not just playing in the snow. They are rolling shields of snow before them so they can make their way into the stone buildings."

A spark of life came into the old man's eyes as he yelled to all the people surrounding the ditch. Soon, he and Sequannah stood alone. The Snake warriors gathered in force upon the rooftops of every building.

"Fools will play as the spirit of death surrounds them," Bakwanote shouted to the rebels in the snow. "You embarrass my warriors to make them slaughter children."

"They were not embarrassed to slaughter women and children when they attacked my village," one of the slaves shouted at the stone buildings. "The games of children will crush you and your warriors!"

The village war chief laughed at the daring slave. "None of you can ever be worthy to be counted among Quiktkoata's empire. Your greatest visions will never exceed those of a child. You will hope and cry, and we will laugh as we spill your foolish blood back into the dirt your kind were made from. You will melt away as surely as the snow you see before you, but unlike the snow, there will never be a season for your kind again." The Snake warriors laughed and growled and whooped, and then laughed again. They jeered at the rebels in the snow, begging them to come within range of their bows.

Sequannah drew himself closer as he saw the Minnecou, the Paccus and the slaves surrounding the small building where they had failed in their previous assault. They had rolled huge balls of snow into lines that surrounded the square stone buildings. The Snake warriors nearly fell from the rooftops in their laughter at the foolhardy rebels. Some of them shot arrows at the slowly advancing lines, but they fell short. "Come closer, little children," they taunted, but now Semmida's archers fell into place behind the lines of mounting snow, while the Snake warriors jeered. Semmida signaled. Each of his warriors rapidly notched their arrows to the bow and drew back hard. The Snake warriors scrambled over the rooftop as they piled themselves down the hole in the roof and then closed the door. One Snake warrior fell from the arrows of Semmida's archers; the village chief laughed from the rooftop of the largest stone building in the distance.

"The loss of one warrior will mean nothing," he shouted. "We both know that is the last Snake warrior to die today. You are leading your children to the slaughter."

But a strange phenomenon was taking shape as Sequannah watched from a distance. The huge balls of snow came closer and closer together until they touched each other. They were now about the height of a man, and after the line had moved a little further, the huge boulders of snow became cemented together. It appeared as if the rebels were rolling enormous white logs. With each revolution, the logs became higher and higher. Arrows streamed out of the stone building, but there were no targets for the Snake warriors to hit; just a mounting white wall, steadily advancing towards the increasingly frustrated Snake warriors. The village chief and his warriors' jeers became fewer and fewer, and increasingly feeble. The Snake warriors inside the stone building threw their lances into the advancing rolls of hardened snow, in the hopes of jamming them up so that they could be moved no closer. But their hopes were lost in the wind as the shafts of their spears snapped as quickly as the Snake warriors' spirits. The Minnecou and the Paccus laughed and cheered along with the slaves as they grunted and rolled the advancing white wall closer and closer to the stone building. The Snake warriors ran out to try and push the great rolls back, but they were overwhelmed in strength and number as the great mound continued towards them, threatening to roll right over them. They were forced back into the stone building, and very shortly after, the rolling snow pressed against the sides, from the ground to the bottom of the rooftop.

The panels on the angled portion of the roof opened and the Snake warriors drew their bows. But there were no open targets below them, only a thick mound of packed snow. By the time they changed their aim to Semmida's warriors, arrows were already hailing down on them, and the panels were quickly shut. Semmida signaled the Minnecou, Paccus and slaves. Then they quickly scaled the mountains of rolled snow, and sat on the panels of the rooftop so that they could no longer be opened. Mokotak ran up with Petawahin and the Wolf brothers and they kicked in the mud and stone chimney that was allowing the smoke from the building's hearth to escape. They sealed the hole with hides and snow, then stood on the door that led from the lower part of the building to the roof. The Snake warriors pounded and pushed to get out from the suffocating smoke.

When enough warriors had mounted the rooftop, Petawahin had everyone draw their bows and step off of the door. Immediately, the wide plank door flew open and Snake warriors began streaming out, coughing and choking and unable even to stand as they gasped for air. The Paccu and Minnecou warriors led them down off the roof under the threat of arrows and lances. The slaves cheered wildly as the village chief looked angrily upon his choking warriors being led away with not one casualty among the rebels.

His anger turned to despair as one building after another fell to the rebels. Even after ordering that the hearth fires be doused, the Snake warriors still were forced to surrender to the rebels who jumped up and down on the roofs until they threatened to collapse onto the Snake warriors below.

By the time the rebels had overcome and occupied all of the smaller buildings, they had collected and corralled a sizable number of Snake warrior prisoners. Quitkwa and Sequannah were charged with overseeing the slaves as they kept watch over the prisoners. Kwoita helped out as well. Sequannah limped around with careful instructions to the slaves, having them force the Snake warriors to remain lying face down in the snow and separated to prevent any uprising, regardless of their lack of weaponry.

"I'm told that the Creator gives you the vision to help us overcome the Snake warriors," the Sikun suddenly appeared at Sequannah's side.

"The Wolf brothers and I, we learned together, after seeing the children play in the snow," Sequannah said, feeling guilty that the Sikun would try to give all of the credit to him.

"I have spoken with the Wolf brothers," Teokahannah spoke again. "They tell me it is you who thinks this way."

"I could not have..." Sequannah tried to explain.

"There is no need to question or explain," Teokahannah looked seriously upon the young Minnecou. "When the Creator points out something to you, he points out something to me. It is you who will bring about the fall of the Snake people. I had suspected before, but now I am certain." Sequannah stood tall.

"Yes. Enjoy the pride you feel for the moment, for it will disappear as quickly as the setting sun. There will be little happiness in your life if you choose to follow the Creator. There will be almost no pleasure if that's what you seek. Unless you learn that to exist is a pleasure in itself.

"You will be burdened with much sadness and much responsibility for the life and death that will surround you. But if you give up or refuse, the end for your people and their way of life shall follow shortly. Quiktkoata's empire will spread to the ends of the earth and beyond. Heal yourself and stand tall, or lay down and die the death to all. That is the choice the Creator gives to his chosen ones. He has placed it before you."

Sequannah didn't feel so confident any more—his pride had been clouded to obscurity well before the setting sun. "I am much too young for anyone to follow," Sequannah insisted. "Perhaps you have not seen all that Semmida has done." The Sikun seemed to ignore him. "I will not leave my people!" Sequannah said obstinately. Teokahannah turned to leave.

As he walked away, several small sparrows flitted around him. One of them darted back, landing on Sequannah's shoulder. It stayed for but a brief moment, then flew back to the Sikun.

From his place among the prisoners, Sequannah now watched the preparations for the moment everyone had awaited. Hundreds of slaves and warriors rolled their huge balls of snow into line for the final assault on the largest of the stone buildings. Bakwanote had retreated deep into the recesses of the huge building, awaiting the fate that had come to all of the smaller buildings. Just as with the others, the huge balls of snow eventually touched together, and with much effort and coordination, they became great rolling logs of snow, pressing in upon the huge stone building from all four directions. All of the hearth fires inside of the huge building had already been doused. Supplies had been stacked to the ceiling to reinforce the roof that the rebels would try to stomp down upon the Snake warriors. The village chief had little else to do but wait. He didn't even send his warriors out to try and push the great rolls back upon the rebels, for he had seen how ineffective this had been with the other buildings. He knew that even all the warriors in this largest building were now severely outnumbered.

He elbowed his way to one of the narrow windows to watch the great wall of snow as it was pressed against the now useless fortress. Closer and closer did the great logs roll. Bakwanote could see the bits of grass and mud, and leaves that were turned up from the ground beneath the snow. This was the fate of him and his own men, he thought to himself. Here he sits with his strong battalion–strong enough even to subdue the white ones–yet under hopeless siege by a group of slaves and nomads. Quiktkoata will be in a rage when he finds that his copper mines have been seized by rebels. Even the fact that they had gotten this far would be enough reason for Quiktkoata to put the village chief and any of his surviving warriors to death, regardless of the outcome. His only choices were to surrender to the rebels or try to escape.

As the village chief watched the mounting snow rolling closer and closer towards the narrow windows, he noticed that the pace of its movement began to slow. But he had seen this in the other buildings as well. As the great rolls of snow were pushed inward towards the buildings, they became heavier and more difficult to move. But eventually they seemed always to crush in upon the buildings in the end. Bakwanote sat resigned, ready to surrender to Semmida and the rebels, yet still determined to think of some means of escape.

Perhaps they could use their surrender as a ploy, and find some way to escape after they had been removed from the building. But he would have to think of a plan now. There would be no time once the building was inundated with rebels. As he contemplated a means, he was suddenly distracted by the fact that the advancing mounds of snow had stopped. As his heart filled with hope, the great rolls began to move once again. His spirit fell. But the snow advanced no more than a few paces, and once again came to a halt. This time, however, it stayed there.

The village chief dashed to the angled portion of the roof and lifted one of the panels. Outside of the great wall of snow he could see the backsides of the rebels as they pressed and grunted against the mound of snow, but to no avail. The logs would roll no further. He scanned the village—there were no other able bodies available. Everyone was either pushing the great mounds or guarding the prisoners. Even the children were among the rebels as they pressed against the snow in a desperate effort to move it, but it wouldn't budge.

After a time, a stream of rebels tried to breech the mound of snow, but the village chief's men easily shot them down, and left them bleeding in the snow. Bakwanote climbed up onto the roof and surveyed the situation from a protected parapet. The battle was now at a standoff. He yelled to his men below.

"We have as much food, if not more than they. When Quiktkoata sees that there is no longer any copper flowing into the city, he will send warriors to find out why, and we will be freed. They have lost!"

His men cheered, but as rumors spread, their cheers became feeble. There was fear among them that even if they were rescued by another group of Snake warriors, they may also be executed, or broken down into slaves. Bakwanote continued to try and raise his men's spirit, until a movement in the distance caught his eye. First he saw a tiny figure climbing over the top of a distant ridge, and then many more began to follow. He couldn't make out who it was, but a number of warriors were obviously making their way down the surrounding slopes towards the burned-out village. Perhaps those warriors who had gone after the white ones were now returning. There may be just enough of them to engage and distract the rebels, allowing he and his men to escape. His heart soared momentarily, but as they came closer and closer, his jaw grew slack.

There upon the slopes, was a group of nomad rebels and the strange white ones returning to the village with them. The great mounds of snow would definitely move now. As the new group set foot upon the flat floor of the village, the chief had already surrendered to the rebels. His warriors streamed over the mound of snow with no weapons of any kind, their hands folded behind their necks.

The rebels had scarcely even noticed that reinforcements were on the way when the first Snake warriors began to surrender. Semmida could hardly believe what he was seeing, but he was thankful that the battle was finally over.

"Make sure that they have no weapons, and separate them," he ordered all of the rebels. "There is still much to do."

Bakwanote didn't surrender first, nor did he wait till the last. He was found in the middle of his hopeless and dejected warriors. He would look up towards the sky or downwards into the glaring snow, but he would not look his captors in the eye. When he was brought to Semmida, he would answer no questions, nor even acknowledge that he had been spoken to.

"Take these men and all of the Snake warriors and Snake guards and set them to work, trampling down the snow that has been piled up around the buildings. These will be our shelters for the winter," Semmida declared.

Sequannah and Quitkwa, and even Kwoita helped the slaves lead the prisoners up to the stone buildings and begin the task of breaking up the huge mounds of snow. They saw a large group of white men coming into the village. Among them, they found the rest of the Minnecou clan.

Sequannah ran with a limp to greet them. Shatomi had blood upon his clothing. Tumaris was being carried upon a travois along with Ketanka. Although Tumaris appeared to be in pain, she was not like Ketanka, who was breathing with difficulty and staring blankly into the sky. Petawahin, the Wolf brothers...everyone gathered to see their relatives once again and pray for Ketanka's recovery. Sequannah was surprised to see Sabatt with a lance and bow, walking proudly among his clan with the hairy-faced ones coming up to feel his muscles and sometimes even bowing before him. It was obvious to Sequannah that they had seen their own terrifying battles as well.

Everywhere around them, people were preparing food for a huge feast and celebration for their victory over the Snake warriors, while the prisoners continued to trample the mounds of snow and bring all of the available supplies in the entire village into the stone buildings.

Although it had seemed a long battle, it now appeared that everything had actually occurred quite quickly. For all of the snow had been trampled down once again, every usable supply had been transferred into the stone buildings and an entire feast was prepared before the sun had come close to setting.

"There is reason to be joyous," Teokahannah spoke. "The Creator has seen fit to rescue his children and allow us to defeat the Snake warriors in battle. Now that we have been given the hand of power, we will use it as the Creator himself would." Everyone jumped to their feet and cheered to the Sikun's wise words.

"But we cannot feast ourselves until we have invited all of his children to victory. Let us free the prisoners now and let them be counted among us." Everyone began to murmur and hiss.

"Would you treat them as slaves and become the same as they were? Would you murder them after they have surrendered to you and accepted your authority? We must accept them and treat them as our own or we will always have an enemy. Those of you who do not accept them are among them. Shall we feast together or always in the midst of enemies?"

The hissing ceased and the prisoners were led in among them. Bakwanote looked somewhat suspicious, but after the feast began and there was singing and dancing, and he along with his own people were asked to sing and dance their own songs as well, only then was there happiness among all of the peoples. They sat together to feast again as the sun went down, and now the people were ready to face the winter that had arrived so early.

But even as the sun's rim touched the emerald horizon, a screeching hiss pierced the village below. And as they looked up, three great hawks circled ominously overhead. The white peaks and ridges around them were lined with thousands of warriors, and even at such distances, the black and yellow war paint of the Snake warriors stood out clearly for all to see. Bakwanote's face became full of anger and suspicion. He regretted the invitation he had so foolishly accepted.

"You have tricked us!" he accused the Sikun. "You knew all along what was to come!"

"But now you have the choice of what kind of men you

wish to be when you leave this earth," the Sikun smiled. "And that is a gift, not a trick."

CHAPTER 23

Semmida cried out over the din of the frantic crowd. "Bring all of the food with you. Do not leave anything for Quiktkoata's warriors. Whatever you leave gives strength to your enemy!"

Ceptke repeated this to the Paccus; the Washan warned the Minnecou. The hills surrounding the mining village became thick with massing Snake warriors, their hard leather armor glistening in the sun; eerie black and yellow jagged lines painted on their arms and faces. A southerly wind blew hard and warm, and most of the trampled snow turned to mud and slush. A droning chant began to build along the ridge tops, echoing in the village like a hornet's buzz in the ear. The rebels' spirits tightened as they sensed the ferocious and imminent strike poised over them. The screech of Quiktkoata's hawks pierced through the frantic scramble of rebels, their shadows drifting ominously over the fearful crowd.

A sudden roar erupted from the hills to the south. The rebels witnessed a visible wave among the hilltops as the Snake warriors set into motion, rushing southward along the ridges on both sides of the mining village, towards a point in the distance. Sequannah raced into the largest of the stone structures and found his way to one of the parapets. The Sikun was already there. He glanced briefly at the young Minnecou, then returned to his southward gaze. In the distance, Sequannah watched a large group of warriors scrambling for cover as Quiktkoata's warriors inundated them, leaving no place to hide. He witnessed their long, straw-colored hair, as screams of death rang out in the distance.

"They are destroying the light-skinned ones!" Sequannah gasped to the Sikun.

"They have more of them in the city," Teokahannah stated unconcerned.

"They are killing all of them. Even those you see surrendering are being killed as they stand!" Sequannah pleaded with the Sikun.

"If there was a way to save them, we would do so. But, as they try to escape, we must remember that they are Yanguis," Teokahannah responded sternly. "White Snake people. They were trying to escape using our deaths as a diversion. They would bring back their own Quiktkoatas, and what would your Minnecou do then?"

The Snake warriors wasted no time in their slaughter of the white ones, and immediately advanced towards the village. The pathways were deserted by the time Quiktkoata's forces were within striking distance. The rebels prepared to defend themselves behind the walls of the six remaining stone buildings. Sequannah scanned the hordes of rebels as they entered the largest structure, but none of his clan were among them. He raced down the stairs to see if any Minnecou were in the building. Most of Semmida's men had chosen this fortress after seeing the Sikun out on the parapet. There were Paccus, slaves and even a couple of the white warriors, but no Minnecou to be found. Sequannah searched until it seemed he had seen everyone in that stone lodge more than twice, before he spotted a Minnecou moccasin in the shadows of a poorly lit room. Here he found Sabatt and Shatomi guarding the entrance. Inside, Shamira huddled against a tall Paccu while several other Paccu warriors sat on the floor, leaning against the cold stone walls.

"Are there any more Minnecou?" Sequannah demanded.

"We cannot find them here," Shatomi looked somberly upon the young warrior. "The crowds knocked us over and we became separated. The Minnecou were not all together. We could not even get out of this building once we were inside because we were always pushed back by the people coming in, even at the holes for viewing the outside."

Sequannah looked casually into the small room. Pointing towards the center with his chin, he spoke to Shatomi. "My sister choose Paccu warriors to protect her?" he said in a voice loud enough for Shamira to hear, indicating that he would no longer speak to her directly.

"We know them," Shatomi shrugged. "They are okay." Sequannah's lips tightened. Shamira couldn't bear to look upon her injured brother. She held the anger in her tongue.

A clamor erupted outside of the building, and the eerie humming of the Snake warriors suddenly burst into a barrage of paralyzing war whoops. Warriors inside of the building began shooting arrows through the viewing holes. The sound of metal against stone clanged through the walls. Ceptke ran past Sequannah, nearly knocking him over. His Paccu companions followed as they clustered around one of the windows. Sequannah saw Semmida and his warriors making their way up the stairs towards the parapets, and limped after them. He became dizzy as he reached the top of the stairs; spots formed before his eyes. The pain of his wounds throbbed and spasmed, and he realized that he wouldn't have the strength to use his weapons. He was defenseless against these Snake warriors, and had to rely on others to save his life. Semmida yelled down from somewhere in the rafters of the strange edifice.

"Forget your wounds, warrior. Get up here now!"

Sequannah ran up next to the entrance to one of the parapets, straining to see into the dark maze of trusses. A strong hand jerked on his tunic, dragging him up into the rafters. Semmida pulled him to the end of the building and propped him up against the stone gable, tying a cord around his chest and under his arms.

"When I tell you to sit, sit!" Semmida demanded.

Semmida disappeared into the darkness, but a few moments later Sequannah was startled as the command to sit was screamed into his ear. Sequannah fell to the floor; a certain creaking sound caused his stomach to turn. The section of roof lifted up before him, as all of Semmida's archers stood at full draw, releasing their quickly-aimed arrows into the screaming Snake warriors below.

"Stand!" Semmida screamed at Sequannah and another warrior at the other end of the building. In the light, Sequannah could see the rope he controlled, threading through a wooden pulley, something he had never seen before. It squeaked loudly as the wheel turned. "They will learn to fear that sound," Semmida winked at Sequannah.

The roof closed, and once again the warriors sat in the darkness. Sequannah followed the command to sit twice more before the Snake warriors abandoned their efforts to capture the largest structure in the village. Semmida commanded Sequannah and the other warrior to sit, so they could view their enemy through the open roof. The Snake warriors had reassembled in the distance, well away from the stone buildings. Swarms of them were drifting into one large mass, larger than any group of warriors anyone had ever seen. They gathered in nearly the same place where Semmida had pulled the rebels together before they attacked Bakwanote and his warriors.

Quiktkoata's litter was carried slowly into the midst of the huge war party, then silence fell over the entire village. Only the wind in the ears and the drip of melting snow could be heard as Quiktkoata's litter was held high over the heads of his vicious warriors. Sequannah heard a low mumbling in the distance as Quiktkoata threw open the curtains of his litter and spoke to his warriors. When the voice stopped, a low humming chant was initiated, slowly intensifying as the vicious warriors began to swirl in a strange and confusing pattern of circles.

At first, the Snake warriors appeared to be walking in unison, but as each warrior suddenly held his hand to the sky, shaking dried-gourd rattles, the strange movement increased until each warrior was running in his own circular pattern. The whole war party looked and sounded like a pile of rattlesnakes, ready to erupt. A booming clap of thunder tore through the village, shaking the stone buildings enough for Sequannah to feel it upon the wooden floor. The swirling mass of Snake warriors suddenly burst apart, and the circles became long thick lines of warriors, zigzagging towards the village. Each line looked exactly like a huge snake, slithering towards the stone buildings. They converged upon the smallest of the stone structures, then another loud clap of thunder released a chorus of blood-chilling war whoops as the winding lines swarmed over the edifice, ignoring the hundreds of arrows emanating from it. They were on the roof in moments. The doors were torn off as hundreds of them pressed into the narrow windows. A short time later, smoke began to drift out from under the eaves of the building, and a stream of Snake warriors poured out of the doors, carrying hacked off legs, arms and heads of their enemies for all to see as the roof burst into flames.

They tossed their trophies into a pile, and as each warrior passed it, they fell back into one of the long and winding lines that began to encircle the next closest building. Another loud boom of thunder shuddered through the village. Sequannah scanned the horizon, but there wasn't a cloud to be found. The winding lines of Snake warriors swarmed the next closest building with chilling war whoops, to paralyze the enemy within. But as they attacked, another war party of Snake warriors burst forth from a different stone structure, and tore into Quiktkoata's forces from behind, scattering the long and winding lines. Quiktkoata stood up on his litter, screaming into the sky and cursing Bakwanote for his treacherous act.

Semmida and the Sikun watched in amazement as Quiktkoata's warriors were caught between two enemies. But, Quiktkoata's warriors knew they couldn't enter the buildings with enemies shooting from behind, and immediately turned on the traitors, forcing Bakwanote's warriors into the charred section of the village, and finally surrounding them.

Backwanote and his warriors hid behind walls, foundations and the furnaces of the great mining village. Quiktkoata's warriors had been thinned from their initial attack upon the village, and now used their warriors sparingly to flush out Bakwanote and his mutinous warriors. Sequannah watched from the safety of the parapets as Quiktkoata's warriors risked their lives to get at the rebel Snake warriors. They forced a few of Bakwanote's men at a time to flee out in the open and expose themselves to waves of spears and arrows. The village was nearly silent as Quiktkoata's cat and mouse game unfolded. Nothing happened for long periods of time until two or three of Bakwanote's warriors were overwhelmed by Snake warriors and a brief skirmish would ensue. Twilight faded into darkness before the last of Bakwanote's warriors fell into the hands of Quiktkoata's bloodthirsty hordes.

* * *

The rebels watched tensely into the dark and moonless night. War cries in distance stabbed into the silence of the village. A spark ignited in the burnt part of the village, and soon, a large bonfire roared in the distance from Sequannah's position. The Snake warriors chanted and whooped, then a tense silence would fall over the village once again. They could see the Snake warriors piling rubble onto the bonfire, but at other times, they appeared to be pulling things out. Sequannah witnessed a lone figure in the distance, creeping along in the darkest shadows towards the largest of the stone buildings.

"Someone finds his way to us in secret," Sequannah warned Semmida, pointing into the darkness. Semmida looked for quite some time before he grunted acknowledgment, then raced off to the bottom floor of the building, taking three of his men with him. The Paccus, Minnecou and slaves whispered amongst themselves, then fell into silence as soon as they perceived Semmida's approach.

Semmida saw a faint shadow flicker by one of the windows. A group of Paccus reached out and grabbed the warrior by the hair, hoisting him through the narrow slot. Ceptke held his knife to the man's throat as Semmida approached.

"Sabanote!" Semmida sneered. "And who do you scout for now? Have you not yet guessed who will stand when the fighting is over?"

"Tarote sends me with information for the Sikun. She fears that her stone lodge or the one closest will be attacked next. There is much food and she does not want it to fall into Quiktkoata's hands. She does not want to spoil it either, because if we survive the Snake warriors' attack, we will then starve. Quiktkoata has no more food," Sabanote solemnly stated.

"How do you know this?" Semmida questioned. "And why should I find reason to trust your words?"

"Look to the ruins of the village...where the Snake warriors have gathered around the bright fire. They are eating the dead from the fighting today. I have heard the soldiers say that they will eat this way until the stone buildings are emptied. And if they lose the battle, they will have to sacrifice their own soldiers to feed their war party until they can get back to the city."

"When will they attack?" Semmida demanded.

"I have not heard this," Sabanote pleaded. "They question each other, but they have no answers. Only Quiktkoata knows."

Semmida tossed his head and grunted, walking towards the stairs to the roof and parapets. Two of his warriors dragged Sabanote behind, while a third held a spear to the back of the spy's neck.

The Sikun turned as Semmida approached the parapet. "Do not let him out in the open," Semmida warned his guards. "He will signal Quiktkoata and his warriors."

"Tarote sends me!" Sabanote pleaded to the Sikun.

"Tarote trusts you?" Teokahannah asked. "She has no one else to carry messages?"

"No one that can slip past the eyes of the Snake warriors," Sabanote said. "I am expendable to her anyway. She has no care for my life."

"There were no Minnecou among you?"

"None."

"I ask this not because I feel you expendable or untrustworthy, but because I question her change of heart," the Sikun held a hand out to the spy.

"There is no change of heart within her," Sabanote said tersely.

"Perhaps now you have the opportunity to bring about that change," Teokahannah spoke softly. "What important messages do you carry?"

Sabanote pointed to a distant building, barely visible in the darkness. "Tarote is over there with a group of slaves and Paccus. There is much food within the stone walls of her building, but it is also the most likely place for the Snake warriors to attack next, unless they attack the other one," Sabanote pointed to another building close by to Tarote's. "She fears that if the Snake warriors are successful, they will have enough food to stay and destroy all of us. She knows they have no supplies of their own left. I have already been among Quiktkoata's warriors and brought this information to her."

"She allowed you to go among the Snake warriors," Teokahannah questioned the spy, "knowing that you could point out her weaknesses to Quiktkoata, and let him know of where the food is stored?"

"I was with Bakwanote when he led us against the Snake warriors. I knew we were all going to die. I am a scout. There was still a purpose for me. I found my way into one of the Snake lines and pretended to join them. In darkness, I returned. Your daughter is in the building that is safest to approach. That is how I know that Quiktkoata will attack there next. Tarote says that everyone must come out and fight if she is attacked or everyone will lose in the end. She says that she worries not for her own life, but for all of us. We cannot let them take that stone lodge. She cannot destroy the food either, because even if Quiktkoata abandoned his anger for us, we would starve in the end."

Teokahannah knew that although he was in the largest of all the buildings, there was not much in the way of food stored there. Valuable copper ornaments and jewelry were abundant, though little else. But Sabanote was guileful. He was more than a spy or a warrior. He was a question with never a clear answer. Did he seek to draw everyone out into the open for one quick ambush by the Snake warriors, then win back his favor in the eyes of Quiktkoata? Sabanote always appeared genuine, but there was always a sense that he knew much more than he conveyed.

"Sequannah!" the Sikun called softly into the darkness. Sequannah limped a few short steps to the parapet. He had heard the conversation clearly as he slumped against the gable, though he hadn't learned enough of their words to understand everything.

"I am here," Sequannah called weakly as he approached.

"I need a Minnecou to bring a message to Tarote," Teokahannah spoke. Sequannah sensed a subtle tension in the spy beside the Sikun.

"There are three of us here in this stone lodge," Sequannah informed the Sikun.

"I need someone that Tarote knows," Teokahannah stated. "Can you move quickly and safely in the darkness with the wounds you have suffered?"

"I can move safely, but I am not sure of swiftness."

"I could be there in an instant," Sabanote offered. "Your daughter, even now, expects and awaits my return. She may kill any other that even attempts to approach her." Both Sequannah and the Sikun perceived the slight rise in the spy's voice.

"If that was the most practical thing to do, you would already be on your way," the Sikun lamented. "But you made your way here safely through the enemies that are scattered in the darkness. Would I not be a fool to send the only logical guide for my warriors to a distant post and leave them to chance? No, I cannot waste a warrior of your talents when my followers are in need." He pulled a long piece of cloth from under his tunic and began to fold it lengthwise.

"Come closer, Sequannah," Teokahannah said soothingly. "I will wrap your leg in a way that will bring strength to it and ease the pain." Teokahannah lifted the young Minnecou's leg onto his lap while Sequannah strained to balance himself in the darkness. The Sikun fumbled and knotted the cloth, wrapping and rewrapping it several times before he felt he had it right. "Try that!" he said with confident delight. "You should feel no pain at all."

Sequannah could almost feel his benevolent smile in the darkness. He placed his foot on the wooden floor and shifted his weight onto it for the first time since the wound was inflicted. Intense pain shot through his body and burned in his neck to the top of his head. He nearly screamed out, but held back, for he was a warrior. "It is no different," he calmly informed the Sikun.

"Let me see that," Teokahannah said in a questioning tone.

"Oh! I know what I forgot to do." He took the wrap off and began folding and unfolding it over and over again. Sabanote began shifting from side to side in the darkness as if his impatience over the matter would cause him to explode.

"If your men were to follow the western side of the stone lodges and lie low in between, they could make it to Tarote without running into any Snake warriors. This is how I got here. I could show them nothing more than you could tell them," the spy finally blurted out.

"Rest while you can, Sabanote," Teokahannah said concernedly. "I don't want a weary warrior to lead my followers into battle. Don't forget that you have been on the move since well before dawn."

A chilling screech descended through the night sky; one of Quiktkoata's hawks drifted overhead, but couldn't be seen. War whoops shattered the silence of the village—another attack was underway. Sequannah could feel the expression of anguish on the Sikun's face, but by his silence, he knew Teokahannah would hold back and send no one.

"Send your warriors now!" Sabanote demanded, "Before it is too late!"

"We must first see where the attack is to be carried out," the Sikun returned. "Do you not agree?"

"If Quiktkoata's warriors seize the food that is in that lodge, they will stay until they have killed us all," Sabanote warned.

"This is where you are wrong, Sabanote," Teokahannah turned to the spy. "Quiktkoata will leave this place tomorrow, no matter the outcome. And you know about this. He has more pressing problems in his own city, otherwise he would have plenty of provisions with him now, and his warriors would not have become so weak on the trail. He must deal with disloyalty before he attempts to destroy his enemy. He will try to punish us and give us reason to fear him more, but as long as we stay within the walls of stone, it will cost him much more than he will gain. You know as well as I, that as horrible as it was for the people in the stone lodge that was overrun today, and the second that was attempted, Quiktkoata lost more than a third of his warriors. He will attempt once more in the night, but tomorrow he must go. The only chance Quiktkoata ever had of destroying us would be to lure us out into the open. That is plain to everyone who ever tried to attack these stone structures. You have now found yourself among your enemies. You will not be given another chance like Bakwanote and his warriors. With no heart, your fear has sent your thoughts in the wrong direction."

Sabanote looked quickly for an escape route, but Semmida had been there all along with three of his guards, hidden in the darkness. They seized the spy and dragged him down the stairs to the dirt floor on the lowest part of the building. The throng of war whoops in the distance began to die down, and soon dribbled back to silence. The attack had been futile.

"The Snake warriors did not attack the building that Sabanote pointed to," Sequannah spoke to the Sikun. "How did you know that he was lying?"

"I did not," Teokahannah replied. "But it is clear to me that Sabanote will always seek to be on the winning side. He wishes to get the battle out in the open so it will be clear to him who will win. He cares for nothing at all in this world but his own survival and a place of power. It is not necessary for anyone to even fight the evil in this world, but only to constantly lean in the direction of what they know is right and good for the whole. And Sabanote cannot even do this. He is a worm in search of a host. He will suffer and sacrifice for a place of power, but he will not do this for his own spirit. He will bend the world to fit him, but he will not bend himself to fit the world. He is just like all of the others who worship Quiktkoata and his ways. He will become a part of the cult that wishes to redesign the Creator's world to fit humanity rather than for the good of all things. He does not know what the world is. This is something you must learn, as well, before it is too late for me to teach you. Do you know what you are and what everything around you is?" Teokahannah posed to the young Minnecou warrior.

"No," Sequannah almost laughed. "No one knows everything."

"Do you know how everything got here and where it came from?" the Sikun asked seriously.

"No!" Sequannah laughed at such a foolish question.

"Think!" Teokahannah said softly.

Sequannah hesitated. "The Creator?" Sequannah shrugged.

"And what did the Creator make everything from?"

Teokahannah would not let go.

"The ground?" Sequannah questioned.

"And what did he make that from?" Teokahannah continued.

"Dust?" Sequannah guessed again.

"And what did he create that from?"

"The sun?"

"Before he created anything, there was nothing but the Creator. If there was nothing else, what did he create everything from?" Teokahannah cornered the young Minnecou. Sequannah shrugged, staring questioningly at Teokahannah.

"Himself," the Sikun said as if it were self explanatory.

"Himself," Sequannah repeated awkwardly. The Sikun must be losing control of his mind for even putting him through all this.

"Himself!" the Sikun said strongly. "Not only did he create everything, but he is everything. You are but a small part of him. He sees with your eyes and feels with your hands just as you do. Whether your eyes are open or closed, you see the Creator, because he is all things. Even the reflection you see at the bottom of a still pool is the Creator; your whole life is but a thought of his. When you feel good in the world around you, the Creator is happy because he knows you appreciate what he has given you. He knows that you are happy to be a part of him. When you feel dissatisfied, he allows you to change the world around you because he knows that in the end you will never find more satisfaction and beauty than you would find if you accepted the world he had given you. Look upon Quiktkoata and his followers. They will change everything that falls in their path until it fits their own desires. But are they ever satisfied? Is there not always something more that needs to be changed to fulfill their futile quest for satisfaction. You have been to Quiktkoata's city. Do you not see that as these people chase their desires, the Creator's world becomes more and more unrecognizable, and everyone becomes more dissatisfied? They become jealous and resentful of each other, and will even deny their need for sleep and rest to chase the satisfaction that comes for but a few brief moments, and is then swallowed up in the desire for more. They cannot see that their own existence is a gift far beyond any desire they will ever have. If the Earth Mother was a turtle, they would be the worms that eventually dry up and blow around in the empty shell. We can become an ally or an enemy to the Creator's body; it is our choice. We can devour it or bring it to fruition, but only one of these ways will allow us to carry on. The Creator is everything and will always be, but the further we stray from him, the more we will isolate ourselves and choke and wither in our own poisons. In the end, everyone is humbled and eventually comes to understand."

"Even Quiktkoata?" Sequannah asked with a doubtful tone.

"To each shall come a sunset of painted sky," Teokahannah replied as if it was self-explanatory. "Do you understand the words I speak to you?"

Sequannah shrugged. "Some," he said in a tired voice.

"You will learn, but perhaps now is a poor time," Teokahannah smiled. "You must get some rest." Sequannah drifted down to the floor of the parapet and immediately fell into a spell of deep sleep.

* * *

Sequannah felt his heart stop and strained to get his lungs breathing as he was shocked from deep slumber, and tossed by a voluminous wave of war cries. The sky was still dark. He had no concept as to how long he had slept before hundreds of Quiktkoata's warriors had crept up to the village and unleashed their fury somewhere outside of the stone lodge. He heard the sounds of many footsteps as shadows raced up the stairs to the parapets. The cries of battle intensified as another wave of Snake warriors ushered into the vicinity of the stone structures—shrieks of death soon began to ring out in the distance.

He caught a glimpse of the Sikun and Semmida as the crowd gathered around them. The rebels listened in horror as the unseen battle raged around one of the stone structures furthest from where Sequannah stood, worrying for the safety of his relatives.

The struggle would die down to almost a whisper, but time after time, another barrage of war cries would ring out, and the battle would intensify to the point of the initial attack. In the middle of one of the loudest attacks, cries of victory began to ring out, then the sounds of whips slashing into the night air. The telltale wisps of smoke and the following tongues of flame sent pangs of misery into the hearts of Teokahannah and his followers; the roof of the distant structure set the western sky aglow, brighter than the rising sun in the east.

The Snake warriors had moved their camp closer during the night. An enormous pile of wood was set to the torch. Drums echoed through the valley as hundreds of Snake warriors came dancing into a circle around the flaming mass, cheering in victory. Their cheers erupted into a frenzy as a large pole, the size of a tall tree, was erected in the midst of the vicious war party. Sequannah focused on the top of the pole–his heart stopped.

As the first ray of sunlight reached over the horizon, it fell upon Ketanka, lashed to the top of the pole. His knees had been drawn to his chest, and his arms flailed convulsively at the morning air as his eyes rolled far back into his head. Only the whites stood out brightly in that first ray of sun. Melonak had been strung onto the pole directly beneath him. Pierced through the back, her limbs hung stiffly below him in sepalic mimicry. The chief of the Minnecou shivered like a dying aster in the late autumn dawn; the night had been too cold.

A large figure escaped from one of the stone buildings and came racing by the parapets. Another smaller figure followed in pursuit. "Mokotak!" Sequannah whispered as the huge Minnecou warrior charged wild-eyed towards the cheering Snake warriors, tomahawk in one hand, his spear and atlatl assembled in the other. Sequannah tensed as he recognized his father several paces behind, screaming for Mokotak to stop. The Wolf brothers had been able to hold Quitkwa back, but nobody could stop Mokotak. As Mokotak approached the vicious army, he reached back far with his atlatl and threw all of his weight forward into the force of his spear. Before the spear had even left its sling, a wave of arrows descended upon the Minnecou giant, and as he fell forward, he never even reached the ground. The dozens of spears and arrows that pierced his flesh kept him propped in a manner where his body could not lay flat. Mokotak's spear continued on and thrust into Ketanka's chest; the chief's arms dropped to his sides, and his head drooped forward onto his chest. Mokotak had ended his suffering.

A few paces behind, Petawahin realized that he had followed too closely, and would never outrun the pursuing Snake warriors. He reached far back and let his own spear fly. Another wave of arrows whistled through the air. Petawahin felt a paralyzing pain as the first arrow pierced his forehead; the dozens of following arrows were like a stinging rain as his last vision of Quiktkoata began to fade into darkness, his spear stubbornly clutched in the Snake leader's torso.

Shamira heard a familiar shriek and raced up the stairs of the parapet to find out what had happened. Semmida and several of his men were trying desperately to hold Sequannah back to keep him from the same fate as his father, but they couldn't protect themselves from Sequannah's ear-piercing howl. She could see them straining to hold the young warrior, alternately covering their ears. She looked to the ground in the village and witnessed Mokotak and her father, dead to the earth, just as hundreds of Snake warriors swarmed the Minnecou bodies. Her vision faded. She heard a thump and a loud buzz as her head hit the cold stone floor.

The Sikun stood before Sequannah. The young warrior's blood-chilling howl turned to a silent scream. "Take heart, young Minnecou," the Sikun said in sympathy. "The evil ones have gone too far. I will give them something to remember."

A look of rage overtook Teokahannah's face before his hood covered it from Sequannah's view. Sequannah had never seen even a hint of anger in the Sikun. His own rage dissipated, and he watched in wonder as the Sikun vaulted from the great height of the parapet and landed on his feet far below with the prowess of a cougar. Teokahannah walked straight into the frenzied mass. They retreated like a herd of goats from a rabid wolf, as they ran in search of their weapons. A large group of Snake warriors raised their bows in fear of the Sikun, but Quiktkoata waved them off as he clutched the spear in his ribs. Quiktkoata's grimace changed to a malicious smile as he looked to the heavens, then sneered at the Sikun.

The three great hawks dove from the sky and drove their claws deep into the flesh of the Sikun's shoulders. Sequannah stared in horror as the three vicious birds of prey, each the size of a wolf, strained to draw Teokahannah away from the earth. It took some time to separate his feet from the ground, but soon they drifted past the height of the stone structures, then rapidly soared towards the heavens. All eyes turned upwards as the Sikun and Quiktkoata's mystical hawks became a speck in the sky, then disappeared. The Snake warriors cheered as the rebels' eyes turned to the ground.

Sequannah heard a crackling noise; the ground brightened before him. The Snake warriors' cheers suddenly turned to silence. He looked up to see a double rainbow, nearly as bright as the sun, glaring in the western sky. The bottom rainbow had a full spectrum, but the crown had alternating arcs of emerald and violet. The crackling sound accompanied the initial flash of the brilliant aura, and like a bolt of lightning, a heart-stopping crash of thunder followed in its wake. The boom was so violent that the stone structures shook to their foundations; partial walls and roofs collapsed. The rebels fled the falling buildings–the Snake warriors couldn't take their eyes off the western sky. Two black clouds appeared on each side of the rainbow and began to grow, then flattened to a thin, black line. The black line began to swell, and a crackling and croaking sound became perceptible in the distance. The sun dimmed, and the brilliant aura of the double rainbow became lost in the thickening black cloud that built up high into the sky, and covered the entire western horizon. A great thunderhead surged as a brilliant band of gold outlined the blackness below.

Sequannah jumped from the quaking parapet, searching frantically for his clan. The stone structures had crumbled; there was no place to take refuge from either the Snake warriors or the impending storm. A blast of powerful wind rushed in from the west. Dust and debris clouded Sequannah's vision as the dawn reversed into darkness. A deafening wave of cackles, caws, and croaks inundated the village as a billowing, black curtain obscured even the closest hilltops. A grackle raced by Sequannah, directly over his head. Several more blackbirds zoomed by, then Sequannah's eyes widened as he turned westward to determine their source. Millions of jackdaws, rooks and ravens streamed through the village, less than a hand's width above his head; there was barely enough room for their wings to flap, as the thick and impenetrable cloud of black birds descended into their midst. Sequannah fell flat, clinging tightly to the earth, as the deafening mass of black wings, claws and feathers roared eastward, just above him. He heard a faint echo of the Sikun's last words: "I will give them something to remember!"

After some time, Sequannah heard the deafening mass suddenly cease, with only an occasional flap of wings racing by. He opened his eyes to find that the sun's rays had once again found their way to the earth, where hundreds of rebels still lay clinging to the ground. To the east, a mass of black birds clawed and screeched violently at the Snake army below as they strained to escape southward to Quiktkoata's city. When the Snake people had been driven far enough away, Sequannah walked towards the large pole from which chief

Ketanka and Melonak had made their final departure. Several sand-colored skeletons dotted the landscape. They had been picked clean by the raging birds. Later, they would bleach white in the sun's bright glare. Before he reached the still-burning victory fire and the erected pole, he found the bodies of Mokotak and his father. The birds had not touched them. He remembered the stern and strong look of his father. He couldn't associate it with the lifeless face that lay before him, an arrow protruding bloodless from the forehead. Arrows stuck out everywhere from the front of the corpse, but the greatest amount of blood was concentrated around his father's hand. A hint of black glistened. Sequannah reached down and opened Petawahin's clenched fist. There in his hand was the long black spear point he had found when they had brought back the grizzly meat. Sequannah remembered the look of admiration on his father's face as he held it up for the council to see. He also remembered how Petawahin had imitated the Paccus in their lovemaking. He could still hear the council laughing. He could still see the Minnecou glint of mischief in his father's eyes.

"I had no time to make it," Sequannah heard a voice behind him. He turned to see Kwoita standing weakly, tears streaming down his face.

"The spear," he cried. "He wanted me to make a spear for him. I had no time to make it. He thought the black stone would give him power," Kwoita squatted to the ground and buried his face in his hands. Sequannah looked away. In the distance, the swarm of black birds appeared as a field of boiling tar, slowly oozing southward; occasional skeletons marking its wake.

They looked southward from time to time, to witness the suffering of Quiktkoata and his followers. The Washan and the Wolf brothers went over to Sequannah and Kwoita.

"I saw it in a dream many years ago," the Washan said softly. "The crows and ravens barely scratch the Snake people, but they trample each other to save themselves in their mortal fear of death. The birds only eat the victims. The Creator's chosen fall humbly to the ground and trust the Earth Mother. But they must also have the trust of those around them."

* * *

Wanachan, the Washan and several healers prepared all

of the bodies for the journey into the next life. Bones had been pulled out of the Snake warriors' fire pit and brought to the base of the Dark Mountains where they would be burned on scaffolds along with the full bodies dressed in red ocher. They wailed and sacrificed in memory of those who had given their lives. When everything was done, they prepared to leave immediately so the spirits would move on and not linger in haunt.

The Minnecou gathered around the Wolf brothers. One of them would become chief. Perhaps the Minnecou clan would now have two chiefs, Sequannah thought to himself in distraction of his sorrow. Two people stood at a distance, and he looked up to see who waited for him. Shamira's eyes were red and swollen, and immediately avoided Sequannah's gaze. The Paccu looked intently at Sequannah, his arm held protectively around Shamira. Nothing was said or gestured for quite some time; the Minnecou and the Paccu stared in silence.

Finally, Sequannah folded his arms across his chest and leaned to one side. "Welcome you to Minnecou stay with," he said in broken Paccu.

"My brother welcomes you!" Shamira smiled widely in surprise. Ceptke shook his head in acceptance, but his face remained solemn. Sequannah smiled, nodded his acceptance of them, then walked back towards the Wolf brothers. Ceptke then smiled, when Sequannah's back was turned, and lifted Shamira high into the air.

Sequannah saw Semmida and his men, assembled and prepared to leave. Semmida seemed to be waiting and searching hopefully among the thinning crowd. "Tarote!" he thought to himself. He had not seen her since before the Snake people had first attacked the village. But each group of the different peoples had already banded together and were now climbing into the hills that surrounded the strange village. She was nowhere to be found. His father was gone. Tarote and the Sikun were gone. Though Shamira and Ceptke would follow with the clan for now, he knew that she would leave too, for Ceptke appeared to be a leader among his people. Even now they gathered around him.

The Minnecou assembled into a line and immediately left the valley of the mysterious mining village. As they reached the first hills, the sounds of soft, grainy snow crunched beneath their feet. Sequannah had cast his eyes downward for some time, and when he looked up, everyone else seemed to be staring into the Earth Mother as well. The wind was warm as it was not yet winter. They trudged their way up the long slope of the hill until the whole western horizon opened up before them at the top of the ridge. Shatomi and Sabatt moved quickly ahead to scout for the clan as they moved northward to meet with Quebathe. They would spend the remainder of the winter in the Dark Mountains.

There was little daylight left—they wouldn't travel very far before they would bed down for the night. Sequannah viewed the vista before him, noting the colorful clouds awaiting the setting sun. Directly in the west was a cloud in the figure of a man. Sequannah studied the figure and noticed it even held a lance. He could see two braids hanging from the obscure looking head. "It is Petawahin!" he thought to himself. "My father walks in the sky!" In the subtle wind, one of the braids shifted until it matched with the other, becoming one braid on the left side of the figure's head. The lance faded away. "It has changed into the Sikun!" he thought to himself once again. "They are together in the spirit world. This is the way they have shown me." A breath of warm wind caused the loose hairs of his own braid to tickle his face, and in the rustling of the breeze he heard the words whispered, "To each shall come a sunset of painted sky..."

Epilogue

To each shall come a sunset of painted sky, where the power of the rainbow dwells within all things. And each spirit shall soar from the shadows of the valley, and out over the highest mountains, to where the rainbow becomes one color and one light. Here, they will shine...and come to understand that light is all; darkness but a shadow. And a gentle breeze from the spirit of all things shall whisper to them:

"Breathe not the smoke of anger and bitterness for the gales to test man's spirit, lest ye yourself are capable of stirring the breath to all things in needed measure. Shrink not from the trials, pains and sufferings that stand where the spirit must tread, for without these, joy and pleasure would have no depth–wisdom, no source. Neither adore the praiseworthy nor condemn the stray, but recognize the consequence of action. Know that naiveté lies not in trust but in distrust, for all things are but a part of one being. Understand that faith and lack of faith are one in the same, but in different directions. Consider that the wise man will follow his heart as well as his logic. Know that to serve the world around you is the sacred way to serve yourself and your kind."

Awaken to the new dawn and put a straight trail beneath your feet. Avoid the mazes of aimless wandering; there are seasons in all things for guidance. Likewise, look not to the darkness in puzzlement, but strive to see clearly in the light. Bring rainbows to your world instead of shadows of concealment. Reach out to the wilderness, for her justice is greater than we understand. Know that the prophet sees not only the future, but also that which once was, and shall come to pass again. See that the creation is not only that which happened long ago, but rather that which is always happening...always has, and forever shall be. Each sunset and each dawn will crave your care and your purpose in all things shall become self evident.

Teokahannah